THE PALM READER

"*The Palm Reader* is action-packed and exciting, with twists and turns, fantastic characters and a truly spellbinding plot—the best book in its genre I have ever read. Highly Recommended!"

—**SUSAN KEEFE**, TheColumbiaReview.com

"Jackson Walker is back in this thrilling, fast-paced sequel to best-seller *Devil in the Grass*, this time taking on evil itself as his family is threatened by the Church of Satan. An edgy, action-packed thriller!"

—**RAYMOND KHOURY**, New York Times Best-Selling Author of *The Last Templar*

"A Florida noir in the vein of Randy Wayne White—with a tight plot, well-drawn primary and secondary characters, and a climax most readers won't see coming, *The Palm Reader* is a most satisfying summer read. One can only hope that the Jackson Walker series continues."

—**BETSY ASHTON**, author of *Unintended Consequences* and *Uncharted Territory, Mad Max Mysteries, Eyes Without A Face*

"*The Palm Reader* is a fast-paced read with twists, turns and excitement around every corner. It is delightfully scary and full of frightening events. A real delight for the imaginary senses. This is the best book in its genre that I have ever read."

—**CHICK LIT CAFE**

"Wow! I absolutely loved this book. Even better than the first, the best-selling Devil in the Grass—could not put it down."

— MAXINE (BOOKLOVER CATLADY) ***** Five Stars—
Top Amazon Reviewer

"The setting for Christopher Bowron's *The Palm Reader* isn't the Florida of blue hair and walkers and early-bird specials and family theme parks—seedy and gritty, *The Palm Reader* will keep you turning pages long past the time those household chores have grown tired of calling your name."

— DAVID PATNEAUDE, author of *Fast Backward* and
other best-selling novels

GOODREADS; BARNES & NOBLE; INDIE BOOK REVIEWERS:

"Sometimes when I read and like a book by an author, I am apprehensive to read the sequel because they are usually not as good as the first. I call it the 'sophomore slump.' But I needn't have worried at all! I was hooked from the first pages of *The Palm Reader* by Christopher Bowron and my interest never faded for a moment!"

— STEPH COLEMAN

"I was impressed with how Bowron can draw out the suspense and high-octane tension through the whole book … even after something crazy happens, there is more to come. A great read that works as a standalone, but I suggest reading the first one of the series (*Devil in the Grass*) for the full effect. Recommend to mature fans of thriller/suspense."

— DARLENE CUPP

"Great writing, great action, great characters, great plot … Overall a terrific read that I feel has really opened my eyes to a new genre of reading for me. The ending was great—Gramps is the man! I can totally see this book being a movie. I hope Mr. Bowron's next book isn't too far off."

—CARLA BIGGINS

"There is such strong, vivid writing, and the characters are all fascinating, flawed, and going through their own problems. Jack is a total badass (can I say that?) and everything just felt 'authentic' for lack of a better word."

—CODY BRIGHTON

"For those who enjoy drama and high-stakes action thrillers that expose the darkest, most vile sides of humanity in a highly readable and 'entertaining' way, then this is a good one for you."

—ANABELLA JOHNSON

"*The Palm Reader* is a Southern thriller filled with supernatural elements. This is one book that I will be reading again. I highly recommend it to all thriller and supernatural lovers and those that are interested in the real-life scenarios of the Church of Satan and the supernatural."

—CHICK LIT CAFE

"Suspenseful, fast-paced, multi-faceted, multi-layered, the plot keeps twisting right to the explosive end."

—SAM LAW, author of *It's Good To Read*

"I really enjoy Mr. Bowron's books and always look forward to the next one. They're a little edgy and a lot creepy. They flow easily and are so detailed that I always feel like I'm there with his unfailingly interesting characters. Lolita? Priceless! *The Palm Reader* delivers, as did the previous book, lots of macabre situations with escalating tension and action-filled endings."

—SUSAN PHEND

THE

PALM

READER

A NOVEL

CHRISTOPHER BOWRON

VIRGINIA BEACH
CAPE CHARLES

The Palm Reader
by Christopher Bowron

Published by

köehlerbooks™

210 60th Street
Virginia Beach, VA 23451
212-574-7939
www.koehlerbooks.com

DEDICATION

Estero Bay

Look away
For the sun is bright
The sand is hot
The sea shimmers in the light

Open your eyes
The stars are shining
The moon sits low
Their reflections dance

I remember you
The way you were
Once again
I sadly close my eyes

To my wife, Carmen, and my children, Molly and Jack—
for your support

CHAPTER ONE

A TALL, MUSCLE-BOUND POLICE officer ushered Jackson Walker reluctantly away from his grandfather by putting a forceful hand on the back of his head, the other on one of his bound arms. The McFadden property, now overrun by cops, news crews and forensic teams, no longer seemed creepy. Lit-up, it looked ready for a film shoot—not the house of horrors it had been an hour back, shrouded in darkness with the smell of the Everglades and death all-pervading. The carnage strewn across the estate would be picked apart, piece by piece, every inch scoured for incriminating evidence until its dark secrets were revealed to all who might have the stomach and desire to know them.

Jack, with the help of his Seminole cousins and a law clerk named Janie Callaghan, heroically brought down the Church of Set, a satanic cult based in Southwest Florida. Its evil leader, Henrietta LePley, along with her henchmen, the McFadden brothers, Eric, Isaac and Jimmy, all found their lives at an end earlier in the evening, and deservedly so. They were evil, hearts rotten to the core, especially the McFaddens, who were killers of a serial nature.

Though Walker would most likely be cleared of the alleged killings of two elderly people a week back in Clewiston, he would first need to be detained. The burly officer ushered him into a police van; the reinforced double-back door slammed shut with a loud clang before the locking mechanism engaged. Sitting across from Jack, to his utter shock, was Mason Matye, a high-ranking leader within the American branch of the Church of Satan. The cops surely made a mistake placing the two in the same vehicle. Matye, like Jack, was one of the few survivors of the haunting events of that evening. Jack felt slightly better seeing the Satanist's hands were similarly bound with plastic flex cuffs. Their eyes met in the dark van.

"Jackson Walker," said the man in his thick, Parisian French accent. His coal-black eyes were like lasers searing into the back of Jack's skull and drying his throat. A wry smile formed on the man's lips. "You have proven very resourceful." His eyes were unrelenting. "You made a deal with the Devil, Mr. Walker, about a week back. I know you remember."

Jack laid into him. "The Devil? Stop with the crap, you satanic fuck. I made no such deal with any Devil: Satan, or Set, or whatever name you want to call him!"

Mason only smiled, the way any Satanist would, his eyes narrowing and his mouth forming a taut smile. "Ah. Perhaps you thought you made a deal with Henrietta. We both serve a higher being—as agents, you might say, Mr. Walker. I hope you will not make the same mistake twice. It's time to pay up, one way or another. You see, the beauty of being a Devil worshiper . . . it's expected of you to be dastardly. I take great pleasure in it." His eyes narrowed as he whispered through pursed lips, "We know where your family lives. We will watch your every move, be it as a free man, or in a prison cell. This isn't finished."

Jack studied the man, his eyes not leaving Mason. "Don't tell me," Jack said sarcastically, "the Church of Satan has connections within the state prison system?"

"Each and every state, Mr. Walker. Your incarceration will be a perfect hell. If you are lucky enough to make it there." He lifted his foot to his cuffed wrists, resting it on the detention van's bench seat. He deftly pulled out a thin blade hidden in the heel of his shoe. With his fingertips he ran the steel edge across the plastic tie and, gritting his teeth, began to cut through the plastic.

Jack couldn't believe this was happening after all he'd been through that day. "Fucker!" He hurled himself at the vile little Frenchman, catching him in the chin with his shoulder. The force of the blow drove Mason's head into the wall of the van. The blade clattered to the floor. Both men ended up face to face on their sides trying to capture the blade.

Mason spit at Jack, covering his face with blood and saliva. "*Merde!* You will die, Walker. Count on it!"

Jack did his best to head-butt the man but didn't have the leverage with his hands tied, so the effort ended in more of a head rub than a useful smack. Mason scrambled to grab the knife. Jack pushed himself up against the bench and tried to regain his footing. Mason pulled his feet back to his hands and, with a couple of frantic pulls, cut his bonds.

Jack, having only freed his feet, hauled back and kicked Mason's throat. There was a sickening crack and Jack hoped something gave way. Mason made a horrible gurgle, like a clogged drain being emptied. Jack kicked him again, this time in the face. He felt the man's nose snap.

Clank. The back doors to the van opened abruptly. Two armed officers jumped into the back, grabbing both of them.

Jack yelled, "The fucker's got a knife!"

One officer grabbed Jack by the hair, expertly herding him out of the van. Within seconds, and with the aid of a fellow officer, he found himself in the back of the police cruiser. Out of the corner of his eye, he saw Matye receiving similar treatment. After that, the night became a blur.

CHAPTER TWO

JACK SHOOK HIS HEAD as he drove down Route 29 to Everglades City, remembering the attack in the van. Amazingly, five years had passed. He'd been pardoned by the governor for all of his transgressions, with the backing of Senator James Hunter. Jack deservedly came out of the fiasco a hero. With his grandfather's backing, he returned to the University of Florida and finished a degree in law. Now he worked for Peter Robertson at Robertson and Robertson LLP.

Jack was visiting his Seminole grandfather, whom he and the rest of his family affectionately called Gramps. A year back, the old man signed on as Jack's first client, much to the delight of Peter Robertson. Gramps invited him down to the Seminole gaming offices to sort out some business. The drive through the Everglades after turning south off I-75 brought back memories, most of them not good. The vast swamp spread out before him, seemingly ready to swallow him up once again; mile after mile of saw-grass savannah and the odd stand of trees, all framed by an endless blue sky, worked to pull at his soul. He loved the place but reluctantly came back, like someone returning to a small town after living in the big city for years. He didn't want to admit defeat, yet it would be easy to fall back into the embrace of the ancient swamp and its simplicity.

Pulling his red Rubicon Jeep into the Seminole Gaming Agency's parking lot, he slipped out of the vehicle and retrieved a satchel containing the requested documents. He two-stepped up a set of wooden stairs and barged into the building.

A young Seminole woman, who gushed every time she saw him, looked up and smiled. "Hello, Jackson. We haven't seen you in months!"

He remembered her: very attractive, tall and slim, with shoulder-length black hair.

"Hello . . . Beth, right?"

"Yes!" she beamed. "Your grandfather asked me to show you right in. Come along with me."

Jack gladly followed the shapely female along the hallway to his grandfather's office. When Beth gave him her best sexy walk, he had to remind himself to *focus*. "Thank you, Beth. I'll see you on the way out." He knocked, stepped inside and closed the door.

Gramps sat behind an old desk made from driftwood, the legs carved by a famous Floridian artist and the top varnished to perfection. Black-and-white Clyde Butcher photos of Florida wildlife adorned the walls around him.

Nathaniel Portman loosened his tie, grinning at his beloved grandson. "Jackson, you leave that girl alone unless you have honorable intentions. Your mother would have loved to see a few little ones running around with the blood in them."

Jack felt talked down to at the mention of kids. Snapping out of the ego-inflated trance Beth put him into, Jack raised his brows. "Gramps, no hocus-pocus, y'all hear? I can handle my own women."

"Really?" The old man jumped out of his chair and hugged him.

Jack nodded and smiled at the distinguished-looking man.

His grandfather was referring to Jack's near-fatal attraction with a satanic cultist. "Point taken!"

"Jackson, I asked you to come down for a few reasons. First, I promised when you were released I'd keep an eye on you." He paused to stare at his grandson, even though he knew how much Jack hated when he did. "I believe in looking people in the eyes from time to time." The old man's eyes probed his until Gramps finally said, "I see no mischief in them. Good." He motioned for Jack to sit.

"So, Gramps, what's up?"

"We have some business to talk about. We've made a few land purchases, and we want you to represent us, but we can talk about that later."

"Okay?"

"Jackson . . ."

"Gramps, you call me Jackson like that when there's something up, like when we were kids and Josh and I did something bad, which was not uncommon."

Gramps suddenly smiled. "You're strong with the spirit." He sat back.

"What's that supposed to mean?" Jack asked with a touch of irritation.

"Just what I said. Jack . . . the cultists were drawn to you and I saw it. I didn't know it to be you, but now I can see your spirit. It shines bright around you, like a beacon."

"So?" Jack chose not to believe in such nonsense, while Gramps was known within the Seminole tribe to be a spirit talker—some called him shaman. The gift passed to Jack's mother, who died several years back. Gramps believed Jack carried the gift to some degree, but it would be hard to tell the strength until the young man openly accepted it. Up to this point in his life, besides when he'd been quite young, Jack utterly denied its existence.

"You, if anyone, should know the truth in what I say. I see danger again, Jack. It's not the same, but it's bad. I have to tell you . . . you attract badness. Evil is attracted to you like when you were attracted to drugs in your youth."

"Aw, come on, Gramps." His short college attraction to a

socialite group heavily into drugs wasn't one of Jack's favorite topics. He wanted to banish all the bad times and the bad people from his memory.

"Maybe not the substance, but surely those people who gave it to you, and the Satanists as well—"

"All a coincidence."

"There is no such thing. These occurrences were meant to happen."

"Where are those real estate files?" Jack messed around with his satchel.

Nathaniel said, "I've experienced a vision for several nights in a row. A raven sits inside a cage, pecking at the lock that binds it, its beak bloodied by the constant pecking. Last night, the bird broke its bonds and flew away from the cage."

"Okay, so how does this concern me?"

"In the vision, I can see you in the distance. The raven flies toward you, Jackson."

Jack sat for a moment deep in thought. *That fucking bird better not cross my path.* He grinned, trying to defuse the old man's bunk.

"Think, Jackson, the riddle is simple."

"I know, Gramps, I'm not a moron. The raven represents someone dark, who has been imprisoned. It could only be Mason Matye. All the rest of those satanic fuckers are dead. That's if you believe all of this nonsense."

"I have lived by these visions my entire life, as have my forefathers. These people, the Devil Spawn, know how to harbor a grudge, or maybe it's the power down below that will not let it go. They will try to find retribution. If in fact this man is on the loose, he will seek you out. I can feel it."

"Okay, so say I believe you, just a little. What am I supposed to do?" Jack crossed his legs uncomfortably. "I haven't heard squat from any of those bastards in five years."

"I would like you to spend more time with your cousin, Josh. I'll talk to Peter and add him to the retainer. A man like Mason does not play by the rules. He will do whatever he needs to do to fulfill his mandate. You . . . are a law-abiding citizen, which puts you at a disadvantage."

Jack tipped his head to the side in semi-acquiescence. "How so?"

"If it's true he's escaped, he'll resort to anything, even suicide, to not go back to jail. You would be wise to keep both your eyes on the lookout, if nothing else, and be a little more careful in the near future." He looked directly into Jack's eyes. "Do this for your grandfather."

"Okay wonderful, Gramps. Let's get to those files. I've had enough mumbo jumbo."

Gramps nodded, accepting his grandson's disdain for the old ways of the Seminoles.

* * * *

Jack pulled out of the parking lot, his head abuzz, the conversation with his gramps still fresh in his mind. He floored the gas pedal as he turned onto the highway, kicking up stones behind him. "Why me again?" he said out loud. "Bullshit!" He punched the hands-free. "Call Perry," he told his Bluetooth and waited for the system to dial.

His friend's voice rang out through the speakers. "Wassup, bro?"

"Bit of a bad mood. Snook fishin' tomorrow morning?"

"Have t'kick the girl out early, but sure, what the hell. Where at?"

"I'll pick you up. We'll launch at the Sanibel causeway, head up to Captiva. We can net some white bait by the bridge pilings . . . 6 AM."

"I'm there, bro."

CHAPTER THREE

LOLITA SHIFTED HER LARGE frame in the overstuffed chair and looked across the small round table at her client. It had been a long day and she slept little the night before. The room glowed softly, lit by an overabundance of randomly-placed candles, the decor heavy and full of warm colors. Her cat, Princess, sat on a chair in the corner preening her black fur. Lolita gently took the woman's small, white hands into her large dark palms, engulfing them in warmth. She rubbed the tops with her thumbs, pulling the client into her presence, Lolita's voice soothing and deep. She turned the hands over, examining them carefully. Each set of hands showed their own story. Sometimes that story came to her as a vision, and sometimes she had to rely on the creases and lines to divine the truth.

The spirits felt strong the past few days, and she was startled by what she saw. Lolita closed her eyes, not wanting her turned-up whites to scare her customer. Once the vision passed, she opened her eyes and examined the lines in the woman's palms, not really taking notice. Lolita tried to come to terms with what she needed to tell her. Sandy Templeton, twenty-six years old, lived in Bonita Springs. She'd been given an hour's time with Lolita by her friends as a wedding shower gift, which was very common. Lolita, by her own admission, could be wrong in her palmistry and even her tarot readings from time to time, but the visions never failed her.

She placed Sandy's hands palms down on the table. "Sweetheart," she said in her South Floridian drawl, "I rarely do this, as I need the money, but this is important. I'm going to give you your gift card back and I want you to make an appointment to come back and see me."

"But—"

"Sweetheart, your fiancé . . . is he tall with dirty-blond hair, and a scar under his right eye?"

"Why yes, ma'am." Fear crept over her pretty face.

"Is he planning on going over water in the near future?"

Hesitating, she grew paler by the second. "He's gonna go fishing with his buddies this evening after work."

"Sweetheart, I want you to go now, and when he comes home, I want you to make love to him like you've never loved a man before. I want you to take your time and ease into making him not want to leave the house. Do you follow?"

"Yes ma'am. What is it?"

"Will he be on the water tomorrow?"

"No. We have plans. He won't be happy."

"Let me put it this way: No one will be happy if you let him walk out that door tonight. I want you to go now and shine up that pretty little white ass and shake it for all it's worth."

* * * *

Lolita turned the deadbolt on the door after the young woman left. She didn't like doing what she'd just done. Sandy would probably be able to seduce and keep her future husband from leaving and there would be no way of proving the vision would have come to fruition. Sandy would think her a crazy old black lady and never come back. It would be a smudge on Lolita's reputation. She shook her head and went back into the parlor, picking up her tarot cards. Lolita eased her large posterior back into her old, rickety chair.

She had seen the drowning of Sandy's future husband. The vision appeared abruptly and was gone within seconds. What appeared immediately after the first vison seemed clearly unrelated to the young woman—an augury jumping over the drowning fisherman. No less important, but the calling appeared stronger. Lolita knew better than to ignore the spirits. She saw two more deaths, one being her own.

Shuffling the cards, she thought about her question until the vision appeared crystal clear. A tall man with dark hair—Seminole blood. Strange how the Seminoles often crept into her head. They were strong in spirit. She'd heard of an old Indian man who lived on the southern edge of the Everglades. She made a pact with herself to bless him with her presence one day.

The young man she envisioned lived locally, somewhat famous for a recent endeavor. He appeared to be in grave danger. She saw his grisly death, a death that needed to be averted. The man looked to be destined for greatness, a champion of South Florida. The vision was conflicted, depicting both their endings, but neither was clear; she saw a vague, this-or-that vision. *Most dangerous.* She shivered.

She flipped over the first card. Strength. Yes, she'd seen strength in the young man's face. His grounding and past? Solid. The Seven of Wands . . . *Yes, there will be a battle, which can be won, but how will I be involved?* There was no doubt she would be. He would spurn her—she would need to be persistent.

Lolita sipped her tea, now quite cold. She turned the next card. The Fool, inverted. *Is he apathetic? Do I dare get involved?* She clearly needed to, but the card indicated that the *quaere*, or "seeker," appeared foolhardy, a risk-taker. She didn't have money to lose, so there was little risk monetarily. She flipped again. The Queen of Swords. There would be a battle of wits. *Very interesting.*

One last card, and when she flipped it, her hand went to her mouth.

The Devil.

* * * *

Lolita gathered the cards together and blew out the many candles spread about the small house, which served as both her place of business and her home. The spirits didn't need any more encouragement today. A cold sweat formed on her brow and moistened her shirt. *Who is this person?* Going downstairs, she turned on her desktop and searched for a while, turning up loose ends and improbabilities. After an hour, she switched tactics and typed *Paranormal/Ft. Myers celebrities.*

She went on a tangent relating to Satanism for a good half an hour before she struck gold. An article in the *Miami Herald* mentioned a Jackson Walker, part Seminole, who brought down a South Florida cult, the Church of Set. Two seconds after she saw Walker's picture, she knew him to be her target.

It began to fall into place. Lolita remembered him as the hero who took down the witch Henrietta LePley. Smiling, Lolita muttered to herself, "Anyone who has the balls to take on that woman deserves to be saved." This was not Lolita's first encounter with the woman. She'd seen her a few times, and each time her inner voice told her to steer clear of *the witch!* That was Henrietta—malevolent to the core, vindictive, evil—a plethora of bad words might describe her. Lolita shivered, crossing herself to ask for a blessing even though she wasn't Catholic.

It was uncommon for the visions to appear in pictures. When the future was painted for her, she would be foolish to ignore it. She felt blessed on most occasions to be close with the spirits. Conversely, she felt wary whenever the omen appeared dangerous. If Jackson Walker was tied up with the Church of Satan or Set, whichever demigod one preferred, he would be a sketchy person to be around. Possibly deadly.

CHAPTER FOUR

JACK DIDN'T SLEEP VERY well through the night. His dreams were jumbled and repetitive. He never slept well when his dreams looped. He remembered a vision of Mason Matye with a big kitchen knife. While Mason didn't try to cut him with it, he carried it around threateningly. Over and over, different situations popped up, until finally Jack woke up in a ball of sweat, the blankets wrapped around his legs.

He'd rented a small bungalow in the south part of Ft. Myers Beach on a little street called Ibis Lane. He loved that spot and the island. The southern end was quiet, while the north tended to be a little more honky-tonk. He made a pot of coffee and went about preparing for his fishing trip with Perry. He packed lots of water, a few beers, beef jerky, and a couple of sandwiches made from the dregs of his fridge on half-stale Kaiser rolls. They would do.

The one luxury he'd afforded himself since being hired by

Peter Robertson was his fishing boat: a 24-foot Ranger with a 250-horsepower Yamaha outboard. It was big enough to take some chop, yet able to get into tight places in the mangroves. He grabbed some frozen cut bait from the freezer, just in case a few tarpon showed up.

Jack pulled out of his driveway with the boat hooked up to his Jeep and headed to Estero Boulevard, where he turned north. Early in the morning there would be no traffic. Coming home, even in May, it would be a different story. Estero was chopped to rat shit for new services and the traffic would be a shit-show. Before picking up Perry, he stopped in at Anderson's Bait and Tackle to pick up two dozen pinfish.

Perry never kept him waiting. He was ready, his rods resting against his cooler—a fanatic when it came to fishing. "You ready to catch some fish, bro?" Jack chortled out the window of the Jeep.

"Hell yeah. Let's get at her!" Perry loaded his stuff into the boat and slid into the passenger seat, handing Jack a coffee.

It didn't take them long to get to the boat launch at the beginning of the causeway to Sanibel. They dumped the boat in the water and parked the Jeep and trailer. Within ten minutes they were jockeying around the pillars of the Sanibel causeway looking for white bait. Jack, being an expert, filled the live well with three casts of his net, and then they were off to Captiva.

* * * *

After a fifteen-minute ride, Jack settled the boat into one of his favorite spots off the edge of the Ding Darling nature preserve. They would hit Captiva if they struck out here. Perry hooked a greenback through the nose and threw it under the edge of a mangrove. Jack tossed a few squished-up baitfish under the canopy to attract attention. He preferred the fly rod and threw a Norm Zeigler Schminnow not far from where Perry placed his live bait.

Within seconds they had a simultaneous hookup, both snook. That's how it was if the snook were biting—life was good. They could turn off as quickly as they turned on. Perry had a twenty-five-incher released before Jack could get his slot specimen in with the much more finicky fly rod.

Perry released Jack's fish. "Amazing how you can't catch a slot snook in season and you get one five days after it closes in one cast." Snook could only be kept within season between twenty-eight and thirty-two inches, which was referred to as *the slot*.

"It's fate, Perry. A pretty fish. We'll get some reds off the oyster beds near Blind Pass."

"Sure. You said you were in a bad mood. I figured you wanted to talk," Perry said, rigging up another bait.

"Yep, but catching a few fish eases the pain, bro. I've been given my first real case."

"Weren't you looking after your grandfather's business?"

"Yeah, but it's pretty mundane shit and Robertson specializes in criminal law. I've been handed a *doozy*! The real estate stuff is something I can do in my sleep."

"Come on, then."

"I'm supposed to help Pete defend a pedophile . . . No. Let me rephrase that to an *accused* pedophile. He wants me to head up the research."

"Christ!"

"Yeah, tell me about it. The guy says he's not guilty, but he's got ten gigs' worth of shit on his computer. Things you don't wanna see."

"You are complicated, Jack. That's all I can say. I'd help you if I could, and you know it."

Jack nodded as he threw another fly under the mangrove canopy. "Gonna get ahead of you," he said as he stripped his line in.

"Not with that pussy buggy whip." Perry baited his hook and tossed it at a stump jutting into the bay. "You got some bug spray? No-see-ums are bad this morning."

"Yeah, under the dash. You need some Seminole blood in you."

Perry nodded as he covered his neck and legs.

Jack threw again and was rewarded with an instant hookup, and a big one. "Monster snook, bro!"

"You fucking bastard!"

Jack laughed. "Remember me telling you about the French guy, the one who headed the Church of Satan? Mason Matye?"

"Yeah . . . watch the prop!" Jack's snook looked to be way over slot and was giving him a hell of a time.

"Gramps thinks he escaped from prison last week. He's the fucking guy who vowed to make me pay for my transgressions against Satan, remember?"

Perry looked at the sky. "Why you tellin' me this? Why don't you stop in at the Catholic Church on Ft. Myers Beach? Speak to a fucking exorcist or something." He scratched his head. "What exactly do you mean by 'Gramps thinks he escaped'?"

"Gotta tell someone." He guided the fish along the boat. Perry picked it up by its lip and belly—a fat breeder. "Says he saw it in his dreams."

Perry shook his head. "This is massive, forty-five inches by my reckoning. Has he ever been wrong?"

"Not to the best of my recollection. Let's get a picture."

The released fish swam away strong. "Can't you call the police? Or the state, or something?"

"What the fuck they gonna do? I'm not even sure he was incarcerated in Florida. It might have been Mississippi. We were told he was wanted there on several charges."

Perry sat and cracked open a Monster energy drink. "Definitely off-putting."

"Just sayin'. Gramps is gonna have Josh hang around with me, like some sort of bodyguard."

"He's probably right for the time being." Perry cast another bait out. "This all comes back to you screwing around with that pussy I told you not to screw around with, remember?"

Jack chuckled. "I got nothin' on the go, pussy-wise. So, you can't gimme shit."

"You get some questionable pussy, you call the Perr guy."

"Oh, come on. It was once, and you sound like a fucking Aircon salesman."

"All it takes, bro. The pedophile?"

Jack stopped him, putting up his hand. "*Alleged* pedophile."

"Ya ya, legal mumbo jumbo. I wish you the best. You know

you can call me if you need anything."

Jack smiled. "Redfish, snapper or tarpon?"

"I feel like eatin' today. Snapper."

"Okay, there's a rock pile close to North Captiva a friend showed me. Snapper will be thick. We can work our way back to the launch after we get our limit, maybe hook up on a tarpon."

Perry smiled. "You the man, Jackson."

Jack reeled in, pulled up the anchor spike and guided the boat out of the mangroves toward open water.

CHAPTER FIVE

THE BASEMENT FELT COOL with the lights dimmed—a reprieve from Florida's midday heat. Solomon liked the anonymity of the basement. Only here could he be himself, away from the prying eyes of society.

He peeled off his work clothes, stripping to his white undershirt and pants. He resisted the urge to pull the paneling away from the wall. Behind the wall were his treasures, treasures he should no longer keep. He sipped a Budweiser and sat on the old orange-and-black couch, derelict and in the same spot since he'd bought the place twenty years ago, the springs allowing his rather large buttocks to sink all the way to the floor.

His workdays were long, and he sat in the darkness for a time before he switched on the television. The WINK midday news popped on, the reporter talking about yet another murder in North Ft. Myers. He removed the hairpiece covering his bald head, throwing it on the back of a chair that was in no better state than the couch. He watched the rest of the news, sipping from the bottle, fidgeting ever so slightly. He eyed the blank piece of paneled wall, downing the remains of his beer.

Coaxing his large frame off the couch, he moved toward the stairs. As he passed the wall, he ran his hand across the indentations in the paneling, lingering on the last ripple. Excited, he took a deep breath, exhaling slowly with a slight whistle.

"Another time, my darlings, another time." He walked up the stairs one at a time, the old wood creaking.

CHAPTER SIX

JANIE WOKE UP DISORIENTED. Sighing in relief, she recognized her own bedroom. *Alone. Good.* The taste of stale cigarettes and fruity drinks lingered in her mouth. Rather than sitting up, she rolled out of bed, stumbling slightly to gain her feet.

"You've got to stop doing this, Janie Callaghan," she said. An important meeting lay ahead of her this morning, yet she'd let some cowboy she met at Sneaky Pete's buy her a bunch of fancy drinks and, worse, feed her half a pack of Marlboros. If there could be any consolation, she remained in her clothes, and the cowboy was gone. She doubted she'd recognize him without the leather cowboy hat.

She made a backhanded oath to be a bit more discerning in the future.

She'd sworn off cigarettes after being shot in the Everglades five years ago; her time in the hospital weaned her off the nicotine.

Lately, she'd been having the odd one. She felt madder at the fact she'd smoked her head off last night than anything else. Whether she screwed the guy seemed irrelevant. Those things happened. There'd been many one-night stands over the years. Janie had to draw the line. Forty-nine seemed a bit too old for that kind of behavior. *Well, unless the guy is gorgeous… and rich.*

Janie wandered into the kitchen, filled a large glass with water, and downed it in one long, slow draft. She popped a couple extra-strength Motrin, hoping they might ease the pain in her head. A bagel and cream cheese would have to do for breakfast.

The hot water of the shower ran freely over her head, face, and body for several minutes before she even thought about washing. It definitely seemed harder to pull herself together as the years passed. If she wasn't careful, one day there might not be much to work with. By the time she'd toweled off and dressed for the meeting, she felt marginally better.

Peter had given her some work over the past few years, which allowed her to get by. He indicated this case might require all of her finesse and might yield a better paycheck. She would be working with Jackson Walker. She smiled. They'd crossed paths a few times since the Everglades but had never taken the time to actually get together and talk about things, life, whatever. It could prove to be very interesting. She liked the young man.

Moving from Lehigh a couple of years ago, she now lived in Bonita Springs. The small house wasn't anything special, but it was closer to the beach. She fired up the old BMW Peter gave her and headed to his office only ten minutes away.

She pulled into the parking lot of the taupe, stucco building. Navigating into a parking space, she felt a bit of déjà vu. Five years ago, almost to the day, she'd met with Jackson's aunt, who hired her and Peter Robertson to determine Jackson Walker's innocence. The woman paid a lot of money to clear her nephew's name.

Janie was ushered into Peter Robertson's office by a new secretary. Peter possessed an eye for large-breasted ancillary staff, and Steff didn't disappoint. Janie chuckled to herself. Peter sat behind his desk in the wood-paneled office. Across from him sat Jackson Walker. She smiled.

The first time she met him, they were in the middle of the Everglades, where he'd been holed up with his Seminole family. He looked much more confident now—not like a caged pigeon. The deep blue eyes were the same, and the athletic build, and a smile that could disarm man or woman within seconds.

Jack, as he liked to call himself, stood to greet her. "Janie"— he gave her the onceover— "you are a sight for sore eyes." She'd saved his life and he appeared more than grateful and truly pleased to see her again. He gave her a quick hug.

Peter grinned. "The two of you will be spending some time together, so let's save the niceties for later." Peter's Southern drawl smoothed out his latent sarcasm. "Please sit down. There's lots to discuss."

Once they were settled, Peter began. "The case we've been asked to interview for will have to be treated with kid gloves. What do either of you know about pedophilia?"

Janie's hangover suddenly worsened. "Pete, you kidding me?"

Peter pushed a dossier across his desk to them. "It's all in there. The defendant's name is Robert Lopez. He's of Mexican decent and lives here in Bonita."

Jack said, "I know what a pedophile is. Who doesn't? This guy diddling little kids?"

"No. It's not that cut and dry. Lee County Sheriff's Department arrested the guy two weeks ago. As I told you the other day, Jack, they caught him with ten gigs of kiddie porn on his home computer. I'm told it's the kind of stuff that makes you want to kill the bastards who film it, box it and sell it."

Jack picked up the folder. "So, what do you want us to do?"

"The guy's got money, evidently, and I will add that you never know where these things go, so let's keep an open mind. Like 99 percent of those we meet, Lopez claims he's not guilty. We'll offer to handle the case if he'll have us, and we'll take a retainer. I want the two of you to see what you can find out about Mr. Robert Lopez. I want to know if we have the potential for a case. If not, I don't want to be wrapped up in something dirty. Let's see what we can find in a week. If he turns out to be a scumbag . . . we'll cut him loose."

Jack nodded. "You're the boss."

Janie couldn't restrain herself. "Never seen you drop a case if there's good money, Pete. Jack, honey, you're looking at the cheapest defense lawyer in Southwest Florida. He'd try to defend Jimmy McFadden if he were still alive."

Peter scowled. "Janie, that's not nice."

Jack raised his brows at Peter. He would have chuckled at Janie's comment if the deranged killer hadn't popped into his head. The wounds were still deep as far as the McFaddens were concerned.

Pete shook his head in mock anger. "I'll take the lead. The two of you speak only when asked. Can you manage that?" His eyes probed Janie's face, but she wouldn't give him the benefit of a response.

* * * *

Roberto Lopez was ushered into the room by Steff. He appeared to look after himself—a tall, lean man, well dressed, with short-cropped hair. In his mid-forties, Roberto looked more like a Hispanic movie star than a pornographer.

Peter stood and greeted him. "Mr. Lopez, welcome to Robertson and Robertson. We're glad you think well enough of us to give us the chance to represent you. Let me introduce you to Jackson Walker. He'll be assisting me with your case." After Jack gave Roberto a professional smile, Peter gestured toward Janie. "This is Janie Callaghan; she'll be our head investigator."

Lopez smiled coolly and nodded, looking directly at Jackson. "That's why I came here, Mr. Robertson." He spoke with very little accent. "Jackson Walker, you're my man. No offense, Mr. Robertson. Jackson beat the odds. Now I want him to do the same for me."

The back of his neck tingling, Jack stood to shake the man's hand. He felt the urge to leave the room and wash his. Instead, he stated, "We'll try our best, Mr. Lopez. Please have a seat." He gestured to one of the green leather chairs, which ringed the front of Peter's desk.

Peter looked at his notes. "Mr. Lopez, during our phone conversation you mentioned that you were not responsible for the files that were seized on your home computer."

"Please call me Robert."

"Okay, Robert."

Robert looked at each of them, possibly scrutinizing anything that could be gleaned through simple expression, looking for any weaknesses. "The computer in question is actually my work computer. I work from home."

Peter made an accepting gesture with his hand and a slight nod.

"You see, I'm no angel, I'll admit. I sell pornography. Did I mention that on the phone?"

"You did."

"I've been set up. I get over four gigs of material a day, sometimes more. No doubt I'm being observed by the police. It's common in this biz. I sort through the shit and rate it, then format it for internet porn sites, name the scenes; you know, 'Skinny girl blasted by big dick.' The sites look different, but most of them are owned by a few large conglomerates. It's big business. I get paid by one of the biggest, City Star Productions. They're based in the Czech Republic."

Janie interrupted, followed by a stern look from Peter. "So how did the child pornography get on your computer and why didn't you purge it when you discovered it?"

When Robert looked her up and down, she squirmed under his scrutiny. "The stuff comes as e-files. Sometimes it takes me a while to get to new product."

Jack said, "We should be able to track when you opened the file, if you opened it."

"Unfortunately, I opened it right away, thinking it to be something else."

Peter drawled, "Possession is nine-tenths of the law, Robert."

"Yeah, but I'm not a pedophile, Mr. Robertson. I watched it for maybe two minutes, then shut it down. I don't like that kind of stuff, and that's the honest truth."

"Why'd you hold onto the material?"

"Mr. Robertson, I don't know. I remember being shocked and I guess I planned on forwarding it to City to let them deal with it. Next thing you know, I'm in cuffs and waiting to get out on bail. All of my computers have been seized and I'm unable to work. In this business, if you're not working it, you're out of it. The accusations could be pretty damning if I'm found guilty."

"Pedophilia is not a good thing to be sentenced with. You're looking at a minimum of five years. Also, I hear pedophiles are not looked upon favorably inside the walls of any prison, if you follow."

Robert looked at his feet. "Believe me, I follow."

Peter cleared his throat. "So where did the files come from?"

"A lot of the sources are anonymous, but these came from an address based in Tampa: *Russians*. I think they control the biz north of the city, all the way through the Panhandle and on up to New Orleans."

"Do you have a contact for them?"

"No. Not really. Like I say, I get the mail and that's it. I did hear, though, they're connected with strip clubs."

"How do they get paid?"

"From City, direct."

"You have their email address?"

"I do, as well as previous statements."

Peter looked around the table. "Robertson and Robertson will not take on a case unless we have a tangible chance of winning it and if the fees are worth our while. We are not cheap, Mr. Lopez. I would be willing to take your case on a preliminary basis. I'd have you pay a retainer of $20,000. I'll then have Jack and Janie look into it for a week. If we're satisfied you're telling us the truth, the whole truth and nothing but the truth, we will agree to represent you. We don't want to be associated with pedophilia, unless we know you are not. You follow?"

Robert looked at Peter, taking a few moments to ponder his words. "Twenty grand seems a bit steep, and I still have to talk to another lawyer."

"As my father used to say, pay peanuts, get monkeys. We'll keep a close accounting of the hours. We bill out at $110 per. The balance will be returned, of course, if we decide not to take you on."

"I'll cut a check for ten Gs and want your answer in four days. I need some resolution."

Peter looked to Jack, raising his brows. Jack nodded.

"Okay, Robert, I'll agree to that. You can see Steff on the way out. She'll take care of your payment."

They all stood and shook Lopez's hand. Jack escorted him out of the room. As he was about to shut the door, Robert met Jack's eyes. "I was referred to you by friends, Jackson. Don't let me down."

"Friends?"

He nodded and turned to leave.

Jack didn't like the way he said *friends* and felt a slight chill run down his spine. Jack stepped out of the office. "Hey, wait a moment. You can't drop a bomb like that without some kind of explanation." *It couldn't be the Satanists. Why would they recommend me? It doesn't make sense.*

Robert turned. "Let's just leave it at that for the time being. If we agree to work together," he smiled, "I might tell you who they are." He walked down the hall, exiting to the front lobby.

Jack hated when anyone did that sort of thing to him. He shouldn't have asked; now he felt at a disadvantage. Robert held something over him before the case had even begun. He would have to be a bit cooler in the future. He returned to Peter's office and sat down.

Peter chuckled at his sour expression. "So, what do you think, rookie? You looked like a jack-in-the-box."

"I'll admit, I felt a bit uptight."

Peter nodded and Janie shook her head, the tiniest of grins crooking her mouth.

"I don't want to appear naive, but his story seems plausible," Peter said.

Janie cut in, "He's a scumbag."

Peter continued, "Point taken, Janie. I don't like the looks of him either, but, by the way, we are criminal lawyers and many of our clients do look and act like scumbags. I'm going to check into City Productions and see what the story is there. I have some connections in California—shady bastards, but they helped me with a similar case a number of years ago. Jack, I want you and Janie to drive to Tampa and talk to the Russians."

"On it, boss."

CHAPTER SEVEN

ELI ROMANOV WATCHED AS his right-hand man, Boris, rolled the body of one of his "actors" onto a white sheet. The young black man, very well endowed, died accidentally of asphyxiation—not a total accident, however. His female counterparts, in the heat of the moment, tipped the chair in which he'd been tied. The noose around his neck attached to a bar several feet above him didn't help.

Erotic asphyxiation was the newest craze in underground pornography. The orgasm achieved when the brain was deprived of oxygen could be very intense and, in Eli's mind, it made for a great scene. Unfortunately, the actor's neck snapped, and he died instantly, simultaneously ejaculating, which was not uncommon among males who'd been executed by strangulation.

Having caught everything on tape, Eli Romanov felt tempted to send the film off to a small group in Charleston that traded in snuff films. He debated whether the risk would be worth the payoff. As much as he seemed up to making a dollar, snuff somehow crossed the line, accident or no accident; there were obvious risks involved.

He'd have to watch the girls. They'd been . . . very upset, but Eli had pacified them by promising a weekend in Vegas. He blamed them for the accident and threatened to turn them in to the authorities if they revealed anything. Truth be known, that was the last thing he'd do. If they squealed, the girls would both find themselves in the same state as his actor. He'd throw them in the cages, then have them dropped thirty miles out into the gulf wearing cement shoes. He'd stolen the idea from the television series *Dexter*. Dexter, however, erred by dropping too many bodies in the same locale. Eli would be more discrete, placing them randomly. In the past, he'd relied upon a family of cleaners down in Ft. Myers to do his dirty work, but, unfortunately, they met an untimely end five years ago.

Eli looked over Boris's shoulder and spoke to him in Russian. "Make sure there are no traces. Did you clean the mess he's made on the floor? Chlorine bleach, Boris."

Boris turned to his boss. He'd been friends with Eli since childhood, following him to America from St. Petersburg, Russia. The scowl was all Eli needed to see. "You know I do anything for you, Eli, but don't make piss with me when I'm doing the dirty work. I know very well how to do this."

"Of course." Eli knew the man didn't like this part of the business, but he'd become good at it. Eli should know better and give Boris his space. Let a killer do what he did best.

Boris turned back to his work, making sure the ropes were tight around the man's ankles. The knots would have to last a few days—long enough for the ocean's bottom dwellers to do their work. Catfish, crabs and pinfish would have the corpse cleaned in no time.

* * * *

Back in his office Eli booted up his desktop computer. The device was a source of pride, one of the most powerful machines available on the market, made by Taihu. Eli, an expert cinematographer, needed the power and memory to compile, save and remaster the thousands of videos that were to be distributed to wholesalers.

He hovered the cursor over the file containing the death scene. *What a shame. A prick that size could have earned him some good coin.* He watched the clip one last time, aroused by what he saw on the screen. Eli found it difficult to get aroused lately. He'd become desensitized by watching so much porn. "Fuck it!" he said, and made a silent promise. *This will be the only time.* The scene looked brilliant, nothing put-on or fake-looking. He wouldn't send this to City . . . no. The Chinese would be all over it and he could remain anonymous. He'd send it to his man in Shanghai, a sick bastard who would pay good money for this kind of shit. The Chinese loved anything with big dicks: the sicker, the bigger, the better!

Once he'd sent the file, he stood and walked through the armor-plated door protecting his office. Pressing the access code, he entered the nightclub. Aversions was one of several strip clubs Eli owned from Tampa to southern Louisiana. The business for the most part could be lucrative, but more importantly it supplied a steady stream of down-and-out women looking for a few extra bucks above what could be earned stripping. It wasn't one of the high-class peeler joints found downtown; he preferred the outskirts and he liked things on the seedier side. The finer establishments attracted clientele from parts of society with important connections, who might be missed if they were to suddenly disappear. The women were more difficult than the men to recruit. It wasn't hard to entice some poor schmuck from the front row with a big dick to perform on camera. Eli contemplated charging for the job, sure the lineup would be long. He chuckled. *How would I even advertise?*

Aversions Tampa was close to the I-75, allowing easy access to clients coming from Naples to Ocala. Here, certain deviances could be found for the right money. Eli paid thousands in fines and kickbacks yearly to keep away prying eyes, which he saw as a necessary business expense.

Eli eased himself into the multi-layered rooms, looking for one of the girls. He had his eye on a young Puerto Rican, new to the state. He craved her dark skin and he loved tattoos, which in her case adorned much of her stunning body. Aversions provided a personal buffet for Eli and the girls never refused— *could* never refuse.

Eli spotted his quarry. There she was, the tattooed vixen, getting ready to start a show. He decided to watch, sitting a few tables back. He could detect the nervousness in her movements. It wasn't every day the Boss sat to take in a show. The girl would know what it meant for him to watch a show. *Girls will talk.*

CHAPTER EIGHT

"DO YOU MIND IF I smoke?"

Jack looked at Janie as he drove through Ft. Myers traffic, heading toward I-75 North. "I know we haven't known each other for a long time . . . Well, we have, but not on a day-to-day basis. Have you ever seen me smoke?" He smiled coyly.

Janie nodded. "Just askin' . . . in case you were a closet smoker, maybe you might have one."

"Not a chance, smoker girl," he smirked. "I don't know why someone like you would even consider having another one. You've got that voice. If I were you, I'd write the thought off. Really, it's not attractive for a girl."

Janie shook her head slightly at the quip. *Girl?* She took the Southern gesture as a compliment. "So, we're going to pay that strip joint up in Tampa a visit first?"

"Suppose. Any better ideas?"

Janie sat up a bit straighter. In the beginning, she'd liked

Jackson. When they first met, he looked almost innocent. He appeared a little *cocksure* since they'd been assigned the case. Janie didn't know if she liked the trait.

"Nope, let's follow Peter's orders and drive to Aversions." She'd checked the place and its location out earlier. There wasn't much of an advertisement on the web page, only a cover stating it was a gentlemen's club, and an address, which usually meant you had to pay a nominal membership fee to get in the door. Your ID would be scanned and they'd know more about you in a few minutes than you could imagine.

Jack's phone rang through on the hands-free. "Jackson Walker?" the husky female voice crackled through the car speakers, sounding South Florida all the way.

"Yes . . ." He didn't give his cell number out freely. Silence.

"Jackson, my name is Lolita."

Jack looked at Janie, shrugging, not recognizing the name or voice. "Okay, Lolita. How'd you get my number and who the hell are you?"

"You wouldn't believe me if I told you, but suffice to say it was easy to locate you if you know . . . how and where to look."

"Okay, you have my attention. For a minute."

Janie gestured to Jack to keep the woman talking, her hands forming a quick little windmill.

"Jackson, do you believe in the occult?"

His hackles went off. His thoughts went to Gramps. He didn't know if there was any validity in what the old man said, but he believed in it with some hesitancy, as did many of his cousins. "I have an understanding of it. I don't know that I totally believe in it."

"Good. Jackson, please listen to me when I tell you this, and don't treat it as horseshit. I don't know you from Cain. But I do have a warning for you, unsolicited. You can choose to ignore my advice, or you can take my help at no cost."

"No cost?"

"Zero. Can I meet with you?"

"You're sure there's no cost? You're not just saying this to get me in there for the sales pitch? I've been to those gigs before."

"I give you my word. I know that's not much because you

don't know me, but it's all that I have to offer."

Jack glanced at Janie. She shrugged and whispered, "Sure, why not?"

"I'll send you a text with the time and location."

"Can I bring someone with me?"

"That's entirely up to you."

The phone disengaged.

Janie shook her head. "Jackson, strange trouble seems to follow you like flies to dog shit."

He smiled. "I agree, though I don't appreciate the analogy."

* * * *

The two-hour drive passed quickly, and Jack pulled off I-75 at the Brandon turnoff. Aversions was located a mile off the interstate. Jack pulled into a parking spot in front of a massive, Southern plantation-style building with a faded gray tin roof. The establishment's only indicator was a five-by-five sign out front announcing the *Aversions Gentlemen's Club*. The parking lot, however, was packed. People clearly knew about the club and certainly knew how to find it.

Janie turned to face Jack. "We're here to gather information. I know you say you want the lead, but I've done this a hundred times. You don't hit it on the head, remember. You're a junior lawyer researching a case, not a cop. Maybe you should follow my lead for your first time?"

"No. I'm good, Janie. I got this!"

"Your call." She touched his arm. "I gotta admit, I feel a little uncomfortable going in. I've been in nearly every beer joint between Tallahassee and Key West, but I've never been in a strip joint."

"No worries. Lots of couples come to these places." Jack tried his best to hide his grin.

"Really?"

"Yep, get primed up for the night, fuck like rabbits later."

Janie rolled her eyes. "So, am I your date?"

Jack pondered the comment for a moment, smiling. "You could pretend to be the cougar with the young guy if you want, but I'm not so sure about the fucking like rabbits later part."

"I don't fuck like a rabbit anymore, Jackson, and that ain't happening anyway. Lead away."

* * * *

The interior spread out before them, dark and vast with several stages where females danced in various degrees of undress. Strobe and neon lighting turned the joint into a decadent playground for the perverted hoard of people filling the place. Jack called prior to the drive to set up a meeting with the owners, but he'd been left on hold for half an hour and finally hung up in frustration. He decided they would risk coming unannounced.

They were required to take out a nominal membership—ten dollars each, to be exact—and their IDs were taken and analyzed. Jack retrieved their driver's licenses after they'd been scanned, giving the woman behind the glass a twenty to cover the charge.

Jack sauntered in as if he'd been to one of these places before. He wanted to appear cool and shot little sideways glances at the girls. Jack played the part perfectly, checking out the naked one on the stage to the left as they passed. He eyed her massive breasts as he approached one of the several bars lining the interior, Janie on his tail. A female bartender, dressed in what could loosely be called a bikini, smiled at them. "Drinks?"

Jack looked to Janie to order first and she said, "Vodka on the rocks."

"Okay," he said, "vodka for her. I'll have a Miller Lite." As the scantily-dressed barmaid poured Janie's drink, he asked, "Is the owner in today?"

Her eyes shot to his. "Why you ask? Eli's in, but he doesn't like to be bothered unless it's for a good reason."

Jack smiled. "We have a mutual friend, who said I should ask for him if I was ever in town."

"I'll let him know. He's only here two days a week, so you're lucky. What's your name?"

"Jackson, Jackson Walker."

"Hey, I know that name . . . and I thought you looked

familiar. You played for the Gators, right?"

Jack took a deep breath. "Yep, a few years back."

"Okay, Eli likes sports. I'm sure he'd have a few minutes for you."

They waited for the better part of an hour. Janie was fascinated by the power the strippers held over the crowd. Though she knew there existed a dark underbelly to the trade, she briefly thought that it might have been a sexy thing to do when she was younger. "You know, Jackson, there was a time in my life when I might have been tempted by this."

Jack turned, his eyes wide. "Yeah, and you would have had it going on!" he chuckled.

She answered his comment with a nasty glare and then a big smile.

"No, really, it's a bad scene. Thank your lucky stars you didn't. I knew a few girls back in high school who got into the trade. One's dead and the other disappeared. Friends of one of my girlfriends. They make good money, but there's a lot of shit that's so easy to access, you know—drugs, prostitution, pornography. Jessica White, she was prettier than all get-out, like a Barbie doll. Heard she died a few years back strung out on heroin. I saw her before the end, barely recognized her."

Jack put a hand on Janie's leg as he spotted a tall man with jet-black, short-cropped hair walking toward them. He was dressed in designer jeans, a white shirt with a suit jacket, and the man's shiny shoes were impeccable. He looked Eastern European and Jack couldn't read his expression.

Before Jack could say anything, the man said, "Jack Walker?"

Jack stood and shook the man's extended hand. "Yes."

"Eli Romanov." The man's thick accent, to Jack's ear, sounded Russian. "My girl says that you are a football star!" He motioned for Jack to sit. He looked over at Janie. "Is this your mother?"

Jack did his best not to chuckle. He saw Janie's consternation. "No, Eli, I *was* a football star, long past that now. And no, Janie's not my mother. We work together."

"Florida Gators. I love Gators." Eli extended his arms, making a chomping motion with his hands to emulate the

Florida Gators fans' signature motion.

Jack smiled. "I love 'em too, but I'm relegated to being a fan like you now. Nine years since I played for the University of Florida. I'll tell you, though, if I could go back in time, I would. Good times!"

"What brings you here, Jackson? I did some checking on you before I came out. You're a lawyer now, is that right?"

Jack saw Janie tense up. He was sure Eli didn't miss the reaction. "I am. I work for Robertson and Robertson down in Myers."

"Criminal lawyers, no?"

Jack got the feeling Eli knew exactly where the conversation was going. "Yes, serving the unjustly accused for over a hundred years."

Eli's face tightened. "Okay, no more bullshit, Jackson. Why are you here? It's not getting a free blow job because you were once famous?"

A bead of sweat formed on Jack's forehead. He pondered what to say before deciding on the truth as the best course of action. Eli had all of the pertinent information before they'd appeared. If Jack hoped to get anything out of the conversation, he'd better appear forthright. "Eli, we're here investigating a case. Your establishment was referenced by our client."

"Client?"

"Roberto Lopez."

"I don't know this name, Lopez. What is this connection you speak of?" He glared at Jack and never wavered.

"Pornography."

Janie groaned.

"Pornography? We run a first-class establishment, Mr. Walker. High-end girls."

A quick glance around gave Jack the impression the man had lofty ideas of where his establishment sat in the hierarchy of strip clubs. The place looked definitely second rate, as did the girls. Many of them looked cheap, little potbellies hanging over their bikini bottoms, overdone makeup. "My client has been arrested and is now out on bail for charges of possession of child pornography."

Eli chuckled to relieve a tinge of nervousness. "And this has something to do with me, of course?"

"I'm not making any insinuations, Mr. Romanov. Just following up on information given to us."

Eli's cheeks reddened. "Like fuck you are." Eli snapped his fingers. Within two seconds Jack and Janie were surrounded by four men. Each had a hand on a gun inside their blazers. Eli stood. "Nice meeting you, Jackson Walker. It's time you left. Too bad. I wanted to chat about football. I love American football."

The four men ushered Janie and Jack to their feet and moved them to the exit. Eli followed. "Let me tell you something, Jackson. The man you speak of is a rogue and a renegade. We no longer have any association with him."

Jack stopped, gaze steady. "Mr. Lopez stated he'd received the files from you a week or so ago. Did you cut ties last week after the porn ended up on his computer? We could file for a subpoena and have your computers looked at, if we wanted. And, by the way, I thought you hadn't heard of Lopez?"

"Maybe you should just do that, Mr. Walker. But you better be correct, because I now know who you are and where you work. We've given nothing to Mr. Lopez. He's delusional."

"Is that a threat, Mr. Romanov?"

Eli smiled, turning his head slightly away from Jack. "I don't make threats. I state fact. If you accuse me of something, you'd better have your facts straight, otherwise I'll find you and cut your fucking balls off."

Jack nodded. "Nice." He grabbed Janie's arm and moved her toward the door.

The four men formed a wall, which effectively pushed them to the exit, Eli looking a bit punk standing behind his men. "Don't come back here, Jack Walker. You're on the blacklist."

As he and Janie were ushered outside, Jack chewed on his cheek for a moment, pausing in his tracks. Janie tried to drag him to the car, but he insisted on getting in a last word. He looked at Eli. "You're hiding something, but don't worry. I feel like I need a shower just being in there. You're on my fucking blacklist, too."

Eli said something to one of the men in Russian. Before Jack could react, he and Janie were physically steered out the door. Once outside, one of the men grabbed Jack's arms, forcing them behind his back while the second man punched him in the gut, doubling him over. The next shot hit Jack's jaw, stunning him. They let him fall to the ground and moved back to the door.

Janie dropped to his side. "Jack, you all right?" She lifted his head from the pavement.

He slowly shook his head, the stars disappearing from his vision, and felt around his mouth with his tongue. He spat a tooth into his hand. "Felt better." When he got to his feet, he stumbled for a second.

Eli spoke calmly at the door. "Just a love tap, Walker. Don't come back unless you want to fuck."

Janie guided him back to his Jeep before he said anything else. "I'll drive."

He didn't argue and slid into the passenger's side as two of Eli's men took note of his plate information.

Once they were back on I-75 Janie asked, "Really, are you okay?"

"My gut hurts and my mouth is on fire. Funny enough, I think we found out what we needed to know."

Janie pondered his words before nodding. "They're in on it."

"Not necessarily, but they knew Robert Lopez."

"True, but I think it might have been better if you'd softened him up a bit before you started accusing him of shit. You know, like talking about the Gators; he gave you the in. It's no wonder you got yourself into so much trouble with the Church of Set. We need to teach you some tact and diplomacy! Well, what's done is done. What's the next step?"

"I hoped you'd tell me. My head hurts too much to think. Besides, this is supposed to be your thing."

"I'm glad as hell to hear you say that. Acknowledging your apathy is a good first step."

"Apathy? What the crap do you mean by that, and first step? Geez, Janie."

She shook her head in wonderment. "Just what I said. If we're working together, we need to be on the same page. I know you're the strong macho type, but if that man had punched me, he'd have broken my face. I don't need that." She tapped her fingers on the steering wheel. "Surveillance! We need to get something on Mr. Romanov."

"We'd need to bring the police in on it, and we don't have anything on him." Jack probed his jaw with his left hand for a moment. "Lopez. Remember I told you that he said he'd been referred to me by friends? There is a connection. I think Lopez needs to come to the table with a bit more info; otherwise, we're at a dead end and it's purely going to come down to the evidence against him, which at this point ain't looking good. We need to talk to Lopez again."

Out of the blue, Jack remembered the lady who called earlier. He checked his phone. He'd received a text with a Bonita Springs address and a time: 6 PM tomorrow.

"That lady, Lolita—do you have a text?"

"Keep your eyes on the road. Yep, tomorrow evening. You don't have to come. This is personal."

"No, Jackson, I'm not letting you out of my sight. I've learned that lesson the hard way."

"Look, I'm a grown man. You and Gramps—"

"What about him? I love that man!"

"He thinks the damned demon spirits are aligned against me again. Called me down to Everglades City a week back; says he's gonna sick Josh on me, like a bodyguard."

Janie nodded. "See, that's it. Your gosh darn apathy oozes out of your pores like sweat. You think you're invincible until it's too late, then all hell breaks loose and we're all pulled in hook, line and sinker to save you."

"Won't happen again, girl. Let's get back to Myers and we'll grab a happy hour drink at the Outrigger."

"You're living on Ft. Myers Beach now? And, by the way, stop calling me *girl*. You've been listening to too much country music."

"Yep, south end. Got a sweet spot on the back bay, boat dock, all I need. C'mon, I'm only saying *girl* 'cause I like you. I'm not fucking apathetic, by the way." He looked out the window. "Just like a spoiled little kid."

"I'm too old for you, Jackson, and if that's the case, start acting like you're not. Face what's in front of you and deal with it. Don't let things fester."

He nodded. "I mean, I like you in a cool girl kinda way, not like I wanna jump in the sack or anything."

"You're digging a hole. You didn't have to say anything."

"Okay, not gonna call you *girl* anymore . . . swear." He prodded his jaw again.

"That's better. You need to respect your elders," she smirked.

CHAPTER NINE

MASON STARED OUT THE window of the prison van as the vehicle passed through the intricate fencing system of the Louisiana State Penitentiary, affectionately named *Angola* by black inmates more than a century ago after the country the original plantation's slaves came from in Africa.

Mason had risen quickly within the prisoner hierarchy. The Satanists were left alone on the inside, free from the sexual bondage the prison was well known for. One stare from the evil little man would freeze the meanest inmate, his mythical reputation preceding him. Angola boasted a population of over forty worshipers of the Dark Lord, ready and waiting to follow the satanic Magus's every word.

It was only a matter of time before an efficient route of escape presented itself. He was one of Satan's most devoted worshipers, and the Dark Lord would show him the way. He smiled, remembering his first day out of solitary confinement.

* * * *

Mason stepped out of his new cell the moment the door locks were released. His roommate cowered in the corner, too terrified to move. Mason smirked, amazed at what the threat of eternal damnation could reduce a man to. Peering into the man's mind and prodding his soul only added to the enjoyment. He'd soon be induced into taking his own life. It would take a few more cellmates meeting the same fate to make the establishment realize Mason had made a request, however subtle it might be, for a single room without cellmates.

He felt all eyes upon him as he walked to the cafeteria. His stride showed he owned the place, and he returned the glares with a sly, devilish grin, which to a man could not be matched. He'd been shoved in the food line, which was to be expected. As he brought his tray into the dining area, he spotted many knowing faces, who saluted him with subtle nods. He sat purposefully among members of the biggest and roughest group he could find, calmly put his tray on the table, and placed his cutlery on either side of his plate.

It didn't take long before one of the prisoners, a large black man with long dreadlocks, stepped in front of him and flipped the tray onto Mason's lap. "Who the fuck do you think you are, *home boy?* You have a death wish or something, or do you wanna be our bitch that bad?"

Mason raised his eyes and never stopped smiling.

Another prisoner rose from the next table over holding a jailhouse shiv—metal torn off a bed frame. It took fewer than five steps to get behind Dreadlocks and jab the razor-sharp weapon into his neck, severing his carotid artery.

Mason froze throughout the expected black backlash against the white killer. Everyone from the table stood to defend themselves from the onslaught and the guards breaking up the melee. When the guards finally gained control, the dead and injured were dragged off to solitary confinement or the morgue.

Mason stated calmly in his French accent, "Who's going to get me my dinner?"

It didn't take long for a fresh tray of food to appear in front of him.

* * * *

The penitentiary owned a golf course located on the prison property and looked after by inmates—its name Angola, naturally. The layout, exceptionally manicured, brought in a good profit from outside golfers. A tee time required booking a month in advance.

Mason placed himself in the good books once the twinkle of an idea formed in his head. He was an expert manipulator of men, with a little help from down below, of course. He needed to be patient. It took him well over two years to solidify a position on the greens-keeping staff—a well-planned, manipulative undertaking. Given time, he could bend any person's mind and free will to his desires.

The prison and its warden and deputy wardens randomized prisoner activities to discourage any sort of plotting; Mason's time at the golf course stayed random. While Mason carefully plotted the timing of his escape during the first year, a rough pattern formed. He contacted his outside sources through coded letters until a plan began to percolate. Today would be his satanic compatriots' third attempt to meet with him on the golf course.

The prison van stopped, letting off those inmates who would be working on the links. Mason walked to the course's work shed in his orange jumpsuit, his hands cuffed in front of him with a long silver chain to allow for raking, or driving a fairway mower. It took Mason months of searching to find the surveillance cameras' blind spots throughout the course. He had found two, one at the bottom of a massive, deep bunker on the fifth hole. He took his time raking the various traps offering angst to golfers whose shots strayed from the straight and narrow along Angola's third, fourth, and fifth holes.

He spied the foursome of Satanists wearing their bright red hats and making their way to the tee at the fifth hole. Mason moved toward the large pot bunker 240 yards out from that tee and stood ready to step into its depths once his counterpart guided his ball into the sand. It hadn't been easy to find a doppelganger with some skill at golf. The follower would be subservient to his death and thoroughly brainwashed by the cult to follow his directive. He appeared to be a close double to Mason, his mustache and beard trimmed to match, and wearing black iris contact lenses—the final touch to be an exact duplicate.

Mason prayed to the Dark Lord that a marshal wouldn't pass through anytime soon. The last escape attempt was foiled by one of the many prison officers who kept a close eye on the course and the inmates to provide a sense of safety for the golfers. As he carefully raked sand from the trap to the lip, Mason watched for a shot headed his way. All four would attempt to put a ball in the trap, which was well-positioned to catch the stray shots.

The first tee shot looked to be heading his way but drew back to the middle of the fairway. The second bounced over it, a towering power fade. The third, a low-running worm burner, rolled into the edge, dropping to the deep middle of the trap as planned. *Perfect!*

Mason raked toward the middle of the deep hole. Once at the bottom, he waited, precious seconds ticking away. His double appeared on cue with a lockpick in hand and deftly removed the cuffs and chains. They exchanged golf shoes for boots, golf shirt and shorts for orange prison jumpsuit. The coup-de-grace to top off the disguise, Mason took the sand wedge and put on the black Titleist golf cap and Ray Ban sunglasses. His double quickly put on the cuffs and chains to resume raking. Mason picked up the ball, tossing it toward the fairway, being a terrible golfer himself.

As he stepped out of the trap, he saw one of the marshals heading for the bunker with a stern look. He pulled up beside Mason, gesturing at his double, now obediently finishing his raking of the trap.

The man asked in a deep Louisianan drawl, "Is this boy bothering you?" He stared over his sunglasses at Mason's double. "Twenty yards, that the rule. You won't see the light of day for a week." When the double nodded, the marshal turned back to Mason. "Sorry about that. We have strict rules. It won't happen again."

Mason did his best to emulate the man's drawl and mask his French accent. "No worries, man. He did stand back. I nearly hit him with my tee shot. I told him he didn't have to move."

The marshal nodded. "Enjoy your round, sir."

Mason nodded and slipped into the empty seat of a golf cart.

He had to dig the homing device out of his back before moving too far from the fairway trap. The man next to him in the cart nodded as soon as the marshal passed far enough ahead of them. "As you requested, Master." He produced a wrapped surgical scalpel from his pocket.

Mason pulled up his shirt and pointed to his left side, prodding the spot where he wanted the other man to feel for the capsule-shaped device and cut it out of Mason's skin. When the small incision was made and the tiny mechanism removed, the follower placed a large, square bandage over the incision to stanch the flow of blood.

"Toss it into the green side bunker up ahead as you've been instructed." Mason reverted to his icy tone as he watched the double making his way to the green.

The foursome speedily finished the rest of the front nine and headed for the exit gate. This would be the tricky part, as they had to pass in front of several cameras while offloading their golf gear. He made it through without difficulty. Within minutes, he was in his own car, heading south toward New Orleans.

* * * *

The duplicate found his way back to Mason's cell following his well-studied mental map of the prison block. Entering the cell, he took off his clothes and lay back naked under the cot's thin blanket. Trying not to think ahead, he stared at the ceiling, remembering how his bottom teeth had all been pulled out a few months back.

He put his fingers inside his mouth and took out the row of false teeth given to him early that morning to wear but not to chew with. He stared at the waxed copies for a long minute, hesitating at the duty before him. The promise of salvation by the Dark Lord for his grand sacrifice was worth giving up his life, but he did not want to suffer. He'd been prepped concerning what the waxen teeth contained and how each one would affect him. If he cracked them open in the order relayed to him, he would avoid the worst of it. Make one mistake and he would stay awake to endure the fires of Hell.

Pulling open the first tooth, he was careful to let the few drops slide across his middle finger. He twisted that finger as far up his rectum as possible to begin the internal combustion. The acid burn crawled up his lower bowel as he swiftly cracked into the second tooth for more of the same. He used his forefinger to twist the next few drops into his ears until the one hundred proof acid burned his ear drums, making him deaf. Two down and eleven capsules to go until he reached ecstasy.

The secretions from the next four had to be spread between his toes and fingers. The thick vapors traveled up his nostrils as he popped the four wax teeth, making him lightheaded. Blinking to stay awake, he cracked open the next four to rub the burn along his legs and arms, front and back. His skin broke apart and the chemical burned and started to eat his flesh.

He had to hurry. Three more to ecstasy. His orders were to drizzle them in his hair and any spot not already sizzling. He could hardly wait to empty the capsules and get to the last one for relief. Smelling his burning flesh caused him to gag, but he did not stop. Opening his mouth wide, he waited for the promised narcotic. Watching the drops hitting his outstretched tongue, he cried. They lied to him. It was not the ecstasy he was promised. He swallowed more of the same chemical, and now it burned down his throat to set his stomach gases on fire. He wanted to pass out but instead gulped the vapors coming off his body. Short chemical flames wound up his spine.

Flaming pieces of hair drifted from his head to his face, but he could no longer move. The excruciating pain and loss of mobility stopped him. The dying man felt betrayed. Where was his ecstasy? Now, he could only pray for his death.

Within the next few minutes, inmates and guards stood outside the cell, not daring to get closer due to the fumes. A few had already taken off for clean air and a place to vomit. Sirens rang, and finally guards dressed in hazmat attire took over. They made all who were not suited up line up to leave the building. This was not a drill!

Unsure what chemicals were at play, the crew watched and waited, unable to spray water or pressurized chemicals at the last of the flames. Sliding open the cell door, the three men who came ready to fight off a major fire arrived to see the indent of a man's body but nothing more.

One of them asked, "Christ, where'd the guy go?"

All three shook their helmeted heads. Another wondered aloud, "Could this be one of those spontaneous human combustions?"

The third guy answered, "I don't know."

For all intents and purposes, Mason Matye ceased to exist in the real world.

CHAPTER TEN

THE AFTERNOON THUNDERSTORM DIDN'T do much to stave off the humidity. In fact, it made it worse. Such was life in South Florida; the moisture would evaporate quickly, adding to the stickiness in the air as the sun heated up the moisture. All things would become sticky as hell.

Solomon made his daily walk, pushing a rusty buggy to the mall at the corner of US 41 and Bonita Beach Road. He'd visit the liquor store, then Publix. He couldn't run out of Budweiser, with Jack Daniels for a chaser—his vices since he'd left the Big House.

He had no friends. People like him didn't want friendship. When first released, he'd moved to Lafayette, a smaller town just outside of New Orleans. People there didn't like his sort. His need to commit crime hung over him like the stench of week-old fish. He swung south along the Panhandle, stopping for a year in Tampa until finally settling in the Ft. Myers area.

When he felt lucky, he'd make the long walk to the dog track. If he won, he'd pop for a taxi ride home. It was cheaper now with Uber, and sometimes he'd spring for both ends of the journey . . . that is, if he picked the correct dogs that day.

Today, he didn't feel like walking to the track. He returned home after completing his shopping to pour a two-finger Jack with ice before he sat at his computer. Being alone and addicted to gambling, the computer was his life breath. He preferred online poker for the most part, and sometimes euchre. He never played for money online; it just didn't seem right.

When he checked his email, Solomon smiled. The file had arrived and he'd paid good money for the material. He couldn't wait to see what his suppliers sent him. *Some little nugget of gold?* His tastes were a little on the dark side. He didn't like anything mundane, or in his face. He liked something with a little thought put into it. Solomon enjoyed a bit of a story, no matter how short it might be. He needed a backstory or it wasn't worth watching. *Yeah, I like watching . . . nothing more.* That was all he allowed himself—all he dared.

CHAPTER ELEVEN

ELI LOOKED ACROSS HIS desk at Boris. His lifelong friend and right-hand man watched him in silence. When they spoke at last, they spoke in Russian. "What you think, Boris? I can tell by the look on your face you're not happy."

Boris chose his words carefully. Even though Eli was his friend, the man had a bad temper and Boris could tell that it currently simmered just below a boil. "Lopez sold us out. The asshole needs to disappear. He crossed the line. If that jerk is not punished, others will see it as a weakness. They will follow his example."

"It's not that easy, Boris. The lawyer football player, Walker, and the blond woman, they know just as much. We must be careful. I don't think the police know yet, or they would have been here before Walker."

"True. Do we take them out as well, I wonder? Now that we've been burned? The country could use one less lawyer."

"I don't know if we have much choice, but it can't be a whack job. We must plan this carefully. I'd like to delay Walker's death, but if he comes back . . . we will have no choice but to kill him." Eli frowned. "And Lopez. You must be careful, Boris. We are close to the edge, here; take your time with it. One wrong step and we could find ourselves in a real mess, but kill him before he causes us anymore trouble. He's a bit of a loner from what we've been told. He won't be missed by many people."

Eli poured two vodka shots, handing one to Boris. "*Vashe zdorovye!*" The two men fired back the smooth Russian liquor. "Boris, take some men down to Ft. Myers and have Walker and Lopez watched. They'll talk to each other again. If we could only be so lucky as to catch the two together, we could plan a convenient end for both of them. Keep me informed."

Boris nodded, a smile creeping into the corner of his mouth. "We will watch them. Don't worry. Am I to use my own discretion?" Coy excitement crossed his face as he waited for his boss's answer.

Eli pondered the assassin's question, knowing that Boris loved nothing more than ending someone's life. Eli could not afford the risks on this one. Boris loved Eli like a brother, and Boris was always willing to do the wet work—the wetter the better; yet Boris could not be left to his own devices. His skills needed to be used cautiously, with purpose.

"*Nyet*, let's watch them first. Wait for my word. I always answer my phone when you call."

Boris nodded. "Okay, Eli, I give you my word." Boris's word was gold when it came to anything relating to their business and personal relationship. The two men got to their feet, smiled and embraced, slapping each other on the back like comrades of old.

CHAPTER TWELVE

MASON RELEASED THE PRESSURE of his thumbs on the young woman's windpipe. Lamenting the fact that he needed to kill her, he pulled the sheets up to her neck and slipped out of the bed. *Oh, how I've craved the touch of female flesh.* Five years locked up in prison did that to a man. It wasn't the act of fornication he missed as much as the touch of a soft breast or inner thigh, looking into the eyes of a female and seeing her soul bared and naked in the heat of sex. Mason's close association to the Dark Lord gave him the ability to see those things clearly. In the end, he reckoned the whore to be a wasted, useless soul who needed to be put out of her misery. She no longer retained the human ability to feel; she existed as a shell of a person, fucking for no reason other than money. She needed to die. That bitch had no right to fuck him like that and she knew it.

Slowly pulling on his clothes, he cursed himself for being so sloppy. His DNA would be detected. *But, in the end, what does it matter anyway?* He no longer existed. His death certainly offered a few fringe benefits.

Mason walked downstairs to the foyer of the once grand hotel. Now it also was only a shell of itself. The old place sat on the edge of Storyville, coined after Sidney Story, an alderman who wrote guidelines to control prostitution within the city. The ordinance designated a sixteen-block area where prostitution, although still nominally illegal, was tolerated for a time. While it was originally referred to as the red-light district of New Orleans, Storyville and open prostitution ceased to exist in the early 1900s. Still, the sex trade continued and could be found readily if one knew where to look or how to ask the right questions.

The night air, delightfully warm, engulfed him as his feet hit the sidewalk; Mason decided to walk to his destination. He needed to clear his head after his disappointing encounter with that woman. His stroll took him down Bourbon Street, which wasn't what he remembered. It looked overcommercialized, like anything and everything in America that had something to it. *How disappointing!*

He passed through the French Quarter and, after several blocks, found himself in a less than savory area. It didn't matter to a man like him, who feared little. In fact, he dared the universe to put some punk in his way to give him a hard time. He'd give that poor sucker a one-way ticket to Hell.

Happily, his destination hadn't changed since he'd been there last. Little Rickard's wasn't a shop in the general sense— nothing but a little hole in a wall, a place not frequented by tourists; but those who *knew* . . . knew otherwise. Little Rickard's wasn't Vodun, or "voodoo," like many of the occult boutiques. Rickard's Shop was one of the oldest purveyors in the dark arts and had existed for centuries. The shop did not need to advertise. In fact, the only indicator was a white hand painted on the door telling those in the know that they were on the Left-Hand Path.

You didn't simply walk into Rickard's Shop. You rang a doorbell and waited for the proprietor, Moses, to respond. An intricate surveillance system gave the quirky proprietor instant access to an extensive underworld data bank. If you were connected in any way, you were already known. A comparison photo would pop up on his computer just in case. Moses would then decide whether he wanted to talk to you or even let you in. The process, in effect, weeded out the police and the pretenders.

The door opened slowly and the dark-skinned Moses peeked out through a crack, scrutinizing Mason with the utmost care. He spoke with a distinctive Haitian-Creole drawl, which didn't necessarily mean he was from Haiti. A subculture ran through the North American occult community in the South. Being extremely insular, the jargon and accents remained eerily similar to what they might have been a hundred or so years ago.

Moses may have found his roots in the Vodun religion, but he was clearly entrenched within the Church of Satan. Satanism found its recruits in all sects of life.

Moses bowed before Mason, the highest level of respect that could be offered within the underworld community. Mason motioned for him to rise, placing a hand on the man's shoulder.

Mason understood, to the word, all of the teachings of Anton LaVey, the father of modern Satanism, and he wanted revenge. The Church of Satan did a pretty good job of softening the less savory elements of their practice. It was easy enough to jump onto their webpage, *thechurchofsatan.com,* and see they espoused non-demonic, esoteric practices. Mason knew better. Before being ensconced as the head of the Church of Satan's Southern US chapter, he assisted in rewriting rituals created to draw upon the power of Satan. Yet, if anyone wanted to put a curse on another, they came here to Rickard's Shop. Moses held a strong understanding of both Vodun and Satanistic rituals.

Mason looked at the man. "Have you prepared the room?"

"*Oui.* I am eminently pleased to serve your needs."

Mason smiled. "Of course." As long as he paid him a ridiculous amount of money. "Do you have someone who can assist me, as per my request?"

"*Oui, monsieur.* There's a young girl, Elaine. She can help you. She's been trained and has reached the second level."

Mason was very familiar with the hierarchy, having attained the level of Magus, second in line to the Grandmaster of the

Church. Disciples of the second level were called Witches or Warlocks depending on their level of expertise. She would do, though he would have preferred a Priestess. A Priestess would have performed the ritual before, without hesitancy. A Witch could very well be working the incantation for the first time.

Moses read Mason's face. "She is well versed in the prayer. We gave the literature to her a few days ago."

"Thank you. I appreciate your expertise, and your optimism," Mason frowned, then brightened. "I do appreciate that you are willing to change suits"—referring to Moses's practice in both of the dark religions.

"Differing views and approaches, *monsieur*. I am a slut to both faiths; though, as you know, I'm a Satanist at heart." He winked. "I must offer what we can to our clients. New Orleans is the heart of darkness. To limit one's self would be . . . foolish. In the end, it revolves around one entity. *Oui*?"

Mason nodded. The man was a religious mercenary, if there was such a thing. Mason needed anonymity foremost, and this is what Moses sold.

"You can take the second door to the right down the hallway." He motioned to his left. "The stairs will lead you to the cellar. Elaine has prepared everything you will require."

Walking to the hallway, Mason smiled, looking back at the man. "Everything?"

Moses nodded effusively.

* * * *

Mason descended the rickety steps to the cellar. A stale smell of moisture and lack of airflow became increasingly pungent as he descended—the smell of death. He knocked on the door and heard a low "Come in."

The dirt-floor, candlelit room appeared much bigger than he would have assumed—maybe thirty by forty feet. Dank and evil smelling, it opened in front of him, filled with numerous devices used over the centuries by the cultists. Whips and chains hung on the walls above strange benches and racks. There were trays filled with wicked knives and bowls. In the far corner, partially covered by a black cloth, was a device that appeared to be an old French guillotine. Mason could only imagine the atrocities that occurred within these sweat-soaked stone walls. He felt mildly encouraged, the dank space offering him comfort.

In the middle of the room, Mason saw a circle of power etched in chalk surrounding a pentagram; black candles made from the fat of an unbaptized baby sat on each of the five corners. At the center waited a young woman sitting cross-legged. She was heavyset with a punk look, hair shaved on the sides with the middle gelled to a fine, short-pointed Mohawk. Her chubby arms, legs and neck were adorned with a mass of tattoos. Beside her sat a thin, black-haired girl, no older than seven, her skin pale and her eyes sunken. Mason surmised she'd been drugged. Elaine raised her eyes to meet his. They sustained contact for what seemed like minutes before Mason broke her gaze. *Impressive. Most don't last ten seconds.*

She returned her eyes to his. "I've prepared all you've asked for, but it wasn't easy. I'll ask you for payment in advance." As Mason moved toward her, she put up her hand. "You can put the money in the bowl beside the door. Five grand." Still gazing at him, she pulled an old-fashioned pistol out of her handbag and placed it on the ground in front of her.

Mason smiled. *Smart girl.* He placed a wad of hundred-dollar bills in the bowl before he moved to enter the circle.

She once more put her hand up to stop his motion. "You must cleanse yourself first before I will allow you to enter my circle."

Mason stared at her incredulously, then nodded. "Wise." He sat cross-legged and performed a cleansing prayer to Satan and the dark spirits, opening up his senses and soul to their influence.

Once finished, Elaine gestured, welcoming him into her circle. "Not too close." She patted the gun.

Mason hesitated, then stepped over the circle and sat three feet across from Elaine, who seemed no more relieved once he'd crossed the chalk. He rubbed his hands together, the smoke from the foul-smelling candles burning his eyes. "Shall we begin?"

Elaine nodded and began the Prayer of Destruction.

Mason knew it would draw upon all of his powers to direct enough energy toward the destruction of Jackson Walker—a prayer not to be taken lightly but nevertheless an important ingredient of the Black Mass he intended to perform in the coming weeks. She evoked the powers of the four crown Princes of Hell, taking a large, lit candle, which sat in the middle of the pentagram, and holding it with both hands. She faced the candle to the east and her voice resonated, "Lucifer, the bringer of light." She turned to the north. "Belial, lord of earth." She turned to the west. "Leviathan, master of the sea." She turned to the south. "Ha Satan, lord of fire, we call upon your powers." She returned to the center and motioned to Mason.

He took a piece of paper out of his pocket and unfolded it. Clearing his throat, he began, "Ha Satan, I call on your eminence and all of your powers to heed my prayer. I pray for the destruction of Jackson Walker. I and the Church of Satan have been dealt a grievous injustice by this man. The despicable vermin killed two of our Priestesses, Henrietta LePley in particular, who was one of your longest-serving disciples and benefactors. He killed members of our church: Isaac, Eric and Jimmy McFadden, Carly and Buck Henderson. I have been incarcerated due to my affiliation with you and the deceased. I deem it to be a grievous injustice to you and those who follow you. I made a promise to the man when I was arrested that I would seek vengeance upon him. I sit here now, open to your powers and your blessed affiliation.

"I call upon you to destroy Jackson Walker. I call upon you to throw down the spiritual support of his Seminole blood. I call upon you to stab him in the eyes, throat, and heart. On his death, I call upon you to give him a thousand years of unrelenting torment in Hell!"

He pulled out a newspaper clipping of Jackson—one he'd been carrying with him for some time—depicting Walker as a hero who broke the back of the Church of Set. He placed it on his written prayer. He lifted his pant leg and removed a thin dagger, his athame, which had been strapped to his lower leg. In a quick motion, he stabbed the sharp knife through the papers, making sure it cut through the head of Jackson Walker.

Elaine pushed the candle in the middle of the pentagram toward him, as well as a stone bowl.

Mason ignited the papers and tossed them into the bowl.

Elaine pushed the young girl to Mason, offering him her arm. Mason looked down at several scars on the soft part of her wrist. He cut lengthwise into the white flesh of her forearm. He didn't want a gush of blood, just a slow, steady stream. He dripped the dark fluid onto the burning papers as they fizzled into dust. The strength of a virgin's blood was renowned for arousing the curiosity of the demons he was evoking.

Elaine motioned, her palm extended toward him, inadvertently getting too close. "That is enough."

He gently let the girl roll to the ground. Before she could react, Mason jumped to his feet, jamming the knife's blade into Elaine's throat. He used his strength to pull the knife up into her chin. Elaine looked at him in shock, gurgling from the gaping, bloody hole in her neck. She dropped, blood seeping onto the chalk pentagram. He smiled. *The sacrifice of a Witch surely won't hurt my cause.*

He wrapped a piece of cloth around the girl's wound and picked her up.

* * * *

Moses watched the ritual with great interest via surveillance cameras. Thankfully, Mason paid him well for the privilege he had taken. The cost of a Witch would well be covered by what the film Moses now owned would earn.

Mason appeared at the top of the steps with the young girl in his arms. He laid the girl upon Moses's desk. "She will live." He met Moses's eyes. "You've received payment?"

"*Oui, monsieur.*"

Mason stepped out the door, the smell of the Mississippi strong now with a change in wind direction. *A good omen.*

CHAPTER THIRTEEN

JACK PULLED INTO HIS driveway and looked at Janie. "You don't have to come, really!"

"I'm not letting you out of my sight again as long as we're on this case."

"This isn't the case." He slid out of the Jeep.

Janie waited until they were clear of the vehicle. "Somehow, I think it is. Bad things follow you, Walker. I don't want to have to chase you all over Southwest Florida again if you get taken away by murderous Satanists."

Jack shrugged. "Whatever." He noticed another car in the driveway, an old Corolla. "Josh," he smiled, walking briskly to the door. Janie followed right behind him. The smell of pot and the sound of Nirvana blasting through the stereo speakers greeted him. He walked through the small bungalow onto the back lanai, where he spotted his cousin lying out in a lawn chair, chin on his chest, snoring nearly as loud as the music. Jack kicked his shoe.

Josh startled out of his sleep. His eyes open, trying to find some purchase on reality, he focused in on Jack, then on Janie. "Fuckin' sore sight, the two of you." He stumbled to his feet and gave Jack a hug. "What's up, bro?" He turned to Janie and hugged her. "Miss Callaghan, it's been some time."

Janie released the embrace, scrunching her face at his smoky beer breath. "Been five years, Josh, and doesn't seem like it. And it's Janie."

Jack walked to the kitchen. "Coors anyone?" Both Janie and Josh nodded. He returned with three tallboy cans and handed them out. The three pulled the deck chairs into a semi-circle looking out on Estero Bay. "So, Gramps made you come up here?"

"You know it. Gramps says something you *damn well* do it. You know how it is. He's got you pretty wrapped now, too."

Jack frowned, the notion dawning on him. "I suppose . . ."

"Said I'm to keep an eye on you."

"Well, let's keep the old gaffer happy. You can hang at the house. You got the boat, and the redfish are running back in the bay."

"I think he meant a little closer than that. He's afraid you're going to get knocked off by one of those Satanist fucks."

Jack rubbed his temples, working to clear his eyes for a moment. He said, "Josh, having you close is a comfort, though I don't know why everyone's being so freaking cautious. Just because Gramps dreams up something, we all go ape shit."

Janie spoke. "What about the call today? You have to go see that woman tonight."

Josh took a swig of his beer. "What woman?"

"Some fortune teller. Palm reader from Bonita."

"She called outta the blue?"

"Yep," Janie was quick to answer.

"Okay, as Gramps likes to say, there are no coincidences." Josh met their eyes. Josh was evidently brainwashed by the old man, just like everyone else.

Janie nodded. "I wouldn't believe it if I hadn't seen the old man at work five years ago."

"Aw, come on, it's all hocus-pocus, mumbo jumbo bullshit!" Jack finished his beer in one long gulp.

"Okay, Jack, I'll not cramp your style, but I'm stayin' close."

Jack sighed, "Okay, you two, have it your way. But I'd appreciate it if you kept an eye on things around here. No more is needed."

Josh half squinted with his left eye, not used to this type of brashness from Jack. His cousin possessed a low-simmering temper, but he'd always been pretty easygoing, not full of the latent sarcasm flowing out of his mouth tonight.

Josh changed the topic. "Nice spot you got here, Jack."

"Yeah, pretty cool for a single guy. Keep the music down—you'll scare the snook from the end of the dock, okay?" Jack took a long look at his older cousin, a native Seminole. Now that Josh worked for Gramps, he'd taken on a cleaner-shaved look. Though he didn't see any merit in the occult warnings, Jack wouldn't mind having Josh around to catch up on things and have a good laugh, maybe get high now and again. He felt terrible shrugging him off. But the psychic shit got on his nerves and he didn't expect it from his favorite cousin. He needed to nip it in the bud.

* * * *

The drive to Bonita went by far too quickly for Jack's liking. Another hour and he would have been happier. He felt edgy about the ensuing meeting. The place was located off Old Highway 41, a plain white house with several signs indicating palm reading, tarot cards and fortune-telling, all in bright neon.

Janine couldn't help herself and commented, "Is this for real?"

Jack blew air through his teeth, not saying a word as he got out of the Jeep. Janie followed him, stepping out of the passenger side. He stomped to the door with a flourish of bravado. Janie couldn't quite put her figure on the purpose of his actions or reaction to the situation. Maybe he didn't want to look foolish for dragging them out on a wild goose chase. *Could it be nerves?* He knocked heavily on the door until it creaked open. Clearly someone expected them, because the latch was not quite engaged.

Janie giggled as Jack backed away from the door. "You scared, Jack?"

He growled something indiscernible under his breath and pushed the door open. Janie peered over his left shoulder. The room looked like a plain reception area—whitewash walls, a small desk; the lights were on, but no one was visible. There were two exits on the far wall, one a closed door and the other an archway leading to a room filled with flickering, orange-and-yellow candlelight.

A couple of steps into the reception area, a heavyset black woman appeared in the archway. Dressed in thick, billowy skirts, her wrists, fingers, earlobes and neck adorned with several pieces of jewelry, she smiled broadly.

"Jackson Walker." It wasn't phrased as a question but rather as a statement of fact.

"Yes, ma'am, and this is Janie Callaghan. I said I'd be bringing someone along."

"Yes. That's quite alright. I know about Janie, though . . . I didn't know her name."

Jack's heart thumped. He could think of nothing better to say than "Okay."

"I'm Lolita. Some call me a fortune teller. I like to think of myself as a white witch."

Jack backed up a step. "The Church of Set?"

Her mouth widened into a big, toothy grin. "Naw, man, I'm on the good team. I know your past, Jackson Walker, and your run-in with the Devil Spawn. I didn't ask you here to scare you. Come in." She gestured for them to follow her into the candlelit room.

Entering the room felt like walking into a Moroccan opium den, minus the drug paraphernalia. Large, overstuffed pillows surrounded a small round table in the center, behind which sat an ancient chair. Incense burned in several locations. In front of the table sat a single small stool. Lolita motioned for Janie to sit amongst the pillows, and for Jack to sit in the spot provided.

Once seated, she looked at Jack. "Are you afraid of the

occult, Jackson? You look apprehensive."

"I don't know what to think, ma'am. Part of me sees the power Henrietta LePley held over others. She was a very strong-willed individual, with a knack for getting her own way. The psychic angle makes me more skeptical, but the old woman, once she looked you in the eyes, seemed to catch hold of you in a way that could not be easily broken. It happened to me twice. I became powerless and couldn't say no to her."

Lolita nodded as if he wasn't telling her anything she didn't already know.

"Here's the root of it for me. My grandfather says there is no such thing as coincidence. I, on the other hand, do believe in it. You can talk your way into believing anything, if that's what you choose to do. I spend most of my time talking myself out of the whole thing. So, I choose not to believe." He took a long breath after his diatribe.

She nodded. "Then why did you come?" She let the words hang.

Jack pondered her question. "It seems this stuff follows me around, and I don't like it. I came here to see what you have to say and debunk it and tell you to stop bugging me. I have enough of you people telling me I'm strong with the spirits, blah, blah, blah. I'm sick of it. Maybe I'm on a mission."

Lolita frowned. "I'm not here to bug you, Jackson. You're free to walk out of here right now. Why don't you just leave, then?"

Part of what Jack stated was bravado. There existed a speck of belief in his mind, not much more—though enough to not want to leave. "Okay, lay it on me."

She nodded. "It's not very often that a witch or medium seeks out another because of her dreams and subsequent readings. My advice to you tonight is free and, I might add, only because I saw myself entangled with the outcome of your plight. I will only say it once, as I know you don't like to hear it, but I have not seen anyone as strong with the power as you. You radiate psychic ability. If you learned to channel the power, I can only wonder."

"*What*? Please don't!" Jack exclaimed.

Janie chuckled at Jack's reaction. "Have you been told this before?"

Jack lowered his eyes. "Gramps says I'm like a magnet for this shit, just like you did."

"He's correct, and that's a good way of looking at it. Your grandfather is the spirit talker from the Everglades?"

"That's what they call him."

"I would like to meet this man one day."

Jack squirmed a bit in his seat. "Okay, so what's got me entwined with you, Lolita? What could be so important you had to track me down?"

"A dream. It appeared two-pronged, which is how these things go most of the time. I saw my death and I saw yours. Now, before you say anything, there will be events that could change. Depending on those events, it will lead to only one of our demises. Do you follow?"

"Nope." He crossed his arms.

"You'll have to choose to believe or not believe." She pulled out an ancient-looking deck of cards from a small drawer in the table. "I verified the vision by consulting with the tarot."

"Great."

"There will be a battle."

Jack blew a deep breath out between his teeth. Janie sat on the edge of her overstuffed pillow, looking up at the large black woman, entranced.

"As much as you don't want to hear it, the Dark Lord will be involved. His presence is strong. I don't tell you this lightly. You are a lawyer, correct?"

"If we've gotten this far, you know that I damn well am."

"You have been given your first big case?"

Jack and Janie looked at each other in disbelief.

"It's all intertwined. You have a knowing look, Jackson. Is there something you're not telling me?" She focused her large dark eyes on his.

"Maybe sorta. Why is it that you occult people all call me Jackson, not Jack?"

Lolita smiled. "If you were so lucky as to be named Chris, we'd call you Christopher. Your formal name brings a little more seriousness to the equation. Your grandfather calls you Jackson, correct?"

"Yep."

"Grandparents almost always use a grandchild's formal name. We are the same. A person's true name holds more power. As they grow older, they cling to whatever power they might have over you. It's an unconscious act."

"Okay, I can possibly see that."

She shifted, the wood of the chair groaning. "Something relating to your case will be deathly dangerous to both of us. I can't for the life of me see why I might be involved, but I will be."

"You asked me if there was something I wasn't telling you."

"Yes."

"Gramps said the same thing to me a week ago, but not so . . . specifically."

Lolita's brows rose. "I need to meet this man. This is a strong coincidence, Jackson. Do you choose to ignore it?"

Jack sat in silence before he asked, "So, what are you sayin'? What am I supposed to do about this shit?"

"I can't tell you that, but I'd like to read your cards." She handed him the deck. He almost recoiled but accepted the tarot. "They will not bite you. Shuffle them please and place them on the table. Cut the cards to the left and flip over the top card."

The Queen of Pentacles turned.

"The Queen of Pentacles represents a warmhearted woman. As a friend, she can provide practical support in a crisis. Is there such a woman, Jackson?"

He looked at Janie.

"Cut the cards again, please."

The next card came up as the Page of Cups inverted.

"Jack, you or someone close could be suffering from bad dreams or nebulous intuitions that are difficult to comprehend. This represents the present. The next card will be unknown influences."

The Sun inverted turned up.

"You will experience failure of some kind. Doubts surround your future plans. Vanity and arrogance are probable blocks to your success. The next card indicates the future."

He cut the cards and flipped the top card. The Devil appeared.

Lolita recoiled. "The Devil has appeared twice now, Jackson. Once relates to devilish circumstances; twice is serious."

"What do you mean twice?"

Lolita chose her words carefully. "After my vision, as I told you, I performed a reading. The Devil came up. The card that comes up in a reading can have a very nebulous meaning all on its own. The cards that come up around them can have deeper meanings. To have the same card come up twice in the same position means it should be taken seriously." She looked at him like a grade-school teacher about to scold her student. "Jackson, I can tell by your body language and what you say that you do not take the occult seriously. Is this because you truly don't believe, or are you posturing?"

Jack shrugged off the question.

"I sense your apprehension. I ask only because you are strong with the spirits. Sorry to say it again, but you do need to claim or show some responsibility here."

Jack rolled his eyes. "Is there anything else that you need to tell me?"

Janie interrupted, "You're being a bit too macho for my liking, Jack. Do you believe in what Gramps says?"

"Coincidences, most of them. Flipping the same card twice. That can happen. I'm willing to take your premonitions more seriously than a bunch of crazy cards. I really can't see how they would work. You're just flipping them over."

"Ha!" exclaimed Lolita. "That's where you're wrong, Jackson Walker. You are the one doing the flipping. The tarot are very powerful. They are a medium's link to the spirits. It's not by chance that a card turns up. They tell a story which is linked to the querent—you, the person who is the target of the reading. I've owned these same cards since I was seven years old. They are part of me. They never leave my person. I would never let another witch or medium use them. Believe me, they tell the truth. Sometimes they speak in riddles, and they need to be deciphered. But on occasion they present a very strong position. Jackson . . . you need to beware of the Devil. It may not be the Devil himself, as he would never do that. Beware of his disciples."

"Mason Matye." Jack said the words without thinking and immediately regretted them.

Janie couldn't hold her tongue. "That's the guy you had the bust-up with back at the McFadden estate. The Church of Satan guy."

Jack squeezed his eyes shut, unhappy now that the cat seemed well out of the bag.

"Who is this Mason?" Lolita prodded him.

Jack slid back in his seat, folding his hands behind his head. "Mason Matye used to be the head of the Church of Satan in the Southern United States. He was affiliated with Henrietta LePley before she died."

"A powerful woman."

"Nasty old bitch."

"Come now, Jackson. As we've already discussed, she was a very powerful witch. Her family, very powerful in Southwest Florida and within the GOP."

"Your point?"

"Within the occult, it is bad karma to not offer respect for those that are strong in the power. True, she was evil to the core, but I will always revere the influence she once exuded. Now, Mason Matye?"

"Gramps told me he envisioned him escaping from prison this past week."

"And you don't believe what's been presented to you? If you are a dumb fool, I can do nothing for you. If my fat ass weren't tied to you somehow, I'd send you on your merry way right now, no more questions asked," Lolita scolded him.

Janie asked, "So, what can we make of this?"

Lolita blew through her lips as she pondered the question. "You can choose to ignore what I've said this evening, or you can heed my warnings. I would ideally like to keep in touch with you. You need my help. I saw it in my dream." She handed Jack her business card. "My cell number is here. Call me, text me if you run into something beyond your scope of understanding—any other coincidence." She smiled. "You will know when. I know you will!"

"I can agree to that." Jack saw no harm in placating the woman, figuring the best way to get her out of his life would be to agree with her and never contact her again.

Lolita stood. "Good. Then we can say that we have an understanding?"

"If that's what you want to call it."

CHAPTER FOURTEEN

A TRAINED KILLER LEARNED to be patient or he didn't remain in the profession for long. Boris sat in the passenger's seat of the BMW 7 Series sedan, his eyes intent on the front door of the law office of Robertson and Robertson. He looked at Leo, his much younger protégé. The young man was his sister's son, just arrived from Russia four months prior. Boris spoke matter-of-factly to his nephew.

"First rule, Leo, you never cross your boss. I don't think that I need to be told when to pull the trigger, but Eli tells me when. Never pull the trigger unless you're told; Eli has his reasons. You cross your boss, you end up dead. It could be Eli, whoever. The consequences for fucking up . . . most often are deadly."

The young blond man nodded. Leo worked for a tough group back in Russia—drug dealers and all that went with drug dealing. His mother thought it wiser to send him to the States to work for her brother in order to keep him out of trouble. If she only knew. Boris found pleasure in Leo's good attitude, always willing to listen and learn. Thus far, Boris more than willingly gave the young man his time. He owed it to his older sister, who'd raised him.

Leo looked at Boris. "Who do we take first?"

"We haven't decided whether or not Walker will live. It depends how much rope his boss gives him. If they back off after we take out Lopez, then we leave him alone. I suspect it will be the end of our work here." Boris spotted Leo's impatience. "We get paid well. Your little whore will be waiting for you when we get back to Tampa. Cool yourself. We could be here for a few days."

Leo sighed deeply. "She's not a whore."

Boris laughed, "If she works for Eli, she's a whore. She's just sucking your fat cock to get on the good side of Eli, don't you forget it. While we're down here in Ft. Myers, she's sucking someone else's cock. They all do. They need the cash to buy their blow. If she's gone when we get back, we'll find another. They're lined up for you from what I hear."

Leo smiled. "Yes, Uncle."

"Good. Now we sit . . . and we wait."

* * * *

Peter Robertson hung up the phone and looked across the desk at Janie and Jack. "As you could probably tell, that was my contact out in LA. They were able to confirm that City Star Productions are not the type of people you want to get tied in with. They're the worst of the worst, and own the market in darker end pornography. They're basically untraceable, moving their headquarters on a near daily basis, and own hundreds of thousands of IP addresses. Some say they are based in the Czech Republic, others say Bosnia, possibly China."

Janie said, "So we're not going to get anything from them."

"No. It's one of those cross-border things. There are no international laws that have big enough teeth to bring them in. The heat gets too hot in one locale, they switch hemispheres. They have feeder sources all over the globe, including amateur, mid-level and professional production companies. I'm also told they double as a policing entity within the porn industry. Evidently, they pay well. But if you start doing things that could affect them adversely, in any way, you pay the price."

Jack sat back, wiping sweat off his brow. He hadn't been feeling well—probably something he ate. "So, these Russians in Tampa . . . where do they fit in?"

"Somewhere between mid-level and professional," Peter guessed.

"They're making the *kiddie porn*?"

"Who knows? They did get their hands on it, which says something. They probably create some of their own smut but have numerous low-level suppliers. Child porn, from what my sources say, is homespun. No one wants to get caught producing it professionally."

"Makes sense. So our client, Robert, he's a middleman between, say, the Russians and City Star Productions?" Jack said, trying to sort out the pieces.

"Exactly. He's a smut merchant. Dirty as all get-out."

Janie exclaimed, "So it's realistic to say Robert Lopez could have this sort of dirty pornography passed through him on a regular basis?"

Peter nodded. "But he got caught."

"So where does that leave us?" Jack wanted to know.

"We could file for a subpoena and have the Russians' computers checked," Peter said.

Jack felt his jaw. "Yes. And I'd be making another *enemy*. I think I was lucky to escape with a sore mouth. So, these City Productions guys get away with this shit and so do the Russians. Our client goes to prison. I have a good picture of things, but something doesn't add up. Do you get the feeling we're getting played by Lopez?"

Janie nodded. "I do. But is that such a bad thing, Lopez getting incarcerated? One less scumbag on the street. I think we should cut him loose."

A slight knock turned their heads. Steff poked her head in to announce, "Your client's here."

"Speaking of scumbags. Show him in, please," Peter smiled.

Robert Lopez entered as Jack rose to greet him, offering his hand. "Mr. Lopez. Please have a seat."

"Robert, please." He sat, crossing his right leg over his left. Jack nodded.

Lopez offered a sly smile. "Well, will we be working together, Jackson?"

Jack paused, carefully choosing his words. "I think we might be able to, but not with the current information you've given us. Janie and I visited your friend, Eli Romanov, the other day. Though they claim to have no connection to you, just the mention of your name got me beaten up a little." Again, he ran his hand across his sore jaw.

"Yes, they can be most inhospitable, those old-world thugs."

Peter interjected, "I've checked out City Star Productions. They're a slippery bunch as well. You don't keep very good company, Robert." The attorney focused his glare on the man.

Lopez nodded. "I didn't give you very much, did I? I've been able to access some more useful intel since we last met." He unzipped a computer bag. "Here are my invoices for the past two years." He handed the pile across the attorney's desk. "They're billed to a numbered company. The number changes monthly and has never been the same since we've been doing business."

"Why haven't you done the same?" Peter asked, leafing through the statements. "I see you bill from Lopez Investments Inc."

"Yes, and each invoice corresponds to the appropriate video file. You may not like what I do, Mr. Robertson, but it is perfectly legal. I have nothing to hide. Now, on the other hand, these bastards are crooked. Why else would they go through the bother of hiding what they do? They're only one of my many suppliers. I have corresponding files for all of my transactions. They can all be correlated with times the files were uploaded to my clients' computers."

Peter nodded. "So, let's be frank. How often does this kind of stuff cross your desk? I mean the taboo stuff."

Robert paused as if calculating. "A lot of it is about the tag you put on it. You've got some guy screwing a young girl. You put the tag on it: 'Stepbrother fucks sister.' They aren't related, but it's the psychological aspect of most porn these days that sells. That's what I do. I'm the king of tag lines. Guys need more than just the visual these days to jerk off."

"Okay, I get that, but you haven't answered my question. What about the taboo stuff?"

Robert sighed. "I know you think I'm a bad guy. I can see it in all of your eyes." He scanned Peter, Jack and Janie. "I've been up front with you. Most of my stuff has a Latin flavor: big-assed Puerto Rican bitch—"

"We got it, Robert!" Peter cut him off.

"So, every now and then, this stuff slips through. I'm very surprised they let it get to me. It's not my thing. Really. It must have been a mistake. Most of the ugly, highly illegal stuff goes to smaller, boutique badasses in the far and Middle East. There are no filters in those places and they like seeing Westerners abuse the kids. I think it's a sadistic form of retribution—jihad. There is no excuse, though. Look, I have two kids. I don't live with them anymore but would cut the balls off anyone who touched them. Just the thought of something happening to them is off limits for me. Same with snuff. Most of what I do ends up on Porn Hub, those kinds of sites. Nothing taboo."

Jack asked, "Where does this leave us?"

Peter put his hand up. "From what I can see, we have the vestiges of a case. We'll have to follow up with what you've given us." He looked to Jack and Janie.

Robert sighed in relief. "You'll take this on?"

Peter hesitated.

"First, I'll call the DA and see if she's willing to investigate the Tampa strip club. Without that, we're stuck in the mud."

Lopez offered, "These guys are not just in Tampa. There's clubs right on through Tallahassee and I think New Orleans."

"Yes. You told us that," Peter answered. Turning to Jack and Janie, he looked both in the eyes.

Jack smiled. "I'm for it!"

Robert jumped in, "Once we get my computers back, there will be enough incriminating evidence to do these guys in for life. I'd check out Eli and all of his locations. He's not stupid. He won't have anything incriminating on any of the strip club computers. You will have to get to his personal stuff. I hear he spends most of his time in New Orleans."

Janie shook her head, not willing to commit.

Peter nodded. "We'll need another ten grand on the retainer."

Robert looked willing and said, "Fine!"

Jack couldn't hold back. "So, who are your friends—the ones who referred you?"

At first, Robert looked down. Smiling, he raised his eyes. "It's not as big a deal as you might think. Ross Finklestein."

"I don't know that name."

"He's a bookie in Orlando. I know him from way back. He said you're a solid bet. Said he was a big fan of yours when you played in Gainesville. His wife's name is Lori. Says she was a playmate. Swingers."

The light went on in Jack's memory. He blushed, trying to spit out his words. "*Oh.* Dark days! That's when I'd hit a real low point. Spent a weekend at their place, real swank. It's a bit fuzzy."

Robert Lopez smiled but would not let it go. "Says he paid you some cash to fuck his wife. Said she got off doing it with athletic celebrities. So did he, I would suspect."

"I don't remember anything about that!"

Lopez showed his wicked smile and stared down at Jack. "Okay, so now we're on an equal playing field. Isn't that right, Jackson? 'Cause that would be prostitution in my books!"

Jack sat up straight, his cheeks flushing. "What's your fucking point?" He shook his head, trying to deny the remark. "And I told you, I don't remember any of that."

"My point is that if you are going to represent me, stop looking at me like I'm some low-life asshole. No one can hide every last one of their skeletons."

Janie chuckled, still frowning. "Got you there, Jack!"

Peter stood. "I think we can see your point, Robert, and it's well taken. Steff will see to the retainer. I'll file with the court tomorrow to have your equipment returned. I'm sure they've sufficiently hacked everything and anything that's necessary at this point. I think we should see the files in question and I'd like to get our own diagnostics performed so we can verify the timelines, etcetera."

Robert nodded, extending his hand to the three one at a time, leaving Walker for last. Jack eyed him, still not happy with the pornographer's accusation.

Robert held on tight and shook while trying to cajole him. "Don't take it personally, Jackson. There are many who'd have paid good money. Consider yourself fortunate." He leaned in to whisper, "I'm sure she was a *hot fuck*, being a playmate and all."

* * * *

Boris and Leo watched Robert Lopez leave the building wearing a satisfied expression. He unlocked and slipped into a black A6 Audi.

"Slowly, Leo. Don't move the car until he's well on his way down 41. We don't want to arouse any suspicion."

They gave Lopez the lead before following his car south toward Naples, eventually turning left on Wiggins Pass Road. Within a couple of miles, they turned into a fairly high-end subdivision. After a few zigs and zags, Lopez turned into the driveway of a nondescript but classy bungalow, fairly standard for the area.

"We watch, Leo. We watch until Eli lets us off the leash."

* * * *

Lopez stepped into the nearly empty house, which held only a few cheap, rudimentary pieces of furniture. His one decent possession was the forty-two-inch LCD television sitting on the floor against a blank wall. He walked into the large master bedroom, where there was a rollaway cot and a table with three laptops. He rolled his suitcase out of the closet and put it on the cot. Robert spent the next twenty minutes packing up what little clothing he had lying around. The laptops were placed into their hard-shell cases.

When his cell rang, he didn't recognize the number but seldom did in his line of business. He answered and waited to hear a voice he recognized.

"Mr. Lopez?" asked a female with a strong Asian inflection.
"Yes."
"Have you completed the transaction?"
"All has gone to plan."
The woman hung up.

Robert sighed. He'd enjoyed the past two Floridian winters. Still, it was time to move on. He'd collect a sizable paycheck and wait for his next assignment.

* * * *

Janie, Jack and Josh relaxed in the lanai behind Jack's house. Sitting around a low wooden table, Janie tapped away at her laptop as the other two passed around the bottom end of a joint. The night was warm and lights from the surrounding homes flickered on the calm water of Estero Bay.

Jack offered a drag to Janie.

"Nope. I know you two can think when you've smoked that stuff, but I can't. I'm fine with my cigs and Miller Lite."

"You're getting right-hooked again, Janie. That's two in the past half hour."

She looked at the Marlboro in her hand, then doused it in the wooden ashtray and sighed, "Yep. I know. Still love' em, though. Wish they could come up with something that emulated smoking. I mean, I've tried the electronic bullshit things. It's just not the same."

Jack hacked away after taking a harsh hit. "You got that voice. It don't sound good."

"Are you kidding, Jack Walker? If I did half the shit you've done, I'd be dead by now. Stop being *Mister Know-It-All*. And really, I've read one hit is worse than twenty cigs."

Jack hacked again after his last toke. "Can't argue."

Josh jumped back in to ask, "So you guys took on the case. What now?"

"We get warrants on all locations of the Russian guy. We fully search Eli, personally and professionally." Jack shook his head. "We don't just get a search warrant. We need to talk with the DA. And organize this properly. Even then, I don't think it's gonna happen. Lopez stated Eli spends time up in Louisiana and Mississippi. We're crossing state lines. We need to get some solid facts before we make those kinds of accusations."

"True," Janie agreed. "We're not the police."

Jack quizzed her. "Do you think Lopez is for real?"

"Not sure. Some aspects of his story jive while some don't. Ultimately, we have to remember we're his representatives. We're supposed to be helping him."

"True. I don't intend to lose the case. Still, we need to know more about him before we can help him. Did you find anything on his background?"

Janie nodded. "I did some digging after we all met today. He has an address in North Naples. It's rented and it looks like he's been there around two years."

"Two years, hmmm. It was also two years ago the invoicing began. You have the log?"

"Made copies. I can't find anything else on him except for his arrest a few weeks back."

"Who put up his bond?"

"Someone named Edward Mann, who also lives in Naples. Ten grand. I can't find anything on him either. Lopez doesn't appear to have kids or a wife, nothing." Janie looked up at Jack, a grin forming. "What about that couple Lopez mentioned? Shouldn't we check them out?"

Jack frowned. "I suppose."

"Who are they?" Josh looked eager to know.

"I'll let Jack explain."

"It's not important, Josh, but yes I'll give them a call. Janie, can you get a number?"

"I'll get it for you tomorrow." Janie added, "It's not in your Rolodex?"

Jack couldn't find any humor in the comment. "You know what you can do, Janie?"

"Testy testy!" she whistled below her breath.

"Well, what do you expect? And who the hell uses a Rolodex anymore? Old people?"

Josh belly laughed. "You two are fucking hilarious. If you want, I can leave. It's like you're a couple." He continued to kill himself laughing. "Who are these people?"

Jack stood up. "I'm not into *wild cougars,* thanks. It's not fucking funny. I'll just say . . . it wasn't one of my finer moments." He looked at Janie. "And don't you say a word!" He walked into the house and slammed the door to his bedroom behind him.

Janie chuckled, "Oh, he's got a temper!"

Josh nodded. "Pretty bad, but it takes a while for it to build. It used to be really ugly when we were kids. His mom used to lock him in his room. Maybe that's why he ran in there like that. We won't see him till the morning. One thing about Jack: once he's cooled down, he's fine."

"So, you gonna give me a ride home?"

"Sorry, girl, not after smoking that shit." He pointed to the small roach in the ashtray. "You can have the small bedroom. I'm fine on the couch. Prefer it, actually."

"Well, if that's the case, maybe I'll have a quick puff."

A few minutes later, she stared at Josh. "What's your story, Josh? I mean, what happens if someone comes after Jack? That's if we all believe in the paranormal religious crap that's being thrown around."

He cleared his throat and thought about her comment before he reached under his chair and pulled a large-caliber pistol out of his gym bag. "I'll not hesitate to shoot anyone who threatens either of you. Gramps told me to shoot and ask questions later."

"Is that wise? There needs to be some form of intent."

"Florida law states you only need to *feel* threatened. You should know that, Janie. Anyway, I can always blend back into the swamp, never to be seen for years. I'm fine with that."

After a few long minutes of silence Janie asked, "Your family reveres Jack; why is that?"

He smiled. "That's easy. He's our only hero. When he played for the Gators, there wasn't one of us that missed a game. He gave us something to look up to and look forward to, being in the stands. He's my brother. I love the guy. Someone touches him? He's a dead man or woman."

Janie smiled. "You think he can't look after himself? He took on the Church of Set."

"We all know he was shit lucky. If we hadn't been there to

help, he'd be alligator bait—long gone." He paused to perfect his next statement. "Jack's fragile; he bares himself to the world and expects everyone will play along nicely. He's apathetic. He's naive. Gramps says he has a purpose. That he's a magnet attracting bad things . . . things that need to be gotten rid of. Jack's the bait, and we schleps clean up the mess behind him." Josh stopped before he asked, "Why are you helping him?"

Janie had never really pondered the thought philosophically. She'd subconsciously thought her connection was purely about the money. *But then why did I risk my life those years ago in the Everglades? Why am I here now?* She didn't need the job that badly. The truth was that she, too, felt drawn to the man. It wasn't a sensual thing. *Can it be a motherly thing?*

She nodded. "I suppose you have something there, Josh. I'm drawn to him at a certain level. I felt really happy to see him again when Peter asked me to help with this case." Now that Janie thought about it, she basically hadn't left his side for nearly a week. *Do I truly fear leaving him to his own devices?*

The answer left the skin of her arms and scalp tingling. *Yes*.

CHAPTER FIFTEEN

SOLOMON PACKED UP HIS buggy to head out for the morning. He'd been edgy for the past few days. It had been hot. He needed to be busy, outside, not inside.

He took a deep breath. The smell of freshly-cut grass and rain permeated the air. Solomon, with great difficulty, mostly managed to behave himself. He followed his parole, not missing a call in twenty years. At some point during most weeks, he struggled. Hard to explain why. Really, he didn't care; it didn't matter. Yet, periodically, he wished for an explanation for why he was the way he was. His thoughts drifted back to his childhood. Funny how things could be traced back to one's youth. *Am I the bad person? Or am I the victim, and my behavior the result of a bad person's abuse?*

* * * *

Louisville, Kentucky, in the 1960s was not an easy place to

live as a young, *gay* Negro. Schools were still segregated and the city had yet to recover from a prolonged downturn in its fortunes. Solomon, a tall, gangly, thin teenager, stayed on the outside of things. He didn't have many friends. His closest, a girl named Sophia, lived across the street. She was perhaps the only person who understood him, at least to a certain degree. She felt comfortable with him because he wasn't a threat to her. In the Sixties, being gay wasn't a subject anyone talked about openly. The same machoism running through the white community manifested in the black community.

Sophia found a strange pleasure in talking to Solomon about his sexual tendencies. One night in particular often replayed in his mind.

He and Sophia had finished school early. They were in the twelfth grade. Solomon remembered it being a cold night, and they huddled together in his family's basement. They were poor, and the room, cold and damp, held only the basic necessities. They shared a cigarette and Sophia cuddled up to him. "You know, Solomon, you could have me if you wanted." She put her hand on his crotch.

Solomon smiled. "That might be nice, Soph. If there was ever to be a girl in my life, it would be you, and you know it."

Looking up at him she asked, "What is it about a man that turns you on? I could suck your cock better than any man does." She batted his hand away and undid his jeans, pulling them down over his buttocks to expose his massive endowment in a state of semi-arousal. When Sophia gasped, Solomon tried to move away. She held him in place. "Can I touch it?"

"Hey, Soph, you know this isn't my thing."

"I know, but . . . I didn't know that a . . . a—"

"Cock."

"Yes, a cock could be this big." She ran her finger down its length, stopping at its head, pinching it between her thumb and forefinger.

"Soph, stop it . . . really!"

"We're just friends, Sol. Nothing more. I don't want to change you." She took him into her mouth, running her tongue down his shaft as far as she could.

He groaned. Her ministrations didn't take long to achieve the inevitable outcome. She looked up at him as she licked the last from his still erect manhood. "You still sure you're into boys?"

"Listen, that can't happen again. Honey, I cannot tell you how good that felt, but you know what the truth is. It won't change." He became quiet, lighting up another smoke. When he passed it to her she asked, "How did you know you didn't like girls?"

"It's not like that. I like girls! You're soft and I can talk to you. I mean, you and some of the other girls at school. I've always known. I just have. I like it when a man's rough with me."

"What?" She took another drag. "I mean, rough? What do you mean, Sol?"

"Can I tell you something?"

"Course."

"No, I mean something I've never told anyone."

She nodded.

"Before my old man passed away, he used to hurt us."

"Us?"

He sighed. "He was a drinker. He wouldn't drink all the time, but when he did he flipped a switch. I used to hear him beating my mom. Real bad. My sister and I hid under the covers when we were little. We shared a bed in the small second bedroom."

"Jeez."

"When we were older, he used to come into our room and take my older sister down into the basement."

"Where we are now?"

"Yep. She didn't talk much after that. Soon enough, she hit the road and ran away. Momma and I haven't seen her since. I hope she's not dead. Then, he came for me."

"Christ, Sol!"

"I've blocked most of it from my mind. Mom and I have an understanding. The day of his funeral wasn't necessarily an unpleasant day for the two of us. Momma struggled to make ends meet, but at least it's quiet, if you know what I mean."

"Is that why you like boys?"

"Fuck no, girl. Don't be pissin' me off. I knew about that long before he came for me."

She pulled Sol's head to her shoulder. "You poor boy. You can be with me and I'll look after you. You know I can. I can see it in your eyes. You're not content here."

"Fuck no. I'm sellin' myself down the river. Like the old days. I like the sound of New Orleans. I might not even finish school. Nothin' for me here. Gettin' beat up every week's gonna spoil my boyish good looks."

"You are pretty. Not like other boys. I think that's what draws me to you. There is a sensitivity I don't see in other guys. You're real and I'm damned sorry to hear what that man did to you. What did he do?"

Sol smiled, still smoking the cigarette. "I've blocked that away someplace safe in the back of my mind. Let's just say he used me like his little whore, broke me like a stallion."

Sophia gasped, hands over her mouth.

Solomon left home later that week. Every day, he wished he had taken Sophia up on her offer to stay with her. Life would have been much easier. *But, then again, would it have?*

CHAPTER SIXTEEN

THE HOUSE LOOKED LONELY, and so empty. Then again, there were no memories to go along with the place—a dry, cool spot to sleep in the stormy Florida heat, nothing more. Robert Lopez finished packing, placing the last of his neatly folded dress shirts on top of a stuffed suitcase. He looked around to make sure he wasn't leaving anything behind. Then he sat for a few minutes and pondered his options. Cracking open his one remaining beer from the fridge, he took a long swig and opened up his Allegiant Air phone app. Confirming the date, he checked to see if his flight to Niagara Falls from Punta Gorda was on schedule. He smiled, seeing no delays. The flight left in five hours—plenty of time to complete what needed to be done. His plan was to lay low for a time. He'd rented a small house just over the Canadian border in a small town called Niagara-on-the-Lake, close to the States but anonymous.

He carried his laptops out to the car first. Then he came

back for his two suitcases, throwing them into the trunk. Within minutes, he was headed inland toward I-75. He didn't notice the black BMW following at a distance.

He would assume a new identity. His handlers were experts at creating and supplying the necessities to make Robert Lopez disappear and Charlie Fernandez appear with a new passport, driver's license, bank accounts, all well established.

First, he needed to sell the Audi. He'd spoken to a dealership in North Ft. Myers, who seemed willing to pay twenty grand. Pretty light in his estimation, but he didn't have the luxury of shopping it around. He pulled off the highway and after a few short jogs he found the used car dealership, just east of Highway 41. Parking at the side of the dealership building, he did not pay attention to the black BMW pulling into the 7-Eleven across the street.

Robert opened the glass door to the modest showroom for their high-end vehicles. His Audi would be on the low scale of what they sold here, which was why he chose to deal with them. He agreed to their price if they paid in cash. They'd make a tidy profit and Robert would be done with the car.

In no time, an anxious salesman greeted him. "Can I help you, sir?"

"Yes, I'm to meet with Albert. We have an appointment."

"Hang on, he's in his office."

Robert looked at a vintage Mercedes convertible coup, shined to perfection, as he waited. How he admired that car. Sadly, he could never own one like it. He needed the anonymity of the much more common Audi—nice, but something that blended in. Within a few minutes a man in his fifties, balding, impeccably dressed, made his way through the showroom toward him.

The salesman, who Robert assumed to be Albert, addressed him. "Let me guess. You're Mr. Lopez, with the Audi?"

Robert shook his hand. "Robert Lopez, and yes, you are correct."

"If you don't mind, I'd like to have a look at the vehicle before I pay you. Albert Henderson's my full name."

"That's to be expected, Mr. Henderson. You won't find a

blemish, and she runs like a charm." He followed Henderson out the door.

If not for Henderson exiting first, Robert's next step would have been to his death. Two men stood beside the door. The tall, blond man put a silenced Beretta to Henderson's head, pulled the trigger, and blew his brains out the opposite side of his skull, splattering the sidewalk. The corpse fell to the ground with a heavy thump.

Robert, being well trained in his line of work, didn't waste a second. He planted the knuckles of his right hand deep in the windpipe of the young attacker, who went to the ground, gasping for air. The second man, tall and husky, aimed his pistol at Robert and fired. The bullet entered Robert's thigh and he lost control of his leg. Dropping to the ground, he was unable to defend himself from the kick to the head. That was the last he remembered.

* * * *

"Bastard!" Boris tried to yank his nephew to his feet, but Leo was dead weight. His windpipe had been crushed. His face was already turning blue, his eyes staring up at Boris as he passed from the world of the living.

"Fuck!"

Boris picked up Leo's gun, stuffing it in his pocket, and then used all of his strength to put the young man's body over his shoulder. As calmly as possible under the circumstances, he crossed the street and dumped the body into the BMW's trunk. He started up the car and pulled next to the dealership. Using his immense strength, Boris stuffed Robert in with his nephew's body. While Boris knew his sister would not be happy with him, more importantly neither would Eli.

CHAPTER SEVENTEEN

JACK WOKE THE NEXT morning to a raging headache, like nothing he'd experienced in a long time. Maybe ever. He stumbled from his bed to the kitchen, noting Josh was sleeping on the living room couch. He'd been a little harsh with him and Janie. They only wanted what was best and he knew it. He blamed his quick anger on how events were unfolding. He wanted more than anything to be able to take care of the work in front of him without all of the paranormal innuendo being flung around. He found it tremendously irritating, and a waste of time and brain matter.

He drank a tall glass of water along with a couple of extra-strength Tylenol. He couldn't remember drinking much, and in fact wasn't a big drinker anymore. Pot didn't usually give him a headache. Some sort of malaise appeared to be slowly taking over his body. It wasn't just his head; he felt it in his joints, achy everywhere. *Could it be the flu?*

When his cell phone rang, he looked at the number. Gramps. Jack made note of the time: *6:46 AM. Too damned early for the old man to be calling.* "Good morning, Gramps."

"Jackson!"

"A bit early, Gramps, don't ya think? Lucky I got this damned headache. Couldn't sleep. Any other day I'd be calling you out on waking me up. Wassup?"

"Wassup?"

"What's up," Jack corrected his vernacular and couldn't help but smile.

"Oh. Couldn't wait to call. I had a vivid dream last night, you know. That's my way."

"Okay, dream walker, I get it." *I just can't get away from this shit!*

"I could see a black fog, creeping out of the great swamp. It formed into a man, a man who carried a long, wicked knife. He stabbed you, and you couldn't feel it, but there was something left in you. I called because I couldn't fully make sense of the augury. I needed to hear your voice, to make sure you were okay."

"Fine for the time being, Gramps. If it makes you feel any better, Josh is here to protect me from the bogeyman," he chuckled.

"Don't mock me, Jackson!"

Jack heard the anger in the old man's voice and backed off. "I will say, this case I've been on is proving to be more difficult than I first imagined."

"How so?"

Jack took the time to tell Gramps about their client, Robert, and the Russians.

"Child pornography. In my books, that's worse than the Devil Spawn. There's something about a child's innocence. It can be so easily taken, and the people who do are truly monsters stealing from them and changing the kids' lives forever. I hope you get them, Jackson."

"Me too, and I agree. Oh yeah, I forgot, I wanted to tell you about the palm reader who contacted me. Lolita's her name."

"Palm reader?"

"Yes. She called me out of the blue. She said—oh, *shit*." The correlation hit him like a slap to the face.

"Exactly. You know my favorite saying is that there are no coincidences. She mentioned the Devil Spawn as well, didn't she?"

"Well, not in so many words."

"Did she or didn't she?"

"Yes."

"Lolita. I've heard of this person, though I know her by another name, whispered to me in my dreams. I would like to meet her."

"If I hear from her again, I'll mention that to her. I'll give her your number."

"Numbers won't be necessary."

"Oh, come on, Gramps. Don't give me that bullshit."

"No problem, Jackson. Then I won't. Is Josh staying with you?"

"Yep. Passed out on the couch. I don't know how much help he would be if we get into a tight spot. High as a kite all day."

"Now, *Josh* I will call."

"Passed out pretty good from last night. I'd wait a bit."

"I want you to promise something to me. Call me once a day for the next little bit. 8:30 AM, every day. You must do this for your grandfather. I have a premonition . . . something bad is going to happen. And you, Grandson, are a magnet for bad things. Bad people. If you don't call me, I'll know something is wrong. Besides, I might be able to help. I'm getting a little bit bored in my old age. There are only so many snook and tarpon to be caught."

"Now, that's the best idea you've had all morning. You still have that old flats boat—the one we used when we were kids. You could get into any tight spot with that old beauty."

"I do. You have a good eye. I dropped a sixty-horse Yamaha on the back last year."

"That old Evinrude had seen its day twenty years ago."

"I got stuck out in Florida Bay. Charlie Turner rescued me. I decided to scrap nostalgia for safety and practicality. Look, you get this case put to bed and we'll go to one of the old hunt camps for a week. The tarpon will be thick as cockroaches in a month."

"I'll call you tomorrow like you asked."

After Jack hung up, he questioned his reason for agreeing to the calls. He didn't believe in hocus-pocus, but the coincidences were piling up too quickly, even for his liking.

CHAPTER EIGHTEEN

NATHANIEL PORTMAN, BETTER KNOWN as Gramps to his family and Seminole brotherhood, fell back into the stiff wooden chair beside his meager dining room table, sighing deeply. He sipped his coffee.

Jackson worried him. He'd known from before Jack's birth that the boy carried the spirit-talker bloodline, as had Jackson's mother before her death. It wasn't just the blood. It was a genetic imprint that allowed the Portmans access to the netherworld—the ability to talk to spirits and have visions from both the future and the past. It wasn't considered strange 200 or 2,000 years ago. It was still a power shared by members of indigenous tribes, usually a shaman or a chief. It was something to be proud of, to be revered. Jack's total denial of his power and lack of desire to understand the events surrounding him frustrated the old man; yet, he understood it. He'd been the same way in his own youth, albeit not to the same degree. He hadn't ventured out like Jackson did, seeing what else the world had to offer.

Jack's mother had been the same in the beginning. She too fought her native abilities. Nattily finished community college in her early twenties. Within a week of her graduation, she'd received an offer to work for a large insurance company and moved to Chicago.

Nattily married Stanley Walker, an ex-jock insurance executive, who possessed good physical genes but also, unfortunately, a penchant for boozing and violence. Nattily spent the next several years living in fear. Stanley, that narcissistic man, wanted to blame his problems on those who surrounded him, never himself. At times the man could be wonderful, but the dark side lurked omnipresent. Nattily and Stanley birthed a son in the third year of their marriage: Jackson Nathaniel Walker.

Shortly after Jackson's birth, Nattily saw no choice but to leave the abusive relationship, and escaped to her roots in the Florida Everglades. Gramps was only too happy to take them in and help raise the boy. During that time, Nattily came to grips with her latent talent. Sometimes that was the way with the occult. Gramps smiled, remembering one of the many conversations he'd enjoyed with his daughter.

Nattily and Gramps had taken Jack and his two cousins, Nate and Josh, to a hunt camp that could only be reached by canoe or kayak. They sat one night beside a fire, the children asleep in one of the crude Chickee cottages adorning the small island. The no-see-ums and mosquitoes were thick, but Gramps burned candles made from an old Native recipe, staving off the worst of them. The night was calm and hot, its silence interrupted only by the odd water fowl whooping, or the swish of a sly gator slipping off the bank after its prey.

Gramps loved his Coors Light, the one vice from the modern world he insisted be brought along. He handed one to Nattily, who accepted. She peeled back the tab and stared at her father, a smile turning up her pretty mouth.

"What is it, Nat?"

"I'm glad I came back, even though I felt there was little choice at the time, and I don't mean that in a bad way."

"Really?" Gramps feared she would regret the move back home.

"No, I am." She took another sip of her beer. "You know . . . I hated this place. I couldn't wait to leave. It seemed like a ticket to salvation when I left for Chicago. Shark Valley, when I look back at what I was feeling, seemed worse than a small town. There's not much here, you have to admit."

Gramps smiled. "It's a big world out there, but it's no different from this place. Bigger city, bigger problems. More money, bigger houses, bigger bills—more headaches. We make lots of money now that we control the gambling. Still, I don't need more than what we have right here. I believe we have something special here, something no one else has. We live in the biggest state park in the United States of America. Our people fought wars to protect our claim to the land. I don't ever want you to feel you have to stay here now that you've come back. Though I will admit it warms my heart and has given me a new lease on life since your return."

"I do see that, and I won't, when or if the time ever comes. For the time being, it'll keep Jackson out of trouble. I can't tell you how thankful I am for you taking both of us in."

Gramps shook his head. "I can't tell you how thankful I am for both of you coming back. I am fearful of the day you might leave, perhaps when Jack leaves. You know I love the boy like my own."

"I know you do."

"He bears the same ability as you and I. I know in the past you've looked upon it as perhaps a curse, something nostalgic, something old and indigenous. Do you still have the dreams?"

"I do, Daddy. I've learned not to fear them anymore."

"There was a time when you would have been revered within the tribe for your ability. Little Jack is already telling me about his dreams. They are simple tales. He dreamed about the big snook he caught today. He looked the fish right in the eye. He knew where to find the old girl. I was with him when he caught it. He stared it right in the eye and put her back in the water. He said there existed an understanding between them. I thought it cute."

"I remember being the same way when I was little. I used to tell you about my dreams."

"Yes, you did. Do you recall the talks you had with your father about them?"

"Vaguely."

"I don't want to frighten you. One day, my daughter, you will need to carry on our family line. You will become chief. We don't really call it that anymore, but your people will look up to you for guidance, like they do me. Likewise, they will look to Jack." He stopped to take a cold sip of his favorite beer. "You know the boy is destined to do great things for his people. I've seen it. But he will attract trouble."

"I could have told you that just looking the little bugger in the eyes," she smiled.

"He does have that look, I have to admit it. But in the end, it will be for the best . . . at least, I hope so."

Nattily turned to her father. "I would like to learn."

Gramps smiled. "We can do that. I mean, I can help you."

"What about Mom?"

"She's lost interest in me and is still shacked up in North Miami."

"I can't believe she hasn't taken the time to see her grandson. And me." A tear welled in her eye. For the first time since his daughter returned, she showed sadness.

"Your mother is a different type. She can be selfish. Needy. I have no wish for a person like that in my life. When she truly misses all of us, she can come back, though I've seen that she never will. She drives fancy cars, eats in expensive restaurants. She sees herself as being lucky."

Nattily shook her head, trying to smile. "I think we're the lucky ones. As we both said tonight, can't think of a place on earth I'd rather be at this moment."

Gramps woke from his stupor, the memory of his daughter briefly bringing a smile to his face, only to be replaced by unpleasant thoughts revolving around her violent death.

CHAPTER NINETEEN

THE HOUSE SMELLED LIKE burnt toast. The smoke alarm sat on the kitchen table with the battery next to it. The house looked a mess, empty beer cans strewn across every available surface along with empty boxes from the Sandbar Pizza Place. The three Js—Janie, Josh and Jack—sat around the table in the lanai, enjoying their coffee and sharing an Entenmann's cream cheese danish, the only reasonable thing left to eat besides burnt toast. A scowling sky and accompanying stiff breeze off Estero Bay made it necessary for the three of them to wear what hoodies Jack could round up from the floor of his cupboard.

Jackson wasn't sure he wanted to talk about the morning call with Gramps, but Josh probably heard the tail end as he woke up. "What did the old man want?"

Jack chose his words carefully. His assumption that Josh unintentionally eavesdropped seemed correct. "Something silly about another dream. Said he saw some dark force rising up from the swamp to stab me."

Janie raised her eyebrows. Josh cut in before she could say anything. "I know what you're about to say, Jack. Before you deny the reason for his call as mumbo jumbo, let me point out that the man is never wrong. At least, never that I know of. You may not need to take it literally, but let's agree to be a little more careful for the next few days or even weeks."

"Okay, I'll buy that." Jack looked as if he meant it. "Hey, I'm sorry I jammed the party last night. I'm a little touchy about the accusations—presumptions, whatever—about all of this paranormal shit. I'll be upfront with the both of you. I would love to believe it all to be true. It's almost like believing in God. I want to be able to believe in it all; I really do!" Pausing for a moment, Jack collected his thoughts. "I don't want to rely on it, though. I don't want to look the fool. I don't want to put us in a bad spot because of some false belief which can't be substantiated."

Josh nodded. "Fair enough. It's hard to put faith into something you can't see or touch. I'd have to disagree about the God part, though. Faith in God is more of a spiritual thing, a parable-oriented belief. Folks can have faith, but they're not going to go out and do something drastic in the name of God, like order a subpoena against Eli Romanov because they believe it's what God wants them to do. That would simply be stupid— blind faith."

Janie placed her cup on the table. "I think you're both wrong. Your grandfather is in touch with his inner instincts. It could be some sort of paranormal ability, or maybe he's simply in tune, and his intuition is really good. As Josh says, *he's not been wrong*! You can pretty much go to the bank with that. Now, on the other hand, what if he does have this supernatural . . . psychic ability? Does it really matter as long as he's always correct?"

Jack canted his head to the side. "Okay?"

"What's the difference? We have to take heed." Janie tried to end the controversy.

"You guys are killing me. Gramps seems to think I have the same ability. Maybe it's that assumption I'm fighting. Maybe I don't want to become . . . the witchdoctor. I don't want to. It ain't happening!"

Josh put his hand on Jack's forearm. "No one says you have to, bro. No one says you have to pray. Personally, I do, but for altogether different reasons."

Jack chuckled. "Yeah, you pray you don't get cirrhosis of the liver."

"Na. I don't drink much. Maybe lung cancer. Those are choices, though. I don't see much reason to pray for something that's under my control. I pray for your soul, Jackson. I pray for mine and for Gramps. And for Janie's." He clinked coffee cups with her.

Jack sighed. "I guess it's a good thing someone's praying for me. I need all the help I can get. Since when did you become an fucking Bible thumper?"

"Really? You can't remember going to church with my mom when we were little kids? I'm no thumper, but I do have faith. That's all."

Jack blew out a long stream of hot coffee breath between his lips to relieve some steam. His phone rang.

"It's Pete. Hello?"

"Jack. I just got off the phone with the district attorney. She told me Lopez's car was found at a car dealership in North Ft. Myers. He made an appointment to meet with a salesman. The salesman had his brains blown out on the sidewalk outside the dealership. Lopez was nowhere to be found."

Jack thought for a moment. "Is there a bill of sale for his car?"

"No. But the car is still parked outside. One of the other salesmen recalls Lopez asking to see the dead salesman, whose last name was Henderson."

"What do you make of it?"

"Not so sure. I want you to check it out. I also have to tell you the place is thick with cops and it would be best if you did not draw attention to yourself."

"How the fuck am I going to do that? You want us to look into it, right?"

"Janie will know what to do."

"Okay, boss." Jack hung up.

Janie jumped right in. "What did he have to say?"

Josh scrunched up his brow. "Robertson, right?"

"Yep!" Jack made an evil face. "Peter said Janie would know what to do."

Janie smirked. "Cream rises to the top, Jackie boy. Now, what did he really say?"

"Just what I said, except for the fact that Robert Lopez left his car at a dealership in North Ft. Myers, where, conveniently, a murder occurred. The salesman Robert was supposed to meet had his brains blown out in front of the dealership."

"Jeepers. And where is Robert?"

"No sign of him. Peter says the place is crawling with cops."

"And he said I'd know what to do," Janie smiled.

"Yep."

"Let's think about this." Josh wanted to ruminate on the facts.

When Jack opened his mouth to speak, Janie held her hand up to silence him. "Off the top, why would he be at a car dealership?" She kept her hand up, anticipating a stupid comment. "Why would he want to sell his car? Now, the only reason I find this important is because he's no longer attached to it, apparently. And it's not sold, and I gather there isn't a contract to sell, or at least a commitment. This would all be ordinary stuff but for the fact the salesman got whacked."

"This is totally fucked up!" Josh shook his head as he lit up a cigarette, offering one to Janie. She accepted and took a light from Josh's pink Bic.

Jack nodded. "They don't teach this kind of stuff in law school."

Janie interjected, "Let's remember, you are a criminal lawyer and this isn't a simple real estate deal. I haven't been on a case in twenty years that didn't require some out-of-the-box thinking. My gut tells me our client is trying to make a dash."

Jack sipped his coffee, placing the cup on the table gently. "I agree—the first thing that popped into my head."

Josh couldn't help but ask, "So, why isn't he dead?"

"The one thing I've learned over the years is these situations don't happen the way they're supposed to. Why whack the salesman? Maybe Lopez is dead," Janie answered.

Josh suggested, "Maybe it was supposed to be Lopez that got shot."

Janie nodded. "Maybe he did but was carted away. But by whom?"

"The Russians," Jack offered.

Janie nodded. "That's the easy answer, and maybe the most logical. Logical doesn't always measure up, though. There is the possibility another outside agency, like City Productions, might be involved."

"I think this would be the time to get the subpoena to search the strip joint up in Tampa. Before they can start a shell game."

"That's if they haven't already dumped him in the swamp. What if Robert is the killer?" Janie said.

Jack paused before he said, "Possible, but I can't see why he'd do it. There's more to this than we're going to be able to figure out sitting around this table. Okay, Pete said you'd know what to do."

Janie rested her chin in her hand, deep in thought. "I think it's time to talk to the police, or the DA. Unless you're thinking of going back to Aversions in Tampa. We can't just walk into that place again or we'll find ourselves dumped in the swamp."

"Unless they didn't know we were there," he smiled.

Janie frowned. "I also don't see what good it would do going to the dealership. We have to hope we can get access to today's criminal report once the Hillsborough Sheriff's Department is finished with it, and that could take weeks."

CHAPTER TWENTY

THE CURSE ON JACK Walker placed, Mason meandered the dark streets to retrieve his car from a remote parking garage. New Orleans, as always, served its purpose. Time to move on; it would be important to do so. The whore in the hotel would be found in the morning when the cleaning staff entered the room. The Witch would disappear. He trusted the anonymity and secrecy promised by Moses. He wasn't positive what methods were used by the peculiar man to dispose of the body and collateral evidence. But really it didn't matter, because Mason Matye no longer existed. The Satanist smiled. It seemed strange but oddly liberating to be dead.

Now, he would put an end to Jack Walker and his family, taking his time, relishing their pain. By the time he finished with those whom Walker loved, family and friends, the curse would have rendered Walker weak. Controllable. He planned to torment the man so that in the end Walker would pray to Mason for Hell. Mason lamented that the McFaddens were already dead. They would have been eminently useful. Those bastards could hold a grudge, and they knew how to torture and kill . . . very well.

He wondered what became of the old estate where the demented brothers once lived. Perhaps he could find some use for the veritable house of horrors, although he doubted that idea would become a reality. The estate had most likely been demolished, but, then again, places that housed atrocities often became fallow. No one wanted to live in the home of dead serial killers; the place would be stigmatized. The first thing he would do when he arrived in Ft. Myers would be visit the old estate.

The Church of Satan created a new identity for him: James Pincton, complete with ID, driver's license, bank account and credit cards. The cult had its fingers in all levels of government, including the US Citizenship and Immigration Services. He'd offered the hooker cash, and thus there was no paper trail from the hotel. There was the slightest of chance of tracing his fingerprints and DNA back to Mason Matye, but he no longer existed. Such tracking would take time and some serious detective initiative. The cult member who'd changed places with him should have gone through spontaneous human combustion. Whatever remained or did not remain erased Mason and any connection to the living world.

He left the city, heading toward the coast where he picked up I-10, which would take him through Mobile, Alabama, then on to the Florida Panhandle and down to Ft. Myers after picking up I-75 in Lake City.

Mason didn't especially like driving. He preferred flying when possible, but it was not in the cards for the time being. Anonymity was the order of the day; there was freedom on the open road. When he stopped for gas in Tallahassee, he stretched his legs and wondered what kept him from changing his life's direction. He could disappear completely now that he'd become James Pincton. It was only a fleeting thought. It didn't matter. The Left-Hand Path, the road to Satan, had him firmly within its grip. Vengeance on his mind, his resolve unflappable, he would kill Jackson Walker.

* * * *

He started to nod off after picking up I-75 and pulled into a rest area. He slipped out of the car to walk for a minute and shake off the cobwebs. He sauntered past an SUV, a young family—parents and two kids—who had the same idea. He felt tempted to warn them against stopping late at night like this, as there were sure to be scary people driving the highways looking for just such an opportunity. He'd certainly killed his fair share. Enough to warrant being branded a serial killer, if they only knew.

Mason smiled as he approached, the father ramping up his wariness, human survival instinct kicking in at the sight of the stranger. The moment he let his guard down, Mason resisted the urge to growl or jump at the man. *Foolish.* In his day, he'd seen many families such as this collected and offered up as sacrifices to the Dark Lord. They would disappear, their relatives wondering, for decades, *What happened to them?* Then there were the self-styled Satanists who simply killed such families, leaving all traces of the grizzly event. An act of terror. They killed in the name of Satan, with no true connection to the Dark Lord. They masked their brutality under the guise of Satanists, but they were simply sick individuals with no right to the claim. Mason resented such self-stylists, who gave Satanists a bad name. He smiled coyly.

Turning when he reached the end of the sidewalk, he walked back to his vehicle. He passed the little family again, walking between them, their belief that he no longer presented a threat strong enough to let him walk between their children. *Fools.* If he weren't in a hurry, he would have found a way to torment them. To teach them a lesson they'd never forget.

He slipped back into his car, plugging his newly-acquired iPhone into the glove compartment jack. He googled *freeradiosatan.com*, a twenty-four-hour talk show preaching the tenets of the Dark Lord. He had little problem staying awake once he tuned in.

* * * *

The sun rose above the trees lining the highway median as he crossed the Caloosahatchee River, the waterway forming the northern border of Ft. Myers. His eyes ached. The drive through the night was long, straight and boring. Walker lived on Ft. Myers Beach. He debated whether to rent a room on the island or somewhere close by. He decided to find a basic hotel room in Bonita Springs, near the south end of the beach.

After a short nap, Mason booted up his new computer, one of his many requests. He found there'd been a lot of press on Walker over the years: his football career with the Florida Gators, followed by the Cincinnati Bengals, and then the fiasco in the Everglades, which tragically led to Mason's capture. Strangely enough, it was Walker's high school football press that offered up the most information. Mason found names of several relatives, Nathaniel Portman in particular. He remembered Walker's grandfather at the McFadden estate that night. That old man would pay for his connection to Jackson. A closer look at the news clippings from that night led him to a few more names: Josh Portman and Janie Callaghan. Both were pictured with Walker celebrating his rescue from the clutches of Jimmy and Isaac McFadden.

He cross-referenced the three names for their places of residence and was able to locate Nathaniel's and Janie's, but not Josh's. He planned on visiting Everglades City tomorrow to see the old man, but not before he took a look at Walker's home. He needed to extend the power of the curse.

CHAPTER TWENTY-ONE

THE DRIVE BACK TO Tampa seemed an eternity, broken up momentarily when Boris stopped at a hardware store to purchase plastic ties. He made sure Robert Lopez was bound and gagged in the trunk of the BMW before he regained consciousness. Boris shook his head over the gray and lifeless face of his nephew, tucked in beside Lopez. The episode had been messy and Boris didn't look forward to talking with Eli. His boss didn't like unplanned contingencies.

Pulling the car into a large, freestanding garage behind the main building at Aversions Tampa, he waited for the automatic door to close before getting out of the Beamer. Walking back to a large work bench with a slotted tool board behind it on the wall, he unlatched a catch holding the bench in place. He pulled one end of it toward him. A section of the wall and the bench swung out from the end of the garage, revealing a secret staircase leading below the main building. The entrance was used for several purposes, many of them clandestine. Eli liked it because it allowed him to slip in and out of the establishment without being seen.

Boris hefted Lopez out of the car, dropping him to the ground. He appeared to be conscious, though the blow to the head seemed to have done some real damage. He lay in a semi-comatose state. His leg wound also looked nasty. Boris brought Leo's body downstairs first. There were two levels to the basement. The uppermost housed the normal everyday workings of the strip club—storage, furnaces, Eli's fake office and dressing rooms for the girls. The lower basement was a totally different world, concealed below the ground. Only Eli and Boris had access to "the bowels," as Eli liked to call the area where the filming took place, the actors sometimes never seeing the light of day again, young and old alike.

Boris placed his nephew's body in the room he used to prepare bodies for disposal. He laid him out on the long wooden table; the corpse lay in a semi-fetal position, already stiffening from rigor mortis.

Boris then retrieved Lopez, hefting him over his shoulder in a fireman's hold. He took him deep into the heart of the place. It was a secret dark space where Eli long ago constructed a hidden lockup. From time to time, they detained individuals who'd crossed the line, which often happened in their business. He doubted Lopez would be of any use to Eli, but it wasn't his decision to make. He pressed a pressure-sensitive panel on a concrete block wall, activating another hidden doorway. Boris pulled open the heavy stone door, entering the dimly lit hallway beyond.

The corridor was sterile and devoid of any decoration. It housed three cells along the left side, thick iron bars separating each cage. Boris steered well away from the first cell. A woman with wild red hair and what could loosely be called lingerie sat cross-legged on a cot along the far wall. Her eyes, black as coal, followed Boris as he tossed Lopez onto a cot in the far cell, leaving a vacant cell between the woman and new prisoner. Boris cut the bonds and locked the door behind him as he exited.

While the woman kept her eyes on Boris, he never

acknowledged *It*. That's what Boris called her: It. She could be cruel. He and Eli didn't quite know what to do with the creature. Boris was sure they would have to shoot her one day, but Eli insisted on keeping It. He wouldn't let her go. They were both of the mind that creature would seek revenge for her forced confinement. Boris shook his head and walked out of the corridor, the thing hissing at him as he closed the heavy stone door.

* * * *

When Eli returned from Tallahassee later that evening, Boris waited for him in his lower basement office, the real office, a bottle of vodka open. He'd taken a couple of drinks—nothing that his large-framed body couldn't handle. He'd needed it after getting off the phone with his sister. She'd been devastated with the news of her son's death. Boris lied, calling the death a workplace accident. In reality, it had been, but he made up something much softer, more acceptable.

Eli came through the back way, not expecting to see Boris, though his car was parked in the garage. He could tell by the way the man sat that something was wrong. Eli knew him well. Boris rose to shake his hand.

"Boris, something is wrong?"

Boris nodded.

A shock of anger colored Eli's pale cheeks. "Why you don't call me if something is wrong, Boris? I sent you to look after Lopez. Did you take care of him?"

Boris nodded. "Lopez is here."

"I don't understand, my friend. Here?"

Boris repeated what happened.

Eli nodded. "You shouldn't have taken your nephew."

Boris cut in and explained, "He's young. I felt it would be an easy job. I wanted to show him around."

Eli walked up to Boris and put his forehead against his, grabbing the back of his neck forcefully. "If I paid you to think, my friend, this wouldn't have happened. Your nephew, did he shoot the salesman?"

Boris nodded.

"Would you have done so?"

"No, Eli. He made a brash move."

"You over-stood your bounds. Now I have blood on my hands because of your fucking stupidity."

Eli's anger was something not to be taken lightly, but, as he stated, it would be Boris's fault if repercussions found their way back to Eli. He knew better than to say he was sorry. Eli would put a bullet in his head if he told him that. *Sorry* was a word for cowards. Boris would take his boss's wrath like a man. He stood baring his chest to Eli as if to say, *Do what needs to be done.*

Eli smiled, his dominance over the man reconfirmed. "Walker?"

"I needed to come back to Tampa. There was no choice, no opportunity."

Eli nodded, pacing the room. "So, we've detained Walker's client. And there can be no question that Robert Lopez must die. I don't know how smart Walker is, but it wouldn't take a fucking genius to figure out we might be behind the event. I mean, it's like two plus fucking two equals fucking four. They will have a search warrant signed tomorrow morning. We can expect them here by early afternoon tomorrow." He picked up the vodka and poured himself a small glass of the clear fiery liquid. He patted Boris's cheek. "You will not go against my orders ever again. Do you understand, my friend?"

Boris nodded. He understood

"I don't give a fuck about your nephew. He possessed promise, but it is your stupidity for bringing him with you that cost him his life—cost me the stress we will now face. You should have killed Walker as well. Now, it's too late. If we touch him, we will be linked.

"Now, let's not fuck up what has to happen tomorrow. Make sure the upstairs computers are clean, and there is no way for the authorities to get down here." He stared at Boris. "Understand?"

"Clear as water, Eli."

CHAPTER TWENTY-TWO

THE BUS FROM FT. Myers to Tampa took a little over three and a half hours. Solomon made the trip every now and again, usually after he'd experienced "a period of edginess," as he liked to call it. He didn't dare buy the stuff online. His internet connection was monitored by the Florida Department of Corrections. He needed hard copies.

He got off at the Greyhound bus lines terminal on East Polk Street, downtown Tampa. From there he took an Uber out to Lumsden Road, where it met I-75. He squeezed out of the back seat, offering the driver a tip if he'd come back to pick him up in an hour.

Aversions existed as a place where things could be had for a price, anonymity virtually guaranteed. Solomon didn't know the place was being staked out by the local police. Everyone who entered was photographed and cross-referenced with state and federal archives, the order coming straight from the district attorney. Solomon even entering the place was a clear contravention of his parole. It would take a few days for the information to percolate through the system, but Solomon would end up paying the price.

He passed his membership card to the female sitting behind a thick, bulletproof glass window. She looked at the card as he slid it through a small hole at the bottom of the pane. After swiping it through a stripe scanner, she slid it back and nodded, giving him the go-ahead to enter.

Solomon didn't like the women there; he had no interest in them at all, but he needed to keep up appearances. He sat at a table near the back of the massive room. A waitress, scantily-clothed, asked him if he wanted a drink. He didn't like fancy drinks. He ordered a Budweiser. He watched the female on stage with passing interest. After ten or fifteen minutes, one of the strippers sauntered up to him. He could tell she found his large frame unattractive. She had no doubt been told to come and see him. He felt sorry for the girls. They lived a dirty life. Sure, they made good money, but it was one of those careers that would always be a dead end, sometimes literally.

She seemed a sweet little thing, very black, a sharp contrast to the shocking pink bikini she wore. She ran her hand along his shoulder. "Hey, daddy, can I offer you a dance?"

Solomon smiled. "Can we go to a back room?"

"You got some money to show me?"

Solomon flashed her a hundred-dollar bill with a few twenties. He stuffed one of the twenties into her bikini bottom. "I'm here to buy."

He couldn't help but notice her relief. "You just come with me then, daddy." She gently took his hand and helped him out of his seat, leading him through a black curtain and into a dim hallway. Rooms lined both sides, black curtains covering each one. In the center was a huge man wearing earphones, sitting at a small table with a board full of switches. He monitored the rooms to make sure the girls stayed safe. The stripper led Solomon to a room at the end of the hallway, where she seated him at a table, a catalog open in front of him. He knew the drill. "Good luck, daddy. I hope you find what you're looking for." She smiled and sashayed through the curtain.

Straight, he would have found some time for that one. Instead, he delved into the book in front of him while he waited for an attendant to arrive. For a price, there was another catalog. He wasn't interested in normal, mundane shit. He needed to feed his sick, perverted cravings.

CHAPTER TWENTY-THREE

JACK AND JANIE SAT across from Robertson's desk, listening as he talked to the district attorney on speaker phone. Peter could be polite as all get-out if he wanted to be, and he needed all the guile he could muster with that woman. Nancy Polk was tough as nails and didn't take anything for granted. She treated her position very seriously, as she should.

"Yes ma'am, I understand we are taking a risk by asking this."

The voice on the other end spoke slowly, deliberately. "Mr. Robertson, I don't see how it could be your risk. I'm the DA, and you are defending the felon in this case. To be clear, you are asking . . . a court order to have the police search an establishment, confiscate their computers, and examine the data? What evidence do you have to substantiate your claim? And it better not be circumstantial."

Peter took a deep breath. "Our client, Robert Lopez, is no

angel, even by his own admission. He is a middle man in the Internet porn biz. Again . . . admittedly, some bad stuff passes through his email. His claim: He didn't have the opportunity to erase the sh—*stuff* on his computer before being busted."

"Tell me something I don't already know, Mr. Robertson."

"I have in my possession two years of invoices from his company and corresponding bank statements, which show the procession of transactions between sources and the company that sent the questionable material to him. All of the data is backed up on disk for us. It shows on several occasions how he'd received questionable content and refused it, or deleted it, returning it to the sender. The string of business from Lopez's company and St. Petersburg Limited is consistently moved on to another, bigger distributer, City Productions, out of Eastern Europe. The child porn that found its way onto Lopez's computer was never moved. Typically, Lopez would move content within three to five days. The questionable content sat on his computer for over a week."

"This is still circumstantial. There could be other motivations in play here, counselor."

Peter paused. "You're making the assertion he might be personally interested in the data?"

"I can't rule it out. Possession is nine-tenths of the law."

"I pointed that out to him, obviously."

"I'm sure you did. What I'm saying is there could be other motivations. Lopez was arrested after an anonymous call, one that hasn't been backed up. What if the data was conveniently left on his hard drive? What if Lopez wanted the data to be discovered?"

"You're insinuating that we might have been played by Lopez?"

"Not insinuating, just open to the possible notion, as you must be. You've indicated Mr. Lopez contacted one of your junior lawyers."

"Yes, Jackson Walker. He's here with me now listening to us on speaker."

"Good morning, Mr. Walker."

"Good morning, Ms. Polk."

"It's not unheard of for a young and eager attorney, such as yourself, to be taken advantage of. Mr. Lopez exists in a world much larger than Southwest Florida, with much more at stake than a child pornography charge. I don't mean to belittle the crime, as I do find it repulsive and a blight on humanity—something which needs to be eradicated at all costs. I want you to be cognizant of the fact . . . there could be more in play than the obvious. Now, the attorney general doesn't take this crime lightly either, which is the reason I'm speaking to you this morning. Please continue." The district attorney was clearly in control of the conversation.

Peter said, "Your perspective is noted. The story gets better. St Petersburg Inc. is owned by Eli Romanov, who also owns a string of strip bars from Tampa all the way through to New Orleans. We have verified the information. The rumor is that Romanov is also a low-level producer of pornography."

"Circumstantial."

"I'm not sure if you heard or not—yesterday there was a shooting in North Ft. Myers."

"Mr. Robertson, this is a normal occurrence. If I had to keep track of every shooting in the state of Florida, I wouldn't be able to find enough time in the day to take phone calls from people like you."

"I appreciate that. The shooting occurred at a car dealership where Lopez's car was found sitting on the lot. The salesman, who Lopez was scheduled to meet, had his brains blown out in the same parking lot. Lopez's appointment with the salesman is verified by the dead man's day timer. A man was seen carrying a body across Cleveland Avenue, stuffing it into the back of a BMW 7 Series. The witness was able to take down the license. It's registered to Romanov Inc., a subsidiary of St. Petersburg Inc. We think our client has been either killed or detained by the owner of this company."

"Okay, Mr. Robertson, you've substantiated your argument. I can't promise you'll get your search warrant, but I can tell you I will contact the chief of police in Tampa and make sure there is an eye kept on the place."

Pete nodded to Jack and Janie and smiled. "That's all we

could hope for, ma'am."

"I'll be in touch, Mr. Robertson, if we decide to grant a search warrant."

"Thank you!" Peter hung up.

Janie spoke. "So what now, Pete?"

"We have to act on two possible assumptions. One, Lopez is who he says he is and the Russians really did frame him. Or Lopez is the one doing the framing. I don't understand why." He paused. "I'm going to speak with my contacts at the Lee County Sheriff's Department and see if I can't pick up a few scraps. I want the two of you to check out Lopez's home, see if he's still around. In fact, it might be prudent to give the man a call, though I have a strong feeling you won't get an answer."

Janie frowned. "What you really want us to do, Pete, is break into the place?"

"No. I'd say watch it, see if he comes back. If there's no activity by sundown, take a look inside."

Jack took an uptight breath. "So, we're going to break in?"

Pete smiled. "Yes. That's what I'm saying. Janie's done this before; she's quite good at it. Don't get caught. You can assume the police already have an eye on the place."

Janie put her hand on Jack's. "Don't worry, Jackie boy, I'm an old pro at this."

Jack shook his head and smiled at Janie. "Oh, those famous last words!"

Peter slapped Jack on the back. "Don't look so worried, Walker."

CHAPTER TWENTY-FOUR

BONITA BEACH ROAD CAME upon him quickly and he swerved into the double left-hand turn lane to exit Highway 41. He dared the old couple he cut off to give him the finger. Evidently, his nasty glare was enough to make them back off. Mason found himself in one of those moods that bad people got into now and again. He knew the evening could end in conflict; thus, he ratcheted up his anger, letting its energy simmer just under a boil.

Once off the stop-and-go coastal highway, he cruised along at 40 mph, the speed limit. He didn't need to get pulled over. After five minutes, Bonita Beach Road veered to the right at the coast. The stretch between the turn and the next bridge was packed with impressive homes both on the gulf and the back bay. Mason found it hard to keep to the reduced 30 mph speed limit, but eventually it picked up as he left the residential area and entered Lovers Key, a beautiful drive crossing three bridges before it reached the lift bridge at Big Carlos Pass leading to the southern tip of Ft. Myers Beach.

The sun began to drop into the gulf, but Mason wanted total darkness for what he intended. Pulling into Santini Plaza, he looked for somewhere busy to lose himself for an hour or so. He spotted a place on the right called Runaways that looked pretty busy. Not wanting to be right in front of the place, he parked a few hundred feet down, in front of a used bookstore.

Pushing the bar door open, he was hit by music from a live band, and the crooning singer sounded remarkably like Rod Stewart singing "Maggie May." He pulled a stool up to a large square bar and was promptly greeted by a bartender with waist-length dreadlocks. He felt almost relaxed and ordered a scotch and water with lots of ice.

Watching the band and the older ladies having a good time dancing, Mason wondered if people ever pondered the wild-ass idea they could be sitting in the same bar as a repeat killer. An *escaped convict*. Somehow the thought made the drink go down smoother. Tonight, they would all be safe, as there were bigger fish to fry. Tonight, they were lucky.

After an hour, he could no longer watch the shenanigans of the ladies dancing, drawing the line when he was propositioned. He retrieved his car and pulled onto Estero Boulevard, heading north. The drive to Ibis Lane took only a few minutes and he might have walked, but he didn't want his car too far away if he needed to get away quickly. Estero Island had two ways in and out; both could be blocked off within minutes. He parked at the Beach Theater and walked up Ibis toward Jack Walker's house at the end of a canal, at the entrance to Estero Bay. Mason frowned. *The sniveling turd moved up in the world.*

He cradled a bottle under his arm containing a complex potion within the thin glass. He'd put a lot of effort into the talisman. All that was needed for the curse-bearing concoction to be effective was a strand of Walker's hair. Mason would break into his house and hopefully find a few on a brush in his bathroom. The spell would guarantee his demise, its power along with the curse placed in New Orleans more than potent enough to stop the strongest mortal in his tracks. The final touch would be maneuvering Walker within a chalk circle created and consecrated by Mason, again using some of Walkers hair.

Without hesitation, he ambled to the back of the house. Seeing lights on and hearing music, he started past the screened-in lanai covering the pool area but was hit by a wafting cloud of pot smoke. One whiff and he could identify the music playing inside the house: classic rock, "Killer Queen." *How appropriate!*

Peering around a stucco corner into the lanai, he spied a single male sitting in a deck chair beside a large, round glass table. While it wasn't Walker, there was a resemblance. He wouldn't be able to get inside the easy way.

He walked back to the front of the house, making sure that no one appeared to be looking, and stepped up to the front door. Before pulling out his lockpicks, he tried the knob. It was unlocked. *How convenient.*

Slowly, ever so slowly, he opened the door, peering inside. There didn't appear to be anyone in the front. The music from the lanai softened coming through the house but still hid any noise Mason might possibly make upon entry. Still, he didn't take things for granted and took his time to move carefully. Tiptoeing like a cat to where he assumed the bedrooms were located, he entered the bathroom that divided two medium-sized rooms. Smiling, he found a brush in one of the drawers. Eyes wide with glee, he plucked off a pinch of hair and dropped it into the blood-colored bottle, re-sealing the lid. Taking another pinch, he put it into a ziplock plastic baggie. He opened the cupboard below the sink and hid the bottle behind a bunch of boxes that looked as if they hadn't been moved in months. It would be better to bury the bottle, but Mason didn't want to risk discovery.

* * * *

Josh stirred from his chair, not knowing why, but he did know he felt damned thirsty and he headed to the kitchen. The front door was slightly ajar. He forgot his thirst and pushed it shut. When he passed it not twenty minutes ago, he was positive it was closed.

Josh turned to the bedrooms. "Naw, gotta stop smoking that shit," he said, and doubled back to the kitchen, helping himself to one of Jack's assorted beers. He chose something Hispanic-looking, the country of origin not clear. He cracked the can and headed back to the lanai and his comfy chair. He didn't know why he glanced at the bedroom hallway again but was glad he did. The bathroom door stood halfway open. His eyes were not fooling him—it had been shut two minutes ago. He veered into the lanai, reaching for the gun under his chair.

The blow to the back of his head knocked him down but didn't stun him enough to stop him from grabbing his Smith & Wesson. The figure behind him darted for the lanai exit. Josh followed his path with the barrel of the gun and fired, the bullet taking out a chunk of the stucco corner where the assailant's head had just been. Josh gave chase, barreling shoulder-first through the lanai door. He turned left toward the front of the house.

Just as the thought ran through his head that chasing the man might be foolish, the flash of a knife caught his eye, but it was too late. It felt more like a punch in the back than being stabbed. His gun flew into the bushes as the knife was pulled out. Josh saw the arm coming at him again and yelled, "Fucker!"

Instinctively, Josh grabbed the descending arm as the blade slashed at his neck. In a fight for his life, he threw out all convention and bit into his assailant's arm; his teeth broke through the bare flesh, the attacker now howling like an animal until he dropped the knife. Josh tried to kick the man's feet out from under him but was hit with an unbearable pain in his back. Dropping to his knees, he grabbed the knife lying in front of him. Brandishing the blade made the man step back out of Josh's reach. Josh got a good look at his face. It took a few moments for the information to connect.

"You're that satanic fuck . . . attacked Jack in the police van. Gramps was right."

The man smiled. "Gramps?" The French accent unmistakable.

"You're Mason. I thought you were in prison?"

"*Was* Mason. Unfortunately for you—I don't know your name, though you bear resemblance to Walker—your recognition of me has sealed your fate. You see, the length of the blade you hold in your hands has passed through your right kidney, hopefully severing the artery attached to it. You will lose consciousness within a minute or so. By my calculations, I have five to eight minutes before the sirens respond to the sound of the gunshot. Then again, it is low season. Perhaps the gunfire went unnoticed."

Josh felt a steady flow of warmth over the muscles in his behind and down his leg. He put his hand back there to feel the sticky blood, sending a wave of shock— *The man could be correct*. Josh's hands numbed and the blade fell to the ground.

Mason smiled. "You see, you are dying and there is nothing that can be done about it."

Josh slid down onto his side, no longer able to muster the strength to remain vertical. He croaked a feeble, "Go to hell . . . *fucker*!"

"No. I'm not a fucker. That is one thing I am not. I am, however, the master who caused your death and I will say a prayer to the Dark Lord to make sure he will welcome *you* to his domain. I think you might like it there." Mason picked up the knife and slit Josh's throat.

* * * *

Assuming the police were on their way, he dragged the young man's body to the canal and floated it out into the waterway. It sank as the air in the clothing slowly bubbled out. Bull sharks were prevalent in estuaries behind the barrier islands. They would no doubt do a job on the body before it could be discovered.

He went back to the side of the house and did his best to rake over the blood spilled in the garden. He retrieved the man's gun and his own knife. Entering the lanai, he retrieved the expelled bullet cartridge in the middle of the cement floor. Looking around first, he turned off the music and the lights.

* * * *

Strolling casually to the end of the street, Mason passed a slow-moving police cruiser. The officer in the passenger's seat glanced at him. They had obviously been called to check on a disturbance. He hoped the dark, now quiet house would be enough to ward off any cursory investigation. They would drive by the address given and, seeing no signs of foul play, go to the 911 caller's house for a visit.

If Mason remained calm, he would be off the island and back out to Highway 41 within twenty minutes, where he would need to find a pharmacy to attend to the bite on his arm. Human teeth could leave deadly wounds if not treated promptly. He sighed. The adventure had been messy. Still, he found some solace in the fact that it looked as if he'd dispensed of one of Walker's family members and he'd extended the curse, and procured some of Walker's hair.

CHAPTER TWENTY-FIVE

IT DIDN'T TAKE THEM long to find Robert Lopez's home in North Naples. It seemed like years since Jack last drove down Immokalee Road. In fact, the last time may have been when he'd been hell-bent on killing the McFaddens. He took a deep breath.

Janie noticed. "What's up? You look uptight all of a sudden."

"I'm thinking that the last time I drove down this road was five years ago."

Janie nodded. "Bad memories?"

"Sorta. Bad isn't the right word, though. Intense memories might be better. The entire time I was imprisoned, I never felt afraid, not for one moment. Anger is a strong energy and a prevalent memory. I was incredibly angry. All I wanted to do was kick Jimmy McFadden's buckteeth into the back of his throat. If it was the last good thing I did before I died, I was going to kill that sick, demented creature. He wasn't even human. He was cunning, like an animal with no remorse—a perfect killing machine, who knew how to clean up after himself."

"Put those thoughts out of your pretty head and concentrate on Robert Lopez."

Jack turned to look at her. "Pretty head?"

"Yes, you have a pretty head, the whole package. You're a good-looking guy, Jackson. If I were twenty—no, fifteen years younger—you'd be in trouble. What are you, twenty-nine?"

"Yep. I turn thirty in January."

"I'm forty-nine, too old for you now. In my thirties, watch out, I'd be all over it. Once you had your birthday."

Jack snapped his head to the side to see if Janie meant it.

When they both laughed she said, "I just like to see you squirm sometimes. For someone that's an ex-sports star, you sure as hell can be shy. That's what I like about you, Jack. You're not so tough that you don't leave your thoughts on your shirt sleeve . . . at least with me."

Jack raised his brows. "If you say so. Be truthful, were you kidding about my thirtieth?"

She giggled at his bewildered look. "You'll find out!"

Jack had to smile, and felt so much better. "Say, isn't that his street up ahead? Longshore Way? Then onto Terramar Drive?"

"Yep, you got it, Jackson. Careful when you come up on the house. Like Pete said, it could be staked out."

Sure enough, as they closed in on Lopez's address, they saw a black Chevy Malibu sitting across the road from the house. The driver looking as if he were reading a book. Standard procedure.

Jack turned to Janie. "So, what now?"

"This golf course seems to twist all through the subdivision. Maybe we can take a look from the backside. Pull around the corner and we'll park and walk up the fairway running in behind his place."

Jack nodded. "Good idea."

They parked out of the cop's eyesight and walked to a tee serving the fairway Janie had indicated. A foursome teed off as they approached, keeping Jack and Janie standing back until the group finished with their drives. Jack was greeted by two of the men. He nodded back and hollered, "Hope you're having a good one."

"The beer's cold," one man laughed.

Another golfer stared at Jack and smiled. "Hey, Jack Walker, right?"

Jack nodded.

"Fred Andres. We played together in a Tampa celebrity event, six or seven years ago."

Jack smiled. As time passed, it seemed fewer and fewer people recognized him—perhaps a good thing. He remembered the man. "Yes. You're the guy who can hit it out of the park. Showed me up pretty good if I remember."

The man smiled. "Can we get a picture with you?"

"Sure, why not?"

Jack cozied up with the foursome and the men took turns handing Janie their phones so that she could snap the shots. After he signed their hats, the group waved and headed up the fairway.

Janie shook her head. "I forget sometimes you used to be a celebrity."

"So do I. That one caught me off guard."

"You're a natural, Jackson. Too bad your other career didn't pan out. You were so good with those guys; they were starstruck."

"Coulda, shoulda, woulda. That's all gone now, Janie. I tossed it away years ago. But . . . I'm kinda stoked to get to the bottom of this case. Let's see what we got in that house."

* * * *

The sun began to sink behind the trees and buildings in the subdivision and there didn't look to be any more golfers following the group on the tee. Lopez's house, Janie figured, was the sixth on the left. The walked casually to their destination. The backyard held no lawn furniture, unlike the neighboring properties.

They stood for a time trying to get a lay of the land. As the sun sank deeper, causing more shadows, the house became darker. Still, no lights went on inside. Jack looked at Janie. "I don't think anyone's in there."

"I agree. You wanna have a closer look?"

"I don't want to waste time if we don't have to."

Jack stepped over the knee-high hedge separating the home from the course and approached the screened lanai. Again, there was no furniture. His hackles rose.

The door from the backyard to the lanai wasn't locked. Jack entered with Janie on his heel.

"Nothing," Jack exclaimed.

Janie nodded, grabbing his hand.

Jack walked up to the french doors. He tugged on them but they were locked. Looking into the interior of the house, he saw it was clearly vacant. "Damn! I need to see the bedroom, Janie."

"Why?"

"This guy could be just cruising on a job, using this place just to sleep. I need to see if there's a bed that's been slept on."

Janie nodded, pulling out her lockpick set. "It might be better to get in through the garage; these sliders are impossible to pick."

He nodded, and they moved to the side garage door. He made sure they were still out of sight of the neighbors and the cop car. It took Janie less than a minute to unlock the door. Inside, the story didn't change, the house empty except for a large, flat-screen television in the living room.

After searching the other levels, they peered into an empty basement. "Lopez is gone."

Janie nodded. "Let's get out of here before someone sees us."

* * * *

They retreated to Jack's Jeep. The sun had dropped, and darkness fell from the sky. Jack drove away from the subdivision, making sure he didn't pass the cop car again.

"So, what do we make of this?" Janie turned to Jack.

"I'm starting to think the DA may have been correct. But what's the motivation?"

"Seems pretty clear to me. For whatever reason, Lopez wants the Russians busted."

"I guess. Why go through all this hassle? An anonymous call would've been sufficient."

"Like the DA said, there's a great big world out there that doesn't revolve around Southwest Florida, and they don't hand out search warrants for anonymous tips."

Jack scratched his head. "The Russians have pissed someone off . . . badly."

Janie cut him off. "Possibly. Still, they're no better. Distributing child pornography, they're doing bad things, and might be producing it."

"Where does this leave us? We no longer appear to have a client."

"Don't we? We haven't been given notice. We have a few circumstantial incidences that might indicate as much. We haven't been given anything concrete to go on at this point. Lopez may have simply moved his residence for all we know."

"Who leaves a fifty-two-inch plasma television behind? For that matter, who leaves his car at a dealership? A man who planned to fly, that's who. You can't take a television and a car on a fucking plane, Janie." He slammed his palm against the steering wheel.

"Calm down. We need to tell Pete what we found out."

"I agree, he's the boss, but it doesn't mean I can't be pissed about the situation. My first big case looks as if it might dissolve right in front of me."

Janie sighed, "I understand. We need to put one foot in front of the other and follow procedure. We have a decent retainer. We need to justify our billing. We follow through on the search warrant. Tampa police have been watching Aversions since we called it in. Jack—" She looked at him, putting her hand on his. "This isn't the first time a client has made an end run on me while working on a case. Things happen and they tend to surface or evolve with new events. Let's be patient and do our job."

Jack nodded. "I can agree with that."

"Okay then. We'll most likely have to drive up to Tampa tomorrow, so we need to get some sleep. I didn't get a wink last night with Josh snoring his head off."

"You were in the bedroom?"

"Yes, but the bedroom window opens up into the lanai. He damn well honked ten feet from my head all night. Can you drop me at my place? It's only five minutes away. I need to sleep and get a change of clothes. I'll see you at Pete's office tomorrow."

"Yeah, sure."

* * * *

Almost on cue, as Jack pulled out of Janie's driveway his phone rang. "Jack Walker."

"Hi, Jackson, it's Lolita."

He recognized the deep female voice. He blurted out, "What's up?"

"I said I'd get back to you. I had another dream last night. Do you feel well?"

"Actually, I feel like shit. The past few days. Crabby as all get-out."

"I saw a cloud hanging over. If I'm not mistaken, it looks like a curse. Now, I don't know what a curse looks like, but it was the first word to pop into my head. There's more. There was a viper that lay watching, ready to strike. As I said when we first met, we are both in danger, and I don't know why. I feel the climax of my premonition is close at hand."

"I don't believe in curses, Lolita. I thank you for the call. It's been a long day." He hung up. The last thing Jack needed now was a bloody palm reader getting him all riled up.

* * * *

He pulled into his driveway, parking beside Josh's beater pickup. Rolling out of his Jeep, Jack walked to the front door and spied a business card stuck in the crack. He read aloud, "Officer Randal Armstrong, Lee County Sheriff's Department." *Strange.*

The door was locked and, too tired to return to the Jeep for the key in the glove box, Jack walked around the house. He slipped on something wet in the grass and grabbed one of the palmetto bushes to stay upright.

Entering the lanai through its side screen door, it seemed odd not to see Josh crashed on the sofa with the music playing.

Distracted, Jack noticed the bottoms of his shoes felt tacky as he walked across the cement floor. When he saw the track of shoeprints he'd left, Jack realized the prints were reddish black. He bent to rub his finger on one of the fresher prints and smelled it. *Blood!*

His inner alarm went off and his knees weakened. Sitting down, Jack pulled out his cell and dialed the number on the business card. Looking around as the line rang, he saw a large hole in the wall beside the lanai doorway. His stress level kept rising. A woman answered.

"Lee County Sheriff."

"I just arrived home and a Randal Armstrong left his card stuck in my door."

"What is your name and address?"

"Jack Walker, 445 Ibis Lane, Ft. Myers Beach."

"Zip?"

"33931."

"Hold on, Mr. Walker. The officer responded to a possible gun shot. One of the neighbors called it in. Is everything okay, sir?"

Jack's mind churned. "No. I just arrived and I need an officer at my premises."

"Is there a problem, sir?"

"I think someone's been shot, but I don't see a body. I'm a lawyer. I know I shouldn't contaminate the area and I'm going to remain inside the lanai until someone can get here."

"I'm sending a response team, sir. Stay on the line with me and please remain calm."

* * * *

Within five minutes there were four cruisers, lights flashing. They parked on the street and front lawn. Jack took off his shoes, leaving them upside down on the cement as he awaited them in the lanai. One of the officers identified himself as Randal Armstrong and sat beside Jack, explaining the gunshot call to 911 earlier.

Jack recounted his discoveries upon arriving home and how he feared the worst: his cousin, Josh, should be there and there was blood at the side of the house. No one moved, awaiting a forensic team. They didn't take long to arrive. They quickly determined there was only one gunshot fired, and the large amount of blood showed there was an altercation followed by a body being dragged to the edge of the canal.

Jack sat sipping a beer, pale, his mind racing, trying to put together possible scenarios. Armstrong watched him.

"Mr. Walker."

"Yes?"

"They're taping the house as a crime scene now. You, of course, cannot stay here, most likely for a few days. Do you have a friend or relative we can take you to tonight? It would be best if you find someplace else to stay. If you can't, you are welcome to stay at the station overnight."

"No, that's okay. I can drive and I have a place to stay."

"Please give me all that information so we can keep in touch. Tomorrow morning, you will need to come in and make a statement."

"I'll do that. Where do I go?"

"Ben Pratt at 41."

"That's what I thought. Any particular time?"

"Not really."

* * * *

Jack dialed Janie's number and waited.

She answered groggily. "Jack?"

He gave her a quick onceover of what happened. "Can I crash at your place?"

"No problem. Are you all right?"

"Yeah, I'm still alive . . . Josh is missing."

"Come right over."

CHAPTER TWENTY-SIX

LOLITA PLAYED HOOKY. SHE didn't have any clients booked for the day. She didn't bother to open up the shop, and instead waddled down to meet the Uber driver. *Anyone in psychic distress would have to wait a day*. The driver took her to the bus station in downtown Bonita, where she planned to get another one to Everglades City. It would take a couple of hours, but she didn't mind the ride.

She stared out the window as the coach traversed Highway 41 into the Everglades. The vastness and stark beauty of the area amazed her. Most Floridians lived on the doorstep of the great swamp, never leaving the confines of their coastal homes to see the real countryside, the real Florida. One of her prized possessions was a book of black-and-white photographs of Florida's wilderness taken by Clyde Butcher. She didn't have time to visit the man and his daughter, Jackie, who'd always been so kind. Alas, her trip today would be purely business.

She'd put off meeting Nathaniel Portman for some time now. He'd come to her in dreams and readings over the years and she'd connected with his grandson—no coincidence. Something needed to be figured out. To ignore things much longer would be negligent. Plus, Lolita always loved her day trips.

Everglade City used to be the capital of Collier County and remained a strange conglomeration of semi-stately buildings mixed with everything from upscale homes to shacks. It sat southeast of Naples and Marco Island, a testament to old Florida. Lolita called it the airboat capital of the world.

She walked to Nathaniel's office, becoming quite hot and sweaty by the time she arrived, her chubby legs chaffing. Going up the stairs to the second level, she pulled open the door. A little bell attached to it by a rusty nail jingled.

A young Seminole female sat behind a desk with a nameplate: *Reception, Beth.* She smiled up at the newcomer and waited patiently while Lolita caught her breath. Lolita toddled into the reception area and paused to wipe the perspiration from her dripping brow. Taking out her freshly-ironed and sweet-smelling handkerchief, Lolita dabbed away.

"Can I help you, ma'am?"

"You most certainly can. I'd like to speak with Mr. Portman. Let him know Lolita is here. I'm sure he will be expecting me."

Before Beth could get up from her chair, an older Seminole man with short-cropped hair, dressed in a fashionable summer suit, came through an impressive wooden door.

Lolita was taken aback by his eyes—black as coal but with a light that could shine to the back of her skull . . . if she allowed it. The distinctive man possessed a guarded yet confident bearing and he was someone Lolita would never forget.

"We have met before," he stated more than asked.

"Not in this world."

He nodded. "Please come into my office. We have plenty to discuss."

Nathaniel gestured for Lolita to sit in front of his ornate wooden desk. While she sat in one of the chairs, her eyes were drawn to the wide expanse of the window taking up one entire wall.

"Nice view!"

It was hard to deny. The office window looked out at one of the local rivers, edged with thick mangrove bushes. He nodded, accepting the validity of her comment. "I'm glad you came. I've felt your presence for a long time."

"As I have yours. Your family calls you Gramps. I'm sorry, but you don't look like a Nathan."

Gramps laughed. "That's okay. I don't think I look like a Nathan either. Feel free to call me what my family calls me, if this is what you were edging toward."

"Okay, Gramps. We share a common denominator."

"My grandson."

"Of course. He's strong with the spirits. I've seen it in him, and I've seen him in my dreams. He doesn't embrace it?"

Gramps nodded slowly. "Jackson is a different kind of animal. He's still young. When I was young I spurned the ability."

"He's nearly thirty."

"This is true."

"I called him last night to warn him."

"He ignored you. I could have told you that he would. He ignores me."

"Basically. Dismissed me and hung up."

"Why are you trying to help him? I know you have a connection, but I don't know why you would come all the way to Everglades City to tell me this. Let's cut to the chase, Lolita. I want to know . . . what is your motive?"

She smiled, showing a full set of perfectly white teeth. "Gramps, I'm an old-fashioned palm reader. That's what I'm best at. I dabble in the tarot." She paused for a moment. "From time to time I have visions. A few weeks back, I saw my own death, and I saw Jackson's death. They are connected. Now, I'm not sure if one will occur if the other happens. This is the reason that I came to see you. I felt that if I could explain to you my vision, maybe you could talk some sense into him."

Gramps stared at her, trying to get a read on the woman. He could not see the motivation behind telling him lies. He had also seen the woman in his dreams. They'd made contact. He did wonder if she had any Native blood. It would be difficult to tell. The Seminoles didn't mix readily with other cultures, especially the African Americans. He turned away from the window they were both staring at and looked deep into her eyes.

"What does your gut tell you, Lolita? Why did you really come here?"

She took a deep breath, nodding. "I see Devil Spawn. Of this I'm certain. I also see another group. It is complex, intertwined, like the dreams often are—clear as the mud of the Mississippi River."

"What else have you seen, Lolita?"

"I should be charging you for this, old man," she smirked. "I've seen the two of us standing on a precipice, Jack and me. I can't tell which one of us will be pushed over the edge, but one goes over in the act of saving the other. I've explained this to Jack. He will have none of it."

"No. He's an idealist and his idealism doesn't involve the paranormal."

"So what are we to do, old man?"

Gramps stood and walked to the window, his hands clasped behind his back. "I've asked my grandson to call me every morning. This is the second day since I've asked him to do so. And today, I've had no call."

Lolita stood up as if her behind had been stung by a bee. "Gramps, if it were me, I'd be calling him right now. I don't know about you, but I just experienced a premonition something bad is in the works."

He turned to look at her. "I don't believe in coincidences. The fact that you are here telling me this is enough to warrant a drive to Ft. Myers. I know you are from that area; I can give you a ride, if you want."

"Bonita, but that's close enough," she smiled. "I'm an old-fashioned girl, growed up poor, and I never turn down a ride, mister."

* * * *

Beth raised her eyes as the stranger walked into the reception room. He was on the short side with dark black hair and a well-trimmed beard. His accent came across as French, but she couldn't quite tell.

"Is Mr. Portman in?"

Beth smiled, her expression soon quashed by the man's sour look. "You missed him. He left for the day about an hour ago. Can I tell him who called?"

The man turned abruptly and walked out of the office.

"Have a nice day," Beth responded to the door closing and the little bell ringing.

* * * *

Mason rolled his eyes as he hurried down the steps. "Satanists don't have nice days!" he mumbled under his breath. "And it just got worse."

CHAPTER TWENTY-SEVEN

THE EAGLE SOARED HIGH above the salt estuary. She saw, with magnified vision, the mullet schools moving down the beach by the thousand. She could see the large sharks that darted onto the massive schools, causing the fish to scurry and leap from the water, the jack crevalle picking up the scraps. A slight adjustment turned the great predator sharply inland, passing over the massive concrete structures, which seemingly reached toward the sky. Storm clouds loomed inland, rising in great plumes caused by the day's heat.

The great bird dove after clearing the buildings, heading toward the bay behind the island. She swooped low to grab a small herring as it skipped to the top of the water but veered away quickly as she neared a strange form. The unmoving land walker floated faceup, its features bloated from the salt water, its eyes plucked by the crabs. The eagle veered upward, toward the sun . . .

Jack startled from sleep, the dream still fresh in his mind. He must have yelled out, as Janie appeared at the end of the couch, the kitchen light shining behind her.

"Jack, you were talking in your sleep. Loudly. I thought there might be someone else in here until I saw you. You're soaked with sweat."

He put a hand up. "I'm okay, just a dream."

"Would you like some water?"

"Sure." He thought about the image of his cousin's body floating in the water. Though distorted, there could be no doubt it was Josh. Jack didn't know what bothered him more: the vision or the fact that he might be considering the vision to have some validity. He'd experienced them before and they were always the same—the bald eagle. When he was younger, he'd told his grandfather about the bird, bringing a broad smile to the man's face. "It's your double, Jackson. Our forefathers called them *familiars*. My grandfather's familiar was a fox. You should be so lucky to have an eagle."

Jack shook his head at the memory. "Bullshit!" he said.

"What's bullshit, Jack?" Janie asked from behind, offering a glass of water.

He took it and shook his head again. "Just bullshit Native stuff. Dreams."

"I'm all ears, now that I'm awake." Janie saw a tremor in Jack's jaw; his distress over Josh was clear. "This isn't an invitation in any way. We're just friends, and don't take advantage of that fact." She led him into her bedroom, propped up some pillows and motioned for him to climb in beside her.

"I'm not sure this is a good idea," he said awkwardly.

"There's no idea, Jackson. You're upset and I don't think you should be alone." She patted the bed. "We both need some sleep and I want to hear about this dream."

He shrugged and climbed in beside her. Janie was right; it felt good to be near a friend.

She turned off the light and made herself comfy. Taking his hand, she rubbed her thumb into his palm. "Tell me about it."

He laid his head on the pillow, staring at the ceiling. "Do you believe in all of this paranormal shit my gramps talks about?"

"He sure believes in it. Let's put it this way: I'd like to believe in it, but I find it hard to. From what I gather, you're kind of the opposite. You don't want to believe in it but find it hard to get away from it."

"Sort of. Gramps says I have a familiar, an eagle. She sees through me, and I can see through her. When I was a little boy, I used to like the dreams. They took me to a place no one else could go. Mostly flying."

"Sounds incredible. Who would not want that? Especially a little boy."

"It was, until I became older. I learned to shut the dreams out. It's when I let my guard down that it returns. Perhaps the stress of the night . . . the bad feeling in my gut, sleeping in a strange place. I think something bad happened to Josh."

"So tell me." She continued to massage his hand, cuddling into him a bit. "I hope you don't mind."

He sighed, "No, Janie, it's actually very nice. I haven't slept with a female in a long time. Well, you know what I mean. It's nice having someone warm beside me."

She smiled to herself. "How long?"

"You might find this hard to believe."

"Don't tell me. The Satanist girl?"

He let out another long breath. "Yeppers."

"Oh, Jack, you poor soul. If it wasn't for the fact it might destroy our working relationship, I'd give you some sympathy sex right now, but that ain't happening. Go on."

"After all that occurred, I didn't want to open myself up again. It's actually okay. Life's been one heck of a lot easier without a relationship to worry about."

Janie pulled his head onto her shoulder. "Tell me more about those dreams." She ran her fingers through his hair, softly scratching his scalp with her nails.

He felt the soft, heavy pressure of her breast against his arm. "Janie, that's heavenly. I've experienced the dreams again lately. I try to ignore them, but tonight I must have let my guard down. When the bird flew along the coast, I recognized the tidal ponds along the southern tip of Ft. Myers Beach. Then it flew out to Estero Bay, clear as day. As it dropped to catch a fish, that's when I saw the floating body, bloated and half eaten. It looked like Josh."

Her hand stilled on his scalp.

"It makes sense. I can't ignore this one. I told you what happened—a body had been dragged down to the back bay. *Josh is gone*." The last words caught in his throat.

"You have to give this dream some serious thought, Jackson. While you don't want to believe, there are those who have lived their lives this way, like Gramps, and they swear by premonitions."

"I don't know. I have the feeling it's true; yet, for obvious reasons, I don't want it to be. And I'm pissed to think I'm actually considering it could be correct. The fucking bird, though. I'm willing to admit . . . it never shows me anything but the truth. When I was a kid, it would show me where to look for the fish. I didn't realize it at the time but, man, I was like a fish whisperer. I could sense the bird finding pleasure in my achievements. I gotta say, it did stop when I started playing football—the drugs. I knew it didn't approve."

"Now, you sound as if you are accepting?"

"Not totally."

"What if it is your cousin?"

"Christ, I don't know. I'm just hoping he's okay. He's a survivor."

"Nothing we can do about it now. The police told you to stay away. Lie back and relax again. We have a big day tomorrow. You need to rest." She continued to massage his head. In no time, he fell asleep in her arms like a baby. She smiled and fell asleep as well.

* * * *

Jack woke with a start. He and Janie were still cuddled in bed. He turned his head to meet her eyes. She smiled. "I couldn't wake you."

"What the hell time is it?" He looked at his watch: 7 AM. "We need to be in Tampa by 10!"

"I'll make coffee. Help yourself to the shower. If we're out of here in twenty minutes, we'll make it okay. We don't need to be there, really."

"C'mon, Janie, we sure as heck do. I wanna see the look on that Russian's face when the police knock on the door. I can only think it might have been me who was supposed to be dead. What if it was them who broke into my house last night? I can't think who the hell else it might be. Think about it. Lopez ends up gone and someone gets whacked at my house. Well, we can't say that yet, but I need to look at his eyes."

"There you go. You're starting to sound like Gramps."

Jack scowled at her.

She caught his look. "Hey, no way to treat someone who rubbed your head all night so you could get some sleep."

He huffed. "See? Women. You can't win. I didn't do nothing and you're holding something over me."

She smiled, trying not to laugh.

* * * *

Two hours later, they were pulling off I-75 a half mile from Aversions when the phone rang. He looked at the heads-up display. "Shit!"

"What?"

"It's Gramps. I'm under direct order to call him every morning."

He put the call on speaker. "Gramps, wassup?"

"You didn't call."

"I was busy, heading up to Tampa and needed to leave early."

"If I was one of your girlfriends, you'd have called me five times by now."

Janie giggled and covered her mouth.

"I don't have any girlfriends, Gramps."

"No matter. I have a bad feeling about something. A premonition. And I have one of your friends with me in the car. Lolita."

"Lolita?" *This is going from bad to worse.* "What on earth is she doing with you? Where are you?"

"She came to my office today to express her concern for your wellbeing. She's with me in the car and I'm on hands-free."

"Hello, Jackson." Her mellow voice streamed into his car, invading his space. He wanted to scream. But knew he had to calm himself. Pushing Janie's hand away from his knee as she tried to pat it, he nearly cut off another car in the process. Jack's voice rose a couple of decibels.

"What the heck are you doing with my grandfather? This borders on stalking. It's fucking grandfather stalking."

Gramps interjected, "I'm a grown man, Jackson. I make my own decisions. Calm yourself. The woman came to me because you failed to heed a dire warning."

Jack's head slumped. "Aw, come on! See, this is why I don't believe in this shit. I no longer control this situation. I don't like that. It's being controlled by shamans and damned fortune tellers. What does that say about the situation? O-U-T of fucking control!"

Gramps distracted him before he hurt himself. "Where's Josh?"

Jack paused too long.

"Jackson, where is he?"

"That's where we have a problem. When I returned home last night, he wasn't there."

"This is abnormal?"

"No, there's more." Jack explained what happened the previous evening, pulling to the side of the road as he neared Aversions.

Gramps went quit for a time. "What have the police come up with?"

"Shit, I'm supposed to go to police headquarters to make a statement this morning. I've not been feeling well either. I've been fighting something off for a few days. I feel like shit!"

"I can't believe you haven't taken this seriously. You didn't call me. This affects me. And this not feeling well could be part of it."

"Come on, Gramps, it's just a bug. I was afraid to call you. Josh could be okay. And I'm already a little worked up about it; don't you worry too."

Gramps used a tone Jack hadn't heard in a long time. "A

little worked up about it. It sounds likely that your cousin was injured and crawled to the water, or his body was dumped there. Are you in denial? Don't you think you should have called me? You are the most apathetic person I've ever met—"

Janie tried to interrupt the tirade. "Jack, you didn't tell him about the eagle."

"*No!*" Jack shook his head desperately.

"What eagle?" the strong voice demanded.

Jack's volume lowered as he explained the dream to his grandfather.

"If you were a little boy, I'd put you over my knee and spank you, and then send you off to the hunt camp for a week. Your cousin could be dead. You need to get back to your house. I'll meet you there."

"Gramps, you'll have to hold down the fort. We've a bit of business to take care of, and I need to stop at the police station on the way home to make a statement."

"What are you doing in Tampa?"

"We've been granted a search warrant to look at a strip joint. It's to do with the child pornography ring I told you about."

"A worthy cause, Jackson, but this is about family. I want you back at your house as soon as you can. We need to talk about a few things. Is the door locked?"

"Left flower pot in the front, underneath. Gramps, what we're doing is connected. I think these bastards are the ones who messed with Josh—that is, if it was Josh. I think they might have been after me."

"All the more reason to come home now. You're in over your head."

"Possibly, but we called in the warrant. I have to be there. I want to see the look in the Russian's eye when we gain entrance."

Lolita exclaimed, "Russians!" The word hit a nerve with her, but she said no more.

Jack was at his wits' end and he wasn't well at all, a low-grade fever and headache ramping up. "Okay, that's enough. Gramps, there is no one more upset about Josh than I am—well, maybe you—but we're gonna do what we have to do, then be back to Ft. Myers Beach as soon as we can."

"So be it. We'll be waiting for you."

"We?"

"Yes, we!"

CHAPTER TWENTY-EIGHT

LOPEZ WOKE LATER THAT night. His head screamed. He'd been hit hard by an expert in the body's weak points. The gunshot wound was crudely bound, his leg on fire as the pain came in unrelenting waves. He lay on an old metal cot pushed into the corner of a cell. He wasn't in jail. You didn't go to jail in his line of work.

He'd been followed to the dealership, most likely from his home. *Sloppy!* He should have performed escape protocol, standard procedure. He deserved his fate. The end play didn't get you the paycheck, but it kept you anonymous and alive, and able to spend it.

A feline form in the cell two over, crouched on all fours, stared at him through the dim light of a nightlight plugged into the hallway socket. The figure's eyes followed his every move. *Where the fuck am I?* He kept his eyes on the figure, sensing that showing weakness wouldn't gain him any advantage. He was being checked out, but not in a sexual way—more the way a caged lion might look at its prey.

The woman smiled. Yes, it was a female; he saw that now. With the dexterity of a gymnast, she stood and moved to the bars closest to Robert to sit cross-legged, her calm gaze never dropping from his. Her hair looked as if it hadn't been combed in a month, but the untamed mop didn't detract from her exotic beauty. Her sharp features and the thin line of her lips were expressive and wild. He knuckled his eyes, returning the smile.

When she spoke, her voice deep, she had an Eastern European inflection. *Hungarian maybe?* "Why did they bring you here? You don't look the type." She looked eager to know.

His voice cracked with the first few words. "Type? I don't know what you mean."

"This is the dead end for strippers and sex slaves. I figure, once they don't know what to do with you, or you cross them, they stick you down here until they can figure out . . . how to deal with you."

Robert nodded and thought for a few moments. "Perhaps they simply don't know what to do with me. Now, of course it's the Russians who you speak of."

She nodded. "You were sloppy; you let your guard down. They got you!"

Robert's hair stood up, heat flushing his cheeks. The female had pulled the thought right out of his head.

She gave him a knowing smile. "Yes. It is possible to get out of here. I will need your help. You do wanna get outta here?"

Robert found her last comment strangely humorous and chuckled, "Who the hell wouldn't?" He stared at her long and hard. She seemed like some dark creature out of a paperback novel.

"No, I'm not a creature from the abyss."

"Stop that."

Having toyed with him long enough, she let her act drop. "I'm nothing more than a Gypsy fortune teller. My mother taught me to read faces. Some are more guarded than others. Yours is like an open book at the moment. Obviously you've been sloppy, or you wouldn't be here, and yes, you want out! Pretty simple when you think of it. You see, the skill in fortune-telling is in reading the client's expressions, emotions, what they wear, how they talk. It's easy to piece together a believable future if you know what you're looking for. *It's in the tells.*"

Robert sighed; somehow, he felt relieved. He wasn't stuck in his cell with a vampire. The thought crossing his mind now: *Okay, so how* do *we get out of here?*

"There is always a way if you are smart enough to see it. If they were me, I'd simply shoot the both of us through the bars and be done with it. A bit messy, but efficient. Eli won't do that. We have some value to him. I think my fate will be in some sick bondage snuff film. He just can't piece it together yet. You, I don't know. I suspect they will kill you soon. Do you have a big cock?"

Robert laughed, his leg suddenly feeling like it might explode from the blood pressure caused by the wound.

"Okay, you don't. But it might have given you some time. Tell me your name."

"It's Robert. And yours?"

"I've been called many names, but my mother called me Zshu—Susan, in your language. Tell me how you ended up in here and maybe we can come up with a plan. Neither of us has much time."

"Susan, you're not just a fortune teller. That's bullshit. Before I tell you about myself, come straight with me."

She smiled, sitting up straighter. "I like to take my clothes off in front of men, more so women. I overstepped my bounds, killing a man who threatened me. Eli didn't like that. So now, I find myself in this damned prison. Boris thinks I'm a werewolf."

"Not that I believe in that shit, but you had me wondering too!"

"The look is the biggest part of it."

"How so?"

"Either you go mainstream in your life's path, or you go against the grain. If you float around in the middle, you end up a marshmallow. I've always taken the more difficult approach. You see, I don't take any shit, but in the end I have no clout to back it up yet. I'm a cheap whore who needs to take her clothes off to make a buck."

"You are a smart woman. You should be in a better situation than this."

"I agree, but I've been driven into a corner. No way out."

"Always a way out. Didn't you just tell me that a few minutes ago?"

She smiled wide and her features softened. Susan almost looked beautiful.

CHAPTER TWENTY-NINE

"JUST AS I THOUGHT, Boris." Eli and his right-hand man sat in the upstairs office, sipping cappuccino. Boris toyed with a biscuit and tossed it into a garbage can. The scantily-dressed girl left the room after informing them the police were at the door wishing to speak with Eli.

Boris sighed, ashamed he'd brought trouble down on his boss. "Want me to see to this?"

Eli shook his head, his scowl enough information. "You've messed things up enough. Make sure things are downplayed. Some of the Russian girls should be taken below, maybe out of here. The last thing we want is for them to be deported. Keep things light; make it look as if this visit is a normal event."

* * * *

Eli calmly walked through to the building, etching a smile across his face like he was chiseled out of rock. Approaching the plainclothes officers in the foyer he asked, "How can I help you?"

The older of the two, of Hispanic decent, stepped forward. "Mr. Eli Romanov? I'm Lieutenant Garcia, Tampa police."

Eli kept the thinly-etched smile, painful as it was, and said, "I'm he."

"I have a warrant to search the premises and to seize all computers and drives excluding point-of-sale equipment." He showed the warrant to Eli, along with his badge.

Eli—having anticipated the visit and removed anything close to being suspicious from the computers—nodded and said, "I suppose I don't have much choice, but I will ask that you respect that this is a business and don't make the patrons or my employees uncomfortable. This isn't my first rodeo, officer, and I know my rights. If I see anything below board, I'll have the Tampa police sued for impropriety."

The officer nodded, raised his brows and turned to his partner. "Tell them to come in."

The second officer exited the building. Within a few minutes, the forensics team carried in bags of equipment, including cameras and cases for removing computers. Close on their heels were Janie and Jack.

Seeing the two of them, Eli turned to Garcia and put up his hand to demand, "These two don't come in. I've agreed to cooperate, but they've been banned from my establishments. Show me where it says anyone but officers of the law can be awarded entry. As I've said, Detective Garcia, I know my rights."

Jack flushed, ready to step into Eli's face. Janie put her hand on his shoulder, but he shrugged it off.

"You know what's going on, Romanov."

Eli smiled. "How's the swelling on your cheek, Mister Walker? Why don't you play your little games back home where you belong? Stick to playing with your ball, football. Am I correct? And a fucking failure at that! You're in over your head here. *No*! You're not coming in. If you try, then we will have a problem, I guarantee it." Eli turned to Garcia. "I'd like him off the property. *Now*! You know I'm within my rights. I'm sure you don't want trouble with me, no?" Eli turned back to Jack. "Besides, we don't want anyone getting hurt!"

"Is that a threat?" Jack turned so red that it looked as if his head might blow. "Were you at my house last night?"

Eli shrugged, but his icy expression remained the same. "If I had been at your house, you wouldn't be here right now." Eli's cruel smile fed Jack's temper even more. "Why do you ask? Did someone get hurt? I hope so, you fucking punk!"

The second officer stepped in and took Jack by the elbow. "Mr. Walker, it's not worth the trouble. Wait outside, please."

Jack spun to get away from his hold, still trying to square off with Eli. The two looked like prize fighters. Within seconds, the cop had Jack in a full nelson, dragging him away. Jack couldn't contain himself. "I know what you've done!"

"Okay, Walker, I'll play your game. What is it exactly that I've *done*?"

Janie and the officer ushered him away from the door before he could answer, but there was no containing Jack. He couldn't stop from screaming, "What the hell? I'm the one who called in this little party. I wanna see what this joker's up to!"

Janie scowled at him. "Are you out of your goddamned mind? You don't know these guys. They live this shit. You're feeding them information. That was . . . not necessary, Jack."

The officer who had him arm-locked released his grip and nodded. "Look, let us do our job. You will be privy to the information once it's been assessed. I understand, these guys are scum, but they have their rights." He looked at Jack. "Hey, I am a big fan of yours, and I know what you are capable of doing physically. Don't listen to him. You were a great football player. This ain't the same. Keep your cool. I'm on your side, okay?"

Jack acquiesced, acknowledging the man's point with a short nod back. Janie led him further from the entrance, into the lot, smiling to placate the officer. "Thank you. We'll not be any trouble." As they continued to the back of the parking lot, Janie let go. "Jeez, Jack, you gotta cool down. Hold your cards closer. We gained nothing by your outburst."

"Suppose so, but I wanted to get a look at his face when I mentioned my house. I'm not so sure I got the reaction I expected. I could tell he didn't know what I was talking about, which leaves me a little perplexed."

"You're right. Who was at your place?"

Jack shook his head. "Only God knows."

They stood for a long fifteen minutes watching the activity at the entrance. All the while, Janie wished she possessed a solitary cigarette. She didn't react to Jack poking her shoulder. She'd been able to abstain from smoking the past few days, but the stress of the past half hour intensified her craving.

"Look at that," he said.

"What?"

"The freestanding garage. You see the car coming out of it?"

"Yeah, so?"

"We've been standing here for some time now, and I didn't see anyone go into the garage. It's not a big structure, and probably hot as hell in there. Where'd the driver come from? And it looks like there's a person in the passenger's seat. The car disappeared into a back exit of the parking lot."

"Okay?"

"There must be another way into that garage. From below?" He looked at Janie, then headed back to the front entrance.

Janie exclaimed, "Jack!"

He smiled, which didn't make her feel any better. "I'm good, I promise." He stepped up to the officer who'd escorted them outside. Evidently, he remained to make sure they didn't try to get back in. Like a traffic cop, he put up his hand at Jack's approach.

"Thought we had an understanding?"

"No worries." The lawman's expression softened. "I want to make sure you find the back entrance to the garage out back." Jack explained what he'd seen.

"Roger that, Mr. Walker!"

Jack returned to Janie. She said, "I don't think there's much more we can do here."

"You're probably right." He paused in thought. "I get the feeling they knew we were coming. I have a sicker feeling we're not going to find anything. I need to get back to meet with Gramps, and I'm supposed to give a statement to the Lee County sheriff. Do you mind coming with me?"

Janie smiled. "Like I said, I'm not letting you out of my sight if I can help it."

CHAPTER THIRTY

GRAMPS PULLED INTO JACK'S driveway—more so onto the front lawn, as two police cruisers and a large white van took up most of the parking. He stepped out of his Mercedes and walked to the front door with a sick feeling in his stomach. The telltale yellow tape stretching across the front indicated his worst fears might be true. Lolita followed meekly a good twenty steps behind him. A police officer standing at the house corner shuffled over after dousing a cigarette.

"Sir, the house is cordoned off for a police investigation."

Gramps met his eyes. "My name is on the lease. I share it with my grandson, Jackson Walker." He'd cosigned the lease a few years back.

"Can I see some identification?"

Gramps fumbled through his wallet, producing his driver's license. The cop cross-referenced it with a sheet of paper on his clipboard. "I have you here, Mr. Portman. I still can't allow you into the house until forensics are finished. It shouldn't be too long."

"I can deal with that. May we go around back?"

The officer spoke into his radio. "Osgood here. Say, Mike, are you finished out back? One of the tenants has returned. He's asking for access. Okay, I'll tell him." He turned to Gramps. "Mr. Portman, I don't want to alarm you, but a body has been found in the canal. You may not want to see this. I advise you to go to headquarters. We'll need your statement."

Gramps regained eye contact with the man before he pronounced, "We're going around the side of the house. That body could be my grandson. Do you have a problem with that?"

The officer shook his head, suddenly unsure of himself.

Gramps turned to Lolita and grabbed her arm. He ushered her to the rear yard, where there awaited all kinds of activity.

"I caught that," Lolita said.

"Caught what?"

"The way you manipulated that man. Our asses shouldn't be back here right now."

He smiled. "I'm old; sometimes I forget that I'm doing it."

"You have a strong spirit, Nathaniel."

He ignored her comment and moved calmly across the yard and onto the dock. Again, he was stopped by an officer.

"Hey, this is a crime scene."

Gramps saw the body in a Lee County Sheriff's Department runabout tied at the dock. "This is my grandson's house, and I have a sneaking suspicion that could be my grandson's body." He pushed past the man but didn't need to get any closer. The body appeared partially eaten, by crabs and possibly small sharks. All that remained was the upper torso, head and one arm. The bloated face, while grotesque, bore enough resemblance for Gramps to identify the remains. Having held his breath on the walk back there, he now let go and heaved a deep sigh of sadness.

Lolita took his hand into her larger ones, her question unspoken.

"My other grandson, Joshua."

The officer overheard. "Are you saying you *can* identify the body, sir?"

Gramps nodded.

CHAPTER THIRTY-ONE

BY NOW, THE POLICE would be investigating Walker's house. The old man would seek out his grandson. Leery about returning to the scene of the crime, Mason still needed to keep tabs on his quarry. He didn't think they had put two and two together just yet. He knew the old man talked to the spirits as Mason did. That Indian shaman would detect his presence and it was only a matter of time before he figured out who Mason might be; although, if he also practiced due diligence, a call to the Louisiana State Penitentiary would tell him Mason Matye died a cruel death.

Will the old man dig deeper, perhaps relying on his intuition? When Walker took on the Church of Set, the affront required a retort; Satanists loved to harbor a grudge, and Nathaniel Portman would know this. *It might be easier to take out Portman first.* The old man was smarter than Walker. Mason didn't need Walker getting any more advice from higher-ups, if it could be helped, and if Portman headed for Ft. Myers, there was no doubt that he would go to Walker's house. Mason arrived a half hour after Portman, in time to see the Native man escorted out of the house with a large black woman. *Who is she?*

There must have been a visible aura around Mason—as he passed the house, the eyes of Portman and the female were drawn to him, meeting his stare. She pointed at the car but he didn't rush to escape. They could prove nothing. He went around a bend and turned into a driveway. A Mercedes left the house; he assumed it to be Portman's car and followed at a distance.

* * * *

Gramps looked at Lolita. "Can I drop you off at your home?"

Lolita rubbed her hands together. "You kidding? I wouldn't miss this for the world. Like I said, your grandson's fate is tied with mine. Besides, you look as if you might need some company. I'm so sorry about your other grandchild. Perhaps it's his death I saw the other night. But I don't feel a pull toward him; there is no connection, not like with you and Jackson."

"I think your intuition is correct. I should call Jackson." Before he could pull out his cell, the old man folded over onto the steering wheel, a low sob coming from deep within his soul.

Lolita placed a hand on his shoulder. "Gramps, I can feel your pain. And I'm so sorry!"

Gramps raised his eyes, focusing back on the road, his heart broken. Josh and Jackson were all who remained of his family. He'd been worried about Jackson, never giving a second thought to the safety of his other grandson. He felt a heavy weight upon his shoulders, like a sack of bricks.

"He was a good young man."

Lolita looked at him. "I never met him, but I can tell by your emotion it must be so."

Gramps nodded. "Thank you. Where to, Lolita? I think I need some time on my own."

She understood, and gave him directions to her home.

* * * *

Lolita waved to the old Indian as he pulled away.

She wanted to put the pieces together to see if she could glean more information. Josh had been shot from one direction and they'd all anticipated the bullet coming from the other. Portman sent Joshua to look out for Jackson. *Now the protector is dead. Why didn't I foresee any of this happening?* Then again, the spirit world spoke in riddles, and reality was even more obscure.

She didn't know why she did it, but she hesitated and glanced again at the Mercedes moving away down the road. Then she saw it: the same car that passed Jackson Walker's house a short time ago. The driver looked at her, their eyes meeting. There could be no denying the dark-haired driver recognized her, as she recognized him. Without warning, dread overwhelmed her—darkness, like she'd never felt before. The car sped away, hot to follow Nathaniel Portman. She would have called him, but Lolita didn't have Nathaniel's cell number.

"Damn!" she said out loud.

* * * *

Gramps pulled away from Lolita's and dialed Jack. Jack picked up on the fifth ring, feeding the old man's irritation.

"Gramps, what's up?"

"Jackson, I told you I would only call if it's important. When you see my name on the phone, you pick up, got it?"

"Whoa, Gramps, it wasn't clicking into the hands-free. I'm driving and had to fish it out of my pocket. I apologize for the—"

Gramps cut Jack off. "Josh has been murdered!"

A prolonged silence allowed both men to bear the horror.

"What?" Jack could only ask.

"Your premonition appears to be correct. His body was fished out of the canal. Well, what's left. The fish have eaten most of it."

"Is this information firsthand, Gramps?"

"Saw his remains with my own eyes and I'm heading to the police station to make a statement. When his body arrives at the city morgue, we must make a formal identification."

"Oh, for fuck's sake, Gramps! Is the psychic still with you?"

"No. I just dropped her off at home."

"Good. Stay away from her. I've got a bad feeling about that one."

"I can take care of myself, Jackson." Gramps heard his grandson hyperventilating. "Pull off the road now, until you can get a grip. Is Janie with you? We don't need anything happening to you; you're all I've got."

"Yes. She's with me."

"Let her drive. Meet me at the sheriff's office on Ben Hearn." Jack hung up.

Gramps was grief ridden. Driving became difficult as tears blinded him. He needed to pull over for a few minutes before he caused an accident. Turning into one of the thousand strip malls dominating the Tamiami Trail, he parked under the shade of a tree. He took a deep breath and flexed his hands across the steering wheel.

As he got a grip on the situation, someone tapped on the driver's side window. The man standing there motioned for him to roll it down. Something told Gramps it was a mistake to do so; still, he might be parked in someone's space. He lowered the window.

A man with strangely familiar features leaned in as if to tell him something. Instead of words, he stuck a .45 Magnum under Nathaniel's chin. "Portman!" he stated with a French accent like they knew each other.

Gramps nodded. The shock of realizing who the person . . . *might be? must be?* hit the old man like lightning.

"I want you to step out of the car slowly. Then I want you to get into the passenger side of the white Toyota sitting just over there."

Gramps turned his head, nodding again as he spotted the car. "Mason, right?"

"Very good of you to remember. I think we met briefly, several years ago."

"It wasn't exactly a meeting. You were getting thrown in jail."

"True enough!" He smiled and almost sang, "Ah, but that was then and this is now, Mr. Portman. Please hand over your keys and get into the car. And here." He handed Gramps two plastic ties. "Place this around your ankles and pull it tight. Then I want you to make a loop with the other one and place your hands through it."

Gramps walked to the car and followed directions. Once the loop was around his wrists, Mason quickly slid into the car, taking the end of the tie and pulling the bond tight.

Mason returned to the Mercedes, placed the keys on the roof and mumbled, "Someone might be kind and steal this." Chuckling, he returned to his vehicle and slipped behind the wheel. Mason placed the gun on his lap and pulled out of the lot to head south.

CHAPTER THIRTY-TWO

LOLITA CURSED. JACKSON'S CELL seemed perpetually busy. She tossed her phone on the coffee table in the reception area and vowed to try again in ten minutes and every ten minutes until she got to him. Leaving the reception area, she entered her personal quarters, consisting of a kitchen, bedroom and semi-finished basement.

In her bedroom, Lolita removed the wig she usually wore when she worked at home. She slipped off her jewelry, several rings and necklaces adorning her rather large frame. Her heartbeat slowed and melancholy came over her. Lolita worried she might become prone to depression. Still, this heartache was different. It seemed like decades had passed since she last felt so sorry for another human being. Many of her clients came to her with their day-to-day troubles, and she gladly took their money, proclaiming to see fates for them via palmistry or the tarot. Seldom did she get involved in another's future. Yes, she warned them, but they lived in their own futures, responsible for their own lives.

Things were different with Gramps and Jackson Walker. She had sought them out in order to deflect something evil, which might be happening to them and her. Somehow, they were tied together. *Could I have been wrong? Was it the death of the other grandson, Joshua, I foresaw?* No, she could not say that emphatically.

She planned to give Jack Walker a little more time before she called again. Undoubtedly, he would be grieving and not answer. She returned to her parlor with a cup of tea, where she lit a few candles and pulled out the tarot.

Deciding to lay out a simple four-card spread to see if it might shed light on the events of the past days, Lolita shuffled her personal deck, which had never been touched by another living soul, and set the tea down to cool. Sometimes, she wondered if the dead might be presetting her deck considering the way the stories often unfolded right before her eyes. Tears fell on her large hands, folded on the table, waiting to shuffle the cards again. She wiped her eyes and tried again. *No.* The deck felt cold. She shuffled again and again until she sensed it was time to lay out her four-card display. All four were placed in a row, facedown.

The first card represented the *past*. It turned up as a Jack: *The Fool.*

She sighed, realizing the card in her hand still felt cold. It related to Walker, Gramps, or one of their adversaries. Lolita thought about them and said aloud, "They are unconventional risk-takers!" She would need to look at the other cards to determine the meaning of the Fool rising in her deck to represent the past.

The second card represented the *present*. It turned up as the Ace of Spades: *Death.*

Okay, the Death card in most cases was not to be taken literally. In this reading, she sensed it warranted its literal meaning of death, even though it could also indicate a new beginning, or even a transformation.

The third card represented the *hidden meaning*. A Seven of

Swords: *Open Battle.*

They were not finished yet. The death of Joshua did not necessarily culminate the warlike events.

The fourth card represented *the outcome*. The Queen of Cups: *Female Psychic.*

Lolita tried to blow her fear out between her teeth. She read the entire story in the cards and knew she would be involved in the outcome. Lolita's lack of confidence became clear, but she did not doubt herself anymore. Packing up the cards, she headed back to the kitchen to make a nice sandwich.

On her way through the reception area, she heard a loud *rap rap rap* on her front door. Through the beveled glass she saw at least two figures standing on the front porch. She quickly retrieved her wig. The knocking continued. "I'm coming!" she hollered loud enough to be heard through the door.

Taking a few seconds to preen in front of the mirror, Lolita made sure that her wig was on straight. When she opened the door, a shock of adrenalin surged through her veins. There were three men: two were correctional officers from the county, the other a deputy from the Lee County Sheriff's Department.

"Can I help you, gentlemen?" Lolita asked in her smallest voice.

Recognizing one of them as her parole officer, she knew her goose was cooked. Since she had been cleared several years back of the requirement to report, Lolita didn't immediately recognize the man. He'd aged and now wore glasses. She sure knew his voice when he asked for her by name. "Solomon Brown?"

She nodded slowly.

"You are being arrested for violation of your parole. Though you are no longer required to report, you still have restrictions. You were photographed entering a strip club in Tampa and we are certain you purchased pornography from the establishment. You were strictly forbidden from entering any place for the purchase of such goods. We have a warrant to search the premises."

The deputy produced handcuffs and snapped them across Solomon's wrists. "Ma'am—Mr. Brown, you have the right to remain silent. Anything you say might be used against you in a court of law."

Solomon's head dropped; he had not removed the newest entertainment from his computer. It would be an understatement to say things had gone from bad to worse, and he wondered why he did not read it in the cards. *Or did I?*

"Can you give me one moment, please?"

The deputy shook his head. "Sorry, I can't do that."

"I know my rights. I'm allowed one phone call, correct?"

He cocked his head. "That right comes after you're booked at the station."

"Will you allow me to write down one phone number from my cell?"

He looked at the parole officer, who nodded. "Okay."

"It's on the table over there. You can watch so you know I'm speaking the truth." Solomon wrote Jackson Walker's number on a scrap of paper and tucked it into one of his pockets.

CHAPTER THIRTY-THREE

JACK DIDN'T NEED JANIE to drive, the fact being she looked even more physically shaken than he did. He pressed his foot nearly to the floorboard, pushing the Jeep over 100 mph and swerving around slower traffic, playing roulette with the hope that the state troopers were not playing hide-and-seek along the trees in the median.

He had not been in such a foul mood for five years, since he discovered he'd been played by Sarah Courtney and framed for killing an innocent older couple up in Clewiston, on the shore of Lake Okeechobee.

There was no denying the truth. His cousin's death was his fault. He'd seen the warning signs. If he was honest, they virtually hit him over the head. Gramps and the psychic tried to tell him, but Jack never faced that he was dealing with powerful and dangerous people. Perhaps he was apathetic like everyone kept telling him. *Why do I have this personal vendetta against anything paranormal? Why not let those who believe in it knock themselves out? Why couldn't I just go along with them?*

"Dammit!" he yelled, smacking the wheel, jolting Janie out of her stupor. As though she'd been following his inner conversation, he blurted out, "Do you believe in all this shit?"

"What? You mean Josh being murdered?"

"No. I believe that's real. Too fucking real. It's the psychic stuff with Gramps and Lolita."

Janie rubbed her eyes, trying to ponder his question. "You're gonna get a ticket."

Jack pulled back off the accelerator.

She shook her head. "I don't know what to think anymore, Jack. You have to deal with the reality of what's going on in front of your eyes sometimes. This psychic stuff goes counter to what we've learned in university, where you're asked to question and not take events or things at face value. Maybe that's why children see things for what they are a lot better than adults. They love to dream about fantastical things: witches, wizards and warlocks. Little ones don't question; they believe what they see. They are molded by their older peers, who try to protect them from disappointment and danger.

"If we were to look at the present situation and what happened five years ago the same way a child would look at it? We would probably be able to deal with it much more effectively. Because it's happening and we . . . you refuse to accept it. Maybe you need to give into the possibility that strange events are more than just coincidence. Let's face it—taking the empirical approach isn't doing you any good. Your cousin is dead. If you'd taken this more seriously, he might have been with us the other night. Like your grandfather wanted."

Jack flushed. "You? Now *you're* fucking blaming me? Don't you think I feel bad enough as it is? I'm crushed. If there was a bridge high enough, I'd be thinking about jumping."

"Whoa, partner. I'm trying to help, and this is no time for a pity party. I'm on the Jackson Walker team; don't even go there. I liked Josh. A lot. Believe me, this has shaken me to the core. All I'm saying, let's try to go along with your gramps, give the psychic woman Lolita's words some credence. See what happens, because the alternative isn't working. Why not embrace the eagle like you did when you were younger? You said it used to help you catch fish. Is that right?"

Jack sighed. "Yep, the eagle's never wrong."

"So why did you stop believing?"

Jack turned off the highway at Daniels Parkway. "It's simple. I felt ashamed being a Native Indian. I wanted to go places. I wanted to rise to be a football star. I wanted out of the small town. I blocked off my past and now I'm being tossed back into it. I'm resisting. Maybe I'm not ready to come back."

Janie smiled for the first time since they'd heard the news about Josh. "Face it, you are a Native. You are special. You can't change what's in your blood, Jack. I think you have a gift, and I wish you would use it. At least try for a time. If you won't do it for yourself, would you at least do it for those who love you? Do it for me?"

Jack grinned. "Are you saying you love me?"

Janie sighed and simply said, "Yes, I do."

When he looked away, she said, "I feel like I need to protect you. Actually, everyone who loves you seems to feel the same. Why is that, Jack? Maybe it's because we have to protect you from yourself? There you have it."

"Okay. I'll try."

"There's a start."

"I'll give into the spiritual side until we get through this. Deal?" He extended his hand. She held on for a few moments. "So, what do we do now?"

"Since we're accepting the mumbo jumbo, can you call up Peter and ask him to check into Mason Matye? Let's see if the bastard actually did escape from prison. Let's hope we can rule out that option."

"That's a better start."

"Then we have to make a statement at the sheriff's department. We're meeting Gramps there. It would be good to touch base with the old guy. I've been harsh with him over all this."

"Remember, Jack, Gramps believes in it all and lives his life by it. He probably takes what you say to heart. I think you're upsetting him. Still, he's smart and understands your apathy. He's a patient man."

"True enough." He pressed his hand to his head. Janie noticed the motion.

"You okay?"

"Actually, no. I haven't been okay for a couple of days now. My guts are ready to come up and I've been getting these waves of head pain, like getting stabbed in the right temple. I just felt one there. It's super painful. Unbearable, actually. They're coming closer together."

"How often?"

"It was every hour or so. Now it's every ten or fifteen minutes with a longer duration. The last one made me feel as if I might pass out there."

"Geez, I'm taking you to see a doctor tomorrow."

"If we have time. Okay, we're here," Jack said, pulling into the lot of the massive one-level building housing Lee County's sheriff headquarters.

CHAPTER THIRTY-FOUR

"NO, WE CAN'T SIMPLY kill him, Boris. I see the look in your eyes and I know you would do a masterful job." Eli put down his espresso. "It must be planned, carefully, like the handling of Lopez."

"Would you like another, Eli?"

"No. That is enough."

"Only thinking of you, Eli. I know the prick wounded your pride. I feel what you feel."

Eli stood, patting Boris's cheek. "I appreciate the sentiment, my friend. We will bide our time. Let things take their due course. We will watch Mr. Walker for the next little bit. I want you to do this for me. If the moment offers itself, remind him of his insolence. We'll take him on a little fishing trip forty or fifty miles out into the gulf." He paused for a few moments, lighting a cigarette. "There is nothing to be found inside what's been taken by the police—the computers. Walker will look foolish. The cops will leave us alone for a time. Think of it as a business expense, an expense that Walker will have to pay for."

"Should I call first?"

"Of course. Why would you ask? You know my rules."

"Just the way you were talking, Eli."

Eli smiled. "You did a good job disguising the lower basement, Boris. I could tell they were looking for something, but your secret doors have done their job. Are you sure we are the only two who know of them, besides Gina?"

Boris chuckled. "The stone masons all went on a little fishing trip. Anyone who goes down those steps is either blindfolded or doesn't come out alive. You know this to be true."

Eli paced as he asked, "What of Lopez?"

"That guy is tough. Still, he should have died by now from the gunshot wound. Is he of any use to us?"

"Not anymore."

"I will kill him soon enough. He is safe where he lies. It's been a long day and I don't want to make mistakes."

"Perhaps by then nature will have taken its course. And the Gypsy?"

Boris laughed. "I think she scares shit out of Lopez. She sits and stares, looking at him with those evil little eyes. Kill her, too?"

"No. I plan on riding her like a wild stallion. She's got something I enjoy: danger sex. I look forward to the challenge because you know she'll try to kill me while I'm fucking her. After I have my fun . . . you can have her. Then she can die."

Boris chuckled, appreciative of the offer.

CHAPTER THIRTY-FIVE

GRAMPS TRIED HIS BEST to remain calm. There was no use in showing his distress. He needed to keep an upper hand, if possible. He watched the little Frenchman, who appeared to be winging the situation, confirmed in the ensuing conversation. Gramps prodded him. "Is this necessary, Mr. Matye?"

"What do you think, old man? Of course it's necessary. I'm going to deliver retribution for the killings of my colleagues, and for taunting the Dark Lord. He is all-knowing and has a good memory, Nathaniel. I am going to kill all those who are close to Jackson Walker. You, unfortunately, are at the top of my list."

"What will you do with me?"

Mason sat in silence for a few seconds. "For now, we're going to take a little ride into the countryside. I think you know the place."

"I know many places in these parts, Matye. Don't tell me you plan on returning to the scene of the crime." Mason wouldn't have had a lot of time to scout places out if he'd recently escaped from prison.

"Why not? The place serves a purpose. It's also a location your grandson will remember. You see, the fly must be able to smell the bait in order for you to catch it. The old estate has lain fallow for the past few years. It's stigmatized; no one wants to live in a place that housed such atrocities. I imagine the county or the state will tear the place down soon enough, but for now it suits my purposes perfectly."

* * * *

They drove out of urban Naples and into the edge of the Everglades, where housing developments became less dense. Gramps remembered this countryside. He'd driven most of the old roads traversing the great swamp. The last time he'd been this far east on Immokalee Road was five years ago, late at night. Still, he remembered the signposts, the occasional stand of trees and expanses of open saw-grass savannah. As Mason cut south on Camp Keais Road, Gramps' fingertips began to numb. He cringed from his increasing sense of dread. They were getting close.

The old estate was built in a bygone era of Southern expansion. The McFaddens came from a long line of Southern gentility. Though their business was of an unsavory nature, they had made a lot of money over the years, with holdings across Southwest Florida still in probate. Now the place sat as an echo of its past splendor.

Mason turned down the road heading for the estate, which backed onto one of the local rivers fed by the Everglades and inland lakes. Chains bound the old iron gate blocking the long driveway. Mason pulled up to the gate and looked at Gramps.

"*Monsieur*, it would be in your best interests not to move."

Gramps looked down at his bound ankles and wrists, now cutting off his body's circulation. The old man smiled. "My best interests. You have to be kidding."

Mason nodded and smiled, acknowledging the validity of Nathaniel's remark. He went to the trunk and retrieved bolt cutters purchased yesterday with this event in mind. He approached the gate and, with a little work, snapped the lock.

Gramps looked around frantically. Mason had taken the keys, but they wouldn't have done Gramps any good. He needed to bide his time, and try to stay calm. The man couldn't be trusted to guide his own destiny.

Mason cleared the debris away from the entrance before he pushed open the barrier. Returning to the car, he drove through weeds nearly as tall as the white rental. Stopping again to get out and close the gate behind them, he replaced the chains to pass a not-so-close inspection.

Jumping back behind the wheel he said, "Almost there, Nathaniel."

The seriousness of the situation ground on Gramps as he shook himself awake from the past hour's ride. With the driver's window open, he could smell the great swamp as they drove along what used to be a grand driveway. He remembered that smell: damp, musty, and charged with a tinge of sulfur, like a newly-scratched brimstone match.

The place and the grounds appeared different in the daylight, and the drive up seemed to take longer than last time. Back then, Nathaniel had been anxious and concerned for his grandchildren. Today, he hoped the drive to the buildings would be slower, stalling the inevitable for him.

Ahead, the disheveled main house sat left of a large asphalt drive. In the distance, to the right, was an old barn on the river's edge. The last time he had been there, the place had been packed with people, cars, and flashing lights from cop cars and news teams. Today, the place seemed eerily quiet, like no living creature had been there since that night.

Mason's voice pulled him away from his thoughts. "It's too bad your grandson killed Jimmy McFadden. He'd know what to do with you."

"Does that imply you don't?"

"Don't you worry, old man, I'm very good at improvising. We might be able to find a few remnants in the McFaddens' workshop to make your life a little more uncomfortable." He sneered. "When I lure Walker here to kill him—and you, of course—I will take perverse pleasure in chopping you both up and feeding you to the gators." He stopped to visualize the scene, ecstatic and losing control. His head fell back as his eyes widened and he giggled. "Oh, how those beauties love fresh meat!"

Turning to Nathaniel, he regained his senses. "There will be bewilderment, everyone asking what happened to you. No one will know, because no one will know who captured you, and when my name is suggested? They'll find out . . . Mason Matye no longer exists. He died in prison a week ago."

Getting out of the car, he walked to the passenger's door and opened it. "Nathaniel, we can do this the hard way—I'm up for a struggle—but it will make your stay here more uncomfortable. If you do not fight me, your last day or so will be bearable."

Gramps swung his legs out of the car. Mason bent and grabbed his tied arms, pulling the old man onto his shoulder. He carried him to the side door of the workshop before lowering him to the ground. Staring at the new padlock, Mason read the notice placed on the door by the sheriff's department. He turned to Nathaniel and said, "Stay put!" Mason retrieved the bolt cutters from the car. Within seconds, he had access to the barn.

He hoisted Gramps back up and entered the dark, musty building. The open door offered just enough light to see. The place appeared similar to what Gramps remembered. An old, multi-colored couch in the middle of the room faced a rabbit-eared television. There were still several TVs dispersed throughout.

Mason placed him on the couch and walked over to the large sliding doors leading to a dock jutting into the river. He cut the chain binding them and pushed them open, the sunlight revealing more of the macabre room's many details. A steel mortician's table sat off to the side, surrounded by odd chairs and machinery in various states of disrepair. The walls were filled with Jimmy McFadden's taxidermy specimens, including fish, large cats, birds and gators, as if every kind of creature found in the Everglades now hung here. A series of rails with large hooks mounted on wheels circled the room. They were used when the estate doubled as a slaughterhouse for cattle in the 1930s.

Gramps shivered at the sight of place, no doubt perfect for what Mason had in mind. The wise old Seminole still bided his time. Mason would depart sooner or later in order to carry out his plans.

"What should we do with you, *monsieur*?" Mason looked around the room, his eyes narrowing when he spotted a door at the back. Walking over, he looked inside. "*Voilà*! It is perfect!" He returned and grabbed the tie binding Gramps' ankles, dragging the hogtied man into the prison where dozens of poor souls, including Jack, had once been locked up. Mason found rope conveniently lying on the floor and tied it to Gramps' feet, slinging the hemp twine over a rafter and raising the man's legs into the air.

"We don't want you moving around now, do we?" Smiling at his handiwork, Mason left, leaving Gramps in the dark.

Returning minutes later, he held a roll of duct tape. Before gagging Nathaniel, he bent over him to ask, "So, who was the man I murdered at your grandson's house the other night?"

Mason could tell he struck a nerve, watching his captive's eyes dilate with pure fury. "No need to answer. You have told me all I need to know." He wrapped the tape once around Gramps' head, covering his mouth. "We don't need you attracting attention." He held onto one of Gramps' arms and reached into his pockets as the old man struggled to resist the search. Pulling out an iPhone, Mason smiled. "*Oui*, this may come in handy." He pushed the access button and the phone came alive. Still looking at it, Mason closed the door behind him, leaving Gramps to wallow in the darkness with only his thoughts of anguish and survival, along with the mice, to keep him company.

Mason spent the next five minutes writing down whatever information could be gleaned from the phone, including Jackson Walker's phone number.

CHAPTER THIRTY-SIX

THE GUNSHOT WOUND OOZED puss and blood. Robert Lopez dropped in and out of consciousness. If he didn't get to a hospital soon, the end would be near. Trying to shake himself from a bad dream, he sat up on the wooden pallet, cringing in pain as he tried to move his leg.

He looked at the far cell. Sitting cross-legged, staring at him, was Susan. She didn't smile as she had in the past. A look of concern now showed. After a few seconds of silence passed between the two, the Gypsy spoke. "Robert, you're not looking good. I think you are dying. I've watched you for the last day and that wound will kill you."

Robert smiled, though it pained him. "I thank you for being so observant."

Susan smiled, nodding. "I don't need to be a fortune teller to see you're ill."

Robert leaned back against the wall, not up to fencing with

the fiery woman. There wasn't much more he could do. His brain hurt too much. He had to force himself to talk. "You said you knew how to get outta here?"

She nodded. "I don't know whether it will do you any good, though. You'll be dead by tomorrow if you don't get that looked after."

"So, what is it?"

"Getting out?"

He canted his head to the side in frustration, the wound affecting the way he thought—a mild delirium, a cross between desperation and pain. "Yes!"

"I've been moving my plate further and further from the bars each day for when Boris retrieves my plate. If pushed, I'm sure I could act quickly enough to grab his arm. I could do it now, but I wouldn't want to."

"What the hell do you mean by you 'wouldn't want to'?"

"Exactly that. I don't want to jeopardize my escape by acting prematurely because of you. You're good as dead anyway. If you don't mind, I'll sit and watch. I've never actually sat and watched someone die. I might gain insight through the process or use it as a diversion."

Robert couldn't believe his ears. "Really?"

She nodded. "Yeah. *Really!*"

"What if I paid you an outrageous sum of money to help me?"

"How outrageous?"

Robert sighed, "You tell me."

"Okay, outrageous to me would be a million dollars."

"Okay, yes, that's outrageous." *Am I worth that amount to my handlers?*

"What's the difference if you're dead? You can't take it with you. So, how about it? I get you outta here, you pay me a mil?"

"I gotta be honest . . . it might be difficult to scrape up that kind of coin on short notice. I could dig up 500 grand in a day. It would take a week or so for the million. I'll get you half a mil right after we get outta here."

Susan frowned. "Are you seriously grinding me?"

"Not so much as I'm speaking realistically. Okay, I can get

you an extra 100 grand within a week, 500 within a day."

"How do I guarantee you will give it to me?"

He grimaced in pain. "No guarantees in life, Susan. You'll have to trust me and it's not like I can run away, right? Look at it this way. You let me die and rot in here, and perhaps you do manage to escape. You're out, but you're still poor. I don't think you have a choice."

"Not a bad argument from someone who doesn't have a whole hell of a lot of leverage. I'll think about it. Not sure I want to be slowed down dragging a sicko along with me. Might mess up my chances. We'll see. Fair enough?"

Robert shook his head. "Suppose I don't have much choice."

"No. You don't." She remained cross-legged, staring at him intently, always watching in case something critical happened.

CHAPTER THIRTY-SEVEN

THE DUTY SERGEANT HANDED Jack back his ID. "Have a seat, Mr. Walker. Someone will be out shortly to take your statement." Jack followed Janie into the waiting lounge, half full of some very interesting characters, to say the least, including hookers and petty thieves waiting to be arraigned.

Jack expected to see Gramps there ahead of him. He'd sounded closer to the station than the two of them when they last spoke. Jack tried his cell but no answer. Over his shoulder Janie sat with her legs crossed, forlorn and pouting.

She felt his eyes upon her and quickly looked up and smiled. "What?"

"I would have figured Gramps would beat us here."

She nodded. "Is he usually punctual?"

"Like a clock . . . usually early. No answer on his cell. Perry should be getting to work about now. I'll ask him to stop by my place and see if he's still there."

Dialing his best friend's number, Jack waited.

Perry picked up instantly. "What's up, bro? Haven't heard from you in a few days."

"Perr . . . I have some real bad news."

"Okay?"

"Josh was murdered last night at my place."

"What!"

"Fucking unbelievable. I don't think it's really hit me yet."

"How, man?"

"Not sure how, I just know he was dragged and dumped in the damn canal. When they found him, his body was half eaten by crabs and fish." Jack sighed, "I need a favor."

"Anything, man!"

"My grandfather was supposed to meet us here at the police station to give a statement. He was ahead of us, but he's not shown. Can you swing by my place and see if he's still there? I'm a little worried."

"Sure thing, bro. Let me know what else I can do." He paused. "Why does this shit happen to you? Something to do with that pornography ring you were telling me about? You need to think about that job of yours."

"Possible, but I'm not about to try a third career anytime soon, I'll tell you. Gimme a call once you've had a look around for my grandfather?"

"I'm just getting onto the island and the traffic's pretty bad. Fifteen minutes probably."

"Thanks, Perr!"

Jack dialed Peter Robertson. It took a minute for him to pick up. "Jack, I literally just got off the phone with Louisiana corrections. The man you're asking about committed suicide a few days ago. They found him dead in his cell last Monday."

"Shit! Then it must have been the Russians who did this to Josh."

"I would be more circumspect, Jack. You have no proof. And until we hear anything back from the Tampa police, you stay away from them. Nothing we can do at this point. You involve yourself, you'll mess this up. And by the way, you're to check in with me once daily. It's been two, by my recollection."

"Peter, I've heard this is how the Russian mob operates. I'm gonna think on things for a bit, but I don't think the police will find anything. That guy, Eli Romanov, looked like he'd been expecting us. Can you ask if the police ever found another way into the rear garage?" He explained what he'd seen.

"That's stuff for another day, Jack. Any sign of Lopez?"

"Negatory!"

"Check back with me once you're finished with the police."

"Will do."

* * * *

By the time Jack and Janie were called in to make their statement, Gramps still hadn't shown up. When Perry reported back that he had seen neither hide nor hair of the old Indian, Jack became even more than worried. They were ushered into a small room. Once they were seated behind a long table, a female officer entered and addressed them. She wore a compassionate look.

"Mr. Walker, my name is Detective Stiner. I'm aware you are the blood relative of the deceased, whom we are asking you to identify. These things are not easy," she said, staring into his eyes.

Jack sighed, "I understand."

"The remains have been substantially altered due to the time in the sea water."

Jack nodded, looking over to Janie. "You don't need to do this."

Janie gave him a stern look. "Not leaving your side until this case is over."

The officer looked at them and questioned, "Case?"

Jack responded, "I'm a lawyer. We've been working for a client . . ."

Janie shot him her best eye dagger, hoping he wouldn't mention that they thought Josh's death could in fact be related. The look wasn't missed by the female detective.

Jack motioned at the manila folder on the desk. "I'm ready."

She nodded. "The photos were taken at the city morgue

an hour ago. You have the right to see the remains in person, but we find most do well enough with these." She spread seven forensic shots out on the table.

Both Janie and Jack recoiled at the depictions. Jack knew the subject to be his cousin within half a second, though what was left of his body looked distorted. Still, Jack could tell it was Josh from his nose and jawline, along with a Rastafarian woven bracelet around his wrist he'd worn for as long as Jack could remember. What shattered Jack the most was the eight-inch slice, which opened up his throat nearly ear to ear, the edges gnawed by crabs.

Jack's jaw quivered and he put his hand to his mouth. He was not quick enough to keep the contents of his stomach from spewing onto the floor. His head barely turned fast enough to miss the table.

Janie put her hand on his back. "You okay, Jack?" she said, rubbing in a circular motion. She looked up to the officer, who was now talking to someone on the intercom.

She motioned to the mess on the floor. "Not uncommon. Someone will be in to clean up. We can move to another room. I'd like you to make a statement, if you're willing. You do have a right to have an attorney present."

Jack motioned it would not be necessary.

"Would you like to step into the restroom first?"

"Yes, please." Jack needed to throw cold water on his face.

The two women waited in the hall until he joined them. The detective ushered them into a similar room and again placed a recording device on the table. She turned to Janie. "Ms. Callaghan, you'll have to wait outside. We'll take your statement once Mr. Walker is finished."

Stiner sat across from Jack and pressed the record button. "Can you confirm for me that your name is Jackson Walker of Ft. Myers, Florida, and that you can identify the victim?"

"I can. He was my first cousin, Joshua Portman."

"Mr. Walker, the deceased was found in the canal behind your house. Can you tell me anything which might help us determine a motive for his killing? I will tell you that we are assuming foul play."

Jack put his hand up. "Yeah, I know. His throat was slashed."

"Why was Mr. Portman at your house?"

Jack decided to be sparing with his words. "Josh was staying with me for a bit. He did that from time to time. We're like brothers."

"Nathaniel Portman is also on your lease?"

"My grandfather. I didn't have great credit a few years ago. He's also—or *was*—Josh's grandfather. He's supposed to be here as well to give a statement, but he hasn't shown up. I will say . . . it is highly out of character for the old man to be late."

"He's a Seminole chief, correct?"

"Something like that."

"Can you tell me anything that might shed light upon the attack?" She crossed her right leg over her left, lowering her eyebrows.

"I'm sure you would find this out sooner than later, and you can check with the district attorney: We have been investigating a pornography ring. In fact, we were just returning from Tampa. The police up there used a search warrant to investigate a strip joint owned by our suspects. Now, I can't substantiate this in any way, but my gut says these bastards might be involved."

"Involved in your cousin's killing?"

"I'm just telling you what I think. I have no proof."

"What would make you think this, Mr. Walker?"

Jack chose his words carefully. "They made a few threats toward me when we had a little altercation earlier this week."

"Why the altercation?"

"My boss, Peter Robertson, asked us to see if we could get any information out of them. When I mentioned my client's name, they basically kicked us out of the strip joint, nearly breaking my jaw in the process."

"Who's your client?"

"Robert Lopez. You'll be able to check your files. He's been arrested for possession of child pornography. The DA can confirm everything as well."

"I'll be calling her office. Anything else?"

"Lopez is missing. I believe he was at a car dealership the other day, where that salesman got wacked. Have a look at the eyewitness accounts. A BMW was spotted leaving the scene, the plate registered to the Russians. Again, check in with the DA. That's as much as I can tell you."

She turned off the recorder. "We'll be in touch. I would advise you to stop with your own investigation until such time as you are told by the DA to move forward."

Jack shook his head. "I still have a fiduciary duty to my client."

"That's fine, Mr. Walker, but I'd advise you to stay away from the Russians."

The way she said it made Jack believe she knew more than she was telling him. He kept the thought to himself. "I'll heed that advice, but I have to follow direction from my boss, Peter Robertson."

Detective Stiner sighed. "You've been warned, Mr. Walker. I must also state you are a possible suspect in this murder. Conduct yourself accordingly. We'll be keeping an eye on you."

Jack's pressure rose. "I didn't murder my *cousin*." He gritted down on his last word. "Check with Janie. I was with her all evening."

"I'm not saying you did. You're a lawyer. You know how investigations take place. Anyone who's been in your house over the past few days is a suspect. Just stating a fact."

Jack exhaled. "Okay, I get it. I'm shook over this. Josh was one of my best friends."

Stiner nodded. "That will be all, Mr. Walker. If anything else pops up, or you can think of anything, please give me a call." She handed her card to him. "And if you hear from your grandfather, please have him call me."

Jack got up, still woozy. "Will do."

* * * *

Janie looked at Jack as he drove home from the police station. She put her hand on his leg. "Say, you okay?"

"Not great. What did you tell them?"

"I couldn't lie. I pretty much outlined what's going on with our case. That's it."

Jack was quiet for a moment. "Yeah, I pretty much did the same."

Janie squeezed his leg. "Let's call your gramps again and then I think we need a drink."

He nodded. "I'm done in. Sounds like a damned good idea."

CHAPTER THIRTY-EIGHT

"CLOTHES OFF, YOU FAT, perverted slob!"

Solomon had no choice but to subject himself to his jailor's search. He took off the dress, followed by the pantyhose, jewelry and lastly his wig. It had been a long time since he was last in the can. *Will this be the end of Lolita?* He had grown used to the cross-dress; in fact, he preferred being Lolita to Solomon . . . if only the tormented thoughts and urges could be purged from his head. He raised his arms, ready for the naked pat-down. He knew the drill.

Two male guards approached slowly, one carrying a handheld metal detector.

"Don't worry, I don't bite," Solomon smiled, flashing his fake Lolita eyelashes.

Grimacing, one guard proceeded to search Solomon's various lumps, folds and cavities by hand. Stepping back, he nodded to his partner and the other guard stepped up to run the detector from head to toe. It did not make a sound. Solomon turned around to let him use the detector on his backside. "You're gonna get some kinda reaction back there from all the metal holding up my discs. I've had three spinal surgeries."

As promised, the cicada-like sound hummed high and low as the guard moved it up and down the newly-booked prisoner's back. Solomon turned around smiling. "I told ya!"

That first night, Solomon awoke in the early hours to the sound of men snoring. The noise kept him awake, but not before he had the dream. It came clear as day: a vision of Gramps, hogtied in a dark place. *The old Seminole deserves better!* Solomon didn't get a look at the old man's captor. He knew it was a singular entity, evil to the core. He shivered.

He waited till mid-morning to stop one of the guards. A tough-looking man did stop at his cell when Solomon addressed him politely. "Sir, I'm allowed one call. I'd like to use it now."

The man nodded. "I'll talk to the chief."

Within half an hour, Solomon stood in his white prison jumpsuit at one of the public phone booths in the rec area. With Jack's number stored in his memory, Solomon dialed it.

CHAPTER THIRTY-NINE

JACK WOKE AS JANIE snuggled up to his left side. After two nights in a row, the occurrence was no longer a one-off. She said before weaseling herself into his bed that she didn't want to leave him alone after his tragedy. Her soft form next to him was very comforting to say the least.

He looked at the clock: 9:20 AM. *Damn!* He'd slept in. Rolling out of her clutches, he slipped into the shower and turned up the heat. The scalding water woke up his senses. He felt like he'd had a bottle of tequila last night, but no, he did not. After toweling off, he walked to the kitchen, picked up his cell and called Gramps. Josh's death was just starting to sink in, and he felt like royal shit. They'd been part of each other's lives since birth. While they were not always close, they were both a reliable presence the other could count on.

"Damn!" The old man either refused to answer the phone, or there was something terribly wrong. Since he'd never known his grandfather to ignore his calls, the latter seemed the only reasonable possibility. As he placed his phone on the counter it rang. Lee County Corrections. Jack cursed under his breath, "What the fuck?"

Still, he answered. "Jack Walker?"

"Jackson, this is Lolita."

"What? Where you calling from? And why are you calling?"

"Bit of a story, Jackson. The long and short of it is . . . I've been arrested."

"Arrested? What? Ya give some bad spiritual advice?" He couldn't help the jab no matter how bad he felt.

"Everyone has their demons."

As much as he wanted to hang up, there were more coincidences occurring than even he with his reticence could ignore. "I'm listening."

"I was picked up shortly after your grandfather dropped me off."

"Wait, I haven't heard from Gramps since last night, which is more than strange. He didn't show up at the Lee County Sheriff's Office."

There was a long silence before Lolita said, "He told me he was heading to meet you there." Lolita took a few moments to gather her thoughts. "Now, Jackson, this could be bullshit, but I could swear that someone followed us. A car pulled out from a parking lot next to my house when he left. I thought it strange at the time and I was a bit worried for him."

"Shit. This is too weird."

Janie appeared at his elbow, her face full of sleep. When she shot him a questioning look, Jack answered, "Lolita."

Lolita said, "Jackson! I know you don't believe what I've been telling you, but things are becoming clearer to me—the reasons I feel we are connected. I mean, I think you and your family are in grave danger."

"No shit, Lolita. Josh is fucking dead."

"Just the beginning, I hate to say. Someone bears a grudge for you, Jackson, with the kind of hate that resonates evil."

Jack blurted out, "The pornographers. They got Gramps."

"Pornographers?"

"I've been working on a case. I messed with some nasty Russian fuckers up in Tampa. They threatened me." Jack relayed as much as he could without divulging names and particular circumstances, as all calls from the correction center were recorded.

Lolita stayed quiet, taking it all in, until she finally said, "This is all very confusing, Jackson. I will tell you, I think I've been arrested because of the same people you speak of."

Jack felt a hot flash. "You're tied in with them?"

"No. Well, I did buy pornography and that's how I violated my parole."

Jack's head began to spin until he exploded, "What the fuck!" Jack felt as if he were being pulled into a vortex, one which he chose *not* to believe in and yet had no choice or way to stay clear of, much like five years ago. Panic surged through his veins.

"I need you to post a bond for my 5,000-dollar bail. It'll cost you 500."

"You gotta be kidding me."

"You have no choice. Without me you won't be able to figure this out. I've seen it and you need to believe me."

"Like hell. This paranormal bullshit is killing me. I swore I'd try, but this is too much."

"Yes, Jackson, it is. Or it will be if you don't take it seriously. Look, I have one more minute. I'm in the Lee County lockup on Ortiz Boulevard. I'll give you the money back."

"I'll think about it."

"Think too long and you may never see your grandfather again. I'm beginning to like the old man. We have a lot in common. Shame to see him come to the same end as your cousin."

Jack thought for a moment. He really *didn't* have a choice. "Okay, I'll talk to my boss. I'm sure he knows a good bond agent. We did this back in law school. I'll need your name, address and file number."

Lolita was ready, reading off the number from a slip of paper she'd been given. "Now, darlin', I don't want you to ever call me anything but Lolita; however, my real name is Solomon. Solomon Brown."

"*What?*"

"That's all you need to know. I'll talk to you once you get me out of here. Again, time is of the essence."

Jack hung up, his head spinning. Things were no longer under control. His spirit spiraled downward quickly.

Janie had been trying to get his attention, until finally she poked his arm.

"Hey, that hurt!" He made a face.

"You mean Jack Walker the football player is capable of getting hurt by little ol' me with one finger?" She smiled and did it again. "What's that all about with Lolita?"

"I'm not feeling so good. I think I've come down with one of those super bugs." He sat with Janie to replay Lolita's conversation.

"What are we going to do?"

"I gotta find Gramps. I can't see we have any better alternatives. I have to post a bond and get Lolita—Solomon—outta jail."

"So, Lolita's a he?"

"It would appear so." He turned on the barstool at the kitchen island. "I couldn't get Gramps on the phone. Something is very wrong!"

CHAPTER FORTY

GRAMPS WOKE UP. HE'D tried to stay awake, but the pain from his bonds left a dull roar in his head. The blood had long gone from his hands and feet, which were now completely numb. Perhaps because of his age and as best as he could figure, he'd slept most of the night. *Who sleeps at a time like this?* He blinked a few times until he could keep his eyes open and see. Beams of daylight threaded through cracks in the outside wall. His throat was sore as hell. The old rag stuffed in his mouth and tape covering his lips did not make it easy to swallow. He tried to wiggle his hands and loosen the rope binding them. Mason had been extra cautious and put duct tape over the knot. Nathaniel was not going anywhere.

A hot flash of understanding woke him from the vestiges of sleepiness. Jackson would think the Russians he had been jousting with were responsible for his disappearance. He would not put two and two together. *Why would he?* Jackson would figure the Russians killed Josh and, though extreme, it could be plausible. They were not nice. They were people accustomed to killing. His grandson was a magnet for evil people. If the pornographers did not kill him, the Satanist would. He was too headstrong and would jump to conclusions. Jack's only hope would be Mason luring him here before he confronted the Russians. He wouldn't stand a chance against them.

Gramps figured he was being held in the same room Jackson was five years back. He could only imagine the atrocities that occurred in the dark and dank space. He remembered Jackson mentioning rats; he didn't like rats. Jackson mentioned the girl, Sarah, and how Jimmy McFadden used her as a sex slave, cutting off her hands and feet . . . Nathaniel shivered. She, too, must have been kept there. The horror of Jackson mercifully strangling her, putting her out of her misery, came back to him. Distracted by the horrible thoughts, he missed the sound of a car door slamming on the other side of the building but not the opening and closing of the shop door. Sweat formed on Gramps' forehead. It was Mason.

Gramps heard his keeper place something down, probably on the metal table in the room next door. He listened closely. Footsteps approached. He took a deep breath as they stopped at the door. He heard the jingling of keys and then the opening of a padlock. The door opened. The light rushed in and blinded him momentarily.

"How are we doing, old man?" Mason walked over to him. "I'm going to loosen your bonds for a few minutes. I wouldn't want you dying on me needlessly." He bent to cut the duct tape and loosened the knots binding his feet, lowering them to the ground.

If the gag had allowed it, Gramps would have screamed in pain as the blood flow returned to his feet, stabbing like a knife. The same stabbing sensation occurred when his hands were freed. Mason left the rope in place, much looser.

"I suppose you would like some food and water." Mason savagely pulled the duct tape off his mouth and pried out the rag with his thumb and forefinger.

Gramps throat was so horribly dry that he couldn't speak. He tried to croak out a sarcastic comment, but the words wouldn't happen. He could only look up at his jailor.

Mason dropped a bag on the floor. "I'm not being a very good host." He reached in and pulled out a bottle of water. He unscrewed the cap and offered it to Gramps, who almost felt grateful and was in no position to decline. He nodded and drank the water as Mason held it to his lips. "You were thirsty. You see, we Satanists are not all bad. I thought about leaving you here to rot. It would have been a lot easier than coming back to tend to your needs. Yes, leave you here to wallow in your shit. It's hot as hell in here. You would dehydrate and die within another day. No one would think to come here to search for you." He looked back out the doorway. "Why the hell would they?" he laughed. "Speaking of shit, do you have to relieve yourself?"

Gramps croaked, "That would be nice of you."

Mason took out a wicked knife. "One of Jimmy McFadden's favorites. Could split you in two in no time. I remember him saying that very same thing from time to time."

"I can appreciate that, but then you wouldn't have your bait. Why don't you just go and look for Jackson? Do you think he's going to figure out I'm here all on his own? You don't know my grandson very well if that's the case." He shook his head.

Mason laughed. "You are more impatient than I am. You see, I have laid a nasty curse on the young man. I'm waiting until he can no longer function properly, then I will lead him here. There's no need to hurry. A simple text or phone call will be enough. I'll give him another day."

Gramps flushed. Another day would give Jack plenty of time to confront the Russians. Gramps needed to get the nasty Satan lover on the right track. He met Mason's gaze. "Why are you doing this?"

"Unfinished business, old man."

Gramps hated being called an old man. "How so?"

Mason laughed lightly, more like a chuckle. "Quite simple, Nathaniel. Revenge. I'm going to kill your grandson to please my savior—kill him because he killed important members of our faith and derailed our plans in South Florida."

"And thank the heavens for that!"

Mason sneered, looking like he wanted to kick Gramps. "And I was starting to like you, old man."

Gramps smiled, fueling Mason's contempt for him. "You sound like a politician. Everything is fine until someone disagrees with you. I'm not afraid of you, Mason. That is your name?" The Satanist's lack of response verified his assumption. "How'd you get out of prison?"

Mason smiled at the comment. "Let's suffice it to say we have friends in low places."

Gramps frowned.

"I've been plotting for this day, Nathaniel Portman. Planning for the day when I can make a sacrifice to my Lord worthy of his greatness. I'm sure he will be more than happy to devour both yours and Jack's souls. Your death"—he looked at Gramps— "will be an appetizer leading up to the main course." He handed Gramps a sandwich that looked like it had been bought at a convenience store.

Gramps took it into his semi-bound hands and ate it thankfully. He would need to keep up his energy to aid Jackson in defeating the evil that faced him. Even the tiniest deflection might prove helpful.

"Time's up, Nate. I hope you don't mind if I call you that. Nathaniel doesn't resonate well with my French accent." He tied back Gramps up, this time relying more on the duct tape, which left a little room for circulation. "Let's sit you up against this pole. I don't want to kill you too soon by hogtying you like last night." Mason proceeded to tape him to the pole with several circles around his chest and the stanchion. "Keep well, Nate, as you know I do have plans for you." Mason took a few pictures with his phone. "A little proof to send Jack." He smiled and walked out of the room, closing the door, once again leaving Gramps in darkness, despair creeping into his consciousness.

Gramps tried to shake off the dark thoughts and did the only thing possible: He opened himself up to the spirits.

CHAPTER FORTY-ONE

"YOU ARE NEARLY DEAD," Susan said, more to herself than to the man two cells over. Robert didn't move, nor did he respond. "I don't give you longer than this night." Again, no response. His chest moved unevenly as if he was in distress. Soon, Boris would be in here cleaning up the mess as she'd seen him do before. She would not spend any more time worrying about Robert Lopez.

CHAPTER FORTY-TWO

JACK HAD VISITED THE county jail a few times in his youth. He was never in the place himself, but he'd seen the odd friend caught on a minor felony, doing a month or so of soft time. He and Janie posted bail for Solomon Brown. It cost Jack $495, which he swore he'd get out of the . . . man when this was all over.

He left Janie in front to watch over the Jeep. He didn't trust this neck of the woods. It wasn't uncommon for cars to be stolen or vandalized close to the prison. He waited in the lounge after presenting the bail bond certificate, vouching for his guarantee that Solomon would return for any courtroom appearances.

The male released into his custody bore little resemblance to Lolita other than his physical size. The man's head was shaved bald; he—she must have worn a wig. When the burly fellow walked closer, Jack saw that he was, indeed, Lolita. The eyes were unmistakably the same. Green like emeralds.

"Should I call you Solomon or Lolita?" Jack suddenly felt sorry for the person.

"I would prefer Lolita," she said with masculine femininity. "You would like her better. Solomon is a sad and troubled soul who emerges from time to time. He's resting now."

Jack could not help but glance anxiously at Janie when they met up with her. She mirrored the same troubled feelings that he had. The hair on Jack's neck rose. He swallowed and wondered if he should have left Lolita in the slammer. The whole situation felt creepy as all hell.

Lolita smiled for the first time. "Remember, Jackson, I'm a medium who makes her money off reading people's faces. The two of you are like open books. Believe me, I do understand your hesitation."

The two guards standing on either side of the exit stared incredulously as the conversation expanded. When Janie picked up on it she said, "Hey, why don't we get out of here? We need to talk, but this isn't the best place." Both Lolita and Jack nodded. Lolita was handed her belongings, a plastic bag bulging with her large dress, bangles and rings.

* * * *

Lolita sat in the front and Janie in the back as Jack pulled onto Ortiz Avenue. Lolita barely fit into the passenger's seat. "Would you mind taking me home, darling? I need to freshen up."

Jack nodded but said, "I don't get it, Lolita."

Lolita nodded. "Neither do I, darlin', but I do know we are tied together in this mess, like it or not."

Jack shook his head. "Shit!" Jack said in exasperation. "Do I not get a choice in this? I'm getting sick and tired of people telling me I'm mixed up in things for reasons that are not logical. Lolita, please show me some reason."

"There often is no reason where the spirits are concerned. To make matters worse, I feel we are battling good spirits against bad. I told you this when we first met."

"I have to give you that." He hesitated and almost smiled. "If we are tied into this, as you say, I need some honesty here. Let me have a crack at putting two and two together."

"Okay!"

"Why were you arrested?"

Lolita took a deep breath. "Lolita wasn't arrested. It was Solomon."

Janie asked, "Are you not Solomon?"

"No. I am not. Solomon comes and goes. At this point in time, he's not welcome."

Jack cut in, "Okay, so tell us why Solomon was put in jail?"

"He's a troubled naughty man, tormented by his inner voice."

Both Janie and Jack said, "Okay?"

"Solomon was arrested for the possession of child pornography."

"*What*!" both of them blurted out.

Lolita put up her finger and said, "Let me rephrase that. He'd been arrested several years back. He violated his parole by entering a place connected with the sex trade, an underground source for taboo smut."

Janie asked, "When was this?"

"A few days ago. Evidently the place was under police investigation and his picture got taken entering the establishment. It was cross-referenced and a few days later . . . here we sit."

Janie's hackles went off. The coincidence seemed too strong to ignore, but then again there had been many of them over the past week. "Where is this place? Tampa?"

"Yes, a place called . . . Aversions."

Jack nearly swerved off the road. "No fucking way! The Russians own that place."

Lolita nodded. "Indeed they do. Nasty people. The kind you don't want to get tangled up with, but Solomon indicated to me they sold good shit—stuff you couldn't get anywhere else, especially online. Tell me about your case, but only if you want to. I'd understand."

It took Jack the rest of the ride back to Bonita Springs to explain what had transpired thus far in their investigation. He explained how Robert Lopez had been similarly caught with child pornography on his hard drive, and how he was now missing. Once he finished, another thought hit him smack in the forehead. "Did I mention the Russians have my gramps!"

Janie squeezed his shoulder from behind.

"The fuckers killed Josh and now they've probably done the same to Gramps."

Lolita did not look convinced. "What makes you think that? It's the reasonable explanation, I'll give you that. But I don't think it's true. I can only back that up with what I've seen in my visions. You and I are in tune with the spirits, whether or not you choose to believe. I'm telling ya, it may not be the logical answer to your question; I believe Nathaniel's somewhere else."

As they neared Lolita's driveway, Jack lost it. "Oh, for Christ's sake. Get out of the damn car! Get out and stay out of my life. That's it!"

Janie put her hand on his shoulder again. "Take it easy, Jack."

"No. You too. You're following me around like I'm going to do something stupid. You're giving me a fucking complex. I'm fine. I finally know where this is all going."

Lolita turned to him as she tried to extricate her large frame from the passenger seat. "Do you, Jackson? Please listen to me. Your grandfather isn't with the Russians."

"*Get out*! And don't you or the other guy damn well be late for that court date, or I'll lose the $495 you owe me."

"I'll go and get it for you right now."

Not wanting to hear another word, Jack said, "No, it's on me. Just get the fuck out. Leave me alone."

She grabbed her plastic bag, her eyes welling. "You know where to find me."

Jack slammed the Jeep into reverse and into the street, cutting off another car, which blasted its horn. He hit the brakes and jammed the car into drive, heading back to the beach. Over his shoulder, Janie didn't look too happy.

"You going home?" he asked.

"If I wasn't so mad at you right now I would. But I don't trust that you will *not* do something stupid."

Jack shook his head and floored the gas pedal.

CHAPTER FORTY-THREE

BORIS SAT IN FRONT of Walker's house. The wait had been eight hours now. He only planned to do another drive-by, the same as yesterday, since the place had been wrapped in crime-scene tape for the past few days.

Today when Boris saw all the police packing up and ripping off the yellow tape, he drove to a nice restaurant and enjoyed a hearty meal. Two hours later, he returned to Jack Walker's house. He felt like calling it a day. The sun was setting on the gulf in a ball of fire when he spotted the Jeep heading toward him. He knew Walker had a Jeep and it was red. This had to be him. Boris slowly moved down the road to avoid drawing attention to himself. He'd already checked the windows a few times while he strolled the sidewalk to make sure he wasn't missing anything. There was no one inside.

The Jeep pulled into the driveway, wheels squealing to a stop.

Walker exited the front seat, storming into the stucco bungalow. The woman with him at Aversions climbed out of the back seat. *Strange*, Boris thought. He'd been about to leave for his hotel room at the Pink Shell Resort but was rewarded with Walker's return. Eli would be pleased. Boris sat back in the driver's seat and watched.

CHAPTER FORTY-FOUR

JACK LEFT THE DOOR open for Janie. She slammed it shut. "What's that all about?" she yelled. "I'm willing to sit in silence as you burn off your male hormones and bad temper speeding your way through Bonita Springs; you're lucky you didn't get pulled over."

He turned to her, putting his hands up. "Whoa, I'm sorry. I really am."

She slapped his face. He recoiled, obviously hurt more by the act than the pain. "Don't do that again, Jack Walker. I'm here because I like you, not because I like being here. Do that again and you're on your own. You're a pigheaded bastard sometimes. You didn't give Lolita a chance. Why in heck do you think she called you? She's not making money from this. She damn well believes what she's saying. And I for one believe her."

Jack paced back and forth in the foyer. "Look, I'm sorry, I really am. I'm just so busted up over this paranormal shit. Josh,

Gramps, Lolita. It's all pushed me over the edge."

Janie nodded. "I get that, but don't take me for granted. I'm not here for the good of my health. Like you, I don't know what the right thing to do is either. I do know you have to stop acting like a child. It doesn't help and I can't take it anymore." She paused. "Did you see the car moving away from your house when we pulled in?"

"No. I must have been focused on the other shit."

"No. You were having your shit-fit . . . just saying. We better be on our guard if we leave here. That car is watching for sure."

"Hmmm. The cops promised they'd be out of here today, unless they put a plainclothes detail on us, but I doubt it." Jack walked to the front window, leaving the lights off in the living room so he wouldn't be seen. He carefully peered out, looking up and down the street. "There it is. A large BMW. It's sure as hell not the cops. They don't drive Beamers." He made out a figure in the driver's seat. Walking back into the kitchen, Janie followed him. "You're right. That makes things more difficult; but then again, maybe not."

Janie's eyes widened. "What do you mean?"

"I'm going in there."

"In where?"

"Aversions."

Janie shook her head. "You're nuts. You won't get one foot into that place."

"Not through the front door. That big garage—the cops couldn't find a way into it from the inside. Like I said, there's something going on in there. I bet there's another level to the basement, or it's cordoned off from the rest of the place. They didn't seem so worried about their computers being taken. They have something else going on in that place. Lolita said that . . . Solomon bought taboo porn from them onsite. You can't just wipe that shit off a computer, especially when you have a business going. We know they're low-level distributers."

"As much as I don't want to agree with you, Jack, I think you are right. But you can't just open up the garage door and walk inside. I bet they have surveillance and the place will be locked up tighter than Fort Knox."

He smiled for the first time in days. "Peter said you are good at picking locks."

"No way."

"You're the one who keeps saying you're not leaving me alone. You wanna keep an eye on me."

"Yes, but now you're taking advantage of me."

"Can't have your cake and eat it too, baby."

"It's reckless. Those guys don't mess around."

"They killed Josh. They probably have Gramps. Maybe they have him locked up in that garage, and we both think they're behind Robert Lopez's disappearance. I'm not going to wait. If you're with me, we're going in tonight."

Janie became quiet for a time, walked over to the fridge, and took out two Coors, handing one to Jack, who gladly accepted. She nodded. "So, what do we do with him?" She motioned to the car parked out front.

"Hang on." He pulled his cell out of his pants pocket and speed-dialed Perry's number. His friend answered on the second ring.

"Hey, bro. Wassup?"

"Did you find out anything about my grandfather?"

"I checked his office and home. No one's seen or heard, which is not his style."

"Perr, I need your help."

"Sure, whad'ya have in mind?" Perry sounded like he'd been napping.

"I need you to pick me up at Doc Ford's in half an hour. I'm going to take the boat."

"Mind me asking?"

"Things are ramping up."

"Christ sakes, bro! How the hell do you get wrapped up in this shit? What's happening?"

"Perry, don't ask. Hopefully we can talk about it soon. Until then, meet me there, please."

"I'm your man. I'll head over there right away."

"Talk to Ron. He's the manager; you know him."

"Yeah, I do."

"Make sure I can tie up there for the night."

CHAPTER FORTY-FIVE

PETER ROBERTSON'S CELL RANG for the third time in five minutes. The call originated from a foreign country. It was 9:30 at night, and he had already put down a few bourbons and was currently enjoying one of his favorite cigars. He did not like talking business after he had been drinking, but the caller seemed persistent and his curiosity was piqued. He pressed the answer button and placed the phone to his ear. "Peter Robertson."

"Mr. Robertson." The voice was that of a female Asian, most likely Chinese, but then again he was not an expert in detecting dialects. "Sorry to ring you so late. I'm calling from Singapore and my message is urgent."

"Okay. I'm listening. Does this have to do with law?"

"So sorry again, yes it does. I am calling regarding Robert Lopez."

Peter put down his cigar and sat up straight. They had not

heard a word since the shooting at the dealership days ago when he was taken, and Robert's phone messaging was full. "Yes. He's one of our clients."

"Exactly. Robert is one of our employees. Your retainer is paid by our company."

"Which is?"

"I'm not at liberty to divulge that information."

Her quick comment angered Peter. "Then there's really nothing to talk about. I can't divulge information from a client to a non-disclosed source, nor a disclosed source, for that matter."

The woman sighed. "Very well. You can track the routing number of the check used by Robert and it will be linked to a Wells Fargo account, which is in turn linked to City Star, Inc. You can take the time to follow the routing and I can call you back. But, Mr. Robertson, what I have to say could be in your best interests."

Peter paused for a moment, his head spinning. "City Productions?"

"One of our many subsidiaries. I have just sent you an e-Transfer. Please check your email. I'm increasing your retainer to $50,000. By you accepting the retainer, we technically become your client, correct?"

"It's a bit loose, but yes."

"Will you accept, Mr. Robertson?"

Peter needed to think this through, but by taking the time to do so he might miss something important. He went out on a limb and said, "Yes. I will accept."

"Thank you, Mr. Robertson. I now assume whatever is said will be in the utmost of confidence?"

"I'm bound by the law, Ms. . . . ?"

"Ling. L-I-N-G. Ms. Ling will do, Mr. Robertson."

"Ms. Ling, I will start by saying we haven't heard from Robert Lopez in several days."

"Nor have we, Mr. Robertson. This is why I'm calling you."

"I'll be honest, Ms. Ling. The whole business is very ambiguous and we were sticking our necks out by taking on the case due to its unsavory nature. I'm fine defending pornography—we are criminal lawyers. However, the child porn angle had me a bit on edge. It was a damned if you do, damned if you don't decision."

"Yet you did take it on, Mr. Robertson. Please don't play coy with me. We chose you because we knew you need the money. Business hasn't been good these past few years, has it? We know your wife likes to spend."

"You are out of line, ma'am."

"Am I? Let me get to the point."

"Please do."

"How can I put this? Robert Lopez is one of our controllers. We often put our people into a situation so they can ascertain if one of our suppliers is overstepping their bounds. You are familiar with St. Petersburg Inc?"

"The Russians in Tampa?"

"Yes. Tampa, Tallahassee and New Orleans, to be accurate."

"Why retain us in the first place? I don't understand."

"We like to handle our . . . situations in a very antiseptic fashion. We have the means to walk in and take out the bad clients. We could simply assassinate them. Robert is more than capable of doing so, but that would be messy. Wouldn't it be much cleaner to have Eli Romanov and his associates arrested on the child pornography charges, after being linked to the material on Robert's computer? The evidence is damning. You were given enough material to have the Russians investigated."

Peter smiled. "You were leaving a lot to chance."

"Perhaps, but we like to take the invisible approach when possible."

"What went wrong?"

"We're not sure. Robert Lopez was in the process of cleaning up and formulating his end game."

"When he disappeared, right?"

"More or less. Perhaps he underestimated the Russians. By now, your district attorney should have had enough evidence to make arrests. Romanov goes to jail, eventually incarcerated. There is no link to us, business goes on. We arrange to have something slipped into Romanov's food in prison, end of story."

"Hmmm, I don't need to hear that, Ms. Ling."

"Tell me, Mr. Robertson, was the DA able to find anything

after the Tampa strip bar was investigated?"

"Actually, I was on the phone with her at about 4 PM. Thus far, they've been able to determine nothing from the computers or forensics."

"That is unfortunate. Perhaps we've underestimated Romanov."

"Maybe so. Tell me, surely you heard that Robert Lopez was last seen at a car dealership in North Ft. Myers, where he attempted to sell his sports car."

"No. Please tell me more."

"The salesman he had an appointment to meet with was shot dead in the parking lot. Lopez's car remained on the lot and there has been no sign of him since."

"Very disturbing, Mr. Robertson. There is only one explanation as to what happened to our agent."

"Yes, he's either dead or detained. So where does this leave us?"

"Mr. Robertson, since you have been retained by us, I would ask that you continue your investigations. But I would exercise utmost caution. Robert Lopez is a pro, very capable of looking after himself. If he's been taken out by the Russians, you would be wise to step back. If Robert Lopez was intercepted, your aids will stand no chance should they be implicated by Romanov. We will need your services to retain some degree of legality in the process, which could become messy. Part of the retainer you just received will hopefully ensure that you are quiet about what has been discussed this evening. Mr. Robertson, we know an awful lot about you and your habits—your family's habits."

"That's a threat?"

"Take it for what it is, Mr. Robertson, but I would say yes." The phone went dead.

Peter poured himself another bourbon. He shook his head, knowing he should have listened to his inner voice and steered clear of the case. Once again, his greed and need for the money came between desire and reason. He picked up his phone and dialed Walker's number. He needed to ensure Walker stayed away from Romanov at all cost. No answer. He left a message.

"Jack, Janie, call me ASAP. Stay away from the Russians.

Don't do anything further in this case until you've contacted me." He called Janie's number. Same thing. He shot back the whiskey in one throw.

CHAPTER FORTY-SIX

BORIS'S SIXTH SENSE NIGGLED at him. He'd seen Walker and his tagalong partner enter the house a good fifteen minutes ago. *No lights?* He called Eli.

Eli picked up on the fifth ring. "Boris, you're interrupting my blow job." He looked down at the cute little French-Canadian number attentively kissing and sucking his semi-erect cock.

"My apologies, Eli. I have followed Walker back to his house. I think he may have seen my car."

"Are you telling me you fucked up, again, Boris?" He swatted away the little slut, his erection instantly losing its rigidity.

"*Nyet*, Eli, but I will not lie. The man is cagey. It is my professional opinion it's time to take the fucker out."

Eli paused. "Okay, Boris." He hung up.

Boris reached into the glove box for his Beretta and carefully screwed the silencer onto the muzzle. Stepping out of the car, he stayed in the shadows on his way to Walker's place. He patted the gun several times as he walked along the desolate sidewalk. Boris enjoyed killing. The act itself dispensed a surge of adrenalin into his veins. The high couldn't be described to anyone who didn't kill human animals for a living as Boris did.

* * * *

Another set of eyes watched the Walker house from the shadows across the street. Mason clearly saw the gun as the large man exited the car. He counted six times the man patted the gun with his free hand as if petting a dog. Mason frowned. *Who could this person possibly be?* It seemed as if Jack Walker made a lot of enemies. However, Mason would not allow another to circumvent his own plan for revenge. Mason moved from shadow to shadow, watching the large figure close in on the Walker house.

CHAPTER FORTY-SEVEN

PETER ROBERTSON'S NAME LIT up the cell screen as the phone rang. Jack looked at it and flashed the screen at Janie.

She shook her head. "What he doesn't know won't hurt him. That's the way you have to be with Pete; otherwise, he'll get all preachy. Besides, if you intend to do what you say you are of a mind to do . . . he won't want to know. He'll look at it like you're contravening the law, which you are, by the way. As much as Pete doesn't mind bending the rules, he would never advocate total disregard for them."

Jack let the call ring out.

Janie took out her phone and held it faceup. On cue, it rang and once again Peter's name came up on the call display. She put the phone back into her pocket, dismissing any message Robertson might have left for the two of them.

Jack went to the furnace room and hauled out his tool chest. Pulling out a multi-use screwdriver, a flashlight and wire cutters, he walked back into the kitchen. "You do carry a gun, right? I vaguely remember you telling me."

"I do. A girly Glock—that's what the gun dealer called it. Although he said it would stop anyone in their tracks."

"Okay, let's get going, then. It's pretty warm out, but you might need a sweater for the boat ride. You can borrow that." He pointed to the hoodie draped over a chair. "We need to be quiet." He escorted Janie through the screened pool area to the rear yard, where Jack kept his boat on a lift.

* * * *

Boris peered into the front window and could not detect any lights on, which again seemed strange, unless the couple was enjoying sex in the dark. If that was the case, it would make his job that much easier.

But then a light went on at the back, maybe even outside. He carefully walked around the house and stepped into the shadows of the backyard. He spotted Walker and the female in a boat. Walker was still standing and pushing it away from the dock with a paddle. Once the boat was afloat, Boris knew they would continue under low engine into the channel.

"Bastards!" Boris said under his breath. They must have caught sight of him. He moved to a vantage point where he might get a few clean shots off before they were out of sight. Leaning down at the edge of the backyard terrace, he took aim. The slight chop in the water made it difficult. The silencer tip bobbed up and down with the figure of Jack Walker as the boat drifted out into Estero Bay.

* * * *

Jack waited for the pre-ignition light to go green after guiding the boat from the lift cradle. Once ready, he fired up the 250-horse outboard and directed the boat to the end of the canal.

All of a sudden, he felt as if he'd been bitten by a monster wasp just above the elbow on his inner right arm. The windscreen on the central consul was shattered, his blood drops circling the small hole in the middle. "*Janie, down!*"

Jack ducked as another bullet hit the consul where he'd been standing. Janie was slow to realize the danger they were in, but the shooter evidently had no interest in her as she fumbled to the deck of the fishing boat. Jack pushed the throttle forward and the boat surged in a wobbly, uncontrolled fashion, Jack doing his best not to expose himself. He narrowly missed his neighbor's dock, the prop now digging into the mud bottom. He could not tell if any more shots had been fired due to the roar of the engine. Both he and Janie were still intact, though his arm burned like hell.

Jack steered the boat out into the channel and pushed the throttle to three quarters, disobeying the idle signs. He prayed not to hit a sleeping manatee—the endangered species slept on top of the water after dark. He took a rag sitting on the consul seat and pressed it to his arm.

Janie appeared at his side. "You okay? Were you hit?"

"I think I'm damn lucky. The bullet nicked the soft flesh under my arm, missed my chest by an inch." He slowed the boat to a stop. "Here." Jack handed Janie the flashlight he brought. He lifted his arm so she could take a look.

"You are lucky, Jack Walker. Hardly a nick. Keep that towel on it." She stared back at the shore. "Now, who was that?"

"Not hard to put two and two together. Had to be Romanov, or one of his thugs."

"Should we call the police?"

Jack thought for a moment. "No. What good is it going to do us? They got Gramps and I don't think they'll hesitate to kill him. I'm surprised they haven't called to threaten me. I don't think they even fathom that we might be coming to them."

Janie raised her eyebrows, wide-eyed, her voice choked with sudden fear. "Jack, I'm gonna say this one more time. Is this worth it? We could be killed. No, I mean . . . we most likely will be killed."

He shook his head. "Gramps and some faraway relatives is all I got. The thought of that gentle spirit being in trouble because of me makes me madder than hell."

His phone rang. He pulled it out and looked. "Unknown Caller." He stuck it back in his pocket, turning it off.

"The Russians?"

Jack shrugged. "No idea, but I'm not in the mood for talking to anyone."

* * * *

Mason watched the large but catlike man maneuver toward the dock. Mason followed, careful not to make a sound, not to snap a twig. The crickets, loudly looking for love on this beautiful evening, gave his footsteps a little cover as he made his way to the dock entrance. Hearing the ignition engaging on the fishing boat and the low rumble as it caught hold of the gasoline, the man raised his arm and aimed a silenced gun. He braced it on the rail, firing off two shots.

Mason heard a low curse in a foreign language, possibly Russian. He couldn't allow anything to happen. Not wanting to use his pistol, which would attract too much attention, Mason picked up a thick piece of driftwood from a fire pit. The sudden roar of the outboard engine, followed by another shot from the man's pistol, was all he needed to cover his own movement. He sprang across the twenty-foot distance to bring down the heavy piece of wood as hard as he could on the back of the big man's neck.

* * * *

Boris didn't know what hit him as he dropped to his knees. Then he felt the hit across his forearm and he thought he felt his bones snapping. His gun toppled into the canal. Instinctively, he turned to avoid another slam. As he did, a small man in dark clothing, with dark hair and a dark beard and moustache, squared off with him, keeping his distance from Boris's long reach.

Boris's sore head made it painful to even think. "Who the hell are you?"

The thin man said lots of words with a French accent. Boris

didn't like the French. "Your reference to Hell may not be too far off the mark, but I don't think you are in any position to be asking the questions." The man pulled a thin-cased Beretta out of his pocket, pointing it at the Russian's chest. "Indeed, I am thinking the same thing, *monsieur*. Who in the Devil are you?"

Boris eyed the gun and made the slightest move toward the man.

The Frenchman stepped back, both hands on the pistol. He shook his head. "Uh uh *uh*, I would not do that. Though I'm curious to find out who you are, it would not pain me to pull the trigger. Don't move again! In fact, lie down facing the grass, arms out to the side."

Boris followed his orders. The little man walked behind him. Before Boris could roll to either side, he felt the hard whack of the gun butt on the back of his head. Then there were stars, and then there was darkness.

* * * *

Mason put the gun back in his pocket and pulled out his cell phone. He dialed Jackson Walker's cell number. Events were ramping up and now another party was involved. Though he could empathize with the man's need to kill Walker, whatever his reasoning, Mason couldn't risk the new entity foiling his plans. Time to set the bait.

No answer. "*Merde!*" He left a message. "Jackson, it is Mason. Could you please call me at this number? We have lots to talk about." He hung up.

Pondering what to do with the man lying unconscious—his body wouldn't fit into the small trunk of his rental car—he went back and broke into the house, searching for something to tie up the big man. It didn't take long to find duct tape in the furnace room. Returning to the man spread out in the grass, he dragged the giant by his feet inside the screened lanai, where he taped his hands behind his back, then his ankles, and finally his mouth a couple times.

He fumbled through the man's pockets but didn't find a wallet. He took his keys, cell phone and a wad of hundred-dollar bills. Staying calm, he walked back to his car while he contemplated taking the luxurious BMW. Unfortunately, he did not want to leave clues behind in the rental car—fingerprints, rental agreement, etcetera. Taking note of the street address, he drove to the corner of Estero Boulevard and Ibis and turned left. He pulled into the plaza he'd visited the other day. Mason found a payphone in the large parking lot, next to newsstands and a mailbox. He dialed 911.

A female voice answered immediately. "Lee County Dispatch."

Mason adopted a Southern accent. "Yes, ma'am. I'd like to report a break-in. My name is Jack Walker." He gave the woman the street address. He drove back a ways, just close enough to see the Walker street entrance. Within ten minutes, two Lee County sheriff's cruisers could be heard, lights flashing in the distance. Mason smiled as they squealed onto Ibis Lane a minute later. The Russian needed to be tortured and left to bleed, but Mason didn't have the time or the strength to pull it off. He would leave him to his fate with the law. Every now and then, the law did come in handy.

He decided some prep work was needed and headed back to the McFadden Estate.

CHAPTER FORTY-EIGHT

PERRY WAITED AT THE dock, a mooring line in hand. His eyes bugged out and his jaw dropped when he saw the bullet-riddled window.

"What the fuck, bro? You're keeping bad company." When Janie frowned, he added, "Except for you, Janie." He didn't really know Janie very well—only met her at a survival party he'd thrown for Jack jointly with Josh and Gramps.

Jack turned off the engine and scampered to the side of the boat to help Perry. "Fuckin' tell me about it, Perr! There's some bad shit going down. Thanks for doing this."

"No problem. He said you could moor here till . . . whenever. He cleared it with Randy. Can I say something? No, I'm gonna say it anyway. You look like *shit*!"

Jack nodded. "I feel like shit! As if I had the flu these past few days, on top of everything else."

Perry only nodded.

Doc Ford's was owned by a successful author, Randy Wayne White, who wrote Florida thriller novels. He was one of Jack's favorites and they'd gone fishing back in his Florida Gator days. Jack felt as if he were in the middle of one of Randy's stories. He shook his head.

The three stepped up to the bar, where Jack gave the boat key to Ron, who smiled and gave Jack an upward-facing handshake. Ron eyed his arm. "Shark get you?"

"Yeah, something like that. Watch my boat, if you don't mind."

"I'll put the key in Randy's office. You look like you need a drink."

Jack looked over at Janie. She nodded encouragingly. "Three double tequilas."

Janie, Jack and Perry all downed the fiery liquor. Jack looked to Perry. "Can you drive us to Estero to pick up Janie's car?"

"Sure. But—"

"*No* buts!"

"I figured you'd say that, Jack. Let me just say, when you left me on the sidelines last time this kind of shit happened? I swore I'd never take a back seat again if I got the chance to help you. Who would figure it would happen again? Where you going?"

Jack took a deep breath. "Tampa."

"Tampa?"

"Yep. Listen, I'll give you the deal once we get in the car." He looked around. "The walls have ears. And I don't want any responsibility if anything happens to you."

Perry smiled. "I'm a chef. Nothing exciting happens to me. I'm in." He gave both of them a fist bump.

CHAPTER FORTY-NINE

BORIS REGAINED CONSCIOUSNESS AS he was being duct taped. He was a savvy operator and knew he stood no chance while the man remained in control. He let him finish his business and waited an extra few minutes just to make sure. Boris knew he didn't have much time. He did not know why, but he had survived this long trusting his instincts.

He reached for his boots; he kept a small throwing knife in each one. It took him a couple of minutes to cut the tape around his ankles, and at least five more to maneuver the knife to cut his wrists free. As he bore the pain, stripping the tape from his face, he considered how the diminutive Frenchman would have to suffer.

Hearing a loud knock at the front door, Boris scurried through the side door to the lanai and snuck over to the neighboring yard. His keys were gone, as were his money and phone. He slipped to the front of the house next door and watched what was going on at Walker's place.

Two Lee County sheriff's cars sat out front. The officers at the front door rapped another time. Boris looked longingly at his Beamer a couple hundred feet down the road; he had hidden a concierge key under the chasse. One of the officers walked around the house. He heard the other on her remote radio.

Waiting until both left the front of the building, Boris jogged across the street, back to the sports car. He retrieved the key and started the engine. The car purred as Boris deactivated the headlights. He backed to the end of the street and around the corner in the dark. Once out of eyesight, he turned the car around and the lights on to make his escape.

* * * *

Coincidentally, Boris used the same public phone Mason used several minutes ago, only he dialed Aversions. Eli would not want to take a call from a payphone. It took some time for the boss to get on the line.

"Boris, what in shit is happening?"

Boris took his time recounting the events of the evening.

"I can't trust you to shit now, Boris? Get back here before you fuck something else up."

"Yes, Eli." He hung up. There were no other words to be said. He'd failed. He must face the consequences. He expected no less. Getting back in the car, Boris headed to the highway.

CHAPTER FIFTY

"YES, I WOULD LIKE you to come to this address. The more strength you can bring, the better. It will be a powerful incantation. If you can find a Priest or Priestess all the better. Yes. I will have everything ready." Mason put the cell phone back on the car's consul as he turned into the McFadden driveway. He moved the old gate to the side, this time leaving it open. It would be difficult enough for his guests to find the place.

He parked the car beside the workshop and retrieved the supplies he had bought: candles, chalk and incense, mostly. He had already secured his live sacrifice. The old swamp hummed, like a massive beehive of nocturnal life. Mason opened the door and dumped the bags on the floor. He walked over to the cupboard and opened it. Blinking at the light, the old man did not look too good when Mason woke him up. "Are you okay, Nathaniel?"

Gramps, thankful Mason hadn't gagged him, spat out a

dusty response. "Okay? Are you for real?"

"Point taken. Anyways, we will be having some guests soon. I thought you might like to keep me company while I put out the decorations."

"Sorry, I'd rather rot in this hovel. I couldn't care less about your party."

"You will be the guest of honor."

"I decline the invitation."

Mason smiled. "You have spunk for an old guy."

"Something you'll never know, Matye. You keep bad company and your god is a sham."

"Is that a curse?" Mason laughed. "I didn't think that Indians laid curses anymore."

Gramps turned his head away from the man.

Mason grabbed his legs and cut all the bonds. "Come with me."

Gramps stood. His legs felt like they might buckle under him. Mason led him into the main room of the shed, which still held many of the stuffed animals prepared by Jimmy McFadden. "Sit!" Mason pointed to a moldy couch.

Gramps scrunched his nose up and sat.

"I'm going to cuff you to the side table. Hold still."

Gramps didn't move as Mason produced a set of cuffs probably more suited to S and M than serious incarceration. He realized Mason was a bit of an amateur. He may have been the grand poo-bah in the Church of Satan, but he didn't know what he was doing when it came to the dirty work. Gramps would watch and find a chink in his armor.

Mason cleared a large space in the center of the massive room. Then, he took out a three-foot-long case, which had been already lying on the floor. He opened it and Gramps saw a very large extendable compass and extendable yardsticks. "Tools of the trade."

Gramps ignored him. He felt dirty watching the man.

Mason put the point of the compass in the middle of the floor. He drove home the nail with a small mallet and extended the device to its maximum of five feet. He placed a piece of divine chalk in the other end and walked the chalk around to make a perfect twelve-foot circle. Folding up the compass, he put it back in the case. He then took out a bag of chalk powder. He said a short prayer over it and spread the chalk around the circle. Gramps swore he saw the man sprinkling threads of hair into the chalk. He stood in the circle and prayed in a language that Gramps couldn't come close to understanding, though he finished with a Latin ode to his god.

"*Ave Satanas.*"

When he finished, Gramps said, "Does that make you feel safer?"

Mason smiled. "From your type, no. From the spirits, yes." Mason continued to plot out a pentagram using an assortment of mathematical formulae and, once again, the compass. Once finished, he performed a cleansing prayer, placing unlit candles at the five corners of the star.

Gramps couldn't help himself. "A lot of crap for a false god."

Mason didn't take kindly to the jab. He promptly walked over and smacked Gramps' head. "Your insolence will not help you when it's time to kill you; I may choose to use a dull knife."

"I'll keep that in mind, Mason. What do you plan on doing to me?"

"To you and your grandson, Nathaniel. You and Jackson will become sacrifices to the one true god: Lucifer. Just like your Abraham did on the mountain."

"He's not my Abraham."

"Then who is your god?"

Gramps kept prodding. "Are you that stupid you can't remember I'm a Native? I believe in an all-encompassing god, a god who is one with nature. Not a one-sided abortion like Lucifer. I think the bunch of you are being hoodwinked. Your sect relies on bullying and coercion. Lies."

"And Christianity hasn't done the same?"

"Good point! However, I'm not a Christian. I believe in some of the Christian tenets—the ones supported by good people."

"Good people," Mason sneered. "Highly overrated. I know many Satanists who are good people."

"Are they an anomaly? I don't know how you can say this with a straight face. You know what you are. The fact that you're plotting to sacrifice Jackson and I is not . . . good. You worship the Devil, Satan and Lucifer. They are noted evil entities."

"There have been more wars in the name of your god in the past 3,000 years than that of Satan."

"A weak argument, Mason. Christianity is the same as Satanism, used as a scapegoat for ulterior motives. It's not the religion; it's the people behind it. Christianity has had its problems, but there has never been any doubt of the motivation behind Satanism. I understand the Left-Hand Path, the right to free thought. The problem is, that's an open-ended premise allowing for . . . bad things. There's no better way to explain it. Everything you Satanists do is in parody of the Christian faith. Is your god so jealous he can't come up with his own pomp and pageantry?"

"A typical Christian response, though I will give you the credit of understanding the Left-Hand Path. All religions borrow from one another, Nathaniel. The Christian Church was created by a bunch of messed-up, drunken Romans who jumped on the bandwagon of a new trend. They chose which scriptures, which ceremonies to keep. I will admit, it was probably one of the most successful marketing endeavors made in Western humanity. Look at the wealth of the Roman Catholic Church. It's gross. Millions of faithful followers living in poverty around the world."

Gramps laughed. "I told you this once, and I'll not say it three times. I'm not Christian, and I, too, am not a fan of Catholicism. I'm a Native American shaman. I am my tribe's spiritual leader. I understand your religion well enough, as I do the Christian faith. I see what goes on in my dreams. I've seen you in my dreams. You are not good. I hate to say this to you, but you are not. So, let's cut with the bullshit. My people are a peaceful group, as are 99 percent of Christians. We are small. We believe in the natural way of things. What you espouse is not natural, so keep your bogus concepts to yourself. You will not sway me. If it makes you feel better telling me all of this, then I pray for your soul, Mason. There are a few bad Christians, let's face it, but most of you Satanists have malice and anger in your souls. I don't care how or what you choose to call it. You are bad people."

"We preach a way of life. A life of greater fulfillment. Freedom to do what one wants."

Gramps turned and stared him in the eye. "Exactly. If everyone thought this way, there would be no law, only chaos, which is an evil tenet. Freedom is earned; it's not a right. My people, the Seminoles, earned our freedom. We were persecuted, hunted down twice by the United States government in South Florida. We survived. I don't know, it seems like you feel that you are owed something, Mason. The American people have been fighting wars to ensure the country's freedoms since its independence, another worthy cause, and I'm proud to say I am an American as well as a Native American. What you plan to do tonight takes away my freedom. Mason, what gives you this right? I don't see the Christian Church gathering prominent individuals within society, imprisoning them to use as human sacrifices. Think about it, you twisted, dirty little man. Who does this kind of thing? Evil people."

"I grow tired of this, Nathaniel. You have your point of view, I have mine. We can banter back and forth for days and it will not get us anywhere. The fact is, you are going to die as soon as I can lure your grandson here, plain and simple."

"That proves it. You are evil. Your personage oozes it. Please tie me up and put me back in the cupboard."

Mason laughed. "No. I want you to watch the process of your demise, old man. Your fancy words will do you no good where you're going."

Gramps caught Mason's gaze. "You are a little man, Mason Matye. You are trying to take advantage of your deity. I don't think any god would like such behavior. Personally, I think at the root of it, Satanism gives you an excuse to do bad things."

"No excuses, Nathaniel, and you don't know the half of it."

CHAPTER FIFTY-ONE

JACK WAITED IN THE car with Perry as Janie went into the CVS to buy bandages and disinfectant for Jack's wound. When she returned to the car, she tended to what amounted to a long scrape.

"You are damned lucky," Janie said, stuffing the used packaging back into a plastic bag.

Jack looked at Perry. "You sure you want to do this?"

"No fear here, bro. Tell me what needs to be done. I would not miss this for the world."

"Start driving toward Tampa. That's a good place to begin."

"I'm on it." Perry pulled onto Summerlin and headed to the highway.

Janie poked Jack's arm from the back seat. "Do we have a plan?" The words came out with a haunting aura of déjà vu. She remembered asking Josh the same question when they attempted to rescue Jack from the clutches of the McFaddens.

At that time, Josh had no idea what he intended to do. Jack differed, in that he knew what needed to happen but didn't have a clue how to accomplish it.

Thinking about her question before answering, he said, "I do, actually. Obviously, we get to Aversions. Perry will drop us off. I don't want you coming in with us."

Perry frowned. "In where?"

"There's an old garage in the back of the strip club. I suspect there's an underground access to the place. They use it to move things, people, in and out of the establishment without being seen. Illegal strippers, dead people, who knows? That'll be how they got Gramps in there. I bet they have a section cordoned off from the rest of the place where they make and distribute their movies, drugs. I'm sure they have their own server and the computers with the pornography stored on it down there as well."

Janie spoke. "You seem awfully sure of yourself. They'll have surveillance on the garage, and you know it. How do we get around that?"

"Good question."

Perry said, "I know a little about surveillance cameras. We have them at the restaurant. It's mostly on the doorways in case we're broken into, so you can see who did it. It's recorded. If that's the case, you put on a hoodie or a hat to cover your face so they can't see who you are."

Jack frowned. "That's fine if there's no one monitoring what's going on. I bet they have the place wired with dozens of cameras. They want to see what's going on in the back rooms, to make sure their girls are safe. I'm pretty sure they have a swingers lounge as well. The patrons need to feel safe. The sick bastards probably film and sell what goes on even back there."

Janie tapped Jack's shoulder again. "You're not going to leave it to chance, then. We need to figure out how to get in there without being seen." After a few moments of silence, Janie clapped. "I've got it! Maybe we want to be seen."

Jack laughed. "Great idea, smoker girl."

"Hey, I haven't had one in two days. Thanks for reminding me. No, seriously, if we can't get rid of the cameras, why couldn't we distract or redirect what they're looking at for a time?"

"Okay, I'm listening," Jack smiled.

"What would happen if you just walked in the front door?"

Jack looked at her, frowning; obviously he was uncomfortable with the proposition.

"Eli and his thugs would be onto you like flies on shit. I'm sure if they're monitoring the activity inside the place, the focus would shift to wherever the point of interest might be. Jack Walker steps into the front foyer, I guarantee the cameras or at least the attention of the person watching the cameras would be on the front door. I don't doubt Eli Romanov spends some of his time spying on the goings-on there. If we time the distraction, Perry and I could get in the back through the garage. I'm sure I remember a man door on the side of the building. If it's being recorded like you suggested, Perry, no one is going to look at the tape unless there is a reason to check back on the recording."

Jack said, "I'm sure I remember the door as well, but this is my deal. I don't want to put you guys at risk. Besides, they'll probably beat the shit out of me." He rubbed his jaw.

"Yes. They will want to get you out of the way quickly, maybe even take you to where you cannot be seen or found."

"Great, so I'm the sacrificial lamb? Now I'm not liking this."

"This is all a big risk, Jack. We have to count on there being a back way into the place. I'm confident."

Perry asked, "Why don't we call the cops? Just sayin'."

"No way. They're gonna get another warrant and embarrass themselves. They've searched the place already. It came up clean. Besides, if my gramps is in there, he may not have much time. I'm not going to risk it. They killed Josh, and nearly got Janie and I tonight. I'm taking this personally." Scratching his head, he said, "What good are you guys gonna be without me?"

Janie smiled for the first time in a while. "I was thinking the opposite. Remember, I've done this sort of thing many times investigating shady people. I can get in that man door in seconds. I have a gun and won't hesitate to use it. If your gramps is in there, I'll find him. We'll keep the car close and make a quick exit."

"What about me? You might get Gramps out and never see

me again."

"Not saying you crash the place, only that you make an entrance and ask to speak with Eli, saying you wanna reconcile your differences. You're the one who wants to be the hero."

Jack flushed. "Like hell, Janie, that's not it at all. I don't care if anyone finds out about this; it's personal."

"We do have to bank on being able to get in the back way. But even if they do try to detain you, you'll most likely find Gramps. Anyone have a better idea?"

Jack thought about it for a moment. "Not really, but let me think about it while we drive."

CHAPTER FIFTY-TWO

LOLITA FELT AS IF she'd been jilted by a lover. The attraction to Jackson Walker was not sensual in any way. It was a spiritual connection. She also felt a connection with Gramps.

She went to the cupboard and pulled out a bottle of Jack Daniels, the only hard alcohol in the house. Lolita definitely needed a shot and Solomon's watery Budweiser would not do. She poured three fingers and knocked it back. Moving to her lounge, she sat in the big, overstuffed rickety chair and lit a few candles, the ones easy to reach while seated. The tarot called her name. She pulled the deck out of the table drawer and held it as if it might make her feel better. It didn't; in fact, it seemed to make matters worse. Her eyes teared up.

She wanted to see if the spirits might talk to her. That didn't occur very often, but it seemed worth a try. Lolita placed a large natural crystal on the round table. Crystal held great power when trying to attract the netherworld. Taking a deep breath, she cleared her mind while the booze relaxed her. She placed her hands on the crystal. What happened next nearly killed her. She felt the blood vessels in her brain expanding, her neck bulge, her eyes nearly popping out of their sockets. Then things calmed.

She was in a car, sleepy, her eyes opening and closing. She looked at her hands. They were not hers. There was a young man driving the car. She didn't recognize him. She could detect the presence of another person in the back, female. They were on a highway, I-75—she saw the signs passing: North Ft. Myers. *She remained for a few more minutes.* Tampa 90 miles. *She settled in.* He's heading to Tampa. NO! He can't go there. *Then he fell asleep.*

The great bird soared high in the moonlit sky. Through her eyes, Lolita saw the Everglades below, a long twisty river. It was a ride like she'd never experienced, nor would she again. Walker possessed a familiar. Amazing, he truly does have exceptional powers. *The bird flew straight up and dove straight down. She felt the wind blowing through the feathers and she tucked her wings to her sides. Then the wings extended, the wind slowing as the massive feathers caught the desired resistance. She flew low, a dozen feet above the water, banking sharply to the left, narrowly missing the pillars of a long decrepit wooden dock fingering out into the river. There was a large shed or barn to the left. A light inside was turned on. To the right, a large plantation house, in bad repair. The grounds were littered with old cars, the grass so long it fell over on itself. Then she zeroed in on one specific car: the car that had followed Nathaniel after he dropped off Lolita.*

"No!" Jack yelled, and Lolita was pushed away from the vision. Everything was pushed away: the bird, the warm night sky, the wind, and the moonlight. Jack didn't recognize the car. But he knew the place.

Lolita woke, her hands cut from gripping the crystal. She yelped with pain and heartache. "Walker is going the wrong way. The Russians. They will kill him. No!" She did not recognize that other place, but she was sure Jackson did. She needed to get to Tampa in a hurry.

She pulled up Uber on her phone. Once her ride was secured, she reached high on one of the kitchen shelves and pulled down a tin box filled with twenty-dollar bills. Once she stuffed a wad of them into a fold in her dress, she ran downstairs and entered Solomon's domain. Lolita seldom went there. It was a place full of bad memories. Peeling back a piece of wall paneling revealed a cupboard stacked full of tapes and DVDs. At the bottom of the shelf was an old paper bag. She pulled it from the cupboard, sealing the space back up.

In the bag was a Ruger LCP .380, no bigger than her wide hand. It was already loaded with five in the mag and one in the chamber. It all belonged to Solomon. He bought it for protection when he moved to wild New Orleans from churchgoing Louisville. The weapon had never been shot in anger. Lolita hoped it still worked.

It was time to bring out her favorite wig. Opening the cabinet, she pulled down a white Styrofoam head with an amazing high wig. Touching the curly cap of dark hair, she stroked the dozens of long dreadlocks sprouting from the built-up back of the wig. Smiling in the dressing table mirror, her fingers searched the high top until she felt the tiny snap. Pulling it to open exposed a small compartment built inside the back rise. The handgun just fit. Securing the snap, then securing the tall wig on her head, Lolita was ready to leave.

She saw her ride sitting out front. The headlights streamed through the reception area bay window. Locking the front door behind her, she shuffled down to the back door of the waiting car. Once inside, she smiled at the young Hispanic male. *Perfect.*

"You goin' to Tampa, ma'am?"

"Yes. You got that right. How fast can you get me there?"

"Two and a half."

"If I give you an extra hundred dollars cash, can you get me there in less than two?"

"As long as you are no uncomfortable, yes ma'am."

"Let's get going, then. What's your name?"

"Hernando."

She smiled in the rearview mirror. "There was a great song written about you!"

He laughed, "*Sí*, the 'Hideaway'!"

They both laughed as he pulled out a device and fastened it to the sun visor, plugging an attached wire into the cigarette lighter.

"You have a radar detector? I didn't think those things existed anymore."

"This is good one. We catch the cops, but cops no catch us."

"I certainly hope not," Lolita said. *Jackson's life might depend on it.*

CHAPTER FIFTY-THREE

GRAMPS WOKE FROM A catnap. He could not believe he'd fallen asleep on the verge of what most likely would be his death. He once again wrote off his need for slumber to old age.

Mason noted his awakening. "Did you have a good sleep, Nathaniel? I hope so. Our guests shall be arriving soon. I hope Jack can make it. He doesn't seem to want to pick up his phone. Never mind, I've left him a few photos. They might help him realize where you are."

A shock of alarm went off in his head. *Jackson?* Worry about what Mason was cooking up overcame him and he needed to know more. "Who are these guests?"

"Our most esteemed guest will be your grandson. I hope he arrives before the witching hour. That will be when we begin our first sermon. Coincidentally, it will also be when we sacrifice you to a particularly nasty demon. Among our other guests will be a few high-ranking members of the Church of Satan, those who might remain of the Church of Set, and an esteemed member of the Illuminati."

Gramps smiled sardonically. "There's no such thing as the Illuminati and you know it."

Mason frowned at the old man. "Oh, but there is, and we take our direction from their wisdom. You see, there is an order to all things. The Illuminati sit at the top of the food chain, just below Satan, of course."

"Of course!" Gramps nodded, his sarcasm evident. "You never heard the Illuminati were invented by a political party to undermine the credibility of the opposition."

"Nathaniel, you can choose to believe what you want. You will be dead to this world by morning and suffering your first day in the fires of eternal Hell. A comforting thought, no?"

Gramps chuckled. "Just because I'm being murdered by Satanists doesn't mean I'll be going to Hell. I do not follow your logic. I have lived at peace with nature and the spirit world my entire life. I will return to Mother Earth in one form or another to be used again to create her many miracles. What you do to my flesh will have no bearing on my eternal existence. You, though, do deserve to rot in Hell." He laughed. "Did he promise you forty virgins?"

Mason only smiled and rubbed his hands together. "I know Satan looks out for those who do his earthly work. And yes, I would expect preferential treatment. Enjoy what time you have left."

Gramps shook his head and settled back into the stinky, broken-down couch. He wasn't able to see much. Mason Matye seemed hell-bent on retribution. In his youth, Gramps would have tried to take the man. Being nearly eighty-one, the struggle would be futile. Logic told Nathaniel he had only one chance: his grandson. Jackson might figure out what was going on at the deserted McFadden place and come up with a solution.

Nathaniel sighed. Jackson was smart enough but so impulsive, often reacting without thinking. Still, his grandson might be the fatal flaw for Mason, who Gramps had to admit was a cool operator. He watched the little Frenchman making room for his guests to sit around the pentagram. He placed dozens of candles in what appeared to be strategic locations, all carefully measured to the inch. The mortician's table was placed over the north section of the pentagram. When he finished setting up the room, he sat beside Gramps.

"I must tell you, Nathaniel, I've placed a strong curse upon Jackson. He will have flu-like symptoms and be feeling weak."

Gramps remembered how Jack complained the last time he saw him about feeling ill. His eyes narrowed at Mason.

"Do you believe in curses, Nathaniel?"

Gramps nodded. "We Natives have been known to delve into the dark arts, though we are more inclined to use the magic for good. To bring two lovers together for the birth of a child. We use words to keep dark spirits at bay."

"This curse will allow me to control him when he gets close enough."

"I wish you luck, Mason." He could not stop staring at the horrible little man frowning back at him for his continued sarcasm. Gramps would have to try to fight off the incantation placed on his grandson. He had but one talisman to work with and feared the pendant around his neck would not have the strength needed.

CHAPTER FIFTY-FOUR

THE MILES CLICKED BY, but Boris was not in any hurry to return to Tampa. The thought crossed his mind that he might be better off skipping past the city and driving to Tallahassee. Though he'd been friends with Eli since childhood, Boris knew how his boss would not condone the level of failure he had attained over the past week or so. Eli would have to be especially hard on him, or else show weakness to the other men.

He pulled into a coffee shop near Sarasota, almost blind because his eyes were so tired. He needed to sit and build up his courage for what lay ahead of him in less than an hour. If he ran, Eli would hunt him down. Boris knew too much and would end up a dead man. His only hope was Eli merely shaming him by demoting him to a lesser job. The demotion would be an embarrassment the others in Eli's employ would see as a punishment. While it would be a tough pill for Boris to swallow, it would allow him the chance to redeem himself. He knew in his gut that time would come.

* * * *

Eli swallowed the sour backwash coming from his stomach. He was in a foul mood, and deservedly so. *How did the Walker scenario pick up steam rather than disappearing?* It needed to go away; it was becoming too public. Boris's failure to take the little prick out this evening could have been their last chance. Now it would be too obvious that they were behind it. News of Walker's cousin being murdered made things even more tenuous. No doubt in the young lawyer's mind Eli was the culprit. There was nothing more to do than lay low, dial back, and wait for the little jerk to come to him.

What to do with Boris? Eli knew the man would give his life for him. Still, there needed to be repercussions for failure. What they did on a daily basis required a chain of command—one seen as unfaltering. This was a tough business. The chain being broken, Boris needed to be knocked down a peg. Eli wouldn't kill him, but he needed to be tough. The hard part was the fact that Boris would condone it. He would expect no less. It would be like beating a faithful dog. He would take it ungrudgingly.

Eli needed to blow off steam and think about what to do. Standing up from his desk in the upper office, he walked out into Aversions. He'd had his eye on a new girl, Tabitha, a very petite blond who looked like a Barbie doll. She would do. He pointed at her. She looked up at him questioningly. One of the other girls was quick to whisper in her ear the nature of Eli's summons. Barbie looked back at Eli with a shocked expression, her lips tightly closed. The other girls practically had to push her to the stairs . . . to Eli.

When she made it to his side, he grabbed her elbow and ushered her to his office, closing the door behind them. "I will be nice to you today. It is Tabitha, no?"

She nodded shyly.

"You know what blow job is?"

She nodded again, slowly, a fearful look in her eyes.

That was her mistake. Eli preyed upon the fearful. Lowering his skintight pants, a nasty smile pulled apart his thin lips, exposing the extra-long top incisors drilled in by a now-deceased dentist. Eli was getting more excited, but he would only nibble on their first date. Second date? He would only draw a few drops of blood from somewhere on her body, usually warm and always wet. And he would share it with her so they both could swallow.

CHAPTER FIFTY-FIVE

JACK KICKED THE PASSENGER-SIDE floorboard as his sleeping body jolted upright to jettison him from the vivid dream.

Perry swerved, caught off guard by the sudden movement. "What the fuck, bro? Ya nearly made me fly off the freakin' highway."

Janie placed a hand on Jack's shoulder. "You okay?"

"Sorta. Sorry, guys, I experienced a dream that felt real."

Perry looked over at him. "Nightmare?"

"No. Not really. Just vivid. As if there was someone with me watching it."

Janie asked, "One of your eagle dreams?"

Perry frowned and looked over at Jack questioningly.

"Actually, yes. I followed her up in the sky. Through the clouds at first, until she flew over the McFaddens' place. I recognized it instantly. She circled several times. The abandoned buildings looked as if someone was there."

Perry sat tall behind the steering wheel, nervously tapping his fingers. "So, what's this bird? And I don't like the sound of the McFaddens."

"The flying eagle is a dream I've had since childhood. Gramps thinks I'm tied into it as my familiar who shows me things. If you can figure out what that means."

Perry brightened. "Like in Dungeons and Dragons, Harry Potter. Wizards can have a special animal friend."

"I guess so, but I suspect my mind is playing tricks with me. I'm a little delirious with this bug I'm fighting. I tell you, if it gets much worse, I'm going to ask you to check me into a hospital."

Janie put her hand on his forehead. "You're burning up, Jack."

"Told ya. I feel like shit."

"Here's our exit! Jack, you still wanna be dropped off a block from the place?"

"Yes. Stick to the plan. I don't like it, but I can't think of anything better." Jack stared out the window. "Don't let me dangle in there on my own for too long. I want you two to get as close to that garage as you can without risking those motorized cameras. When I make my move to enter the place, I'll text you, Janie."

"Okie dokie!" She fumbled around in her purse to locate her lockpicks. Taking out her handgun, she stuffed it into her jacket pocket. "I'm ready as I'll ever be."

* * * *

Perry pulled to the side of the road about 200 yards from Aversions. When he sped off, Jack was left on his own, standing on a rough sand-and-cement sidewalk. The clear sky made the half-moon look even brighter. Still hotter than hell, it was even more humid than the norm for this time of year.

No one around, Jack realized he had not been on his own over the past week and felt an urge to run. Gramps and Josh came to mind, and Jack steered away from his anger and sadness. He walked slowly, still not sure what he was going to do or say when he got to the entrance. *Never been a planner.* Jack relied on his gut instincts. Pondering that thought, he chuckled; his usual approach never did him a whole hell of a lot of good. In fact, Jack knew deep down that he had failed miserably with most of his decision-making over the past dozen years, since leaving the University of Florida.

Gramps was right! he admitted to himself. Jack Walker needed to make a better attempt at recognizing what was out of the ordinary. There was irrefutable evidence that abnormal things happened to him. By ignoring the possibility of a reason for all the crazy shit, he negated the one possible way of dealing with it. Stopping in his tracks, Jack wondered, *What if I do have a gift, or I'm a shaman, as Gramps describes himself? What if I'd accepted those truths when I came down to visit Gramps?*

He would not have left Josh on his own. He would have accepted the idea that Josh was there to protect him. *Why didn't I allow my cousin to do his job?* Jack could have given Josh a fighting chance.

What about Lolita? She begged me to listen to her. What's in it for her? Jack had put up roadblocks at every opportunity. As a kid, he never fought off the visions. Often, his ability seemed like having an unfair advantage. He knew where to find all the big snook and redfish, like shooting fish in a barrel. He never balked at his natural advantage then. *Why am I making it so difficult for myself now?*

Anger boiled on top of his high fever. He smacked his forehead. The flying eagle had always told him where the fish lay. He felt sorry for that bird. Over the years, she made an effort to tell him what she saw while flying in the sky. It should have seemed important to him. *Is Gramps the fish now?*

Trying to clear his aching head, he realized that, twice this week, he had refused to listen. Lolita was telling him shit, Gramps was telling him shit . . . *Why did I put up road blocks?* Simple; it did not seem logical. It seemed like believing in Harry Potter: *Macho football star believes in witches and warlocks.*

He knew it ran deeper, and he had rationalized it. *Did I want to embrace being Seminole and taking up all that goes with being a Native?* The truth as he faced it now was . . . *no.* While he had always taken his grandfather seriously, respecting the American Indian background, Jack envisioned his adult lifestyle as being grandiose. He could not admit to his grandfather that communing with nature, as was the way of the Seminole, did not seem good enough for Jack. Therefore, when told he shared a similar calling to use his natural abilities—the same as his grandfather and his mother—high and mighty Jack rebelled.

The truth was out and, deep down, he could not deny it any longer. Tears filled his eyes and ran down his cheeks. He felt like a little boy. His apathy allowed Josh to be murdered, and Gramps to be taken, and perhaps killed as well. Jack Walker felt like a fool.

Wiping his face, he saw his past life from a grown-up perspective. "Okay, Jack, from this day forward, you're gonna believe in mumbo jumbo." He had to laugh at the new sound of his voice making the promise.

Nearing the front door to the strip club, he saw a short line waiting to file into Aversions, giving him a few minutes to catch his breath. After his grand epiphany, he questioned why once again he was doing something totally off-the-wall crazy. Had he listened to Lolita and Gramps, he would most likely not be standing here, suffering with a god-awful flu, waiting to get his brains bashed in by a bunch of mad Russians.

The line moved steadily and, within ten minutes, he was next. Pulling out his phone, he texted Janie, *Give me five!*

CHAPTER FIFTY-SIX

"PARK HERE!" JANIE POINTED to the tight spot—close enough to the garage, yet mingled with the vehicles of other patrons so as not to give away any ill intentions should they be caught on a security camera. Janie felt like she might throw up; the anticipation of what they were embarking upon suddenly became reality. "Sure you don't want to wait in the car, Perry?"

"Look, five years ago if you said Jack Walker was going to take down a satanic cult, I would've laughed. I'm the one getting into trouble most of the time: bar fights, couple of B and Es." He squeezed into the narrow space.

"Really?"

"Yep. I went through a bad patch. Had my wallet stolen by a hooker once. I called the police and told them she robbed me at gunpoint. Next thing I knew, the cops were everywhere and I end up on WINK News. It was a mess. And no, they don't find a gun on her. Get the point."

Satisfied with his parking, Perry turned off the engine. When he smiled at Janie, he looked handsome. "No fucking way you're holding me back, Janie. I'm going with you. You need me."

Her tummy stopped flipping, and Janie was surprised at how much she'd hoped he would say as much. "Okay, Perry, glad to have you. Keep your eyes and ears open and follow my lead."

"Yeppers. Say, don't you think you should let someone know why we're heading in there? What if we're captured and no one on the planet knows we went inside the club?" Perry winked, making him look even better.

Janie smiled while she thought for a moment. "You have a point there. I'm going to send Pete, our boss, an email. He doesn't want us to be here, but he doesn't check his email regularly, so by the time Pete reads this we'll probably be in his office talking about it."

She typed: *Pete. I know you will not want to know about this, am sending note as a failsafe should we not succeed. Jack believes the Russians killed his cousin, Josh, and have taken his grandfather prisoner. We're attempting to rescue Gramps. About to enter Aversions. 9:55 . . . Janie.*

She hit *SEND*. "Done."

Perry nodded. "Can't hurt."

Jack's text came in and Janie's heart jumped to her throat. "Time's up, Perry."

He nodded, ready to jump out of the car and start their end of the plan.

She grabbed his hand and held him back to ask, "Are you a good kisser?"

Perry eyed Janie and softly asked, "Whad'ya mean?"

"I wanna be careful here. Let's set up our charade. They'll know we haven't walked through the entrance yet, so we are arriving patrons who are already hot for each other. We act excited back here in the lot as if we wanna make out. We kiss and keep looking around to locate the camera. Should only be one out here scanning the lot. You act aggressive to cover our searching for that camera; push me around the lot and keep trying to feel me up with your hand inside my dress. Be an animal—we can't fake it! Give it a minute or so, and the guy inside the club who's monitoring the lot will no doubt continue to change views."

"You're giving me wood, Janie." A sly smile crossed his face.

"Don't get any ideas. This is strictly business. Two minutes of you and me dancing with bodies entwined while we whisper and embrace our way to the garage. When you spot the camera turning away, that's where we change tactics. I want you to pull me over to the garage and turn me around. Make it look as if you're all over my backside, taking me from behind. Don't push too hard though. I'll be picking the lock on the door."

"Wood!"

She reached into her purse again and pulled out a tiny box of white breath mints. Shaking out two, she pushed one into Perry's mouth before popping the other between her lips. They both burst out laughing until she said, "Okay, let's go. *Showtime!*"

* * * *

As they strolled arm in arm away from the car, Janie pulled him back and slid her left arm to his right shoulder. Perry smiled. Grabbing her hand, he led her in a tango-walk as they both searched the poles for cameras. He stopped and pulled her close, and together they swayed in place. Laughing, she teased, "Didn't think you could dance."

"I'll show you who can dance."

He swirled her into a waltz, turning Janie in circles until she spun so fast she laughed and stepped on her own toes. She pulled him close to whisper, "I'm dizzy!"

Perry kissed her face, moving his lips down her throat, deep into the low-cut dress until she nodded—they could move again—and he led her into a slower dance. Moving in a tight embrace, she hummed an old Sinatra tune to keep time.

Perry smiled and sang the next line of lyrics, "No one knows better than I that love keeps passing me by."

Smiling, Janie sang along with him, "That's fate!"

She covered his mouth to stop him from singing. Pulling him into a wild embrace, Janie nibbled on his ear and whispered, "*Camera!*"

His eyes followed hers to the closest post to the left. They both eyed the red-glassed security camera aimed at them but laughed and smooched as if they could not keep their hands off each other. Perry danced her over, pushing her back against the cement post. Smiling like a ghoul, he spoke up for the microphone. "You're gonna get it!"

"Oh really? What am I gonna get, *smart guy*?"

He stared down, and for a second she forgot they were only acting.

Perry brushed away her hair as he bent over her. Acting half drunk, he squinted and yelled about all the fun he planned to have with her. She squealed as he covered her face with baby kisses. Playing her part, she moaned as loudly as he groaned, both declaring their enchantment with each other.

Within seconds, they heard the whine of the camera motor turning to zero in on the front end of the lot. When they looked at the entrance, a pickup was turning in. She gained her composure and ran to the garage with Perry in hot pursuit. His body-slammed her against the garage wall. When she turned to kiss him on the mouth, she placed her hand behind his head. At first his muscles tightened in surprise, until her arms encircled his neck and she pulled him closer. He relaxed into her sensual embrace and extended their play kiss into a lover's kiss. Pushing past her closed lips, he probed her mouth open with his tongue.

Janie bit down on entry as if he had entered a no-go zone. He chuckled. Still holding her tight, Perry kissed her softly until his male instinct took over again. While she might have wanted to push him off, she knew better. To do so would jeopardize their plan.

Janie stared up at Perry's sweet smile when he asked, "You ready?" Knowing what he was going to do to her, she smiled back. He lifted her up by the buttocks. They were no longer concerned about the surveillance camera as she sighed, his body slamming hers and knocking out some of her wind. When he pulled her legs up around his thighs, Janie felt his erection through his jeans. Leaning back, she kissed him even harder. His left hand reached up her skirt aggressively, while his right hand held her up to him by the cheeks of her ass.

Suddenly, she slid off to pull Perry around the corner of the building, toward the side door. Standing in front of it, he knew what to do. He pulled her shoulders back and spun her around, pushing her toward the door, face-first. Pushing her hips against him as planned, Janie relaxed and fell back on him. Perry caressed her all over as she tried to pick the lock.

Janie swooned as he softly touched between her thighs. "Perry!" she protested.

"Open the fucking door!" he growled.

"It's already open."

He burst out laughing, still pulling at her silk panties.

"No! Perry!"

"Then hurry up and open the door."

He released his hold on her to unzip the fly on his jeans.

She retrieved her lockpicks and inserted the largest prong into the keyhole. While bent over with her back to him, Janie felt his extended manhood. *Click!* She had the door open.

They slid inside the narrow opening, quickly closing it behind them. Turning around to face Perry, they both still felt their unexpected passion but knew it was the wrong time and place. Instead, she reached down and stroked him tenderly, but only once.

"Now, put that away, my sexy man, and save the thought for another time. We must hurry. I will say, though, you are one hell of a kisser and I hope the person watching had the good sense to go to another camera." Still not ready to separate, she leaned against him for another embrace and short peck. Straightening her summer dress, Perry fastened her top button.

Before they explored, Janie pulled out the flashlight from her purse and handed it to him. The garage appeared empty besides a workbench backed up to the wall facing Aversions.

Perry pointed to the bench. "That's never been used." Walking to its right side, he looked curious. "Aha!" Perry pointed to the three sets of hinges on that side. Moving to the other side, he found a padlock and proudly looked up at Janie.

"I'm on it!" Within thirty seconds, she had her picks out and the lock open.

He pulled the corner and the workbench swung out, revealing a staircase leading down.

"Pay dirt!" Janie smiled and took the first stair.

CHAPTER FIFTY-SEVEN

JACK FELT AS IF he had stepped through a wall of charged energy as he passed the guards eyeballing him at the door. The inside was lit up, the opposite of its regular shadowy effects where customers could hide. He heard and felt the live band rocking in the giant room. What caught him off guard were the couples standing around him in line. When he got to the lady in the glass booth, she spoke to him through an intercom. "Sir, do you have a Unicorn Pass?

"Sorry?"

"Single men are not allowed on Friday nights without a pass."

"I don't get it."

"Friday night is 'lifestyle' night."

He still could not figure out what she was trying to tell him and could only shrug.

"It's Swing Night."

"*Oh.* Why does that mean I can't get in?"

The lady laughed. "You do look cute enough. Can I see your ID?"

He smiled, knowing his fate was in jeopardy. "Here." He produced his driver's license.

She pulled it through the tiny slit in the bulletproof glass and slid it through a scanner. Soon enough a frown froze on her face. "Would you mind waiting to the side, Mr. Walker?"

He nodded, retrieved his license and stepped aside. *Here we GO!*

Jack swiftly found himself surrounded by four bouncers. All were as tall, or taller, than his 6'2" frame. Their jackets fit tight around muscled shoulders and arms, making him look small by comparison. The shortest of the four addressed him with a heavy Russian accent.

"Mr. Walker, what an unpleasant surprise! You were told not to come here again. Is there something about these instructions you do not understand?" Before Jack could answer, the inquisitor snapped his fingers and the other three moved around Jack for a fast pat-down. Their trained hands and fingers felt inside his clothes and swiped every part of his body before they pronounced, "He's clean."

The guy in charge rubbed the end of his clenched fist as if getting ready to punch him. Jack recognized him as the man who nearly broke his jaw the week before.

"I came to speak to Eli. It seems we've had a bit of a misunderstanding."

"Misunderstanding?" The bold voice from afar carried over the other conversations in the swanky foyer. Eli meandered through the crowd until he stepped toe to toe to Jack. "What misunderstanding do you speak of?" His mouth smiled but his eyes remained cold. "Please, come this way so we can talk about misunderstanding. We do not want to make the guests uneasy hearing about our mutual distrust. Come, I buy you drink."

Jack expected to get his head knocked off and tossed out the door. Eli offering him a friendly drink made him even more uneasy. Being friendly with Eli was not part of the plan. While he did not know what to expect, he could only hope Janie and

Perry were having luck.

Eli put his hand on Jack's back and ushered him past the security check and into the nightclub. "This is special night, swinging night. It is brilliant. See all these couples." He pointed around the room and Jack's eyes followed, picking up how sexually charged the place was. He felt it in the air. "They pay me to come here and fuck."

At this point in the night, strippers were on the tables dancing with only their G-strings for cover. The guests were coupling up in a variety of configurations; women were topless, being fondled by their male or female counterparts, and the same for the males, who were often seen in threes. Having only heard about these kinds of places, Jack's eyes were wild as he shook his fevered head.

"You see, Walker, we have special rooms out back. You want fuck some guy's wife? You pay and you take her there. Brilliant. You want threesome, foursome, whatever you want. I set you up." He waited to see Jack's innocent reaction. "Now, you and I have things to talk about. Come." He ushered Jack to a corner booth where the music was not quite as loud. Sitting, Eli waved off the brutes following him. "What drink you like?"

Jack needed a little liquid courage and did not turn it down. "Stella."

Eli looked at him. "How about shot of tequila as well? I share with you." He ordered the drinks before Jack could refuse, and turned to him. "Why do you come back here, Jack Walker? I'll tell you no lies. If I were not so curious, you would be downstairs right now getting shot. By morning, you would be at the bottom of the gulf wearing cement shoes. Talk to me."

Jack drew a heavy breath, happy the drinks had already arrived to give him a few moments to put something together. He thanked the scantily-dressed server and took a quick sip of his beer before picking up one shot glass of tequila and passing the other to Eli. "Go Gators." He tipped the shot glass with Eli and downed the fiery liquor. Eli followed right behind him.

"You no come here to talk about football. Cut to the point, or you will be taken downstairs." He smiled, but Jack sensed that something simmered behind Eli's exterior.

It would have been easier if the Russian accused him of doing shit. But the man was smart. Eli would not offer any help, letting Jack squirm as he drew a blank as to what to tell him. Taking another sip of his beer, Walker finally began, "Your computers came up clean. But I know you're selling illegal porn from this establishment."

Eli laughed. "If I had drink in my mouth, I would spit it across the table. What kind of establishment do you think we run here? Of course you find no porn on the computers *we gave you*. You think I am fucking stupid? You are in over your head, Walker."

"What about Lopez?"

"What about him? He is low level. He fucked up. Let me tell you, Walker, this is boring. What can I tell you? He got caught with some bad shit on his computer. I will not admit in court of law—it did filter through here but never took hold. It was just a pass-through. You never find that shit on our CPUs. Not safe!"

"What happened to him?"

"He got popped. I not know who did it."

For the first time that night, Jack did not believe the Russian. *What game is he playing?*

Eli changed the subject. "Like I say, Jack Walker, this is boring."

Jack tried to read the brutal man, but his face was like porcelain without a crack in it. "My cousin was murdered a few days ago."

"You want pity party, Walker. We no do it, if that is what you want. What is his name?"

"Joshua Portman."

Eli shook his head back and forth slowly for emphasis. "We no do that . . . kill family members. Although I might have wanted to kill you. There is no benefit in killing your cousin."

Staring at Eli, he saw it was true. "I believe you, but now my grandfather's missing."

Eli shook his head and laughed, "You come here? You think I tell you if I killed your cousin and grabbed your grandfather? I promise you right here, I did not do any of it."

Again, Jack believed him. A jolt of electricity passed through him as he realized that he shouldn't be here. He'd been wrong. He needed to get out. Now!

"You come back here after you call police on me. What is your purpose? Cut to the chase. I tell you yes or no. I thought we might have a little fun tonight. Like, you tell me what you want, we get that over with and we talk about your Gator days."

Jack's head swam. The illness plaguing him was taking a strong hold. He found it difficult to think clearly.

Eli showed the first signs of irritation. "Look, you are sweating all over my furniture. You have a minute left to tell me something interesting."

"Or what?"

"Your time is dwindling."

CHAPTER FIFTY-EIGHT

BORIS PULLED OFF THE highway, driving slowly along the ramp, turning onto Lumsden Drive. For his entire life, the man had never experienced a moment of failure. During his criminal career, he often got only one chance. Two chances? You were a dead man. Everyone knew that, but Boris hoped he had not overstepped his boss's lenience.

The club was always busy on a Friday. People came from all over: Orlando, Ocala, St. Pete's. He pulled in front of the garage and pushed the auto button above the rearview. He wondered if it was for the last time. Only time would tell. He loved the big BMW, a present from Eli a year back for long-standing loyalty.

The door opened and he pulled inside, like he had done a thousand times before. He realized something was not right. The workbench had been left open against one of Boris's rules. Even the police had not found the secret entrance a week back, but if it was left like that?

Boris worried their hidden agenda had been found out and cursed. Another thought crossed his mind. *What if it was not an accident?*

He stepped out of the car, careful to not make unnecessary noise. His gun was in the bottom of the canal, back at Walker's place. He cursed again. He would need to manually take care of any intruders. Boris smiled and his eyes brightened. He liked snapping necks. It was easier than one might think, especially with the great strength he possessed in his hands.

He stepped onto the descending staircase, pulling the bench door shut behind him.

CHAPTER FIFTY-NINE

LOLITA WASN'T SURE THE vehicle could handle the 110 mph it cruised at. A slight wobble in the tires made the ride most uncomfortable and nerve-racking. Hernando did not seem to have a problem with it, though she questioned whether he was in the bliss of ignorance as he operated the car.

"Maybe you should slow down to catch the next exit. You've earned your bonus."

"Okay, lady." He slowed to a more comfortable speed, the wobble not so noticeable.

"Take the first right." Within a few minutes, they pulled into Aversions' lot. She paid the driver, who happily accepted the cash on top of the credit card fee.

At the front of the place there appeared to be a long line of mostly couples waiting to get in. *What does it mean?* She ambled over, moving up with the line. With all the people around her, she easily found the opportunity to talk to a group of younger couples who stood waiting. Ignoring their questioning looks trying to size her up, Lolita asked, "Is there a special function here tonight?"

One of the girls laughed. "You don't know?"

She shook her head while reading the girl's face, which said: *What are you doing here, anyways?*

"It's lifestyle night."

The light went on. Being a very sexual being, Solomon had attended such events in his youth, though in a homosexual setting. Orgies, they'd been called back in the day.

She shook her head and asked sweetly, "They allow that here?"

"It's a club, ma'am. As long as you're a member, no one can do anything. If you don't mind me saying, I doubt they'll let you in as a single. You have to be a couple, or a guest of a couple, if you know what I mean."

Lolita smiled. "Yes, honey, I do. These big ol' bones have seen more than you can imagine. What if I bought you all a nice bottle of whatever you're drinking tonight? They do have bottle service to your table, right?"

One of the guys spoke up. "Why not? We get you in and you're on your own."

Lolita stared him down. "Don't you worry, big fella, you couldn't handle what I have to offer." When she laughed, the young man did not retort. Instead, he got a pensive look. "So, we have a deal?"

The group of six looked at each other and, when no one rejected the plan, the first girl said, "Sure, why not?"

"I'll not bother you when we're inside. Here's a hundred bones—it should take care of the bottle. I'm Lolita, by the way, and thank you."

The girl happily accepted the cash.

Eventually, they made it to the front of the line. Lolita became quite antsy, troubled about Jackson—worrying she might be too late. She could not have arrived much later than him, and was surprised not to see him in line.

The seven of them paid their fees to the woman behind the glass. Lolita was last in line and the woman stared at her and frowned.

Lolita smiled a wide, toothy grin back at the cashier. "I know what y'all's thinking. I'm a sex therapist, honey. These kids have paid me to show them a thing or two." She passed across her Lolita ID.

The cashier slid it through the scanner and shrugged. "Okay, have a good time."

Lolita separated from the young people once they approached the security room. While civil rights disallowed civilian pat-downs, guns were plentiful and the club crowds loved to bring them along. Everyone had to do the "perp walk," as it was lovingly referred to at Aversions, when the guests stepped through the metal detector. It was the same operation as the airports, except the machinery was bought secondhand and might not pick up everything.

Her companion group had already passed through security and hit the stairs to the night club. Lolita heard them clapping and congratulating each other. They finally got inside. Lolita knew the drill and stepped onto the foot patterns on the floor, following them while the large machinery got busy winding around her body. She smiled, seeing the man with the wand standing at the end of the line. Although he was so much shorter than her, he never got on his tiptoes to wand her hair. Instead, he bent to wand her shoes. Lolita took a deep breath as she was cleared to go in. If she'd been caught with a gun, she would be facing big time. Three strikes and Solomon was a lifer.

She entered the massive club, filled with gyrating, dancing couples along with the strippers on multiple stages and tabletops. The entire scene seemed tantalizing and hedonistic to Lolita. Still, she had to ignore it and focus on faces to find Jackson. It took her a good ten minutes to locate Walker, and to her shock she found him sitting with a man who fit the description of Eli Romanov. Not knowing what else to do, she ordered an iced tea and tried her best to find the ladies' room. There was another line there and it took her longer than expected. When she returned and tried to blend in with the wild crowd, it was not easy—a big and tall man dressed as a female.

CHAPTER SIXTY

JANIE AND PERRY STEPPED carefully down the stairs. A motion-detector light flickered on as they reached the bottom. In front of them was a heavy steel door with a coded entry lock. She cursed under her breath. "Damn!" There was a keyhole on the lever. These types of locks could be a bugger to open. She got on her knees, knowing it might be a finicky mechanism.

Jamming the lock with picks she said, "That was quite the performance back there."

"You made it all the easier, Janie. Never kissed an older woman." He looked boyishly shy. "Now, in my mind, I know we wanted it to look believable."

Janie blushed. "A good hard kiss might have sufficed?"

"I didn't detect a lot of resistance coming from you."

"The situation was complicated. I couldn't—"

"I'll remember that in the future."

Janie probed with the picks. She smiled. She had not minded

what took place between her and Perry, though she did feel like a wild cougar during the act. *Click.* She turned the handle and the door opened.

"There ya go, girl." Perry almost clapped.

"Not you, too. Don't call me *girl*."

"Whad'ya mean?"

"You and Jack, you both listen to too much country music."

"It's not so much that; it's just how we talk."

She lowered her voice. "We need to be quiet now." She opened the door to a thirty-foot, lit hallway with two doors on both walls and a single door at the end. They moved quietly and tried both doors on the right, which proved to be storage closets—one full of files and the other loaded with cleaning materials.

"I'd love to get my hands on those files," Janie commented, and Perry nodded.

The first door on the left led to a massive room. She flipped on the light to get a better look. The space was full of props, sets, beds, S and M paraphernalia, along with lighting for photography and filming. Farther into the room, there were a couple of offices behind large glass windows, full of monitors and computers. The far wall was a little out of context with the rest of the area, being made from concrete blocks.

She peeked through the other two doors. The one on the end appeared to be a staircase heading upward. "Jack was right," she muttered. The next door opened up to a large, opulent office with a mahogany desk. The walls were filled with monitors linked into the building's surveillance system. Three other screens were tuned in to various sporting events. The fresh smell of cigarette smoke indicated someone had been here recently.

She returned to the room with the cameras and sets. Pulling Perry in behind her, Janie closed the door and explained, "I don't know what it is, Perry, but I don't think prisoners would be held close to the brains of an operation. That room has to be Eli's private office. We don't want to get caught in there. It'll be game over."

"Okay. I'm getting a little creeped out. You think they make snuff films in here?"

"Do not want to think about that, but sex films for sure." She stared at the stone wall. "That damn wall looks out of place."

"Yeah! It reminds me of *Lord of the Rings* when Gandalf and the fellowship end up at the door to the Mines of Moria."

"What?"

"No, really, if these dudes want to use prisoners for snuff films, whatever, they want the product close." Perry walked closer to the wall and Janie followed. "Look at that." He traced a line in the sandstone brick. Then he found another four feet over, and one running across the top. "That's a door. It's not well hidden, which normally isn't a problem if you're not worried about close inspection. I feel like I should be making a few mighty incantations like Gandalf. Hey, look at this." He pointed to a solitary block with no mortar around it. He pushed it and the door swung inward.

Janie looked up at Perry and planted a sweet kiss on his lips. "I didn't bring you along for no reason."

"Help where I can, my queen."

Janie pushed the section of wall as far as it would go. Stepping in, she pulled Perry along with her. Her shoulder against the door, she pushed the lock mechanism shut behind them. "We don't need any surprises."

Perry nodded, looking around at what appeared to be an actual dungeon. The only light, a small nightlight, was plugged in the wall near the entrance.

It took a moment for Janie's eyes to adjust, but the room was a large rectangle, with jail cells along one wall filling up most of the room. "Hand me that flashlight. If they took Gramps, this is where he'll be!"

Janie turned the light on and scanned the first cell. She nearly jumped back into the wall as a scruffy female with catlike reflexes pounced at her. Landing on all fours, the scruffy creature was only inches from the bars when she started snarling.

Perry steadied Janie, grabbing her shoulder. "What the hell is that?"

The drawn-up face in the cage softened when she heard Perry's voice.

The limited light revealed a dirty face with pretty features and eyes as black as coal. She watched the two of them without moving.

Janie moved to the next cell, which appeared to be empty, but she couldn't be sure, as there were several old blankets on the cot in the far corner. She pulled out her lockpicks.

"Careful," cautioned Perry.

The feline answered in a Transylvanian accent, "The cell is empty."

Janie turned to meet her eyes, gesturing toward the last cell with the flashlight.

"The man in there is in bad shape. He hasn't spoken in a day."

"How long has he been in there?"

"Several days, but it is hard to tell how many. There are no windows, as you can see."

Janie walked over to the third cell. Gramps had only been missing for a little over a day. *Couldn't be him*, and yet her heartbeat doubled as her mouth went dry. A man lay on the cot against the far wall. She smelled infection, wrinkling her nose. She took the picks out again and within seconds had the door unlocked and open. She walked over and peered at his face.

"Christ, it's Robert Lopez!"

"Who's that?" asked Perry.

"Our fucking client who's been missing for nearly a week." She lifted the sheet off him. His pants were still on, but he'd probably been shot in the leg. The swollen wound threatened to burst open his dress slacks. She used the pen knife on the other side of her picks to cut the pants above the wound, pulling the lower part off his leg. "Man alive, that's bad. If he doesn't get to a hospital, he'll be a goner. In fact, it may be too late as it is." Lopez's breathing sounded shallow, almost nonexistent.

The caged female was eager to ask, "You know this man?"

"If *you'd* been paying attention, you'd know. I do know this man."

"No need for sarcasm. Just trying to find out which side you're on. Is it the Russians'?"

"Hell no!" Janie blurted out.

"Can you get me outta here?"

"Are you with the Russians?"

"If *you'd* been paying attention, *you'd* see I'm locked up by the Russians!"

"Okay. I had that coming. Will you help us get out of here? Do I have your word?"

The female looked calmer and nodded.

Janie pulled the gun out of her pocket, took off the safety, and handed it to Perry. "If she makes one wrong move, you shoot her in the head."

Perry took the gun and nodded. His stern expression showed he would do just that.

The caged female stood with a smile. Wearing nothing but a bikini bottom, her firm perky breasts were exposed as she rose. "You won't need to shoot me."

When Janie opened her cell door, the prisoner stepped out calmly.

Janie took off her own jacket and handed it to her. "Do you have a name?"

"Susan."

"Okay, Susan, we're going to get you out of here." Turning to Perry she said, "We can't move that man without killing him. He needs an ambulance." She pulled out her cell.

Susan put her hand out as if to stop Janie. Perry pointed the gun at Susan's head. "Nope, don't do that. Back away."

Although Susan complied, her smirk held a challenge. She could avoid his best efforts to shoot her . . . if she wanted.

Janie hit up Peter Robertson's number.

Peter picked up almost instantly. "Janie, what the hell? Where have you two been? I've been worried. Plus, I have some important information."

"Hang on, Pete. We found Lopez!"

Silence.

"*Really*?"

"Yes, we did, locked in a dirty cell. Looks like the Russians shot him at the car dealership and took him back to Aversions to die."

"Aversions? I told you two to stay away from that place. The DA will have a fit. This is against the law. Is Jack with you?"

"Sorta."

"What do you mean *sorta?* You do know Jack's on his way to getting disbarred."

"Calm down, Pete. Jack figures the Russians killed Josh and now his grandfather's missing. We're trying to find his gramps before it's too late."

Peter sighed, "Did you find Mr. Portman?"

"No. Not yet, anyway."

"There isn't going to be a 'not yet.' I'm calling the DA, even if it is late, and we're going to get the police in on this. How is Lopez?"

"Lopez is in bad shape, close to dying. I wouldn't dare move him."

"Okay. How'd you get in there and find him in the cell?"

"Perry and I sorta backed our way in; long story, and we'll laugh about it later."

Peter's voice rose. "Look, I want you to get out of there. Now. I'm calling the police and an ambulance. I need you outside, so you can direct them to Lopez. We'll need to get a judge to grant a warrant ASAP. Won't be easy and could take some time. For now, leave Lopez where he is."

"Okay, Pete, we'll get out of here."

* * * *

Boris looked into the film room. He found it strange the lights were on at this time of night if they were not shooting scenes. He pulled his head back and went to see if Eli was in his office. After knocking, he walked in and looked around. While no one was there, Eli had been there recently because the room smelled of cigarettes. The televisions and monitors were all on. *Strange.* There was an odd pull at the back of his mind; before he went upstairs, he wanted to have another look in the film room. Something appeared out of place.

CHAPTER SIXTY-ONE

"THE GUESTS ARE ARRIVING, Nathaniel!" Mason kicked the man's shoe to wake him. "For someone who is about to suffer and die soon, the old Indian sure likes to snooze a lot."

Little did Mason know, Gramps had not been snoozing. The old Indian had been doing his best to relay psychic messages. While he did not know whether they were being picked up or even noticed, Nathaniel had no better way to use the time left to him. At one point, he felt he connected with Lolita. The connection was fuzzy on her end and he was not sure. There was another, but, again, the link was unclear. Most psychics did not practice spiritual connection these days. It remained more of a Native ritual, often discussed but not used or even believed in anymore. Plus, it required all the planets and stars to align. Gramps had only connected with animals throughout his life. Still, ancient lore promised connectivity through the spirit world to all creatures, living and dead.

Gramps sighed, sad because he had failed. Instead, he created a psychic note to be delivered to his grandson upon his death. Nathaniel did not want his Jackson to feel guilt and regret over the loss of both his grandfather and cousin.

When he opened his eyes, Mason was smiling at him.

"You sleep too much, Nathaniel. You take the fun out of killing you. I would like to see you wide awake, shedding a few tears about what lies ahead. Most men beg for their lives, or beg for a quick death. How humanity hates to suffer. Keep this up and I'll suspect you might be one who loves the *pleasure of pain*. If that is true—and I dearly hope it is—you and I will stay strong and go long, rejoicing our pleasures together!" Mason's face quivered with glee as he tried to catch his breath. "I cannot wait to administer to your dark passions. Masochists and zealots last the longest. I bet you did not know that. We do respect both for joining into the rhythm of the ritual to obtain their own passion. If you can last, Nathaniel, you will be in for a real treat before you draw your last breath. A surprise awaits! I cannot wait to show it to you. Let's hope your grandson, Jackson, has a bit more life left in him when he arrives."

"What makes you think he's coming?" Gramps became interested.

"An *augury,* Nathaniel. I have seen it! He will be present. Maybe too late to save you, but I feel we will be blessed with his presence. Better late than never. You see, we need to sacrifice both of you between the hours of midnight and one—the witching hour, of course."

Nathaniel shook his head. "However, much I do not like what you say, I must agree, that hour holds special power over the spirits."

Mason gave Gramps a little wicked grin. "I appreciate your concurrence."

There was a sharp knock on the door to the workshop. Mason went over to it.

Nathaniel looked around. Mason had lit all of the candles and the large room was awash with a golden glow. At the door opening, he held his breath. His heart sank as three robed men stepped inside. Mason bowed his head to them in respect.

"Gentle greetings to you, fellow man-brothers!"

"*Ave Satanas*," they responded as one.

"Please, make yourself comfortable. I've placed wine and hors d'oeuvres on the table by the deck."

Gramps saw a bar and food set up on an old chopping block where Jimmy McFadden had often cut up people.

One of Mason's guests appeared at least seventy years old, bearing a wizened appearance. "Mason, the Church appreciates the sacrifices you have gone through in the name of our Deity, Lord Satan. The death of Henrietta LePley was a blow to our fellowship. Though she'd only attained the level of Witch, she held more power over men than any Magus. She acted as a major benefactor and our hand in the sugar and cattle industry here in Florida, which is now suffering. The bleeding hearts and their salt water estuaries will win out over our interests if we don't regain control of South Florida."

"I agree, though I'm not familiar with those politics. I do thank you for coming all this way from Poughkeepsie, Your Grace. We are blessed to have the benefit of a High Priest of the Church present. I look forward to your participation in the Mass."

"It will be my honor. Your perseverance and dedication to our alignment is worth the trip here, Mason. Besides, your weather is much nicer than Upstate New York." The high priest turned his head, noticing Nathaniel tied up on the old couch.

Mason caught the man's thought and answered, "Our sacrifice tonight. Chief of the local Seminole tribe, and Magus."

The High Priest's eyes widened and he looked impressed.

Gramps had a strong urge to rub the horrible little man's face into the floorboards but remained calm, hiding his anger. If he died tonight, he wanted to retain some dignity.

CHAPTER SIXTY-TWO

"I'M GLAD I CALLED the authorities in on you. You deserved it. We may not have accomplished much with their search, but now your name and business will be on their radar."

Eli smiled. "You suddenly grow balls, Walker?"

Jack tried his best to smile. "Perhaps I have. Here's the deal. I'm willing to dismiss the pornography angle, Eli. What I really want to know is what happened to my cousin and my grandfather."

"Now, you bore me again. Not only do you bore me, but you *really* fucking bore me. I could put naked ladies on our laps while we talk about Sugar Bowl." He pulled out the black Glock under his hip and placed it on the table. "Is that it, Walker? You drag me from my sports to talk about nothing. You come to waste my time. I was getting nice blow job." He shook his head. "The girl, she was nervous. You'll enjoy this, Walker. The girls here, they no want to do blow jobs. They are smart and charge the customers the most money for a lick and a promise. Those silly men—and women—pay their price to get it. But girls know . . . when it comes to the Big Boss, they must do a good blow job for no money. It must seem like a gift they are giving me. When you are boss, it is best you take away their innocence, and then?" Eli gave Jack a devilish smile. "You own them!"

He could tell Eli was baiting him. Jack had done his best to prolong their conversation but was now at a loss besides talking about fucking football. *What the hell.* Jackson Walker, ex-jock and newly-appointed barrister, looked straight at Eli and smiled.

"Like the blow jobs we got from the football groupies. You could get three of those cuties at a time if you wanted, Eli. Difference is, they fucking wanted it!"

"Three at a time? Come on, Walker. You imply there are females who want blow jobs?"

"Straight truth, didn't you just tell me you enjoyed the fact they were nervous?"

"Yes. But I always jerk them around. Give them a jolt of fear so they want to please me. Why else would females do blow jobs? What do you say? Treat them like ponies. Give them the carrot or the stick. Fear of a beating or lots of cash?"

"What do you want to talk about? Gators, NFL, after-game orgies with underage girls?"

"I get the feeling you are stalling me, Walker. You have a bug on you?" Eli flushed at the idea of being played. "You come with me." He motioned Jack off to the right and pushed him to a back door with a keyless access.

Jack's heart pounded and he damned himself for not making an attempt to leave the club. Instead, he antagonized a man who could not believe young females would offer blow jobs unless they were coerced or paid. Now, he had no choice. He had to follow Eli. If he made a mad dash, he would be taken down in seconds. Evading tackles had never been one of his strong points. Eli pushed close to Jack, the gun in the small of his back. They approached the door and Eli pressed the five-digit code to give them access to a large office.

Jack did not see or hear it coming. All he heard was the

close-range retort of a firearm that made him blink. Opening his eyes, he saw Eli's brains splattering against the door and onto the office floor. Before Jack could process the audio and visual messages beating on his brain, his body was manhandled and pushed into the office along with Eli's shaking corpse.

* * * *

Like a hawk, Lolita kept her sharp eyes on Jackson. She read both of their expressions and could almost follow their conversation, which went from grimace to smiles. Jackson did not look comfortable. She sensed the tension between them and knew, when Eli put his gun on the table, Walker was in dire trouble. Reaching behind her high wig, Lolita opened the snap, the small handgun falling into her oversized hand. She snapped the secret space closed and it was all done without anyone noticing. Turning back, she spotted Eli's face burning bright red. When he stood up and pushed Jackson to leave the table, Lolita knew it was time to act. She moved fast to get behind them. Eli's gun was pressed into Jack's back. Her senses lit up, knowing it was time to kill Romanov. She never debated whether death might be necessary for such a cruel man. Lolita had already seen the answer: Eli Romanov needed to die, hard and fast.

Moving through the crowd, she easily got behind Eli as he entered the code. She waited for the door to unlock. When it opened, Lolita raised her gun within an inch of Eli's head and held on tight, because her small firearm had one hell of a kick. Without recourse, she pulled the trigger and dropped the Russian just as all three of them moved through the doorway. Grabbing both men, she used all of her great strength and energy to heave the two down a set of stairs opening to a brightly lit office. The door behind them was already closing electronically after their quick entry. The sound of gunfire caused a screaming riot behind them, but the chaotic sounds stopped once the door clicked shut.

Lolita was sure she'd seen a few of Romanov's men, who would have seen the shooting and would be at the door in seconds. She closed a second door at the bottom of the stairs and jammed a chair under the door lever, hauling Romanov's shaking body on top of it. It wouldn't hold for long.

She looked at Jack, who had not quite registered what happened. "We're both alive, Jackson."

"What?" Jack had not seen it coming, but he was certainly glad Lolita was there to help him. "A bit excessive. What are you doing here?"

Lolita looked at him, the large whites of her eyes bulging from the exertion. "You'd have been deader than dead if he had another few minutes. I wouldn't have been able to get through that door, and we'd never see you again."

"What did you mean by 'we're both alive'?"

"My vision, remember? From before we met. We were both in danger. One of us dies."

"We're still in danger." He pointed at the dying Eli Romanov. "There's one good thing to come from this."

"You need to disappear, Jackson. If you want to keep your career going, you can't be seen here if the police come."

Someone began pushing on the door, which would soon dislodge the chair. They heard several voices at the bottom of the stairwell. "Janie and Perry are below. I acted as a distraction so they could sneak in the back way to the basement, which we think is below. They're looking for Gramps."

"Think? I hate to tell you this, Jackson, but your gramps isn't here."

Jack frowned. "Hold your gun on that door. How do you know?" Jack was confused and tried to think clearly. "If there is a way down from here, it would have to be connected to the other staircase. If there is another basement, it has to be below this one."

"Let's get out of here and I'll explain later."

Jack moved close to the mirrored wall beside the door as the chair bulged, ready to snap with the weight of several men behind it. Noticing handprints on the glass, he pushed the mirror and it clicked open on a hinge; behind it was a secret door, but it had a keyless entry. "Dammit. Gun."

Lolita shoved it into his palm. "Hold on tight!"

He fired two shots into the other door. The pushing stopped, but the yelling escalated. He turned back and fired two shots into the lock. The device exploded into a pile of screws and twisted metal. "Come on."

Lolita followed him through the doorway, which led to another set of stairs going down. She pulled the mirror shut behind them.

CHAPTER SIXTY-THREE

BORIS SURVEYED THE ROOM. Nothing looked out of place, except the light had been left on, and it was late. As he turned to leave, the secret panel leading to the dungeon slowly pushed out. He heard gunshots from up the stairs. He cursed the fact that he had lost his pistol, and hid behind a prop used to depict a palm tree on a sunny beach. He couldn't afford to be stuck between two potential adversaries and hoped it was Eli coming from the dungeon, but it seemed unlikely.

* * * *

Once the stone cleared the edge of the wall, it swung sideways on two large hinges. Perry prodded Susan ahead of him with the muzzle of Janie's handgun. Janie followed last, leaving the stone door open. She wanted the police to be able to easily find the dungeon and Lopez.

Janie caught the movement out of the corner of her eye but

was too late to react. A large man brandishing a small knife emerged from behind a beach scene prop. He brought his fists down hard on Perry's forearm, instantly freeing the gun from his grasp to fall to the floor. The man followed up with an elbow to Perry's jaw, and Perry dropped to the floor like a dead weight, his head hitting hard.

Janie dove for the gun, getting a hand on it, but their assailant stomped his boot on it. She knew one or more of her bones were broken. The man kicked her ribs, launching her thin body a few feet to slam into the brick wall. The wind knocked from her lungs, Janie could only groan.

Before he could turn back to grab the gun, Susan kicked it halfway across the big room. Crouching low, her feral eyes stared up at the man. He did not move and looked wary of her.

"So, Boris, I've been waiting for this day." She followed his every move, mirroring it with her own.

Footsteps approached the doorway.

* * * *

Jack and Lolita came through another doorway at the bottom of the stairs. There was no lock on it. It led to a fairly chic office filled with dozens of television screens and monitors and at least five separate computer stations.

"Pay dirt!" yelled Jack.

They both ran for the only other exit. Their pursuers were hot on their tail, their footsteps clamoring down the staircase. Finding themselves in another hallway, Lolita rolled her eyes. She was already huffing and puffing. Jack felt no better, still suffering from the flu, or whatever it was that ailed him.

Jack heard a commotion from the next room, specifically a woman's voice. He stepped into the doorway with Lolita's gun raised, ready for anything. A large man squared off with a rough-looking woman. They saw Janie crumpled against the far wall and Perry motionless on the ground, blood seeping from the corner of his mouth.

Jack stepped into the room, waving the Ruger .380. "Okay, who's on our side?"

The distraction was all Susan needed. She sprang like a cat and attacked Boris, one of her thumbs landing in his right eye socket. She wrapped her legs around his chest and grabbed the back of his head, driving her thumb into his skull. He howled in pain and utter fear, trying to pry her off him. She was relentless and drove her other thumb into his left eye, ripping the eyeball out of its socket. The massive man fell to his knees, then toppled to his side, still trying to shake his assailant free.

Janie yelled as best she could, trying to catch her breath. "She's with us . . . I think." Climbing unsteadily to her feet, Janie stumbled over to where Susan had kicked her gun and picked it up.

The sound of running down the hallway grabbed their attention. Jack moved beside the door with Lolita's gun pointed and ready. Janie made it to within a few feet when three men, all carrying guns, charged into the room, no doubt following the loud sounds of Boris wailing in agony. Janie dropped to one knee, her gun pointing at the first man.

Jack had to yell above Boris, "Drop your weapons!"

He placed the barrel of his gun against the head of the last man to enter. Feeling the gun and hearing the screams of pain, that last man dropped his gun. It took the first man a moment to compute what was happening. He made the fatal mistake of raising his weapon at Janie. She and Jack fired simultaneously and the man staggered, dropping to the floor.

Now, Janie aimed her gun at man number two. Sensing he was also in the crossfire, number two dropped his gun and went to his knees.

Jack wasted no time, yelling above Boris, "On your bellies, hands behind your backs!" Janie picked up the loose weapons while the men followed Jack's orders.

The screams ended suddenly. Jack and Janie saw Susan wipe the blade Boris had been carrying. His throat was cut from ear to ear.

"The bastard deserved it. Now, if you don't mind, I'm getting out of here."

"Hey, not so fast," Jack said as he went to check on Perry.

Janie said, "Give her all the money you have in your wallet

and let her go."

Within a few seconds, the exotic woman named Susan smiled and was through the door, running for the back exit.

Perry began to come around. After being knocked cold from the slam to his jaw, the bruising was coming up quickly. There could be a break.

"Okay, what now?"

Lolita exclaimed, "If you don't get your white ass outta here right now, you're gonna be up to your eyeballs in cops. Your grandfather's life may depend on you getting to him."

"What about these guys?" He pointed to the men lying on their stomachs.

Janie said, "Let's get them into the dungeon."

Jack looked at her, ready to ask.

"No time to explain. Just get' em moving."

Jack got them on their feet and through the stone doorway. Janie opened all the cells and Jack ushered them inside one. Janie slammed the door, the lock clicking into place.

Jack looked over at the last cell where Lopez still lay. "Gramps!"

"No. Lopez," Janie answered.

"What?"

"He's not in good shape. I've called Peter and he's getting a warrant. The police have been called as well as an ambulance. Now, I should stay here and help clean up this mess. The cops won't know where to go. Perry's in no shape to move, so you two need to get out of here."

Lolita nodded. "She's right, the cops will be here any moment."

Jack whispered in Janie's ear, "And Lolita blew Romanov's brains out in the night club."

"Geez, don't tell me any more. The police could already be here."

"And there could be a mass exodus from the club happening as we speak."

"Good, a little confusion couldn't hurt."

"I think I've had enough confusion for one night. Give me the three guns from the thugs."

Janie handed them to him. He gave one to Lolita, stuffing the other in his pocket. He went to Perry and removed his car keys from his pocket. "Where did you park?"

Janie responded, "Against the back fence, directly behind the garage."

He looked at Janie one last time. "So, Gramps wasn't here?"

Lolita said, "I told you he wasn't."

"Yeah, I have to start giving this hocus-pocus some credence. Where is he then, Lolita?"

"Only you can tell us that, Jackson."

* * * *

Jack and Lolita carefully made their way to the back entrance through the garage. He eyed the 7 Series Beamer wistfully.

Lolita cut off his thought of taking it. "They'll see us leaving. Keep walking."

She would have been correct, as the parking lot was already full of panicked partiers, and the blue-and-red lights of several police cruisers flashed by the front entrance.

They needed to get out of there. Without running, they found Perry's car and within a few minutes were following a steady stream of vehicles out of the busy parking lot.

CHAPTER SIXTY-FOUR

"THE WARRANT'S BEEN EMAILED to the Tampa police. They should arrive soon."

"Warrant or no warrant, Pete, they're already here."

"What are you talking about, Janie? The call went in only minutes ago."

She paused, trying to figure out how best to explain to Peter what had taken place. "Things got a little crazy. Eli is dead, as are a few of his henchmen in the other room. We found Eli's secret office, where I'm sure we'll find all the porn to prove it is being stored and shipped from this place."

"Eli Romanov is dead? Let me guess—Jack?"

"Nope! He's clean on this one. The palm reader, Lolita, killed Eli up in the nightclub to save Jack's life. Eli had a big gun pressed into Jack's back and was rushing him downstairs. She got behind the Russian with her small gun and put a bullet through his head."

"Pardon my French, but who the hell is the damned palm reader?"

"Lolita. It's got something to do with Jack's grandfather and their spiritual connection."

"The woman shot Eli Romanov and now he's dead? Where is she?"

"Actually, turns out *she* is a *he* and *they* are with Jack. They got outta here before the police arrived and are on their way to search for Jack's granddad, Nathaniel Portman."

"You're not making any sense, Janie."

"Sounds crazy, but we'll hammer it all out when the lurid details are in front of us. It does sound like we might be able to find some resolution in the Lopez case."

Peter paused. "I was contacted by City Star Productions. They upped their retainer to find out what happened to Lopez, and to push harder at the Russians."

"How much?"

"Fifty grand. *American*!"

"Easiest money you've ever made."

"Maybe. I still don't like some of the implications, and I really don't like Jack taking off like that without talking with the police. He's beginning to show he can get a bit squirrely."

"True. He gets confused and headstrong. So do I, and a lot of crap's been fired at him this last week. There've been some strange occurrences that might not be related to the Russians. While Jack still figures they killed Josh, and kidnapped Gramps—here's where Lolita comes in—she's saying her psychic senses scream about a revenging entity out to raise hell for past transgressions. In fact, Gramps got the same message from his Seminole spirit guide."

"I vaguely remember Jack telling me over a few drinks how he'd been threatened by the head of the Church of Satan, in the prison van."

"Yes. We checked that angle. Supposedly, Mason Matye committed suicide over a week ago while still in prison."

"A bit of a coincidence?"

"I don't know, but Jack and Lolita were outta here like a bat outta hell."

He chuckled, "That's the second time the word *hell* has come up."

She took a deep breath. "Pete, can you call the police again and ask them to meet me and Perry at the garage behind Aversions? I'm headed out with Perry, who looks like *hell*. His face is swelling from his broken jaw and Lopez could be on his last leg. If you want any sort of resolution on this case, you want Lopez alive, able to make a statement."

"Okay. Are you all right, Janie?"

"A couple of broken fingers, but my gut's not swelling from a drop kick that sent me across the room. I'm hoping the paramedics are outside with the cops."

* * * *

Janie opened up the side door to the garage and found herself greeted by about ten squad cars and more than twenty officers standing behind their open doors with guns drawn.

A strong voice hollered out to them, "Disarm and drop your weapons!"

All eyes and handguns panned to her. Perry tried to stay on his feet, showing no appearance of being a threat. Janie held up her damaged hand and retrieved her handgun with the other, pulling it out of her pocket by the muzzle.

"Put the gun down."

She dropped it on the cement floor, holding both hands over her head. "I'm with the good guys," she yelled out. "We need paramedics. *NOW*!"

CHAPTER SIXTY-FIVE

"I WAS WITH YOU, Jackson. You know that I was. You had to sense my presence."

Jack was not willing to admit it out loud. He could only go so far with accepting the unknown. To admit to Lolita, or anyone, that he shared a vision would be twice as bad as admitting he actually had a vision. But he did know someone else had been there.

Lolita shuffled her feet on the passenger's side, trying to get comfortable. The Chevy Cruise designers did not have extra-large people in mind. "If you're not willing to admit it, Jackson, let me tell you what I envisioned."

"Let it go, Lolita." Jack took the onramp toward Naples.

"You're heading back to Ft. Myers. You know where you're going."

"Let's just say I have a premonition."

"I saw the bird fly along the muddy river. It's dark. She veers toward an old, rickety dock between a rundown plantation house and an old slaughterhouse sitting on the river bank."

Jack stayed quiet and listened.

"You were there with me."

Jack flipped on his phone, which took a few seconds to boot. He nearly swerved off the road when he eyed his first text: a picture of Gramps, bound on an old wooden floor. He knew that floor. The caption read: *You owe us, Jack Walker*. It was signed, *Mason*.

He passed the phone to Lolita. She gasped. "Who is Mason?"

"He was the leader of the Church of Satan." Jack explained all that had happened between him and the Frenchman.

"Are you willing to admit now how I could know the place?"

"Okay, I am. I'm guessing . . . I simply don't want to admit it."

"I won't tell you again that you have psychic abilities, as I know it upsets you."

"Right now, I have to concentrate on saving my grandfather." Jack texted Mason back, one eye on the road, and asked, "Where?"

"You should not text and drive."

Jack turned to give her an evil look. "I could simply stop and let you off in Sarasota. Are you going to keep badgering me? I don't need your help."

"Yes, you do. I've seen it. You haven't managed to get rid of me up to now. Do you think I'm going to let go now that we're at crunch time? You'll have to manually pull this fat ass out the car—and it is fat, I will tell you."

Jack shook his head, the vestiges of a smile forming. There was something he liked about the sincere creature sitting next to him. His warm thought disappeared to be replaced by cold reality. Jack needed to know what awaited him.

"I have to find Gramps. Since you're the only one here, and I can't seem to get rid of you, maybe you could help make sense of all this."

"Hallelujah! This is what I've been trying to do for the past week and a half. Now, I'll only do this if you promise to open up to the fact that there is more going on here than the reality in front of your nose, and that spirits do exist. They're not as strong and as influential as what people think. Believe it or not, Jackson, they have been trying to help you. You create bad karma with them and the law of attraction can turn into the law of detraction. You've been putting up a bloody dam and it's hurt the people you love."

Jack gripped the steering wheel even harder. "I'll be honest, I've had those thoughts over the past two days and I've been trying to reconcile what you've been saying. Maybe I can see what you're talking about and maybe it exists. I'd have to be blind at this point not to. I've rebelled against the notion that I'm strong in the power, and that one day I'll be my people's shaman like my grandfather, like my mother. All I want to do is hunt, fish, go to work and have a good time. I can do all that on my own and be perfectly happy."

"You should have been a country singer, Jackson."

"I suppose so, but I can't hold a note."

Lolita shuffled around again, still trying to find a comfortable position where her feet would not fall asleep. "Those days may come, but you have been grossly negligent up to this point. Look what it caused. I've talked to your grandfather about most of what transpired. We have a connection, and I'm worried about him as well. I do not need to tell you that if you'd heeded his advice and let your cousin, Josh, keep an eye on you—"

"You don't need to remind me. I've thought about Josh and my grandfather every day."

"Somehow, you opened up to the evil spirits lurking on the other side of reality. Tell me about your past. I hear you were a pretty good football player, leading your college team to a bowl game, where you won. What happened after that, Jackson?"

He did not want to go over the messy details, having already done so a thousand times in his head. "I became a drug addict. It ruined my professional career. It ruined me and I became weak."

"You turned off the faucet. You were no longer in tune with the good spirits."

"Gramps has said as much."

"They don't always come to you with life-changing scenarios, like what is happening now. They can come in subtle ways. People can sense things in others, but most don't know why. The spirits are always in tune. This is the world in which they live. You have an aura, like all of us. If your aura fades or darkens, other souls will shun you. Your aura is bright right now. Believe me, Jack, I see it. It shines emerald green."

"I take it that's good?"

"Let's not get too carried away; it's promising."

"Let's say I'm on board with all of what you and Gramps tell me. How's it going to help get him out of whatever situation he's caught up in?"

Lolita pondered her words. "You have to be wholeheartedly committed, or it will be like bringing a knife to a gunfight. The entity who detains your grandfather is evil incarnate."

"Yeah, he's the fucking head of the Church of Satan."

Lolita closed her eyes and nodded. "Mason is his name?"

"Yes. He's the one who texted the picture of Gramps tied up. And you know what? I recognize the floorboards and the couch."

"We both saw the vision of the bird. You know where this is located." She stared at Jack.

"The McFadden Estate." He did not want to admit it because the place brought back so many horrific memories. Still, he knew it to be true. As much as he hated to admit it, the bird never led him astray.

"Darlin', I have to ask you, what on God's green earth did you do to have that enemy?"

"It's quite the story. The long and the short is I got wrangled into doing a few things for the matriarch of the Church of Set, Henrietta LePley."

"I knew of the woman—strong with the spirits."

"I was fooled and ended up being captured by the McFadden brothers: badass swamp people. I ended up killing all of them. The old woman was shot when the police arrived at the plantation."

"Mason?"

"He was on the side, so I thought, but evidently he played a big part in the South Florida cult, offering support from the national Church of Satan."

"Are you leaving anything out?"

"Yes. Mason swears that I made a deal with the Devil."

"That's a strong statement, Jackson. Is it true? Did you?"

"Maybe, halfheartedly. I'm not sure."

Lolita rubbed her forehead as if she did not want to bear bad tidings. "The followers of Satan take our halfhearted proclamations seriously. Tell me about it."

"Henrietta made the statement. She promised me a walk-on tryout with New Orleans."

"Yes, and there's always something that you need to give back in return. This is how the Devil works, and believe me, he exists and his followers will do anything to please him."

"I promised to fulfill a few requests for her from time to time. I was to look after Sarah Courtney, and treat her well. I ended up having to take some cash up to Clewiston, where I was fingered for a double murder."

"The Devil never asks for little favors. If you cross him, he will see his enmity through to the end. Tell me more about Mason."

"We got into a pretty good tussle inside the prison van. It came about after he made a vow to avenge the breaking of my deal and the deaths of the members of the Church of Set."

"How many did you kill?"

"Six, to the best of my knowledge. There's the Freshwater Bill as well. I think, ultimately, I was being used to bring down Senator Hunter, who was out to get Big Sugar and the cattle industry, who not coincidentally were backed partially by Henrietta."

"You stirred up one big can of whoop ass. And look at you now. You don't look well at all. I suspect they may have put a curse on you."

"What? Now that kind of shit I'll never believe. I have the flu."

"Curses are real and can have serious consequences. So, what are we doing here?"

"I'm going to resolve this once and for all. I'm going to find out if my gramps is okay or not before I shoot Mason Matye between the eyes."

"Sounds simple enough, but I don't think it'll be so easy. He is using your grandfather as bait. Mason knows he's no match physically for you. That man didn't rise to the top of his hierarchy without being conniving and clever. He'll have some sort of trap set in place. Don't discount the fact you may be cursed. Could we not call the police in on this?"

"We need to keep that thought in our back pocket. I wouldn't want Mason to kill my gramps once the police show up. Plus, what am I going to say?" Jack sputtered. "I think my grandfather was kidnapped by a bunch of Satanists? I want to see what's going on first. I need to see that my gramps is still alive. If what you say is true, this guy Mason will harbor his grudge for life. Is that right?"

"He will, or he's not a proper Satanist."

"I don't want him getting arrested again, and coming back for me in the future. I'm going to finish this correctly. Once and for all. I'm going to feed the fucker to the gators. Then we call the cops. Maybe."

CHAPTER SIXTY-SIX

PSYCHIC RUSH, THE INFUSION of power from human sacrifice, was an experience that truly could not be explained. Mason felt the rush when he slayed the witch in New Orleans. The power he released killing Nathaniel Portman would be heady, but nothing compared to what he would experience in slaying Jack Walker. That human being had damaged Satan's power dramatically in the South. Senator Hunter's Clean Water Bill, championed by the state senate, passed two years ago. Already, profits from cattle and sugar were on the decline as measures were put in place to re-energize the ancient flow of the Everglades from the great interior lake system down through to Florida Bay. Still, it was not too late.

Mason's bid to perform a Black Mass was well received within the Satanic Brotherhood. He'd attracted some of the major players, including the Grand Master himself along with high-ranking Magi, members of the Illuminati, Witches and Warlocks.

Mason would reposition himself into a place of influence. He paid a heavy price during his incarceration at Angola Prison. Now, he would be rewarded for his devotion to Satan.

Attention would be given to the Florida problem, which he would oversee. A void had been created in the slaying of Henrietta LePley. Mason envisioned himself filling that position, open once again to the pipeline of funds available within the Church. Unlike many religions, the Church of Satan kept expanding at an incredible rate throughout the world, attracting the fringe sectors within modern society—those full of anger or looking for an excuse to rebel against the norm. It was happening in politics. Leaders with aggressive mandates for change were being elected, for better or for worse; the same had started in religion. Satanism did not espouse mindless faith. It required the ability to think for one's self and form one's own opinion.

Since he'd been in Ft. Myers, Mason had inquired about the old McFadden estate. Stigmatized by its past, the county appeared unable to sell it at any price. Mason could find the resources easily enough. Stashed away in offshore accounts was enough money to purchase the place and bring it back to its former splendor. The history, rumors and lore of what transpired there meant nothing to him. Mason would blend into South Florida society seamlessly with his new identity, while building a new coven, stronger than LePley's network.

She'd grown old and complacent. He didn't want to take anything away from her accomplishments because she had been a devout follower of Satan and garnered much power from the relationship. Still, she'd only risen to the level of Witch. Powerful, yet nothing compared to a Magus. Mason would right the ship in no time. But first, he needed to complete the Black Mass, one of the most powerful devotions to honor one's Divine Leader. The ritual was not to be taken lightly. Once completed, he would have the support of those who traveled to Ft. Myers. Mason tried his best not to get giddy over the ramifications of a successful ceremony.

Paramount to the success of the ritual was the inclusion of Jack Walker, who was strong with the spirits and a lightning rod for everything bad within the Church of Satan in South Florida.

He'd been baited and powerfully cursed. He would not know why he'd been called to that place, but he would come. Full of bravado, thinking he could rescue his grandfather, that he could dispatch Mason, the man didn't stand a snowball's chance in Hell. The power within the room would be able to grab hold of the roots of the curse, leaving the despicable creature soft like putty in his hand. Mason's joy would be in making Walker watch as they slew his grandfather. Walker's hatred would surely attract the strongest denizens of the abyss and, most positively, Satan himself.

Just thinking about what was ahead so excited Mason that he had to stop and brace himself. He knew what was coming and it was only seconds away. The Magus learned to perform the self-imposed act; the zap of electricity, rippling down his spine and crossing his hips, only increased his anticipation. Breathing heavily, he felt the hot pain in his heart as it strained to pump double time. Only true Satanists who enjoyed the excitement of whipping the innocent were able to conjure the self-induced climax. He held still as his muscles stiffened, waiting the few more seconds for it to come. He was not disappointed when his pleasure exploded without anyone or anything touching him.

Mason gave himself a few minutes to come down from his euphoria and thank Satan.

He had already placed Nathan back in his prison, not wanting to show off one of his prize catches until the time was ready. The Mass would be a show, which would build to a crescendo, culminating with Walker.

Many of the guests had arrived, though more would filter in throughout the night, a quorum of thirty being easily attained. Most of the congregation wore masks, some in the form of a white-faced devil, while others wore the face of a horned goat. Those who didn't wear masks were split almost evenly between male and female.

Candles were lit, along with a choking ensemble of burning incense: henbane, *Datura*, dried nightshade and myrrh.

A few caught his attention, one group of three in particular. Two females and a male, though he wasn't sure he'd be able to confirm gender. The male wore a black robe, with a necklace made of finger bones, his face painted white, lips and eye sockets black in typical Vodun manner. What caught Mason's eye in particular were the blood red lips. His lip color was not painted on, and his eyes were black as coal. Through the white paint, Mason saw deep wrinkles, which gave away his age.

The stranger stood tall. His hands stayed on the much shorter females beside him. One looked quite plump and wore a purple robe, denoting her rank as Witch. Her stare looked delirious, Mason guessed from bloodletting or some sort of opiate, which was not uncommon among the satanic hierarchy. The other female, thin and exotic, wore little clothing: a black leather corset and black tape to cover her nipples. He hoped they were not stylists just there to sit in on the Mass. Word of the gathering would have charged around the Satanist networks over the past few days. He did not doubt there would be pretenders presenting themselves. Looking back at the tall man, the lips continued to disturb Mason. They were most unnatural and he did not recognize the man. But then, why would he, having been in prison for the past number of years.

Another mixed group arrived looking ready for the orgy that usually sprang up from such occasions. Mason hoped the night would be more spiritual, but letting go of inhibition was one of the satanic tenets.

The Mass would take place in four parts. The first was a cleansing of the spirit and mind, where the congregation opened itself up to the spirits who might be present. The Catholic Church would call it the Greeting and Penitential Act.

By custom, Mason deferred to the High Priest to perform the first prayers. The seventy-year-old Graham De Foe from Upstate New York stepped into the chalk circle and pentagram after cleansing himself. He wore a red robe like Mason, a silver amulet depicting a horned goat embossed on a pentagram around his neck. He raised his hands. The crowd's mumbling quieted. He stood in front of the metal mortician's table, set at the north end of the pentagram to use as an altar. He gestured to a middle-aged woman to enter the circle.

Disrobing, she dropped the black garment to the wood floor before she cleansed herself with a short invocation. *A beautiful creature.* Mason's groin came alive again in anticipation. She lay on the cold steel table, her feet pointing north, her head to the south.

One of the High Priest's acolytes rang a heavy bell, the chime resonating through the room, the congregated Satanists becoming quiet. The priest moved toward the center of the circle and pentagram. Once there, he spread his hands wide and chanted.

"*In nomine magni dei nostri Satanas, introibo ad altare Domini Inferi.*"

As he finished the words, the assembled resonated as one: "*Ave Satanas.*"

He chanted again: "*In nomine dei nostri Satanas Luciferi excelsi.*"

Again the congregation responded: "*Ave Satanas.*"

As the High Priest sat in the pentagram, the rest of the followers circled the outside. Stragglers continued to enter the smoky, candlelit room. Mason estimated fifty people at this point, the room getting somewhat crowded. He began the summoning of the four Princes of Hell, lighting a candle procured from Moses, made with the fat of an unbaptized baby. The wick fizzled and crackled as the flame came to life.

He pointed the candle to the south and chanted in his deep, resonating voice, "Hail Satan."

"Hail Satan, unholy father," they responded.

He pointed to the east. "Hail Lucifer."

"Hail Lucifer, who is never questioned."

He pointed to the north, where the woman lay on the altar. "Hail Belial."

"Hail Belial, god of the wicked, bringer of death."

Finally, he pointed to the west. "Hail Leviathan."

"Hail Leviathan, god of serpents."

The energy in the room was palpable, electric. The congregation wanted more. For many, the ceremony was akin to a close encounter with their favorite rock stars. The High Priest, as well as Mason and some of the lesser clergy, all represented the highest levels of attainment within the Church of Satan. The High Priest stood and motioned to Mason that it was his time to lead the rest of the Mass.

Mason moved to the center of the room, bringing with him a reluctant, handcuffed Nathanial Portman.

CHAPTER SIXTY-SEVEN

A PLAINCLOTHES OFFICER FROM the Hillsborough Sheriff's Department stepped forward. He looked to be of Hispanic descent. She vaguely remembered his face. "Is your name Janie Callaghan?"

Janie sighed and smiled. "That would be me, sir."

"Then you're the one who called this in?" He brandished a piece of paper. "I'm Deputy Garcia. The DA reluctantly issued a warrant to search the premises." He flashed his badge for her to see. "I don't know if you remember, but I was here the last time this place was investigated. We take these things very seriously, ma'am."

"I do remember you. And"—she pointed to Perry, who stepped out behind her, his face bloodied and grossly swollen— "I too take this seriously. Actually, it is my boss, Peter Robertson, who made the call."

Garcia could not hide his agitation. "Now, tell me this isn't a coincidence that Mr. Robertson called this in at the same time as a reported shooting took place inside. We can find no evidence of the shooting, yet there are several eyewitnesses claiming to have heard the gunshot or thinking they saw somebody or some*bodies* getting their brains splattered."

"There are no coincidences in life, Garcia"—borrowing the line from Gramps—"and there have been a number of shootings. You were not able to find the Russian's hidden basement the last time you searched. There are a number of men down, including one of our clients, who's been held prisoner inside for nearly a week."

Garcia motioned for his men to enter the garage. Eight men dressed in combat gear and carrying assault rifles filed past Janie and Perry, entering the garage through the side door.

Janie waved when the ambulance arrived. The paramedics calmly exited the large white vehicle and came over to Janie and Garcia.

Garcia said, "We're doing a sweep of the interior before I can let you down there."

The thirty-something female nodded. "Can you give me an idea of what we're in for?"

Janie spoke. "You'll find three deceased males from gunshot wounds. Another male with his throat cut and missing eyes. The other gentleman is in a cell at the back of the first room on the right. He's been shot, maybe four days ago, and doesn't look good. He's a client of ours held prisoner here by the owner of this establishment. He's integral to determining the legalities of the whole situation. I'd ask you to attend to him first, as we'd hate to see him die."

"We'll do our best as soon as we're given the green light."

"In the meantime, Perry here looks like his jaw is broken."

The EMT took a cursory look at Perry, and pulled him aside to look closer at his injuries.

Janie said to Garcia, "There are two thugs in one of the cells. I'd be careful of them."

"Ms. Callaghan, what the hell happened here tonight? Who's been shooting whom? It doesn't add up. Do you mean to tell me you took out all of these men?"

"Garcia, I'd be lying if I told you that I had. Let's say it's complicated. I'm going to need to make a statement, but I'm not going to do so until my boss and legal counsel arrives—Peter Robertson. It might be best to make that statement at your headquarters."

"You can sit in the back of my car. It's the black Impala over to the right." He ushered her to the car, opening the rear door for her. "I'm going to have to lock you in, ma'am. Until we find out otherwise, I'm going to have to detain you. You are a lawyer, correct?"

"Close enough."

"Then you know I have to read you your rights."

CHAPTER SIXTY-EIGHT

VENICE, NORTH PORT, PUNTA Gorda—Jack drove slowly past the signs, trying to keep awake. Nodding off and being sick did not help how he felt. He wished someone could teleport him from where he sat behind the wheel to his bed. Looking over at Lolita, her chin still on her chest, he figured she fell asleep not far out of Tampa. With all the craziness that had happened, staying awake was a major problem. He tugged on her elbow, jolting her large frame to sit up.

"What the hell, Walker! I was having a helluva dream. Why'd ya wake me up?"

"I'm about ready to fall asleep behind the wheel. Besides, we gotta figure out what the heck we're gonna do here. You said this . . . whoever-he-is would be ready for us? For me?"

"Yep!" She yawned. "You've been cursed and are being reeled in like a fish on a hook."

"Knowing this, why are we going to where we're going, besides the obvious?"

"Like I say, you're being played. And very skillfully, I might add. This Mason character knows you're coming. Hell, he's counting on it. We must find a way to use this knowledge against him. Here's a point: he's not expecting a 400-pound medium to be accompanying you. Plus, we have guns. He'll expect you to storm the door alone, without weapons, and be controllable due to your feeling the way you look right now. There's no way you could defend yourself. Picture this—we allow him to take you into his clutches. Making him think he's in control. When he least expects it, I'll come in and blow his brains out, *POW*!" She stopped to laugh. "We find your grandfather, and we skedaddle. How does that sound?"

"Let's say I accept your take on the curse shit. How do you or I end it?"

"That's easy. The curse layer must undo it, or the one who cursed you must be killed."

"Okay, sounds good. But let me put one caveat into all of this. I'm feeding his guts to the fucking gators. I want to make sure he's good and dead, and never coming back."

"I will not hold you back, Jackson, as that seems to be the reason why you've been brought in contact with this evil man. Our world is all about good versus evil."

Jack enjoyed a breath of relief as they crossed the Caloosahatchee, meaning they'd arrived in Ft. Myers. Within a half hour they would arrive at the McFadden estate. For better or worse. Jack felt his stomach rise at the mere thought of the old decrepit place.

CHAPTER SIXTY-NINE

THE BELL RANG AT midnight to announce the witching hour. Nathaniel Portman lay in the middle of the pentagram, his feet and knees bound together tightly. One of the young acolytes acted as guard by stepping on the old man's shoulder to keep him pressed to the floor. He held out the Seminole leader's wrist.

Mason stood close, holding his athame and a silver chalice. Grasping the outstretched wrist, the little man in the ruby red robe deftly cut the soft underside of Nathaniel Portman's wrist. Not enough to kill the elderly gentleman, but enough that he bled slowly into the chalice. After the bowl filled a few inches, Mason wrapped the arm in a bandage, stanching the flow of blood. He didn't want to kill his sacrifice—not just yet. The smell of fresh blood made him lick his dry lips. *Oh*, how he wanted to dip his finger into the rich blood and lick the drippings off his finger, but Mason held back; the magic moment was not even an hour away.

Mason eyed the supine female. Her mouth open, taking fast breaths, she was caught up in the rapture of the moment. In most satanic ceremonies, it was time for the priest to enter the female and masterfully copulate until orgasm. The semen would be added to the blood, creating the sacred mixture to be shared from the chalice. Mason, however, did not want to expose the diminutive nature of his manhood. Instead, he decided to ad lib. Bending between her spread legs, he made a small cut on the bottom edge of the vagina, adding to the bowl. As the flow of rich red liquid slowed, he inserted a tiny clip to pull the sides of the minute wound together. The pinpoint of pain sent her high arousal into orgasm and her body recoiled as she screamed out her divine love for Satan.

He turned to the worshippers and saw their bobbing heads and blinking eyes, all ecstatic with their own physical excitement in anticipation of the rapture soon to come.

Mason proceeded with the Midnight Evocation of Satan. He held the chalice in both hands, as if offering it to the congregation. "*Ya! Zat-i-Shaitan!*"

The gathering responded, "*Ave Satanas.*"

"By the Gate of the Black Light, when I name the words against the Sun, O' Fire Djinn Azazel, Set-heh, I summon thee forth with Serpent's tongue. That my oath before this blackened flame, ignited within, in the dreaming aethyr shall I be known in the wisdom of the Moon."

Pausing, he raised the cup higher while once again motioning as if to offer it to the gathering. "Al Zabbat, Hekas Hekau, serpent soul, I do summon you. Rise now from thy black light, that I see what has never been known. Akharakek Sabaiz!

"I call forth the shadow of which I am and have always been, the darkness, which I nourish in between the light. Eclipse now the face of God that I become in this darkened image."

Mason gestured to the chalk circle. "By this circle do I become." He pointed to the candle in the center of the pentagram. "By this flame do I emerge. I am the peacock angel, beauty revealed unto those who may see. As the black sun rises, I become in this emerald stone. I am the imagination, the seed of the fallen angel. In darkness exists my light. My will gives birth to the kingdom of Incubi and Succubi, to nourish their desires in the blood of the moon, Lilitu Az Drakul."

He took a small sip from the chalice, then exclaimed, "So it is done!" He handed the chalice to the High Priest, who in turn handed it to the person to the left of him, and thus the cup holding the blood of a Magus and Holy Priestess was shared by all who bore witness to the ceremony, adding collective power to the incantation.

As the bowl found its way throughout the room, always being passed to the left, Mason returned his attention to Nathaniel Portman, who now sat with his knees pulled up to his chest. Mason enjoyed what he interpreted, for the first time, as fear upon the old man's face.

CHAPTER SEVENTY

GRAMPS WATCHED THE CEREMONY with utter disgust. It was all poppycock. None of it made sense from a spiritualistic point of view. The only true part of the whole thing was the bloodletting. The rest was just made-up words. No self-respecting spirit would pay attention to such crap.

Satanism seemed like so much shock-and-awe to him. Nathaniel wondered how many followers stayed with the religion. He guessed there would be the diehards, who truly wanted to believe because it made them physically feel good with all the sex. Then, there were those who used the satanic excuse to rebel against society and their families, because most were losers. They would never be a success no matter what they tried.

There were, however, a few who caught his attention out of the fifty or sixty people in the room. *Mason and the high priest, definitely*—they were both in tune with the spirits, in a very *physical* religious way. He detected a few witches, who were easy to spot by their auras. There were two others Gramps was not able to get a read on. *Can they be fey?* When he met their eyes, there could be no misunderstanding the contact. Their auras differed from those of the Satanists. They seemed disconnected from the hedonistic urgency revved up by the Black Mass. They were present, but not because of devotion to the Satanic Mass.

One was a thin, redheaded female with streaks of gray across her temples, eyes yellow like a wolf. She bore a look of concern, and her eyes held his whenever Nathaniel glanced her direction.

The other was male with bluish-gray hair pulled back in a ponytail. His skin was tan and he had dark brown eyes. Like the female, he seemed to try to capture Gramps' attention, offering him reassurance. *But is it encouragement to bear my death with humility and purpose?* He could not be sure. Regardless, they did not belong.

There were tales of the fey in Native lore as well as Celtic myth. Some called them elves. Nathaniel might have been fishing for an answer, but there could be no other way to describe their auras, gold ringed with a deep green fringe. When he saw that they alone refused the unholy sacrament, an old Muskogean legend came to mind. It spoke of a husband and wife who looked after the great swamp, protecting those who championed the Everglades.

Gramps shook his head, thinking he must be losing his focus from the blood loss.

He turned to smile at them once again, but they were gone. They must've disappeared into the crowd, having made their point. *What was their point?* Gramps could find a few arguments. *For instance, what right do these upstarts, their religion relatively new, have to kill a Native shaman, whose faith is possibly tens of thousands of years old?*

There was one other who did not pretend to believe: the man with the blood red lips. He did not bear an aura. Gramps could not hold his gaze.

CHAPTER SEVENTY-ONE

JACK DROVE ON AUTOPILOT to the old estate, amazed that he remembered the signposts and curves as if it were yesterday he'd last driven along the country roads, the Everglades at night passing by like a deep darkness …unending. He envisioned Jimmy and Isaac McFadden chasing him crazily through the river of grass in their prop boat—how freedom had been snatched from him after a frantic paddle run on his kayak through the intricate canal system. Remembering it all made his heart beat harder; nearing the place made his heart beat faster.

Lolita picked up on his edginess. "Bad memories, Jackson?"

"Kinda."

"Let them pass. We need to be on our game."

Jack fell into a line of three cars. The front one seemed to be lost, very strange for this time and location. On a normal night, he might encounter one or two cars on an entire trip. He fell in behind them, not wanting to pass—they must be close to their destination by now.

The brake lights of the train of cars came on in succession, from the leader back to Jack and Lolita. "We've got to be here. This is very strange," he said.

"What do you mean?"

"I think we are there, and all of these cars look as if they're turning into the estate."

This was indeed the McFadden Estate, as shown by a crude, white, hand-painted wooden sign stuck in the ground beside the driveway. It allayed any doubts. "Follow them in, Jackson."

"You sure?"

She smiled. "We're on the crazy train to Hell. Don't you dare think about hopping off."

"Crazy train to Hell? You don't think that's a bit dramatic?"

"Perhaps a touch, but if you drive past and come back, we won't have the luxury of blending in with whoever these folks are ahead of us. Obviously, the Devil Spawn have something happening here. I might not be, but I know *you* are invited. Obviously, others were too."

Jack turned into the long driveway, not acknowledging her words. He followed the other cars, bouncing in and out of the massive potholes. After several hundred yards, the old manor house appeared, silhouetted in moonlight, memories from the place stirring intense anxiety. Jack began to hyperventilate.

"Jackson, we will be okay."

"Like fuck we will! I wanted to come in here and put a bullet in Mason's skull and leave." Spread across the weedy lawn and parking lot were dozens of cars. "Last time I was here, I basically went Rambo and killed all the bastard Satanists. There were a few glitches, but the McFaddens came to a timely end, as did Henrietta. Gators were fed, everyone went home happy. This does not look so good." A throng of people in long black robes pushed to get into Jimmy McFadden's workshop, like a mosh pit.

Jack pulled the car into the lot and followed the direction of a parking attendant, who wore a goat's mask.

"What the fuck!" Lolita burst out, getting a look at what was to come.

"My sentiments exactly." Jack shook his head.

When they stepped out of the car, they both turned to the car four spots over, where a young couple were fornicating on the hood, their robes discarded on the ground. Jack put his hand to his head. "This is out of control."

Lolita motioned for him to follow her, putting a finger to his mouth to shush his next word. They moved behind a row of cars. The screwing couple were in front. "Grab the girl."

Jack followed Lolita as she moved up behind the male, in the throes of finishing the act. Lolita slammed the back of the man's neck with her handgun. He fell off his partner and rolled to the ground unconscious, his penis waving around like a lost beacon.

Jack grabbed the girl, covering her mouth as she wailed in fear. Lolita brought the gun down on the back of her neck. Jack cradled her to the ground as she fell limp into his arms.

Lolita searched the couple's car for the keys and opened the trunk. "Help me get them in here." Jack dumped the woman into the trunk first. It took their joint strength to get the man inside next to her. The quarters were close, but Jack managed to slam the lid. It was an older model Mazda and he couldn't see an inside release. It might be there, but it wouldn't be any easier for the two Satanists to find in the dark.

Lolita picked up the man's robe, handing the smaller one to Jack. Lolita could hardly fit the costume over Solomon's frame. Once in it, the robe flared out over her immense hips.

Jack chuckled. "You look like a big black pylon." He put on the other robe, the size just fitting, and Lolita harrumphed.

They walked to the shed. A television screen set up on the back of a pickup truck showed a simulcast of the interior events. Twenty or so people diligently watched, not able to get into the venue. Jack stopped in his tracks, seeing his gramps laid out in the pentagram. The camera zoomed in on his stricken face.

Jack felt the hair stand up on his head. He looked at the building, the glow of candlelight flickering from within, and couldn't fathom how or why there were so many people there. It looked as if they'd arrived by boat as well, since five decently-sized crafts were tied at the dock.

Lolita read Jack's wonderment and said under her breath, "This is how the Satanists operate. They get out the word and use social media. If Mason was jailed five years ago and now there's news he might appear at this gathering? The Church of Satan could call this a miracle, if not a resurrection. People would flock to see a man who might be considered the son of Satan and take part in a ritual being performed by him."

"Great, to see me and my grandfather sacrificed."

"Not specifically."

"To tell the truth, if I didn't have to rescue Gramps, I'd need you to drop me off at a hospital. I'm really not well. Everything is blurring in and out of focus."

She felt his head. "Hard to tell in this heat, but you're burning up. Want some water?"

Chanting came from inside and from the monitor. "As one, there. *Ave Satanas*!" resonated through the night air.

Jack ignored her question. "I gotta get in there. Even if I die, I can't let him go it alone."

"Remember, Jackson, only one of us will die on this night. I have nothing much to live for and you're still young. Let me go in. They'll be all over you if they find out you're here."

Jack stood back and stared at the ridiculous creature in front of him. "You don't look like a Satanist. There's no way you're barging in there, looking like that."

"What do you have in mind, my young, precocious friend?"

Jack looked crestfallen. "I was hoping you might pull out your cards and give us a reading. Honestly, I'm not sure."

"Are you admitting to the viability of the tarot?" she smiled.

"Possibly, but I don't think it practical to set up out here. I was just talking out loud to hear myself think." He became quiet for a moment until his eyes brightened. "Not much of a plan, but it's the best I can come up with. It looks as if the porch cantilevered out over the river is packed. We're not going to get in that way. The door at the side is a no-go. There's thirty people around it trying to watch the Mass from there. If I remember correctly, there's a lean-to storage room on the far side of the building. It wasn't much of a structure and it's probably rotted to nothing by now. We might be able to pull some boards off the wall and get in that way, unseen by prying eyes. If what you think is true, they will be watching for me."

"They may already know you're here. There's a link between the cursed and the curse-giver. At least you'll be entering where they won't be on the lookout for you. Once you're in there, you're on your own, baby. You'd have to pull down half a wall to fit me through."

Jack nodded and headed to the far side of the structure. Lolita took off the robe, its tightness restricting her ability to catch up to him. They had to take a circular route around an outcropping of thorn bushes and animal pens. Jack vaguely remembered Jimmy McFadden mentioning hogs and the animal's ability to grind down bones to an unidentifiable form.

The shed sat where Jack remembered it to be, and he was pleased to see the corner of the building had sunk a foot or so toward the river, exposing the bottom edge to the water. Directly around the corner, Jack and Lolita spotted the backsides of many participants edging out onto the rickety decking.

He needed to be quiet. Fortunately, the boards were so rotten that he could easily pry them up and to the side, creating a hole big enough to slide through. Once in the hole, he looked back at Lolita. "Do you have a cell?"

"Yes."

"If this thing seems as if it's going sideways, call the cops."

"You think they'll get here in time to be any help?"

"I'll share a contact with you. Peter Robertson, my boss. Call him—he'll know what to do." He gave her the number along with smile. "I'm sorry for the shit I put you through."

"Everything has a purpose."

"That supposed to make me feel better? Here I am trying to give you an apology."

She smiled. "Get going. I'll call that boss of yours and hear what he has to say."

Jack disappeared into the darkness.

CHAPTER SEVENTY-TWO

MASON TRIED NOT TO get caught up in the rapture of the moment. Word had certainly spread through the satanic community about their special Black Mass. There were few familiar faces besides the High Priest and his acolytes. The rest seemed to have come out of the woods. He smiled at the size of the crowd. His Mass would always be remembered and written about in the annals of Encyclopedia Satanica. *After all, have I not risen from the dead?*

It was time to make the first sacrifice. He stared at the old man, who was weak from captivity and blood loss. Mason had set up the cameras and television screen outside the building. He hadn't been sure he'd get a good response to his invitations, but, just in case they all showed up, he wanted Walker to be able to see what happened. If Walker was indeed there, he would make an appearance soon with what was planned next.

Higher-ranking members of the Church performed such

rituals hoping to find a miracle, a tangible sign from Satan. Mason did not have any false ideas about the ritual. He knew fame would follow if he succeeded. He sought revenge. If Walker didn't show, there would be no such occurrence, and Mason would look the fool. He didn't need a petty sign from his Deity—women crawling on the ceiling, blood pouring forth from holes in his hands or any other nonsense. That was stuff for movies. Tonight was real.

The Mass called for a sword, but Mason made a slight change, using one of Jimmy McFadden's wicked long knives. It was long enough to be called a short sword—good enough in his books. The tool was most likely used to skin gators. He called for the bell to be rung. Its impure note rang unremorsefully into the night. The gathering once again became quiet.

Mason raised his hands before the makeshift altar, the woman lying naked before him, Nathaniel Portman stretched out, ropes binding his hands and feet to four of the five points of the pentagram. His head turned to Mason. Mason looked down upon him now, smiling, mouthing a silent "Soon!"

He spoke in a loud, clear voice: "*In nomine Dei nostri Satanas Luciferi excelsi!*"

The congregation responded: "*Ave Satanas.*"

"In the name of Satan, the ruler of the earth, the king of the underworld, I command the forces of Darkness to bestow their infernal power upon me! Open wide the gates of Hell and come forth from the abyss to greet me as your brother and friend. Grant me the indulgence of which I speak!"

He turned to address the other side of the room. "I have taken thy name as part of myself. I live as the beasts in the field, rejoicing in the fleshly life. I favor the just and curse the rotten. By all the gods of the Pit, I command these things of which I speak shall come to pass. Come forth and answer to your names by manifesting my desires!"

Mason licked the tip of the long knife before making a cursory incision from the supine female's pubic bone to her navel. Once again, within the Black Mass Mason was required to enter her sexually. Not wanting to expose himself nor turn the Mass into an orgy—just yet—he had devised an alternative measure. Pushing his first two fingers far inside her warm wetness, he looked out at his audience and smiled. They hunched forward to watch as he gave her long, rhythmic strokes. Her blood bubbled out of the incision. When she screamed out Satan's name, he raised both fingers to his lips. All watched as his serpent tongue wiggled between his lips to slide across each of his fingers, leaving his mouth and chin covered with the bloody sacrament.

The congregation could not hold back. They hooted and hollered but did not know which direction to take. Normally, the gathering would now open up into a sexual free-for-all.

Mason raised his hands again. "Children of Satan, hold your tongues for a time. We are here to exact vengeance before we partake in the gifts of the flesh. We are here to make sacrifice before we rejoice." He stepped around the altar, pointing the long knife toward the five corners of the pentagram.

"I call upon the Princes of Hell to manifest their power through my sword." He turned this way and that, pointing the "sword" at the crowd, whipping them into a frenzy. Standing over Gramps, one foot on either side of him, Mason raised the sword high over his head and turned to the crowd. Once again smiling and looking for their approval to make the strike, Mason dropped to his knees. The blade flashed down like a bolt of lightning to the middle of the man's chest. Mason halted his thrust an inch above his target, his eyes locked onto Nathaniel's. He was disappointed the shaman didn't flinch, instead bearing his imminent death stoically. Mason stood again, raising the sword with more resolve, the crowd revved up to watch the kill.

* * * *

Jack pulled open the door, and three or four participants looked at him questioningly. Still in the robe, he wore the hood low over his face, hiding his eyes.

He mumbled in a matter-of-fact way, "Pissing." They stood aside and let him pass.

While he pushed toward the spectacle, Jack gazed around. He could not see Gramps but knew he had to be somewhere on the floor close to Mason. He paused, watching the creepy little man perform his version of the sacrament. As Jack's fevered brain wondered how the place could possibly hold so many people, he swore the building groaned, wood rubbing against wood. When the room hushed, Jack wondered if he was mistaken, until the hum returned.

* * * *

Lolita watched Jack disappear, knowing she wouldn't see him again—that had been her premonition all along. Hearing the building shift, she saw the corner in front of her sinking deeper into the water. An idea popped into her head. A wide smile crossed her black face as she looked around for something to use for leverage. She found an old shovel handle, the blade having rusted off years before. She pulled out her phone and punched in the number.

"Peter Robertson?"

"Peter, my name is Lolita."

Peter had just finished hearing all about the woman from Janie. "What can I do for you, Lolita? Where's Jack?"

"He is in grave danger."

"If I hadn't been through this a few years back with Jack, I would find this hard to believe."

"Believe what you will, but he's about to be sacrificed in the name of Satan."

"Where the hell are you?"

"Close. A place owned by a family named McFadden."

"Christ!"

"Yes. Jack may need His help as well." She hung up.

As quietly as she could, she slipped her massive body into the warm, muddy water. The deck hung a good twenty feet into the river. It was dark, and the last thing she really wanted was be in the alligator-infested water. She prodded ahead with the long handle. A small gator swam away from her and she prayed she wouldn't encounter a much bigger and more ornery one.

Light filtered through slits in the floor planking. She trudged through the water until she heard a man calling forth the creatures of Hell.

"Okay, close enough." She studied the structure of the

building, noting how the wood pilings looked to be rotten and shifting toward the corner where she had entered.

A sudden swirling in the water close to the foot of the building grabbed her attention.

"Holy mother of God," she blurted out, realizing she had disturbed a nest of water moccasins. One very large snake came straight for her, its fangs extended. She whacked it just behind the head, killing it instantly. There was nothing she could do as dozens more of the black snakes swam toward her. The tiny serpents probed her clothing for bare flesh. She was lucky for a time, but then one of the small vipers sank its teeth into her ankle. She flinched in pain as the burning hot venom took over the flesh.

* * * *

Mason enjoyed stirring up the crowd. Once again, he had the blade raised, ready to strike. As he dropped to his knees, a sudden movement caught his eye and he stopped to look. A man in customary attire forced himself through the crowd, charging toward him. When the running man was close, looking as if he would try to tackle Mason before the sacrifice, he crossed the chalk circle and collapsed. On the ground, he lay unable to move due to the spasms passing over his entire body.

Mason grinned, lowering the blade to his side. "Jack Walker."

The congregation chanted as one to repeat, "Jack Walker!"

Mason raised his hands and the blade. "Let this be a showing of the powerful god in whom we place our faith." The buzz died down so all could hear the man's words. "I placed a curse upon this man, Jack Walker, seven days ago, and promised he would be delivered to me. Let this be a sign that Satan is with us, that the Black Mass is all-powerful. Because this is indeed a miracle. Satan be praised."

"Satan be praised!"

Mason, in full control of Jack, moved to him, lifting his chin with his index finger, and beckoned him to crawl to the middle of the circle. And he did, following his antagonist. Mason pushed him down beside his grandfather.

"Tonight, we will avenge the deaths of our brethren: Henrietta LePley, Buck and Carly Henderson, Isaac, Eric and James McFadden. All were staunch followers of our Deity. Jackson Walker and his shaman grandfather, Nathaniel Portman, will be sacrificed in the name of Satan and will die for their transgressions against the unholy father for making a deal with the Devil, not willing to pay the price."

"Pay the price!" the congregation chanted as one, though a few remained silent as they watched and listened to the spectacle.

The building groaned once again, shuddering as the soft, rotting wood found new resting places. The rumble under Mason caused him to stumble, but he quickly regained his footing to look around. Picking up that the lack of foundation might upend the building soon and cause the demise of the waterfront slaughterhouse, Mason decided to shorten the Mass. Still, before the Satanists retreated, Walker and his grandfather needed to die. Standing over Portman, who would be first, Mason signaled for the acolytes to bring the silver chalice to him.

* * * *

Lolita's foot went numb from the snakebite. She gave up trying to shoo the snakes from her robes as they slithered and swam around her, searching for flesh. When the old place groaned again, one of the rotten pillars fell sideways into the water. Surveying the structure, she didn't need to be an engineer to see that the place was resting on two piers further out. She moved toward them, out into deeper water. She saw the water swish made by the tail of a much larger gator. As she went deeper, the snakes gained access to her upper torso.

"Wonderful," she said aloud. "The serpents of Hell, no doubt."

As she pushed her great weight into one of the piers, a small viper leaped from the water to latch onto her nose. She grabbed it behind its head, ripping it off. Blood spurted into her eyes and into the water. When the wooden post wouldn't give, she felt around the bottom with her foot. It was rotten—about an inch of thickness remained holding it up. She wedged the shovel handle between a rock and the bottom of the pier. The snakes continued to attack as she put her prodigious weight behind the lever. Lolita felt the post give way, hopping off the stub on the river bottom.

The building groaned, yet the last pier still held.

* * * *

Jack remembered pushing through the crowd, the knife raised over Mason's head. The man sure hadn't changed much in five years, and Jack would never forget those hateful black eyes. The bastard meant to skewer Gramps. He charged Mason, hoping to tackle him before the knife could be driven home. As he crossed the line into the circle, everything went fuzzy. He caught his breath. Unable to draw another, he felt like he was having a heart attack. Falling to the ground, the last thing Jack remembered was his head hitting the floorboards.

* * * *

The acolyte returned with the heavy silver chalice, placing it on the ground by Mason's feet.

Mason raised the blade one last time. "By the power invested in me, oh Satan, I make sacrifice of this servant of Yahweh, shaman of the Miccosukee people, who have hurt our interests in South Florida. Grandfather of Jackson Walker, he of vile intent, killer of members of the Church of Satan and Set."

The building shook once again.

* * * *

Lolita could hardly bear the pain inflicted by the aggressive black serpents. She saw one last opportunity to bring the building down. Diving under the water, snakes circling, she squatted at the base of the piling. Like the other, it was held together by soft rot. She used the long wooden handle once again, wedging it under the rotting wood and heaving to push the upper part of the wood pier off the base. Lolita groaned—her last breath leaving her.

It didn't look as if it would go, but a sudden weight shift above must have been all that was required. The pier popped off, snagging her dress as it slammed home into the soft river bottom.

When the building began its slow, laborious slide into the river, Lolita did not have enough air in her lungs to get back to the surface. The last thing she remembered of her earthly existence was the weight falling on her. Lolita's last hope was for Jackson, and that her final efforts were enough to aid him and Nathaniel. Looking down, her body was no more. Looking up, there was a beacon of light, just past the surface of the water. She smiled.

* * * *

This time, the structure pitched sideways as the rest of the pilings gave way, snapping or toppling. The river side of the building dropped, slicing into the water. The eighty or so people inside the building were thrown into the water . . . along with thousands of pounds of broken-down machinery and furniture, crushing limbs and dragging bodies beneath the brown, brackish water.

Jack, Mason and the naked female on the altar piled up against a pillar. The water came up to their necks and only the woman swam free. Mason and Jack ended up face to face. Perhaps it was the jolt of being thrown in the water, or maybe the curse was broken and Jack was no longer in Mason's circle of power. Either way, Jack snapped awake. Taking in a big gulp of dirty water, Jack felt alive and well again.

Mason still brandished the knife and tried to stab Jack's chest. Jack rolled to the side, the knife piercing his shoulder through to the floor.

Snakes, big black ones, came at both of them. Mason, showing his fear of snakes, turned from Jack and tried to swim away. A voice called out and Jack saw a red-robed man beckoning Mason to swim to the dock. Mason watched for an opening between the huge debris and swam away with haste. That was when Jack remembered there were powerboats on the water.

"Dammit!" he yelled after his archenemy.

Looking around, Jack spotted Gramps, still tied to the stakes. His head was under the water, but Jack was relieved to see the old bugger trying to free himself. Before he could move to help him, a hand rested on Jack's shoulder. He turned to see a Native American. Jack looked back at the long knife pinning him to the canted floor. The man nodded, pulling out the blade and handing it to him before diving into the water, disappearing into the night.

With all of the strength left to him, Jack slid further into the water and cut Gramps' bonds. Once cut, Jack heaved the man to the surface, coughing up water. Jack touched his grandfather's face, kissing his forehead. "You are one tough old Indian."

Gramps smiled. "Only so tough, Jackson. My breath was about done. Thank you. What on earth is happening?"

"I don't know, but I have the sneaking suspicion Lolita had something to do with it." He looked out to the river, where Mason stepped down into one of the bay boats moored on the dock. Jack shook his head. "That fucker can't get away."

Gramps noticed it too. "I couldn't agree with you more, Grandson."

"I'm not letting you out of my sight." A water moccasin swam at them. Jack chopped it with the knife, severing its head. Out in the small cove, all Jack and Nathaniel saw was chaos. The gators were swimming in and looking for an easy meal; the snakes defending their lair attacked anything close to the toppled building. Bodies floated facedown, no doubt crushed by falling debris. Others swam for the far shore—unknowingly toward the gators, which were easy to see from Jack's vantage point.

He smiled and called after them, "Hurry!"

Gramps followed Jack and they found an old ladder to the dock. They scampered onto the rickety structure and turned to see Mason's boat roaring away, slamming through swimmers still trying for the far shore. Without a care, their prop sliced open a near-naked female Satanist.

There was one boat left, and Jack saw the owners walking along the dock to leave. Sprinting as best he could, he made a run for it. The boat owners saw him coming and tried to hurry.

Jack faced two males and one female until he remembered the snub-nosed .45 in his pocket. He pulled it out and, without jumping into the boat, Jack brandished the weapon at the three.

"Get out of the fucking boat, or I'll shoot you all. Believe me, it won't take much, you satanic fucks. Just try me." He kept the gun leveled, watching them reluctantly climb out of the low-riding bay boat.

Gramps was limping behind and Jack yelled back to him, "Get in."

The spry old Native climbed aboard and set himself up at the steering wheel. The motor was already running. On the dock, Jack slipped the mooring lines from the metal cleats before climbing into the boat, the gun panned on the three former occupants, who looked as if they might try to retake the vessel.

The stare-down proved Jack's smile held more promise of evil than they had seen that night. "Do not fucking tempt me!"

Gramps, an expert skipper, moved the boat away from the dock, avoiding the remainder of people in the water—those still alive and the floating dead. Jack never dropped sight of the three left behind on the dock. Once clear, Nathaniel gunned the motor and headed after the boat carrying Mason. He yelled to Jack, "They're headed back into the Everglades!"

Jack finally turned away from the dock and relaxed. "I wouldn't have expected that." He leaned against the center console, his body aching and his shoulder oozing blood. He took off the robe and sliced a few long strips from it. He motioned to Gramps that he wanted to drive, handing the strips to the Native healer. Gramps understood and did his best to tend to Jack's wound.

Mason's boat carried six. Gramps and Jack only had two aboard and experienced no problem closing the gap. Jack motioned for Gramps to take back the wheel. "Here." He handed Gramps the other gun he'd taken from the Russians back in Tampa, which seemed so long ago.

"Where did you get the weapons?"

"Tell you later."

As they got closer, Jack took aim and fired a shot into the middle of their boat, not really aiming at anything in particular.

The boat swerved, one of the passengers falling to the deck. He fired again, this time aiming at the outboard motor. It took a direct hit but kept going. He fired again, this time hitting something important. The motor whined to a stop, the boat surging to a glide. Gramps pulled up within a few feet.

"That's the high priest, Jack," Gramps said, recognizing the man and both of his acolytes, the other passengers female and scantily-dressed. Another man lay on the floor, having taken the first shot fired in the middle of the back.

Jack nodded. "I don't have a beef with any of you except that little fuck." He pointed at Mason. "You can all go. There will be no enmity from me, and hopefully none from you, by me letting you go. I should shoot you all right now. I'm not built that way. I don't practice evil like the bunch of you."

The tall older man spoke. "And say we don't agree to hand Mason over to you?"

"Then I will start by shooting you and will continue to do so until we're left with only Mason. Okay, I'm going to treat you like little kids and count to ten to talk it over."

Without warning, Mason jumped overboard. He swam toward the saw-grass shoreline.

Jack nodded at the people in the boat. "I'm sure there are some paddles in the boat. It's the law."

Gramps backed the boat away and maneuvered to cut Mason off from the shore. The man decided to tread water, no doubt to catch his breath.

Jack yelled down, "Whad'ya think of my deal with the Devil now, Mason Matye?"

"You're not free from your bargain yet, Walker."

"You know what? I am. I've suffered enough because of the false deal you speak of. My family has suffered. You were about to kill both of us."

Gramps nodded. "There's something else you have not taken into consideration."

Mason was huffing, his breath short from exertion. "What's that, Nate?"

"Swamp justice." Gramps pointed his gun at Mason and, without flinching, shot the nasty little man in the head. Mason's final death throes kept his body afloat until it finally stopped thrashing. It floated on the water for a few moments before drifting below the surface. Nathaniel turned to Jack, placing his hand on the back of his grandson's head and bringing their foreheads together. "Will you listen to me now, Jackson?"

Jack offered the beginnings of a smile. "Suppose I'd better from now on." He turned back to Mason's watery grave. "The gators will take care of the rest of him."

"We can't go back to that place. One of the hunt camps is only a few miles from here. I think it would be good to disappear for a short time."

"I'm in your hands, Gramps." He didn't want to admit it, but he felt better.

Gramps gunned the engine, heading off into the darkness of the great swamp with only the moon and stars to guide his way—as it had always been before him, and would be after him.

ACKNOWLEDGEMENTS

Christopher would like to thank:

Agent Mary Ellen Gavin from the Gavin Literary Agency

Jean Young, editing

Old Nick

John Koehler and the wonderful people at Koehler Books.

Readers: Sarah Gleddie, Philip Bowron, Bonnie Grimm, Bev Matychuk, Jessica Schmitt, Carmen Bowron, Graham Heyes, Bryan Funk, Marilyn Francis, Jewell Betts, Jodi Gribbons

BIOGRAPHY

CHRISTOPHER'S ROOTS ARE IN Canada, and his two children make the fifth generation to live in Niagara-on-the-Lake, Ontario. His second home, in Southwest Florida, is surrounded by the Everglades and the ocean. Both provide ammunition for his imagination and his love of storytelling. The diversity of the Everglades became the backdrop for his first published and best-selling novel, **Devil in the Grass,** and now the sequel, **The Palm Reader**, both published by Koehler Books.

Considering himself fortunate, Chris enjoys living his own great story. After earning a BA in history and graduating from Brock University, Chris is now surrounded by a wonderful family and runs a real estate brokerage. Whenever possible, he enjoys getting away to do some salt-water fishing in Florida.

Christopher Bowron's stories leave the humdrum train station of life behind to travel through dark tunnels into the unknown. Readers may need to buckle up and hold on tight as his stories lead them to the sharp edge of reality, where they get to peer into the paranormal.